Readers love *A Little Side of Geek* by MARGUERITE LABBE

"I adored this book. I'm talking read it twice, and probably going to read it a third. All I can say is, if you haven't read it yet, why not?"
　　—The Novel Approach

"The author did a great job with all the characters, and I can hardly wait for the next book."
　　—OptimuMM

"*A Little Side of Geek* is at its heart a sweet love story about two men from very different worlds who find love unexpectedly."
　　—*Divine Magazine*

"This book has it all. It's definitely also going on my Best of 2018 list."
　　—Scattered Thoughts and Rogue Words

By MARGUERITE LABBE

All Bets Are Off
Ghosts in the Wind
Make Me Whole
Other Side of the Line
Playing Ball Anthology

GEEK LIFE
A Little Side of Geek
A Whole Latte Sass

TRIQUETRA TRILOGY
My Heart is Within You
Haunted by Your Soul
Our Sacred Balance

Published by DREAMSPINNER PRESS
www.dreamspinnerpress.com

MARGUERITE LABBE

A WHOLE LATTE
SASS

REAMSPINNER
PRESS

Published by

DREAMSPINNER PRESS

5032 Capital Circle SW, Suite 2, PMB# 279, Tallahassee, FL 32305-7886 USA
www.dreamspinnerpress.com

A Whole Latte Sass
© 2019 Marguerite Labbe.

Cover Art
© 2019 Kanaxa.
Cover content is for illustrative purposes only and any person depicted on the cover is a model.

Trade Paperback ISBN: 978-1-64405-009-5
Digital ISBN: 978-1-64405-008-8
Library of Congress Control Number: 2018956389
Trade Paperback published January 2019
v. 1.0

Printed in the United States of America

This paper meets the requirements of
ANSI/NISO Z39.48-1992 (Permanence of Paper).

Now Felipe just has to convince his family—and Trask—
that Trask has more love to offer than he ever dreamed.

This is for my mama and my sister Amanda. You both are an inspiration. I admire how you keep fighting the fight, and I cannot tell you enough how much I am proud of you. I love you.

Chapter One

TRASK BRISCOE dug through the boxes of role-playing accessories stashed underneath the convention table. He had dice here somewhere. He should have anticipated needing to replenish more often and kept them on top. This show boasted a game room for diehards who had to have another fix and several panels covering different tabletop and role-playing topics. Including a well-attended one on gamemastering that featured Trask as a panelist. Dice were fundamental.

He shoved aside a box of various card decks and another one of role-playing modules, and huffed when he found the one he needed. He opened the box, noting the array of dice, dice bags, and other paraphernalia. Finally. He needed more structure. He organized his store. He should bring more of that system to the shows. He made a mental note to discuss the issue with Ryan.

Trask peeked out over the table and caught the customer's gaze. "Did you want to see the sets, too, or just the loose dice?"

"Do you have any of those boxes of six-siders?" The man peered over at him. "I'm getting killed in Warhammer. I need a new set before we get together if I don't want to come out dead last in our tournament."

Trask pulled out several in a variety of colors and stood up. "Have you tried out War Machine?"

"I keep hearing about it, but I don't know. I've invested a lot of money over the years in Warhammer," the man said as he picked up a plastic box full of tiny six-sided dice.

"Haven't we all." Trask plucked one of his business cards and handed it to him. "If you're in the area and have time, stop by the shop. We have a regular group that gets together for various war games. They're doing War Machine right now if you want to see what it's like."

"I might check it out." The man tucked Trask's card in his back pocket and held up a set of bloodred dice. "I'll take this one. I have an orc army. This has to give me good luck."

Trask rang up the sale and made small talk with the man before he wandered off to rummage through another booth. For the first time all day, no one browsed at the Magick Den's table. He checked his watch with a sigh. Three more hours before they could begin to pack the van. At least he didn't have long boxes of comics to load like he used to back when he first started doing cons. It was the last day of the show. He could relax tonight with a video game and sleep in tomorrow.

He glimpsed Ryan's tall, slumped figure making its way down the aisle, balancing a tray of coffees in one hand and a grease-stained box in the other. "Here you go." Ryan edged around the booth and handed Trask the tray. "I'm sorry it took so long. Everybody was getting fresh donuts today and the line was out the door."

"You're here now. That's all that matters." Trask picked up the largest coffee and sipped it. He could practically feel the aroma and richness charging up his blood. This was one of the few indulgences he allowed himself, and he enjoyed it to the fullest.

"I don't understand how you can drink it black and decaf." Ryan slid the carton of donuts beside their cashbox and popped up the lid. "What's the point?"

"The taste. The scent." Trask took another appreciative sip. "A good cup of coffee is a gift from the gods. An amazing dark roast, brewed just right, can change my whole day."

Ryan stuffed half a donut in his mouth. "You are weird, man," he mumbled around his bite. "After all these years, I should be used to your oddities."

"You'd think." Trask had given Ryan a job when nobody else would after he left rehab. Since then he'd become one of the rare people Trask considered family. He crouched down again to reorganize the boxes he'd mixed up. "This weekend may have started out slow, but we made a killing today."

"Sometimes they want to shop around before committing to buying." Ryan pulled out another donut and closed the box. "Did we make up for the last show?"

"Yeah, I think so. I suspect we might get a few online orders out of this weekend too." Trask pulled out more card sleeves. They were getting low on those. "And if there are new repeat customers at the store, that's the real win. The last guy I talked to might come by and check out the war game merchandise."

"Oh boy, here comes trouble," Ryan said with a soft groan. "Literally the harbinger of doom."

Trask glanced up to see a familiar figure clad in almost nothing but silver paint from head to toe and carrying a silver surfboard. Somehow, Trask could picture Felipe Suero on a beach, hitting the waves from dawn till dusk. He could also picture Felipe being the herald of an impending disaster. Still, something about the young man made Trask sit up and pay attention.

"He's not all that much trouble." Trask stood up. "He doesn't hang out for thirty minutes in front of the table posing and distracting people from browsing through the games."

"No, he only hangs out for thirty minutes to flirt with you," Ryan muttered under his breath. "That kid is fixated on you."

Felipe was a flirt, no lie, and he didn't just flirt with words. He did it with his eyes and whole body. Harmless fun and nothing to take seriously. He sure as hell wasn't serious about flirting with Trask. He was old enough to be the young man's father.

There was nothing kidlike about that broad-shouldered, lithely muscled body in those teeny, tiny silver shorts or the smirk of that heavy-bottomed mouth. Felipe sauntered toward them, completely at ease with the stares directed at him. Felipe knew the power of his looks and reveled in it.

"Hey, Felipe," Trask said as the young man stopped by their table. Even Felipe's scalp was silver. Trask tried to ascertain if it was only a trick of makeup and prosthetics. Felipe was a master. He was also dedicated enough to nail a role by shaving off his gorgeous black hair. Trask hoped he hadn't but had to admire his dedication if he had. "Did you stop by to try to strong-arm me into running a game for your group?"

"Among other things." Felipe cast a slow smile and a caressing glance at Trask. "You're looking delicious today. I see that the fall weather has brought out your lumberjack style."

"Lumberjack." Ryan snorted. "The flannel may be right, but I've never met a hipster redneck. The hair is all wrong."

"Looks fine to me." Felipe set the surfboard down, angling it out of the way so it didn't block the table. "You haven't had a dedicated group in a while. You must be craving a good game."

"It has been a while," Trask admitted.

Felipe eyed Ryan's getup. "Nice Eleventh Doctor Who jacket. Where'd you get it?"

"My fiancée bought it for me as an engagement gift." Ryan eyed him, apparently deciding that since Felipe kept the snark down, he ought to be nice in return. He held out the donut box. "Want one?"

Felipe eyed the box with an air of longing regret. "Can't but thanks, man."

"Worried about your figure?" Ryan asked with an incredulous expression.

"Please. My figure kicks ass and asks who's your daddy." Felipe flexed, striking a pose. Trask took another sip of his coffee to hide his smile of appreciation. Felipe did not lack for confidence. "Nah, it was a pain in the ass getting all this paint on. I had to call in reinforcements. If I eat or drink, it'll come off my lips and I'll be pissed. I'm doing a photo shoot in an hour."

"'Scuse me."

Felipe glanced down, and a sweet smile crossed his face at the sight of the little girl at his side. He should smile like that more often. It suited him. "Yeah, kid?" His smile widened. "Want a picture with me?"

The little girl nodded vigorously, her hair flopping in her face as her parents stood off to the side with beaming smiles. "Come on." Felipe stepped away from the table and laid the surfboard down in the aisle. Moments later the girl balanced on the board with Felipe crouched behind her, both their arms spread wide in imaginary flight as the mom took pictures.

"Say what you will about cosplayers—" Trask began.

"Oh, trust me, I do," Ryan cut in.

"But they do bring people in." Trask eyed the delighted little girl. "And they make it magical for them."

"If only the people they brought in bought more instead of ogling," Ryan said sourly. "Then I'd say it's a plus. And if there weren't so many jerks who think the show runs around them."

It was a familiar argument, one that Trask had heard from many other vendors. The small cons were changing in response to the megacons. They tried to draw in more mainstream people. As a result, attendance increased, but the mainstreamers weren't interested in the cost of original art or searching for rare comics. It was a double-edged sword. Not all cosplayers were prima donna assholes, despite Ryan's opinion. Most of them were pretty chill.

Felipe rose with the surfboard in hand and gave the girl a last wave before turning back to Trask. "I don't often use props like this. I hate maneuvering through a crowd and getting through prop check, but it has attracted attention."

"How'd you do in the costume contest?" Trask asked.

Felipe shrugged. "Fourth place. I kind of expected it. This was fun and the makeup was a pain, but there isn't much to it other than the paint. There were some elaborate contenders today."

"True." Trask eyed the skintight silver shorts. "But you are more covered than the man who ran around as Conan the Barbarian a few months ago."

"I loved that dude." Felipe grinned mischievously. "I hope I have the balls to wear nothing but a loincloth and fake sword when I'm seventy. Seriously, back to our discussion. We're an awesome group. We've been together for years. You know Dakota and you know me. I'm not sure about the others, but if you can hang with Dakota and me, you can hang with them. They're more laid-back."

Trask missed playing a long campaign versus the one-offs he was doing now at the shop. His last group had fallen apart after two of the members who'd been dating had a nasty breakup. Players took sides. Drama ensued. And Trask had zero patience with drama. "Didn't you and Dakota used to date? How's that working out with your group?"

"Oh fine." Felipe gave a dismissive flick of his fingers. "Dakota's all flash of temper and then clear as a summer day. He's not one to hold on to issues."

"I notice you didn't mention your attitude in all that," Ryan said with a bland look.

"Bite me." Felipe shot him a glittering smile. "Don't you have inventory to take?"

"You make it so easy to bait you." Ryan moved to take care of a customer who had wandered over.

Ex-boyfriends would be precisely the kind of drama Trask wanted to avoid. But it seemed to him, from his observations of Felipe, there was far more bark to him than real anger over his split with Dakota. "He does have a point, you know. You didn't mention how you're handling the breakup in your group. I've dealt with that as a GM and it's no damn fun."

"Yeah, I get it. We wanted to avoid that too. I saw the writing on the wall long before Mr. Clueless did." Felipe glanced away with a shake of his head. "We're cool. We're friends." Then that sharp, wicked smile came into play. "I kick his ass in board games, honey, and it's fucking sweet."

Trask's lips twitched. "I see."

"A bunch of us are getting together after the show for dinner. I need sustenance for the drive back home." Felipe cocked his head. "Why don't you join us? We can discuss the pros and cons of our group then. And I can fortify my lonely heart for the next week by ogling you through dessert."

Trask hesitated. He wasn't one for hanging out after shows. Many of those dinners included an excuse to get sloppy drunk, and that wasn't his scene anymore. "I don't know. It'll take a while to pack up the van and get it back to the store. I can't leave it sitting outside the restaurant. You heard about Pete getting robbed, didn't you?"

"No worries. It'll take me a while to wash off this makeup and get my gear together. You're not the only one who'll want to get their things back to the store. That's why we set it for eight." Felipe grimaced. "Which means I probably won't be on the road until ten and home till almost midnight, but whatever. We won't linger because Morris has got to get his fiancé's brother home. School night and all that. I could've driven my car, but that's one boring-assed drive after dark. Nothing but trees and winding roads."

Trask followed Felipe's rambling as he finished his coffee. Felipe did love to talk, which was okay by him because it meant that he wasn't expected to talk much himself. He liked people, liked interacting with them. He just preferred listening. And Felipe did not seem at all bothered by Trask's short answers.

Felipe cocked his head and gave Trask a sly smile. "So, what do you say? A wild night of dinner and discussions of gaming joys?"

Ryan snorted and shot Trask an amused glance. "That might constitute a wild night for this man."

Felipe had been after him every show since midsummer to check out his gaming crew. Persistence did deserve a reward. "You'll keep at me until I say yes, won't you?"

"You do understand when no means no, right?" Ryan cut in, and Trask stifled a sigh. His friend was determined to stick his nose into this because of his irritation toward cosplayers. The same friend who hounded Trask about getting out more.

"I haven't heard one 'no' from Trask." Felipe gave Ryan a cool glance. "There have been 'maybes,' 'ask again later,' 'I'm busy,' 'not sure,' and a hundred other noncommittal answers. I can tell when I'm not wanted in a conversation." He flicked his hand at Ryan. "Unlike others. Go play, Ryan. Trask doesn't need your white knight bullshit."

It might do Trask good to get out once in a while. Somewhere that wasn't a meeting, work, or a show. He'd gotten too used to silence, and it was a little lonely. "Okay, kid, you've worn me down. I'll be there."

"You keep calling me kid and I'll start calling you old man. I'm no longer a kid." Felipe's eyes glinted with naughty intent as he leaned closer and gave Trask a slow, raking glance. "And you most definitely are not an old man."

Felipe was trouble in metallic paint, and Trask had not been attracted to trouble in a long time. At least he made life interesting when he was around. "I'll keep that in mind."

"You do that." Felipe picked up his surfboard and winked at Trask. "I'll text you the directions, but it's that BBQ place on Broad Street. You can't miss it. You'll smell the goodness from the road." He glanced at Ryan. "You're welcome too if you want in."

Felipe didn't wait for a response, as if it was a given they'd attend. Trask's gaze slipped down to Felipe's tightly muscled ass as he sashayed off. Absolute trouble. Ryan crossed his arms, giving Trask a resigned look that he caught out of the corner of his eye. "You of all people are going to a BBQ joint?"

"Seems that way." Felipe disappeared into the swirl of attendees, but Trask could track his progress by the surfboard sticking up over everyone's heads.

"You're vegetarian."

"BBQ joints have vegetables too." Trask shot an amused glance at his employee and friend. "And usually amazing mac-n-cheese."

"If I thought you were going for the mac-n-cheese, I wouldn't worry." Ryan twisted his lips into a sour expression.

"If it's the age difference thing—"

"Nope," Ryan interrupted with a shake of his head. "You're both grown adults, and I have no doubt Felipe knows what he's doing. You've been alone a long-assed time. I know I've given you a hard time about finding someone, but a guy like that will break your heart and move on to the next conquest."

Ryan was in love and headed for years of wedded bliss, and ever since he got engaged, he'd obsessed over the idea of Trask finding someone. As if he hadn't been taking care of himself for years. As if he had a heart to break.

"I'll keep that in mind." Trask grabbed his coffee. "I'm going to check out how the gaming tables are going. See if anybody needs anything."

To his relief Ryan didn't attempt to get in a final word. Trask was sure he'd get an earful about Felipe in the next few weeks. The cosplayer was already in Trask's thoughts enough without the added reminder. And he wasn't quite sure when Felipe had taken up that quiet space in his brain. It was something to consider.

Chapter Two

"JUST BECAUSE you two have unnaturally long legs, I don't see why I have to sit in the back," Felipe complained.

Morris glanced at him in the rearview mirror, and Lincoln ignored him, his head down over a game on his phone. "We're all making sacrifices. I have a surfboard on top of my car. Do you know what a pain that's going to be when I go down that dinky-assed road of yours after dark?"

"You loved my cosplay." Felipe slouched in the seat and stared out the window restlessly. He wasn't entirely sure Trask would show up despite his words. He was the ultimate definition of a lone wolf, a sexy, silver, drool-worthy wolf.

"That's not the point." Morris pulled into the parking lot, and Felipe got a whiff of smoke and meat that made his taste buds sit up and take notice. The food was killer here, and the fact that the restaurant could usually accommodate their crew when they descended after a show was a huge plus. "What's got you so worked up tonight?"

"Nothing," Felipe scoffed. "I'm fine."

Morris parked the car and shot Felipe a disbelieving glance. "Whatever." He nudged Lincoln. "The next time there's a show in Richmond, I'm kidnapping your brother. He would salivate over this place."

"Good luck with that." Lincoln smirked. "I plan on rubbing it in his face how much he missed out."

Felipe envied Morris and the happiness he'd found with Theo. They were the most unlikely pair Felipe had ever seen, and yet they made it work. Felipe had been skeptical when he'd met Theo. He was a jock, for Chrissakes, and a non-geek, foodie twerp, but he gave back sass for sass, and Felipe had to respect that. Besides, he'd never seen Morris so happy and relaxed, and he'd known Morris for years.

Felipe wanted that joy for himself. He wanted the house, the dogs, and the happily ever after that went with it. The only thing he didn't want out of a connubial blissful future was kids. Nobody was going to out-drama-queen him, and he knew his DNA. If he bred, he'd be forever competing with a mini-him, and that would be good for no one. He planned to be a doting uncle for all the twerps Morris and Theo were likely to get. Those two screamed parenthood and adulting.

The early-fall night air held a chilly nip after the recent rain. Pumpkins, sheaves of Indian corn, and a scarecrow decorated the raised wooden porch of the restaurant. This was Felipe's favorite time of year. It was a nonstop celebration from Halloween to New Year's. The Ren Faire was going full tilt, which gave him extra excuses to wear costumes when there wasn't a show.

The restaurant was long and dark with the aroma of smoked meat lingering in the air. It made Felipe think of a village tavern. In the kitchen window, one of the cooks carved a brisket into slices, and Morris's eyes lit up with glee.

Felipe peered over into the bar area, scanning the clusters of rough wooden tables and booths filled with con rats. Out of the many familiar faces, the one Felipe wanted to see was missing. His stomach dropped with disappointment. He'd thought he'd made his interest clear. Well if Trask wasn't going to bite, that was his loss. They were the best fucking gaming group this side of the Chesapeake Bay. They could find another GM.

"Come on." Morris plucked his sleeve. "Stop daydreaming. I'm hungry."

"You're always hungry," Felipe muttered and followed Morris back to their usual corner. A quick glance at his phone showed no new messages. He tried telling himself that maybe Trask got held up packing and unpacking, but he wasn't an optimist. He let Theo own that cheery shit.

Felipe stalked over to a table and sank down in the chair. Not even the scent of slow-cooked ribs could cheer him up now. He wanted to bitch to Morris, but Lincoln was there. Besides, Morris found his fascination with Trask amusing. Morris always did have a problem with seeing potential in a relationship. He focused on problems that weren't really problems, like age differences, which didn't mean shit if you were compatible.

Morris eyed him with one heavy brow lifted but kept his commentary to himself as he doled out menus. A flicker near the door caught Felipe's attention, and he sat up straight as Trask came into the restaurant. Damn, he was sexy. It should be a crime to be that yummy. Angled black brows arched over eyes almost as dark, and his hair was mostly silver with some black still woven in. He had a short silver beard, also shot through with a little black, but it had to be a genetic thing because he wasn't really that old. Still, the silver hit all the right buttons for Felipe.

He was lean and covered with tattoos from his entire torso and arms down to the words emblazoned across his fingers. Felipe had seen them enough to be intrigued. "Clean" and "Life" on the left hand and "Death" and "Love" on the right. There was a story about them, he just knew it.

Felipe lifted his hand and caught Trask's attention. "Move your oversized self next to Lincoln," he ordered Morris. "We've got company."

Morris shot a startled look over his shoulder, then slid in next to Lincoln as they switched spots. "You invited Trask? Don't get me wrong, I like him, but I know your agenda."

"I'm just trying to talk him into running a trial game with us." Felipe pulled out Trask's chair as he approached. Clad in jeans distressed enough to be interesting, an open flannel shirt with a tight black tee underneath, he looked good enough to eat. The scooped neck of his shirt allowed Felipe a glimpse of the top of his chest tattoo. Some kind of tree with fully leaved branches spreading across his shoulders. Undressing him would be like unwrapping a gift, and Felipe was dying to know what other pictures decorated his body and what they all meant.

"That would be kind of cool." Morris rubbed his hands together. "At this point, it's been so long I'll take anything, even a pity game."

"That bad?" Trask asked as he got close enough to hear the tail end of Morris's remark. He swept the table with a measuring look, then met Felipe's gaze with a slight smile. "I'm very relieved you didn't cut that gorgeous hair. I was a little worried when you stopped by my table earlier."

Startled, Felipe put a hand to his hair. "Cut my hair? For a costume? Aw hell naw. That was a prosthetic." He thought about it a second. "Okay, maybe for the right costume. It would have to be a killer, though. I love my hair."

"Yeah." Trask's smile widened. "It looks good on you."

Felipe preened. He did have amazing hair. "Trask, you know Morris, and this is Lincoln. Morris is going to be a stepdaddy when he gets hitched."

"Brother-in-law actually," Morris said as Trask sat down. "Felipe likes to tease. Lincoln does not need another mother hen."

"Dude, I love your store. Old Dominion Magick Den, right?" Lincoln asked. "How long have you had it?"

"About twenty years now." Trask opened the menu. "It's almost walking distance from here. It started off as more of a New Age thing. I still have some incense, tarot, crystals, that sort of stuff. Then I went into comics for a bit, still have some graphic novels, but the last ten years or so it's been mostly games of all kinds. People come, hang out for a bit. It's a good gig."

Twenty years. Felipe was toddling when Trask owned his own business. That was kind of cool. Felipe did have a type. He liked men who were enterprising and not afraid to take risks.

"It's a pretty cool place. I've been there a couple times. Wish it was closer to Southern Maryland. We only have one game store. I'm greedy. I want more." Morris set down the menu as the waiter approached.

"At least you have the one." Felipe grimaced. "We have nothing in Chuck County."

"You could move to Richmond. You've got some serious talent," Trask suggested. "I carry some of your compilations, so I know you have fans. You'd do well here."

A pleased smile crossed Morris's lips. "Good to know, but I'm afraid I'm pretty settled where I am. My fiancé owns a family restaurant back home, second generation."

"There will be blood in the water before Theo gives up the bistro," Lincoln said. "But I'm not sticking around Solomon's Island. It's too quiet there."

"Oh yeah, you're not going anywhere." Trask looked around the restaurant. "I keep hearing about this place. It's pretty popular, been around awhile, I think. Not sure if it's family run, though."

"Enough chitchat." Felipe crossed his hands together on the table and caught Trask's gaze. "How about a test game? We could come to your shop," he added in a wheedling tone.

Trask pursed his lips, hollowing his cheeks in a way that emphasized the fine bones of his face. "Look, I'm not against the idea, but you guys are pretty scattered to come all the way down here. How can you get together regularly?"

"It's no different than making the time to go to a show. Sometimes we plan it around a con if we're all going to the same one." Felipe shot Trask a winning smile. "We make it a point to get together once every four to six weeks. We usually take turns going to each others' houses."

"That time frame seems doable. I don't get many days off from the Den," Trask replied slowly. "So, if you wouldn't mind hoofing it down to Richmond, I'll run a game or two to see if we mesh."

"Whoever is hosting usually does the bulk of the feeding, but even if we use the Den as our central place, we can still take turns potlucking it," Morris added with a hopeful smile. "Like Felipe said, we're used to traveling all around. The only ones it was sometimes an issue for were Brett and Daphne since they have a kid, but they're actually the closest to you, so they'll probably love the idea."

"Do you have any particular game in mind?" Trask asked, his expression thoughtful.

Felipe and Morris exchanged excited glances. Oh, this was going better than he hoped it would. "Before our last GM was deployed, we were doing a sweet campaign of Shadowrun," Felipe said. "Though we're open. We've done all kinds of campaigns, some home brewed."

"We like a good character-driven campaign," Morris added. "Not so much into the hack-and-slash and treasure grab. We've done some Call of Cthulhu, D&D of course, just about every edition. Feng Shui was fun. Scion…." Morris trailed off, tugging on one of his long dreads as he thought. "So many games, really. We've been doing this for years."

Trask nudged his chin toward Lincoln. "How about you? You've been playing too?"

Lincoln shook his head. "I joined in after their GM left. Mostly we've been playing card or board games. I haven't really role-played, to be honest."

"I think you'll be a natural," Felipe assured him with a wave of his hand. "You make up character backgrounds for your Munchkin cards."

"That would be a telling sign," Trask agreed. "We could easily do a one-off *Star Wars* game. I'm assuming everyone knows the world. The D6 version is an easy game to pick up, and it doesn't take long to make characters."

"I thought it would take more to convince you than this." Felipe sat back as the waiter came to take their orders. Trask had caved in like a sandcastle under a coming wave. Maybe it meant his resistance to the idea of a date was crumbling too. Felipe would pounce all over that weakness.

"You have been nagging me for months." Trask folded his menu and added it to the stack. "I gave it a lot of thought when I was unpacking the van. You're right. I've been feeming hard for a good game. If you can convince the others to come to Richmond, I'll give it a try."

Felipe gave his order, and to his surprise, Trask only asked for the salad bar and some mac-n-cheese. It was like the man lived off caffeine and air. Felipe leaned over and lowered his voice. "The ribs really are good here. So's the sausage. I promise."

Trask leaned in as well. He had super dark eyes. Darker than his own. Felipe just wanted to sink into them. "I'm a vegetarian."

Felipe wrinkled his nose. "For real? Why?"

"It's one of my rules. I gave up meat ages ago." Trask sat back as Morris regarded him with a horrified expression.

"One of those superhealthy things?" Morris asked. "My mom's into that craziness, and Theo's managed to get me to give up processed food, but there's no way I'm ever giving up meat."

"Something like that." Trask tapped his tattooed fingers on the table. "No drugs, alcohol, caffeine. After a while of doing that, I ended up going vegetarian too. I seriously considered going vegan, but damn, I do love cheese. I ended up never making that jump."

"No caffeine? You mean all that coffee you suck down is decaf?" Felipe shook his head as Trask smiled in acknowledgment. He was crazy. "I'm sorry. I could've suggested another place for dinner." There were plenty of options around here.

A pained expression crossed Morris's face, but he nodded in solidarity, and Trask laughed. "It's okay, really. I don't mind. A few years ago, the aromas would've seriously given me second thoughts, but not anymore. Besides, I'll go out of my way for a good mac-n-cheese."

"You should try Theo's," Lincoln said. "He makes it from scratch."

"Those are the best," Trask agreed. "I don't have the patience for it myself, so it's a real treat when I get it."

"So are there any other rules I should know about?" Felipe asked. He admired a man who had a code. He had one himself. But he had no time for someone who was too rigid.

Trask's eyes smiled, though his mouth remained straight. "No dating players. Leads to too much intergroup tension."

Felipe turned to Morris and Lincoln. "Sorry, we're going to have to find a new GM."

The corners of Morris's eyes crinkled in a smile. "You're staking a claim?"

"Totally." Felipe smirked at Trask, who looked thoroughly bemused, as if he couldn't figure out if Felipe was serious about his attraction or teasing him. Felipe liked that look on him. He usually had this unapproachable attitude, an air of solitude about him that always seemed a little sad. Like the Tin Man who wanted to be a part of a group and loved but didn't know how to find his heart. "No casual dating. Okay, then. How about marriage?"

He caught Trask at the wrong moment, and he sputtered out the sparkling water he'd just taken a sip from. Felipe handed over a wad of napkins as Trask thumped his chest and coughed. "Sorry about that."

Morris shot Felipe an exasperated look. "Trask, please ignore my friend. He goes from zero to a hundred in no time, and anything is liable to pop out of his mouth."

"I'm flattered, really I am." Trask wiped his eyes as he recovered. "But I'm not the marrying kind of man. Come to think of it, I'm definitely not a casual dating kind of guy either, which probably explains my lack of a sex life. But there you are."

"Your problem is too many rules. Rules are good for a guideline, but they can be taken too far." Felipe made room as their food arrived.

Morris rubbed his hands together, eyeing his platter with an unholy gleam in his eyes. "If you want me and Lincoln to hold Felipe back, just give us the word. Theo gave me that exact same determined look when I was laying out all the reasons why we didn't fit. We even quizzed each other on our lack of knowledge about everything that was important and failed. Both of us botched."

"Now look at you." Lincoln snickered and nudged Morris. "A total goner."

Felipe glared at Morris, but his friend did not seem impressed in the slightest. "Yeah, such a hardship for you," he said sarcastically. "You're so upset over being nabbed."

"Good point." Morris tied back his hair and picked up a rib. "Just don't say I didn't warn you."

"On that note, I'm running away to the salad bar." Trask picked up his plate and sauntered off. Felipe watched him go and turned to his own food with a shrug. He had his sights set on Trask. The man wasn't going to escape that easily.

Felipe pointed his fork at Morris. "Just you watch, that man is mine."

"It'll be a mess," Morris predicted. "Your personalities couldn't be more different."

"Your track record for recognizing compatibility is suspect." It had taken Morris forever to recognize he was in love with Theo. Felipe had seen it before him. But he had to give it to him; once Morris committed, he'd done it wholeheartedly with no reservations. "Just watch and be amazed. That man is going to adore me."

Chapter Three

TRASK CHECKED the stock of snacks in the Den's small pantry and went into the back room to get more sodas, packaged cookies, and chips. They disappeared faster than the protein bars. The store was empty on a midmorning Monday, and he expected it to remain that way. There might be a regular or two to come in and clean out their comic stash, but most of them wouldn't show up until after this week's new issues hit the shelves.

There were no tournaments or games scheduled for tonight, though a few kids might pop in after school for a round or two of Heroclix, Pokémon, or Magic the Gathering. He liked to keep his Mondays quiet so he could recover from the weekend and the cons. He never missed his home group meetings on Monday night, so he tended not to schedule events that evening for Ryan and Gillian to juggle.

With his phone pumping out ska, Trask grabbed a bottle of glass cleaner and started wiping down the windows and the long glass case holding various rare items he had on display and a few really kickass figurines and busts. His favorite first edition comics, some of which he'd even managed to get signed, hung on the wall next to photos of the stars he'd met over the years going to cons all over the world before he started slowing down to concentrate on the ones closer to home.

The crowded front of the store held short aisles stuffed with game paraphernalia and anything else that warmed the cockles of a geek's heart. And it all collected dust like a magical conduit. Trask traded in his rag and bottle for a duster and went to war. By the time he'd finished dusting the rows filled with a hodgepodge of gamebooks and the miniatures that went with them, the wire stands with comics, and the jumble of New Age paraphernalia, he wanted a break before he even considered touching the back room. That was a whole different chore with its long tables and war game terrain models that collected dust into every nook and cranny. Once Trask got started back there, he wouldn't want to stop until every last piece was done.

Trask brewed himself a pot of his favorite dark roast decaffeinated coffee, sat down in the comfortable chair he'd placed behind the register, and pulled out his battered copy of *Zen and the Art of Motorcycle Maintenance* from the little bookshelf that contained all of his favorite books. He'd give himself half an hour, then clean the back before tackling the online orders.

He propped his feet up on a stool and took an appreciative sip of his coffee before turning to one of his favorite passages. His thoughts flicked to Felipe. The cosplayer had popped into his mind every time he'd given himself a quiet moment since they parted last night. He wanted to pass off Felipe's interest as just teasing and flirting. And it was flattering, but Trask's ego didn't need bolstering by a fling with a guy barely old enough to drink.

He had to admit he enjoyed Felipe's company. He was amusing, confident, and hell, really sexy, with his rich dark brown hair, light brown eyes under heavy brows, and a mouth that just begged to be kissed. Trask had no doubt Felipe could bag any single gay guy he wanted and probably a couple who considered themselves straight too. He didn't see what the interest was in himself. Trask was no prize. He could be considered unexciting if you didn't like the introspective type.

His phone dinged, interrupting the music, and like a Pavlovian dog, Trask picked it up. He really ought to shut it off every once in a while, instead of being a slave to it.

Felipe's picture smiled up at him. *I am stuck at work bored off my ass. What'cha up to, Tin Man?*

Felipe had this uncanny knack of knowing whenever Trask was thinking of him and choosing that moment to contact him. He couldn't picture a man like Felipe stuck in a highway toll booth for an entire shift. That had to be a nightmare for him. *Taking a break at work, sitting down with a book. What made you decide on that career path?*

Even if I had the patience to read, they'd never let me take one into this cage hell. It's close to home & school, good benefits, & I needed to get away from working w/family. Why're there so many stupid drivers in MD?

Trask set aside his book. He could sacrifice his reading time to entertain Felipe. He sympathized. He hadn't wanted to work with family either. His old man always figured that Trask would toil with him in the garage. Trask couldn't run away fast enough. *They're everywhere. Trust me.* Curiosity got the better of him. *If you don't mind my asking, what happened with you and Dakota?*

There was a long pause, and Trask was about to apologize. Some people didn't want to discuss past relationships, him included, but before he could, Felipe texted back. *We wanted different things. He wanted to keep it kind of casual, I wanted something a little deeper. We agreed to stay friends.*

From the way Ryan made it sound, it seemed like the other way around, but Trask had spent some time with both men, and he couldn't see Dakota settling down with one person anytime soon. He was usually flitting from one guy to another, so when his name had been linked with Felipe's for so many months, many assumed he'd met his match.

No drama between us, I promise, though I do adore a bit of theatricality.

Trask smiled at that. *I never would've guessed. Working on any costume commissions?*

He'd seen the fruit of Felipe's labors on more than one cosplayer. That kind of work took time and attention to detail. He'd also seen the number of panels he'd appeared on at conventions, and Trask knew he went to as many shows as he could. Felipe was serious about cosplaying. Trask respected that level of dedication.

Honestly, it's to the point where it's more than I can handle. It's time to make some decisions, cut back, or find a partner & go at this full-time. I could make a career out of this if I do it right.

Well, that showed ambition and drive that men his age rarely displayed. Trask didn't want to think about what he'd been doing at twenty-two. He'd either been stuck in county jail or rehab. He'd hopped back and forth between the two enough. It had taken more than one wake-up call to get on the right path. Even then, the road had been long and treacherous, and he'd stumbled more than once. Sure he'd had the Den, but he'd almost lost it before he'd gotten his shit together.

I hope it works out for you.

Yeah, me too. Look, gotta go, traffic's picking up. Talk to ya on the other side. Stay sexy. I need the hormone boost when I look at you.

Trask chuckled at the last message and set aside the phone with an air of regret. After Felipe's marriage announcement last night, he'd been braced to dodge a lot of uncomfortable come-ons, but Felipe had acted like he always did, snarky and funny, with wicked observations about everything and everyone. He'd even included Morris's kid friend, who'd tried to keep up with equal snark that they both clearly delighted in. Felipe had been concerned that Trask enjoyed his meal and had enough to eat, but not so much that Trask felt he had to defend his choices, which had been a problem in the past.

He'd had fun. Maybe Ryan was right and he should socialize a little more, because it had been nice without being too much. He glanced at his watch with a sigh. And now it was time to get back to work. He wanted to have that back room straightened before the open role-playing night on Tuesday. A couple different campaigners used his back room as headquarters.

The chime over the door jangled. Trask glanced over and his brow lifted. Dakota Nye, king of the podcasts, surveyed the shop from the doorway. What were the chances that Felipe's ex would come in today? If Felipe got him caught up in a relationship triangle, this gaming trial would be over before it started.

"Hey, Dakota." Trask lifted his hand in greeting. "You didn't head back home last night with everyone else?"

"Nah, I caught the train into Richmond on Friday. I have an interview later on today for *Geek Wars*. Then I'm heading back up to Baltimore." Dakota crouched down in front of the glass case. "Wow, that's a sweet Cyborg bust."

Trask leaned his hip against the counter. "I picked it up at Wizard World. This guy was trying to sell off most of his stash, get out of the business. I spent a lot of money that day but made a killing."

"I bet you earned it all back after a month online." Dakota straightened and met Trask's eye. "I hear you're going to give our group a trial run."

"That didn't take long to get out." Trask poured himself another cup of coffee. "Want some?"

"Sure, got any cream and sugar?"

Trask pulled out the stash he kept for Ryan, set them on the counter with the cup, and filled it. Dakota quickly doctored it up, then took a sip and hummed in appreciation. "That's good. Morris pretty much squealed with excitement while you were still eating dinner. He blasted everybody with it."

Trask remembered Morris texting furiously, but he hadn't let anything else show but cool pleasure. "Don't let that excitement get out of hand. We're just going to see how it works. It's a long drive if you're not happy with my style or y'all get on my nerves."

It probably sounded more pessimistic than Trask meant. He didn't want to get anyone's hopes up and squished if it didn't work. That was all.

Dakota shot him a grin. "We're an interesting mix of personalities, but we mesh well. I don't think anyone there is going to have a problem being on display in your back room. Well, maybe Lincoln, but he might not join in. I think he's still in high school or something."

On the counter, Trask's phone dinged with an incoming message, and Dakota glanced at it. "Giving Felipe your cell phone number is an invitation for nonstop chatter."

"I'm coming to realize that." Trask stuck the phone in his back pocket and grabbed the duster. "I was heading to the back room if you wanted to talk."

"Wow, it's been a while since I've been here. I love the changes you've made." Dakota made a slow circuit around the room, examining the fantasy maps and star charts Trask had used to paper the walls.

"Yeah, it needed something. It was starting to look a little dingy, and this at least adds to the ambiance." The Den was more Trask's home than the loft he lived in.

Three tables dominated the back room that took up almost half his shop space. The long cafeteria-style table with its built-in benches was mostly used for card tournaments. It usually had kids there in the summer and on weekends. In the back, next to a series of built-in cabinets, was the bar-style war game table set up for a moon base siege. The group using it was in the middle of an ongoing battle, but he had more scenery in the cabinets for all kinds of other campaigns. Trask didn't play that much himself, but he loved to make miniatures and scenery. He either kept it at the Den or sold it online. The round table sat up to eight players and was ideal for role-playing. Big enough to lay down scene maps and minis, but not so big that you felt like you were shouting at your fellow players.

Trask had to admit, he missed playing with a group. He'd sulked long enough, nursing his irritations in isolation, which was a bad habit he needed to stop. Another one of those toxic thinking attitudes he was struggling to put in his past, one at a time. He knew everyone in Felipe's group at least casually, and they seemed like a cool bunch.

"We usually take turns at other people's houses. That way we're all taking part in the traveling. But I suppose having us play here will help you sell games," Dakota observed with a shrewd look.

"And dice, maps, and everything else that goes with it," Trask agreed. "If you miss your old GM, have you considered doing a game online? Using Twitch maybe, or Discord, Roll20?"

"We tried, but it wasn't the same. It's okay. I don't mind coming here. I'm in and out of Richmond all the time." Dakota spread his hands as his expression became more intent. Trask had heard that he was a man who usually got what he wanted. Trask was curious to know what that was today. Because if it had to do with Felipe, he was ready to shut that shit down now. "I was just thinking that since you're going to get some monetary value out of this, maybe you could spread the love."

Trask eyed Dakota, trying to figure out the angle. "Sounds like you've been listening to Brenden."

"Yeah, he's a bad influence," Dakota agreed easily. "Believes in reciprocity. He's drilled that word into my head."

"What do you have in mind?" Trask already had a number of items on sale from people in his circle, and they made a nice exclusive addition to the Den.

Dakota reached into his messenger bag and pulled out a stack of postcards. "Would it be a problem having these on your countertop?"

Trask glanced at the image of a guy dressed in a generic comic book hero cape and mask facing off against a woman who looked like a cross between Red Sonja and Xena with the words *Geek Wars* emblazoned over them. "This Jackie's work? It looks like her style."

"Yeah, we must've spent a month haggling over the design." Dakota looked at the postcards with obvious pride. "I really like how they turned out. I think they've helped get the word out. It's slow, but the downloads are increasing."

"I don't mind setting them out. It's an entertaining podcast." Trask set the cards aside. "I can also put a link on my website for a small ad fee, unless you want to maybe mention me from time to time on your show."

Dakota grinned. "Now who's sounding like Brenden? I'd be happy to shill your shop. To be honest, I think this mutual backscratching is working out better than paying off some of the bigger venues for advertising."

"Have you been able to quit your day job yet? I know you were considering it last time we talked." Trask finished his neatening and deemed the back room ready for the players later on. He'd tackle the dusting after Dakota left.

"I've cut back to part-time, but I'm not quite there yet. Thinking about moving back in with Brenden to cut costs. Not sure, though. He might strangle me in my sleep. I opened an online store, and that's helping supplement my income. Have you thought about that? Adding T-shirts and mugs geared to your store, tchotchkes stuff?" Dakota followed Trask back into the main room as another customer entered.

"Not really, I have my hands full with the online sales as it is. It would be just something else to track." Trask dropped the postcards on the counter and nodded to the customer. Didn't look familiar, but they usually got some new foot traffic after a show.

"I've got to go and get ready for my interview. Thanks for this." Dakota tapped the postcards on the counter. He gave Trask a considering look and then leaned in. "Word is Felipe's got his sights set on you."

Trask shook his head. "I don't discuss stuff like that, true or not."

Dakota hesitated, studying him. "I'm not big into gossip myself, so I'll leave it at this. He's a good guy and a hopeless romantic. I don't want to see him hurt again. So if you're not interested, let him know early before he builds it up in his mind."

"Duly noted."

Dakota paused, but when Trask didn't add anything else, he gave a little salute and walked out. Trask watched Dakota go and glanced at the phone, at the last text Felipe sent.

Look what that mom from yesterday forwarded to me. It was the picture of Felipe on the surfboard with the little girl. The way their eyes were both lit up called to that place inside of him that had been empty for so long.

"Well damn," Trask muttered.

Chapter Four

THE SOUND of yipping puppies scattered Felipe's concentration. He cussed under his breath, finished the seam, and straightened from the sewing machine. His neck had knotted into kinks, and he took a moment to roll his head from side to side to work them out. His eyes burned from the strain of staring at one spot. He'd been at this for a while now. It was time to take a break before he started making mistakes.

Felipe cut the thread, lifted the stiff fabric free from under the presser foot, and shook it out. He held it up so he could get a better look at the progress on the tunic. *Perfect*, he thought with a thrill of satisfaction.

Tomorrow he'd work on finishing the armor before turning to the final touches. He arranged the tunic on the mannequin in the corner and took a quick picture for his customer. At this rate, he might be able to squeeze in an extra project before the next show if his schoolwork didn't get too crazy. And he had to finish the cape he was wearing for the Ren Faire this year.

More yipping attracted his attention, and Felipe walked over to the large box in the corner where a pile of squirming, floppy-eared, four-week-old puppies was waking up next to their mama. Lady lifted her tawny head and gave Felipe a long-suffering look. "Does Mama need a break?" Felipe asked, sitting cross-legged next to the box and rubbing under her chin where she loved it best. "I bet you're bored in there, kiddos. I get bored in my box too."

One by one he lifted them out, let them nuzzle his face before setting them on the ground. They ranged from tawny to a coppery red-brown with whipcord wagging tails and paws too big for their bodies. "We've got to see about getting you all a home," Felipe crooned as he lay back on the floor and let the excited puppies crawl all over him. "But not yet, me and your mama get you for a while longer."

It was hard to remain irritated over Trask's silence with such wiggling adoration. He picked out his favorite, a rust-colored girl with a silky coat and ears that didn't know if they wanted to point or fall over. "I'm going to miss you, baby. I need to find you a special home." He'd tried so hard to talk his mom into letting him keep her, but she refused. They had enough critters crawling all over their land, and he was away from home often. "You're the smartest one out of a pretty smart batch, Sophie. Maybe I'll give you to Jaydon. He's dying for a puppy."

Brett and Daphne's son had a special place in Felipe's heart. He was always at the cons, catching naps under his mom's table, fetching drinks for those stuck by themselves, generally making an amiable nuisance of himself. He adored Felipe's costumes and was trying his own mix of cosplay at seven. And like Felipe, he had a foot in two different cultures with his white Jewish dad from upstate New York and African American mama from Mobile, Alabama. Felipe knew what that felt like. How it could be incredibly cool and confusing at times. Jaydon was mature enough to have his own dog. It was just a matter of picking out the one perfect for him and sweet-talking Daphne into allowing the puppy to come home.

Sophie found the string to his hoodie and began to tug on it, shaking her head in mock ferocity. "Nope, not that." Felipe gently tapped her nose and held out a toy. "Chew this instead."

As he played with the puppies, his thoughts went back to Trask. The man was attracted. Felipe had seen the admiring looks, and he never tried to dodge Felipe's conversation, which was a telling sign. He knew when someone was only interested in his ass and not him. If he was just wanting a booty call, he would've pounced. That he hadn't was, in a way, a relief. Felipe did not want to be that guy again. Nor did he want to be somebody's closet dirty secret. He wanted a friend and a sexy lover.

"Fuck, I'm pathetic." Felipe got up with a disgusted groan for his moping. "And sadly desperate and it shows."

It wasn't that late. He could go out and have some fun, only there was jack shit to do in Charles County, Maryland, on a winter weeknight unless he wanted to go to a vape lounge or redneck bar. At least in the summer, there were baseball games, fairs, and racing. Going to DC was no fun alone, and Morris was probably at the bistro's bar mooning over Theo, which would only make Felipe feel worse.

The text ping that came through struck another sour note. Abby Albion. The bane of his existence since his very first day of kindergarten when she'd tried to steal his pink crayon and he'd retaliated by drawing an ugly face on her worksheet. They'd both ended up in time-out on their nap mats, and a war started that continued to this day.

Felipe pulled up a picture of Abby in a *Fifth Element* Leeloo costume, complete with the orange wig. It suited her long, leggy figure, but he'd be damned if he said it. *This beats the hell out of your Silver Surfer.*

Felipe snorted with a grin. *Please, Duchess, you may be able to sew, but your makeup and prosthetic skills are nowhere near my league.*

He didn't actually dislike Abby. She was cool even if she was a constant thorn in his side. And he could admit privately that she was some serious competition for him. If he lost first place in a contest, it was a sure bet that she had a hand in it somehow. At least it went both ways. He had upset her plans for con domination more than once. If they banded together, they could make a killing, but that would require one of them to extend the invitation, and hell if he'd bend first to a crayon thief.

Asswipe

Beeyotch

Felipe grinned. An exchange of words with Abby always amused him. *Hey, did you hear that Brenden's setting up a bigger con in Annapolis next year?*

Yeah, I heard. Not his usual style.

Felipe had to agree. Brenden was very hands-on and meticulous. He liked to control every detail himself. There was a rumor that he carried around a notebook he called his Con Commandments, but Felipe had never been able to get a hold of his clipboard and accessories to check.

With a bigger con, Brenden would have to delegate and refrain from micromanaging, and that was going to be difficult for a man who let go of nothing. Good thing he was already bald or else he'd tear out all his hair in the coming months. It would be amusing to watch him come apart at the seams. Felipe felt that he was owed a little entertainment at Brenden's expense, considering how hard the man rode him while Felipe was dating his brother, and it wasn't even the fun kind of riding.

He'd have to hit up Morris and see if he could cozy Brenden into adding a panel on cosplaying. He'd seen the flyers and promo. There would be a costume contest, and the prize was sweet. It would be a perfect time to plan a parade. Annapolis was gorgeous in September.

Want to see if we can headline a panel together? As soon as Felipe sent the text, he winced and wished he could recall it. Didn't he just say he would not extend the first invite? He had serious diarrhea of the brain issues. Something popped into his head and he just had to air it. But they could really kick ass together. Like quit the stupid government day job and really make a go at designing costumes and accessories. He just didn't want to trade one aggravation for another.

Have you been drinking?

Felipe glared at the phone. Try to be nice to someone and they immediately suspect you of having ulterior motives or apparently being drunk. The only person Felipe drunk texted was Morris. *You know what? Nvrmind.*

Fuck Abby Albion and her superior Duchess attitude. He needed a pick-me-up, a date with sexy-assed Trask if he could get the man to agree. Felipe started to text him and then made himself stop and think it over. He shouldn't hit up Trask now. Felipe knew how he was when he got in a mood, reckless and pushy. Didn't he just have the thought that he needed to pause before texting or talking? Yet thinking hadn't ever stopped him once. Time to find out if there was a chance to get Trask out on a date or if he should just forget it.

Hey, going to be in Richmond Friday. Wanna go out for a drink? I know a great bar.

The response was quick and pointed. Felipe got the picture immediately. *Don't drink.*

Felipe stared at it with a sinking heart. Well, he wanted his answer. He had it. It was time to say fuck it and move on. He'd harass Morris, indulge in some wings and a beer, and let himself sulk for one night, no more. There were other men who were more than happy to spend an evening with him.

Felipe's phone pinged again. *How about getting together for coffee?*

As quickly as his spirits plummeted, they soared again. Coffee? Yeah, he loved a good latte or a dark roast loaded down with cream and sugar. Hell, he'd take mineral water if it meant he could spend an evening with his favorite silver fox. *Love to. Know a good place?*

Yeah, Perk it UP. Not far from the Den. Meet me at 7?

Felipe rescued a tennis shoe from one of the puppies, humming happily to himself. His week just got a whole lot better. *I'll be there.*

He really needed to practice some meditation to balance his moods. He was mercurial. He'd always been like that, bouncing from mad, to happy, to sulky. The only time he seemed to be in a calm zone was when he was concentrating on a project. People found it exhausting, and sometimes Felipe wondered if he were more like others, calmer, maybe he'd have more friends, but then he wouldn't be him either, and he just couldn't see changing himself for anyone.

He cleaned up after the puppies, put down fresh pads, and set up the pen so they'd have room to explore without getting into anything. Lady was dozing in the relative quiet, taking advantage before her brood decided they were hungry. Felipe took a picture of them tumbling about and sent it to his friends. *Want one?* The only people who were getting Lady's babies were people he trusted.

A harvest moon was out, gleaming, a huge, gorgeous ball of orange shining through the black half-bare branches of the trees. Felipe took a moment to drink in the sight. He loved it back here, tucked in on the southern end of La Plata, Maryland.

Their home was hidden a good mile into the woods with no neighbor in sight. The sprawling farmhouse held three generations of family. His mama's parents occupied the built-on in-law suite on the southeastern side of the house. It had its own door near the garage and no stairs. His parents and sister lived in the main house, and so had his abuelo until he went back to Colombia after Felipe's graduation. Then there was his apartment tucked in over the kitchen on the opposite side of the house. It had its own entrance and appliances, so he could see as much or as little of his family as he wanted. The setup couldn't get any better.

It was tiny, but it was all his. He paid his rent and utilities, which gave him a sense of independence and the feeling that he was helping his parents. As Felipe headed to his car, he checked out the rest of the house. The lights in the suite were low, so his grandparents had settled in front of the TV to doze and talk before they retired. His dad's truck and mom's car were in the driveway, so everyone was home. Felipe glanced through the wide french doors as he passed by on the patio. His sister Mariana was at the kitchen table, finishing her homework. His mom, Ratree, was making her evening tea, still dressed in her hospital scrubs, and talking on the phone.

Felipe slunk by guiltily. He should be doing his own homework, not spending his entire evening on a costume before heading out to spend the rest of the night with friends. He had the first of several projects due in a few weeks. He was so close to graduating with his associate's degree in business management in December. He couldn't blow it off now.

He didn't have a show this weekend. He was off from toll bridge duty. On Saturday, he'd hole up in his apartment and knock a chunk of it off. He was invested in the work. He'd designed his project to fit what he wanted to do with the degree. He'd make damn sure it was the best project in the entire class.

Morris texted him back as he reached his car. *No! Cassie would murder me in my sleep if I got a dog. Do you want that on your conscience?*

You're that cat's bitch. Felipe hit Send and slid behind the wheel. *You at the bistro? On my way. Order me some wings in about 30.*

It was a long drive to Solomon's Island, but at this time of night, the roads were quiet and Felipe knew he could get there in decent time. He waited for Morris's answering text and then edged out of the crowded driveway. Other than the single lamppost, there was no light under the trees as Felipe took the winding dirt road to the highway. The bumps reminded him that he'd have to help his dad level the road before winter came, just in time for the snow and ice to add new bumps and dips.

By the time Felipe pulled into the parking lot near the bistro, he was more than ready for those wings and a beer. He spotted Morris's long, lanky body at a high-top table near the tail end of the bar, where he could watch the football game and keep an eye out for glimpses of Theo at the same time. His friend was such a goner, and it had been hilarious to watch his fall.

As Felipe neared, Morris half turned, and he spied the tiny baby that Morris cradled to him with the ease of a man who was not terrified of squirming, smelly creatures. "Man, what are you doing with a baby at a bar?" Felipe asked as he approached.

"Babysitting for fifteen minutes while Jill has some adult conversations." Morris grinned down at the little bald-headed munchkin with a pink bow wrapped around her head. "This is Olivia, Theo's niece."

Felipe peered into wide gray eyes. "Whose idea was it to wrap her up like a tamale?" The blanket completely encased the baby's arms and legs, leaving only her blinking face free.

"Babies like being wrapped up. At least they do at this age," Morris assured him. "Later on she won't be such a fan."

"The fact you know that is a little disturbing." Felipe pulled up another stool, eyeing Olivia's face again. She did seem content enough. Seemed claustrophobic to him. "Sure you don't want a puppy? They have more personality."

"I hear you're hogging my niece." Theo came out of the kitchen with a plate of wings that he sat in front of Felipe. "Give her to me. Hey there, troublemaker," Theo cooed.

Morris handed her off, and Felipe rolled his eyes at the looks of adoration the two suckers were giving each other and that little bundle of gas that came out both ends. If Morris didn't watch it, he was going to be married by spring and trying to figure out a way to get kids of his own by fall. "Felipe wants us to adopt one of his new puppies," Morris announced, sitting back on the stool.

Theo shook his head with a frown. "I like dogs just fine, but when would we have time to take care of a dog?"

"Might I remind you Morris is home all day every day, well mostly every day." Felipe added a little extra hot sauce to the wings. "He's home enough to love a dog."

Theo turned a speculative look on Morris, who shook his head. "And might I remind you, Boarman, our place is not big enough for the three of us and the cat. No way a dog is going to work until after the move. So don't get any ideas."

"And then we'll have other things on our mind," Theo said with a wicked laugh as he kissed Olivia and handed her back. "Got to run, just saw a six-top walk in and we're going to get hit."

"What's that supposed to mean?" Felipe asked as Theo hustled back toward the kitchen. "Other things on your mind?"

There was a slightly panicked look to Morris's eyes as he turned toward Felipe. "Wedding planning, man. Who the hell thought it would be this complicated? All the sisters have gotten involved."

Felipe snickered and took a bite of his dinner. The bistro had the best wings in Southern Maryland. He knew how much Morris loved Theo and the idea that they were a permanent item. It was just that he'd been so leery of dating that the idea of permanence still made him twitchy. But the one time Felipe suggested Morris step back and rethink things, he'd gotten a twenty-minute lecture on letting Morris make his own decisions. "He's talked me into naming a date. Next Memorial Day weekend."

"So you want me to have the getaway car ready?" he suggested innocently and grinned as Morris shot him a horrified look.

"No!"

"Then chill the fuck out. If you're not going to run, enjoy the ride." *Estúpido.* He didn't get how Morris, of all his friends, had fallen for a guy like Theo, but somehow they balanced each other out and it worked. If Morris fucked it up, Felipe would kick his ass for him. He'd never seen Morris this happy.

"You're right." Morris gently patted the baby's back as she let out a soft whimper. "I wish we could get away with a small, chill affair. My sisters are driving me nuts. I think that's what's got me in such a panic. I just want something cool, something that fits both of us without all the fuss."

"Like superhero capes for all the guests and handmade canapés from Theo's kitchen?" Felipe teased until it hit him that he could see them suggesting that.

"Something like that." Morris eyed Felipe. "You going to be my best man, right?"

"Do I get to wear a skirt?" Felipe glanced at Morris's kilt. He'd never worn one before. He'd probably look ridiculous, but hell, it would be fun.

"I'm working on that. I think I could get away with it if I went with the full deal. Scotsman all the way. Theo does have a thing for kilts." Morris propped his chin on his hand. "What's got you in such a good mood?"

"I have a date." Felipe smirked.

"With Trask?" Morris shot him a disbelieving look. "You are serious about him. I have to confess, I don't get it. I mean, he's cool enough, in a standoffish kind of way, and I suppose he's good-looking if you like that type."

"Morris, we've always had opposite taste in men. You like apple pie, I like something with a little more edge." Like cherries jubilee.

"Edgy he is," Morris agreed. "And completely in another generation."

Felipe rolled his eyes. He knew Morris was going to be a stickler for that one little fact. "He's only about ten years older than you."

"And I'm ten years older than you, which makes him old enough to be your daddy." Morris bounced Olivia as she began fussing. "Let's go find your mama."

"You're a killjoy," Felipe shot after him as Morris walked away. He wasn't about to let his friend sour his mood. It wasn't like this was unusual for him. His ex, Dakota, was in his thirties, and most of Felipe's friends were Morris's age. People his own age annoyed him. Maybe it was the influence of his older cousins, who'd always allowed Felipe to hang with them. His lola said he had an old soul. Felipe didn't know about all that. He just knew what he liked, and Trask Briscoe hit every one of those buttons.

Chapter Five

TRASK WALKED into his favorite coffee shop, struck by the scent of roasting beans, an aroma that evoked a sense of comfort and home. The large roaster sat in the window, its wide stirrers moving gently through the browning beans. Perk it UP was usually quiet on a Friday night. Most of the people who came here to hang out and enjoy a cup were at a bar right now, as Felipe had suggested. There were a few college kids studying in a corner booth, some hipsters and aging hippies scattered around, and the two loner gamers who came most nights. Trask fit right in.

It was probably not Felipe's dream first date. But Trask had vowed never to step foot inside a bar again. Besides, this place had a kind of quirky charm that Trask enjoyed, and he thought Felipe might appreciate the vibe too.

He decided to wait for Felipe to arrive before ordering and turned toward the array of low-slung couches covered in cushions of various hues and the retro tabletop arcade games. His favorite, *Galaga*, was free and had a clear view of the door. As he sat down, he wondered, not for the first time, what he was doing. Felipe and he were worlds apart despite having many of the same interests.

It was crazy, but Trask couldn't deny how he felt whenever Felipe breezed by the booth for a hello and few words and flirt. Seeing Felipe was like that first sip of a perfectly brewed cup of coffee. It woke him up and made him take an interest in everything else around him.

The chime of the door sounded over the murmur of low conversation and the digital noise of games. Trask glanced over and stood as Felipe entered. The button-up white shirt emphasized the richness of his skin tone, and the rolled-up sleeves gave him a casual, gorgeous air. Trask felt incredibly awkward. He couldn't remember the last time he'd been on a date, probably before Ryan met his lady. Which would make it a sad almost two years.

Felipe spotted him, and the crooked grin that crossed his face was full of delight. He strolled over to Trask with no hesitation or shyness and brushed his lips over Trask's cheek. Then he stepped back, gave Trask a once-over, and winked at him. "Sexy. I like your look."

"Me too." Trask found himself reaching for Felipe's hand for a warm squeeze. He nodded toward the counter that led to the kitchen. "Hungry? They have pretty decent food as well as coffee and tea."

"Yeah, actually that would be awesome. I was trying to start this project for school, and I haven't had anything since a late lunch." Felipe plopped down on the couch and moved in closer as he pulled out the menu. "Have you tried the veggie flatbread?"

"Many times. It's good. So's the black bean nachos. I can't vouch for the meat items, but based on everything else I enjoyed, I don't think you'll be disappointed." Felipe's hair smelled faintly of citrus, and the warmth of him near Trask felt right. He slipped his arm across the couch behind Felipe.

Felipe set aside the menu. "Nachos it is. They are a weakness of mine. And a latte with whole milk. I don't believe in denying myself one bit. So waistline be damned."

Trask looked Felipe over. Those silver shorts Felipe had worn at the con had not left much to imagine. He didn't think Felipe had anything to worry about. "Your waistline is just fine. I doubt that either the nachos or the whole milk will make a difference considering the amount of energy you expend."

Many might consider Trask's philosophy on life as entirely different from Felipe's. That he denied himself everything, but he didn't see it that way. He looked at the way he lived as a conscious choice, to live the best life that he could. Instead of thinking he was making some kind of sacrifice. Attitudes like that had led him right back into bad habits.

And now he was completely overthinking the symbolism of a whole-milk latte.

Shaking his head, Trask went and put in the orders for their food and came back carrying Felipe's latte and his own coffee. Felipe had turned to the game and was firing away at the alien ships swooping toward his digital fighter. "Thanks, man," he said as Trask set the coffee down. "I haven't seen one of these games since I had braces. My orthodontist had one in his waiting room. It's the only reason my mom was able to get me through the door."

Trask took the seat opposite him and fired up his own console. "Somehow I cannot picture you with braces."

Felipe flashed him that crooked smile. "Oh yeah, I was an awkward teenager, braces, acne, and a gay geek who liked to sew? About the only friend I had in middle school was also my rival. But don't tell her I consider her a friend. We have a complicated history. Our rivalry makes us better."

"Was she awkward-looking in middle school too?" Trask found it easier to talk when he was half concentrating on the game. He didn't have a chance to overthink every word.

Felipe made a disgusted sound. "She was adorable from birth and knew it. I was a pretty cute kid, but man, puberty was rough."

Trask glanced at him and decided he'd have to have picture evidence to believe that. "So what turned you from the ugly duckling into the swan?"

Felipe grimaced. He had a wide range of grimaces, this one self-deprecating. "Manual labor. My dad's a contractor. There is always construction going on in my county. One summer spent sweating in the sun, drinking gallons of water, and working my tail off made vast improvements. It didn't hurt that the braces were gone by the time I went on to high school. How were your school days? Did you hit that awkward stage, or were you as sexy then as you are now?"

School had been a series of suspensions, hazy memories, sex, and fights. Trask had looked exactly as he'd been nicknamed, Trashy Trask from the other side of the tracks. "Actually, I dropped out." Trask met Felipe's shocked gaze. "I ended up getting my GED later."

"And now you own a successful business," Felipe said and to Trask's surprise, didn't try to pry further. "Which just goes to show there are many paths. I tried working for my dad for a couple years after high school. It wasn't what I wanted to do, but it seemed like a good option while I figured out what I did want. I hated every minute of it. If I want to sweat, I'll go to the gym or have sex."

Trask couldn't help the chuckle. He never knew what would come out of Felipe's mouth. "Did you figure it out? Is that what you're studying in school now?"

"Well, I always knew I wanted to turn my hobby into a career. It got to the point where I was so wiped out from work I didn't have the energy to work on my costumes. So I quit Dad, got a job with the DOT, and started taking classes in business at the local college." Felipe looked down and shook his head at the sound of an explosion from his console. "The aliens skewered me."

"Me too." Trask sat back with his coffee as the serving man came by with their food and a couple small plates. One of the things Trask appreciated about the place was that they didn't skimp. The nachos were piled high, smothered in cheese, black beans, scallions, and peppers with a healthy dose of sour cream and guacamole on the side. The flatbread was easily big enough for two people and loaded down with vegetables and cheese from one end of the crust to the other.

"Oh man." Felipe eyed the food with a greedy expression. "Halvsies?"

"I was hoping you'd say that." Trask put a portion of each on a plate and handed it to Felipe. "Some guys don't want to share a taste."

"You won't have to worry about that with me. I'm all about the communal food." Felipe sat back as Trask served himself. "So what made you change your mind about the date? The last time we talked you were big on rules."

Trask ate a nacho as he considered his answer. He wasn't entirely sure what had prompted him to suggest this when Felipe hit him up. He did have his rules and he had them for a reason, but he'd also learned that some rules were outgrown and no longer needed. Maybe it was loneliness. Hell, he didn't know. He glanced at Felipe, who waited with an air of quiet patience that he was sure wouldn't last. "I wanted to see you smile."

He felt like an idiot for saying something so sentimental, but the grin that blossomed across Felipe's face quelled that emotion. When Felipe smiled like that, with his whole being, it was like a light dawning. "That has to be one of the best answers I ever heard." Felipe leaned forward and brushed his fingers over the back of Trask's hand. "You mean that?"

"I wouldn't have said it if I didn't mean it," Trask replied gruffly, and to his surprise, Felipe glowed even more. "What's got you so happy? I'm sure you've heard better lines."

"I've heard just about everything." Felipe shrugged. "Most of the time it's just words and said just to get me naked. You meant it. Nothing more, nothing less, and that's rare. I appreciate honesty."

"I promise I'm not trying to get into your pants." Maybe that sounded churlish. Trask would have to be a monk not to appreciate the thought of getting into Felipe's pants, and he wasn't that much of an ascetic. "At least not tonight."

"Well, I'm definitely trying to get in your pants." Felipe gave an airy wave as he picked up a slice of the flatbread. "But not tonight." His dark eyes twinkled wickedly. "We've got to save some things for other dates."

Other dates…. Just how far did Trask plan on taking this with Felipe? One date and coffee did not make a commitment. Felipe had been hounding Trask for a few months now. He had to give him points for persistence. Planning another date so soon might give the imp ideas that Trask wasn't ready to tackle. Still, Trask couldn't deny that he wanted to see Felipe again. He enjoyed the hell out of their conversations.

"You've gotten awfully quiet on me," Felipe said with a shrewd look. "The thought of more dates have your tongue tied up in anticipation or terror?"

Trask smiled faintly. "Maybe you can come down early, before our game in a few weeks," he suggested. He definitely wanted to see if this zing he got when they were together had a little more chemistry than just attraction. He wasn't going to jump all over a man twenty years younger than him for fleeting hormones. "We're not getting together until the afternoon. Ryan's watching the store in the morning. We could do something."

Felipe tapped a finger thoughtfully against his lips. "That depends on two things."

"Okay, one." Trask raised a finger.

"How do you feel about puppies?" Felipe asked, cocking his head.

"I like puppies just fine," Trask said slowly, mystified. "Why?"

Felipe blew out his breath and ran a hand through his hair. "My old girl had her last litter. I'm going to miss her babies. She's always had the best. Super-smart sweeties. I've been taking care of them until they're old enough to go to new homes. I'd like to bring one of them down to give to Jaydon, Brett and Daphne's son. I'd trust one of my puppies with him. If we make a day of it, I'd like to bring my favorite too. By then most of the rest of them should be adopted. But Waldo shouldn't be alone all day until Jaydon claims him. And Sophie's really special."

"You're not trying to talk me into one of them, are you?" Trask hadn't had a dog since Spaz died years ago. He didn't have it in his heart to replace the guy. Spaz had been with him through the worst. There had been times when he hadn't left Trask's side even to eat. Trask still missed the silly, overactive mutt.

"No, I just don't want to leave Sophie all day and half the night. My mom's working at the hospital that day, and Dad's taking my sister to DC for some nerd thing. I suppose I could ask my grandparents to keep an eye on them, but… don't laugh; these puppies will be gone soon, and they're the last. Could I bring them with me? They will have had all their shots. They'll be weaned. They're learning to go outside. If I bring their box and their toys, they shouldn't be a problem."

Felipe was serious, and the pleading look he sent Trask's way would've been hard for anyone to resist. Spaz used to come with him to the store, Trask remembered with a smile. He'd loved it. He had his own dog bed behind the register and his favorite customers who stopped by just to see him. Trask had even built a little fenced-in yard out back and a doggie door so he could come and go.

"If you keep an eye on them, I don't mind. We can go for a walk by the river, wear them out before the game." There was a little spot in the back room where they could put Felipe's box. "Though you might have plenty of adoption offers before the end of the day if they're as cute as you say."

Felipe whipped out his phone and brought up a picture of an adorable rust-colored pup with lively eyes. "That's Sophie. She's got a lot more of the Irish setter in her than the others. But she's the smartest one of the bunch."

"What else is in their mix?" Trask asked, picking up the phone. His heart tugged at the sight of those eyes starting up at the camera with bright curiosity. Oh, she was going to be a heartbreaker.

"They are mutts through and through. Mom's an Irish setter, golden retriever mix, the dad's German shepherd and black Labrador, though there may be something else in there as well." Felipe made a face. "He's getting on there in years too."

"They are going to be big dogs." Trask handed the phone back. His Spaz had been part Jack Russell terrier. He'd had to be inventive to keep up with him, give him things to do or else his dog got bored. And when Spaz had gotten bored, he'd lived up to his name. He could see from the expression of pride on Felipe's face that he loved his dogs as much as Trask had loved Spaz.

"No lie there," Felipe said easily, "but eager to please and easily trained. I'm really working with them now to get the basics down before they leave. A dog like that, with that much energy, will get into anything out of sheer curiosity."

Trask was taken in by that picture of Sophie, but he wasn't sure if he was ready for another dog in his life. Spaz had left a hole when he passed, old and full of his dignity. "It'll be good to have a dog at the Den again, even if just for a day. The place felt empty without my boy."

"You had a dog there once?" Felipe's eyes lit up with interest.

"Yeah, he passed on about five years ago." Trask pulled up a favorite picture of his, of Spaz sitting on the stool behind the counter, looking as if he was ready to have a conversation. "That was Spaz."

Felipe took the phone and grinned at the picture. "I imagine he kept you hopping."

"You'd imagine right."

Trask's worries about knowing what to talk about faded as the evening continued. Felipe was never at a loss for things to say, and he drew Trask in without leaving him feeling like he was being interrogated. They traded pet stories as they finished their meal, and then Felipe bought another round of coffee before they attempted to one-up each other in their *Galaga* scores.

When the after-bar crowd came in, Trask realized with a pang how late it was. "You going to be okay getting home?" he asked as Felipe rose and stretched.

"With the amount of caffeine I have pumping through my veins, I'll be wired until I hit the bridge. My house isn't far beyond that." Felipe held out his hand and tugged Trask to his feet. "Walk me out to my car?"

"Yeah." Trask left extra tip money on the game top and headed out with Felipe. The night air was a cold slap in the face after the warmth of the coffeehouse, and Trask slung an arm around Felipe's shoulders. The parking lot was dark, the dim streetlamps on the corner providing little illumination, and the lot needed to be repaved, which was a common enough sight around the city.

Felipe paused by a battered, used four-door sedan with a dog bed in the back seat. "Does your Lady give you sad eyes when you take off without her?" Trask asked as he turned toward Felipe. They were almost the same height, and when he slid his arms around Felipe's waist, he fit against him like he belonged there. Once again Trask wondered what the hell he was doing, but then Felipe's strong arms wrapped around his neck, and Trask told that nagging voice to shut up.

"Every damn time," Felipe breathed before his lips were on Trask's. It was like a shooting star, a burst of bright light on the horizon and then a long streak of fire. Trask pulled Felipe closer, learning every nuance of Felipe's generous mouth. And underneath the fire of that kiss was the realization they were both holding back. Any more and he suspected they'd scorch each other.

The night air ceased to be cold as Trask eased back with reluctance. Kissing Felipe was an experience he'd remember for a long while. "You never mentioned the second condition for our pregame date." It was a stall, and from Felipe's smile, he recognized the tactic.

"Next weekend is the last weekend for the Renaissance Faire. You should meet me there." Felipe's gaze dropped to Trask's lips. "I'm going with some friends. That will take the pressure off it being a date, and we still get to see each other."

Trask hadn't been to the Faire in Maryland in years. He'd always had a good time, though. "I'll think about it." It was a long drive, and he'd need to make sure the store was covered. But he hadn't taken a full day off since last Christmas, so he doubted Ryan would mind. "What about your puppies? They going to be fine by themselves?"

"I won't be gone as long, and I'll get Mariana to entertain them. She'll love it." Felipe caught Trask's lower lip and gave it a friendly nip. "Don't disappoint me."

"Can you be an absolute brat if I do?" Trask asked, still holding Felipe close to him. He had missed this, a touch of the hand, a close embrace. And the thought of a bratty Felipe was more amusing than off-putting.

"Absolutely." Felipe brushed his mouth across Trask's, leaving him wanting more. Then he slipped away. Trask watched him back out of the parking lot, his lips still tingling as he half smiled. Well, at least Felipe was honest. And if Trask were honest with himself, he'd admit that he'd dearly love to see Felipe again before their game.

Chapter Six

"I FEEL completely underdressed," Theo said as he turned around in a slow circle, goggling at everyone thronging the Faire before eyeing Felipe and Morris as he faced them again.

"Told you," Morris grumbled, raising his eyebrow at his fiancé. "I even offered to not wear anything under my kilt as an incentive, despite the chill, and you still didn't take me up on the idea of dressing in a costume."

Felipe rolled his eyes and adjusted his hat with its long, elegant plume. "You have your priorities screwed." He scanned the crowd and the jumble of costumed people, both visitors and staff. Trask's last text indicated he was parking, which meant he should be here soon. "Not only are you missing out on the fun, you denied yourself one of your fantasies. Silly man."

Morris had gone full out, but then again he always did. He'd chosen to add a rich blue old Eliot tartan to his collection, and he'd bought new knee-high leather boots and a kilt pin for the occasion. The wide belt, sporran, broach, shirt, and leather vest were recycled from last year. With his hair down around his shoulders and a claymore in a sheath at his back, Morris looked ready to kick some serious English ass. "Probably for the best," Morris admitted. "This wool is itchy."

Theo made an exasperated sound and put his hands on his hips. He definitely looked out of place with the group in his jeans, T-shirt, and worn denim jacket. There were plenty of people running around without costumes on, but within their group, he was utterly alone. "What are you supposed to be?" Theo asked, jutting his chin out toward Felipe.

Felipe swept off his hat and gave Theo an elegant bow. "Spanish ambassador to the king's court." He'd made the doublet, cape, and hat himself, though he'd bought the hose and used his Link boots to complete the look. He'd decided not to bother with a weapon this time. To be honest, the damn rapier got in the way of his flourishes, and he'd never look as competent with it as Morris did with his sword.

"If Lincoln hadn't opted out today, I'd be seriously outnumbered. He was worried about being the fifth wheel, but I'm the odd man out." Theo threw his hands up to the sky. "This guy Trask is on his way, right? Maybe I can count on him to be on my side."

"I wouldn't." Morris raised up on his toes and shaded his eyes. "Because I think that's him right there. You might want to hold Felipe back before he spies him and drags him off to his sex bower."

Hello, that sounded promising. Felipe leaped onto a tree stump and looked down the path. It took him a moment to pick out Trask from all the other people taking advantage of the clear weather on this last weekend. When he did, a shiver of pure heat went through him. "Oh, fuck me sideways." He laid his hand on his heart as Morris snorted with laughter. "I think I might swoon."

Trask had gone for the Dread Pirate Roberts look sans the mask. Dressed head to toe in black, his billowing shirt partially open, baring his chest, his silvering beard neatly trimmed, he was the sexiest fucking man in the entire Faire. Trask spotted him, lifted his hand, and Felipe's hormones jumped in response.

"Excuse me." Felipe leaped down from the stump and adjusted his hat. "I have someone to abduct and molest."

"Which one of them is dressed as the pirate?" Felipe heard Morris ask as he made a direct line for Trask. Behind him, Theo groaned, and Felipe smirked. He bet that before the day was over, Morris was going to get that man into one getup or another.

Trask whistled appreciatively as Felipe sauntered toward him. He stopped, crossing his arms as he gave Felipe a raking once-over. "Okay, that is fantastic. Did you make the whole costume?"

"Hold that thought." Felipe threw his arms around his neck and settled for a hug. He'd dearly love to scandalize everyone within eyesight of them, but he didn't want to be walking around in his tights afterward. It might be a little embarrassing. He brought his lips to Trask's ear. "Please tell me you later plan on having your wicked way with me while holding me for ransom."

Trask's arms slid around him in a warm embrace. "That thought has definite possibilities." He pulled back reluctantly and looked around him at the colorful array of booths with a wistful smile. "Thank you for insisting I come along. I'd forgotten how much I loved the Faire."

Felipe winked at him, though he was inwardly relieved. He wasn't sure how much was too much with Trask yet, and he knew he could be a pushy, nagging bastard. "Now you don't have to worry about disappointing me," he said airily. "Come on. You need to meet Theo, our pet non-geek, who is very disappointed in you for showing up in costume. He was counting on having a bosom buddy."

As they approached, Theo threw his hands up in defeat. "Okay, I give. I'll wear something, but not the tights. I don't have Morris's sexy legs."

Morris lifted his fist in victory with a broad grin. "Yes! Felipe, take him in hand. You're the best one to pick out something appropriate."

Felipe studied Theo, walking around him slowly as he considered the options. Any kind of nobility was out. Theo would not be comfortable in all the frippery that Felipe adored. He'd look good as a common mercenary, a little leather, a little chainmail, but that would have to wait until next year. There wouldn't be anything good at the rental shops. He'd work with Morris over the summer to get Theo properly outfitted for the following Faire.

"I'm thinking peasant," Felipe said at last and held out his hand to Morris. "Give me your credit card."

"Peasant?" Theo's brow furrowed. "Wait, he's a sexy Scottish warrior, you're a rich Spaniard, that one's a pirate…. How come I get to be the peasant?"

"Because you snooze, you lose." Felipe caught Theo's arm and grabbed Morris's credit card. "We'll get you something more appropriate and in keeping with your dignity next year. Trust me, you'll look good and fit right in with Morris. Until then, common peon, you are of the lowest rank."

Felipe led Theo over to his favorite place to rent costumes. This wasn't the first time he'd come to the Faire with somebody who'd realized they wanted to be dressed up after all. He began going through the racks, tossing various breeches and shirts over his arm. He eyed Theo's complexion and hair and picked colors to suit. "Okay." He turned on Theo, who watched him apprehensively. "Into the changing room." He pointed imperiously toward a canvas-walled area in the crowded back.

"I feel silly," Theo complained as he disappeared behind the strip of fabric, carrying the pile Felipe handed him.

"It's all in the spirit of fun. Don't be such a curmudgeon." Felipe went through various accessories as Theo changed. The good thing with a peasant was that he didn't need a lot of decoration. "You're acting like an old fart."

"No, the old fart is dressed better than me," came the muffled reply.

Felipe rolled his eyes and stole a peek out the storefront. Morris and Trask were leaning against a tree, talking as they watched the shop. His gaze lingered on Trask. He had an aura about him that went so much deeper than being one hot silver fox. Every time they had a conversation, Felipe couldn't wait until the next one.

"He's not an old fart," Felipe said with irritation.

"I know. I'm just screwing with you." Theo stuck his head out. "Okay, did I do it right?"

Felipe looked over the rough breeches, the flowing coarse-spun shirt, and the outer long vest, all in varying shades of brown that set off his tousled, honey-haired cuteness. He was a walking case of diabetes. God help Morris. "You'll do."

"Killing me with praise." Theo glanced at the belt in Felipe's hand. "Where are the holes?"

Felipe shook his head. "Wrong era. I'll show you how it goes." He circled it around Theo's waist and looped it into a knot. He stepped back to study the results and met Theo's curious gaze. They hadn't hung out too much, and most of what he knew about Theo was through Morris and Lincoln. Still, he'd seen the influence Theo had on Morris, and Felipe felt it was time he said something. "Hey, just between you and me, say a word to anyone and I'll kill you. You and Morris, you're good for each other. I like seeing him so happy."

Theo's eyes glinted with a teasing light. "You going soft on me, Felipe?"

Felipe shoved a finger at him. "You tell anyone and I'll deny it to my grave. Now come on and let's get out of here. I have a pirate to ogle, shows to watch, and a giant-assed turkey leg screaming my name."

"Let's do this." Theo stuck his thumbs in the belt and struck a pose. "Dilly dilly!"

"No." Felipe gave Theo a gentle shove toward the counter. "No dilly dilly from you. No huzzahs. Nada. You're trying too hard. Just have fun. Follow Morris's lead. Should be easy enough with as much as you googly eye him."

"You're having that problem yourself." Theo put his hand over Felipe's as he pulled out Morris's card. "Let me pay for my own getup. Morris can buy me one of those turkey legs he doesn't shut up about."

"Now that's more like it." Morris straightened and clapped as they emerged. He gave Theo a look of loving approval that had Felipe raising his eyes heavenward even as his inner romantic did a happy squeal. Those two. "Let's party."

Felipe met Trask's gaze and preened at the way he smiled in appreciation. Felipe loved having his ego stroked, and Trask was able to do it without words. He fell in next to Trask and brushed his fingers over the back of his hand. "Did I warn you that those two newly engaged fools are probably going to make us roll our eyes several times today?"

"No." Trask cocked his head as he looked at Theo and Morris. "It's good to see a happy couple. The world needs a little more of that kind of eye rolling."

"You're going to make me reveal that I'm a secret sap and not a cynic, aren't you?" Felipe sighed as Trask gave him a gentle smile.

"Your secret is safe with me." Trask pulled a map and program out of his belt pouch. "So what's it going to be first? I haven't seen the jousting in years, and it's cold enough that sitting on the benches in the sun won't be a misery."

Felipe peered over at the map. "I could be down with that. I want to see Shakespeare's Scum, too, and one of the madrigal acts."

"Food first," Morris demanded over his shoulder. "I'm hungry."

"Dude, you were born hungry," Felipe retorted.

"Actually, I wouldn't mind eating first either." Trask tucked the map back in his pouch. "It was a long drive from Richmond."

Felipe shaded his eyes against the midmorning sun. "Why don't we go down one of the lanes instead of hitting the tavern? It's early enough that the booths shouldn't have long lines."

Morris turned and headed down the lane that narrowed to a rough, knobby walkway of pounded dirt. They were forced to walk single file as a stream of people came from the other direction. Felipe fell in behind Trask. He still couldn't quite believe he was here. He'd thought he might've pushed him away with his nagging. Maybe Trask really was as chill as he seemed.

"I'm glad you came," Felipe said softly.

"How could I not?" Trask reached back and caught Felipe's hand. "First there were the texts, then the pictures from Faires past. Let's not forget the reminiscing about your favorite acts to entice me."

Felipe smirked. "Never let it be said I'm not persistent."

"And you know just how to tempt a man," Trask replied soft enough that Felipe wasn't quite sure he heard him right.

"Are you freaking kidding me?" Theo stopped in his tracks and pointed at a man striding by with one of the turkey legs. "No one person can eat that entire monstrosity."

"Care to wager on that?" Morris asked, looking back the way the man came.

"It's bigger than my arm!" Theo jabbed a finger in Morris's side. "And no short jokes from you either."

"What are you going to get?" Felipe asked as they reached the line of food booths. He scanned the menus as more than one item caught his eye. He did love the turkey legs, but he didn't want to get anything on his costume either. He'd steal a bite from Morris instead when he wasn't looking.

"The berry muffins, I think, and a large coffee." Trask ate like a bird. He claimed to be hungry and he wanted a muffin. It was like he subsisted on deep thoughts.

"Let me get the food while you grab a table." Felipe gave Trask a nudge toward the eating area. "You treated me on our last date, and I think my budget can handle some measly muffins and a coffee."

He headed toward the nearest stall before Trask could protest, and when he returned, carrying a tray with their drinks, a paper holder with two muffins, and Felipe's crab cake sandwich, he found them at a table under the spreading branches of a tree. Both Morris and Theo had turkey legs and a stack of napkins in front of them.

"I want a bite," Felipe said as he slid in next to Trask.

"I'll tell you what I told this moocher." Morris cast a narrow-eyed glare at him. "Get your own or suffer the consequences."

"You ain't going to do anything, bitch." Felipe smirked and yanked off a piece dangling on the side. It tasted as good as he remembered. "I've got too much dirt on you."

"Leave the man's meat alone." Trask broke open a steaming muffin and made a sound of appreciation as he took a bite.

"There are so many places I could go with that comment that my brain doesn't know where to start." Felipe glanced at the enigmatic man beside him with a snicker. He was so hard to read, so quiet at times that he just didn't know where he stood with him, and it drove him batty.

The corner of Trask's mouth lifted. "You, at a loss for words. I don't believe it."

Trask did have the ability to tie his tongue and put him off-balance. "What made you decide to come, other than it's been a long time since you've been to the Faire?" Felipe asked, lowering his voice.

"I'm not entirely sure," Trask admitted with a long sideways look at him. "I went back and forth on it, impulse maybe. Not because you're not cute, because you know you are, not because I'm not attracted, because I am. It's just complicated."

Complicated. Felipe had heard that one before. "Is it the age difference?"

"Twenty years is nothing to sneeze at." Trask sipped his coffee, looking off into the crowd. "But it's more different life experiences. We don't have all that much in common."

Felipe couldn't argue against that. Not that he knew as much as he wanted about Trask, but he suspected Trask was right about different upbringings. They did have mutual burning interests, though, and that had to count for something. "Seems like we're moving forward in the same direction now."

"You are a persistent man." Trask shook his head with a smile. "I've got to admire that. And I have to admit, I just wanted to see you again, even more than I wanted to see the Faire. Though I'm not sure what you see in me. I'm pretty quiet, borderline boring."

Felipe didn't think Trask would want to hear a comment about his drop-dead sexiness. "We both like the same things and we sizzle. That's a good basis for starting out."

Once again Trask shook his head, but he didn't offer any further argument. If Felipe took him on his surface attitude, he might consider looking elsewhere. But he was a big believer in actions speaking far louder than words. Trask's words made it seem like he came here on a spur-of-the-moment decision. You didn't throw together a costume like that without putting thought into it, and you sure as hell didn't drive all the way from Richmond to almost Annapolis on a whim, not when you had to get coverage for your store.

Trask was interested, and Felipe would follow this road as far as it took him.

Chapter Seven

THEO SNUGGLED closer to Morris and into the warmth of the tartan he had draped around both their shoulders. The Renaissance Festival had been interesting, with so much to do and see. He'd had more fun than he thought he would. Granted he didn't get into it at the level of Felipe and Morris. Those two ought to go into theater, but it had been fun. He'd actually felt far less self-conscious in costume than out of it, and Felipe's promises to make sure he was properly outfitted next year no longer filled him with wariness. Just as long as they didn't put him in a short shirt and tights, he'd be good.

Raucous singing filled the night air, and torches guttered at the corners of the outdoor tavern as the diehards gathered to send off the Faire for another year, which seemed to involve a lot of bawdy songs. Not that Theo minded a good bawdy song one bit. It was all in good fun.

Morris slipped his arm around Theo's waist and took advantage of the fact that they were sitting on the fringes of the tavern in the dark to steal a kiss. He tasted like the hard apple cider the tavern served, and if Theo wasn't the designated driver for this outing, he'd probably ask for another glass himself. But really, all he needed was Morris.

"So what do you think?" Morris asked as he pulled back. "I told you it would be awesome."

"I think you need to kiss me again." Theo rubbed his cold nose against Morris's cheek. "I still have numb extremities." Once the sun set, the temperature dropped. The wind had picked up, sending occasional gusts that cut right through the clothes. At least it was warmer here, huddled among the crowd.

"Come on, no hedging." Morris nudged his side. "Did you have fun?"

"You want me to say it, don't you?" Theo gave a dramatic, long-suffering sigh worthy of Lincoln. "You were right and I was wrong about the Faire and the dressing up." He supposed that if he managed to get Morris to give up most of his processed food, he could admit to enjoying a bit of geekery now and then.

Morris beamed his broad-cheeked smile but didn't gloat more than that. "So, what do you think about them?" Morris jutted his chin out to where Trask was returning to the portion of the bench he shared with Felipe, carrying another round of hand pies and coffee. The couple sat in front of them, curled in almost as close as Morris and Theo.

Theo studied Trask and Felipe as they talked with their heads near, though given the way the rest of the day had gone, Theo was sure that Felipe was doing the talking while Trask got by with the occasional comment. "I think with the both of them wearing all black like that, we'll never see them leaving when they opt to slip away to make out in the back of a car."

Actually, Theo thought that sounded like a wonderful idea, and he wondered what his chances were of getting Morris back there so he could get his hands under that sexy kilt. Every once in a while his fiancé still got shy, and Theo loved to witness those moments.

Morris made an exasperated sound and nudged Theo's ribs. "For real? That's all you have to say?"

Theo gave Morris a mystified look as the band of singers launched into another song that had most of the crowd joining in. He leaned in closer so Morris would hear him without giving away the fact that they were sadly gossiping. "I'm lost. What's got you so agitated about Felipe's date? They seem like they mesh pretty well. They definitely have the same fashion sense."

"You're impossible." Morris worried his lower lip. "And I'm overanxious. I just don't want to see Felipe get his hopes all wrapped up again. I can't deal with Felipe's sad puppy eyes."

Theo turned his attention back to the couple in front of them. Felipe's face turned in profile to them as he laughed at something Trask said. He looked happy. "Felipe never struck me as the kind of guy who listened to advice unless he asked for it or wanted people butting in. Well-meaning or not." He paused a moment and gave Morris a significant look. "Like your family."

Morris grimaced. "I hate it when you're right. Maybe I just feel guilty about the situation with Dakota. I could've issued a stronger warning. Though he surely didn't listen to that one either. Which just proves your point."

Theo didn't know Felipe that well, but he suspected a stronger warning would've had the opposite effect. "You, Morris Proctor, are a mother hen. You know that, right? Always fussing over people and details."

"So says the man who tries to single-handedly feed the world, starting with me," Morris retorted. "Don't think I didn't see you trying to mooch some recipes today."

Theo decided that comment didn't even deserve a response. He'd just wanted to know what the ingredient ratio had been in those spinach pies because they'd been delicious.

"And who personally examines every plate that leaves your kitchen to make sure all the details are right?" Morris continued, and Theo could only nod to that as well, though he'd argue that Morris was just as picky over his own details.

Theo watched Felipe and Trask, trying to see them from Morris's point of view. They looked good together. Trask seemed laid-back from what he could tell from hanging out over the day. Definitely not as volatile as Dakota and Felipe had been together. The first time he'd met them, Felipe had threatened to throw a plate at Dakota's head.

"You know how you were convinced we'd never be more than a fling," Theo reminded Morris. "Because we had such different interests?"

"You were kinda set on the fling idea too." Morris chuckled in a low rumble. "Too busy, remember? I hear what you're saying. There is a lot more to us than on the surface, so shut up and give it a chance because there may be a lot more under their surface."

Theo rubbed his fingers over the soft wool of Morris's kilt. "You know how to speak Theo."

Morris settled down and joined in on the next song, singing in an off-key baritone. When it was over, the remaining crowd called for an encore, and Theo realized that this group could probably go all night long if the drinks and food kept flowing.

"Felipe was asking if we're going to have capes and canapés at our wedding," Morris confided. "I laughed it off, but I kind of like the idea."

Theo closed his eyes with a shake of his head. "Scottie would murder me and hide my body in the walk-in freezer if I tried to put him in a cape."

"Yeah, so would my sisters." Morris sighed. "It would be cool, though."

Theo heard that underlying note of nervous tension in Morris's voice. He supposed it would make another man anxious, like Morris was having second thoughts, but Theo didn't think that for a second. It was just the idea of a big event that got him so antsy and the desire to please everybody. Theo's thoughts whirled as he looked at the people around him, the people who made up Morris's world. The world that his family didn't entirely get. "You know, I'm having a crazy thought."

"Just as long as it has nothing to do with extending the hours of the bistro until after the honeymoon. Things are going to be insane enough as it is."

The honeymoon. Wow, Theo could not wait for that, for real. It had been years since he had a vacation. The thought of it being just him and Morris at Disney and Universal Studios for a whole week of crazy fun. No work allowed. None. May couldn't get here fast enough.

"No, I was thinking of your capes and canapés idea." Theo turned toward him and lowered his voice. "What if we did both, had the big celebration that fits our families' idea of weddings and something small, zany, and fun earlier? Just us and the handful of people closest to us who can keep a secret."

Morris turned toward him, his eyes widening with hope. "Are you asking me to elope with you before our wedding that our sisters are going mental over?"

"Yep." The more Theo thought about it, the more he loved the idea. Jill and Morris's troop of sisters had taken over. Which was probably partially their fault for letting them in the first place.

"Didn't I warn you that we would have to face the gauntlet of the sisters if you talked me into a plan like this?" Despite the warning in Morris's voice, Theo could tell he was considering it.

"That's only if we get caught." Theo hugged Morris's waist. "They wouldn't even think we'd do such a crazy thing in the middle of planning a wedding with a couple hundred guests." The size and scope of it was part of what had Morris so on edge.

"I can't even believe I'm seriously thinking about agreeing to this," Morris muttered.

"We can clear off the tables one morning on the bistro deck or go down on the waterfront with just a few people. We can have all the crazy silliness we want. It'll be our secret. And then whatever tizziness our families get into, it won't matter because the important part, you and me and to death do us part, will be done. The rest is just dressing, and we can have fun." The more Theo thought about it, the more he wanted to have that quiet, crazy day just for themselves. They were getting married. Who said they couldn't celebrate that twice?

Theo felt the tension drain out of Morris's body. "You had me at capes and canapés, for real." He brushed his lips over the top of Theo's head. "I love it, especially the thought of doing it at the bistro. Just a few of us, right? Felipe, Scottie, Laila, and Lincoln? Lincoln can be trusted not to tell our sisters, right?"

Theo pondered that a moment. It touched him that Morris had thought of Lincoln too. He weighed Lincoln's desire to be a part of the secret against his ability to hide anything from Jill. Lincoln had a pretty good poker face and great instincts for survival. "He'd probably blurt it out a decade from now at some family function, like 'Hey, guys, remember when you eloped,' but by then it won't be such a big deal. What about Laila? Can she keep it quiet?"

"Oh hell yeah, she'll tease us, but no threats would ever get that info out of her." Morris nodded, his broad brow creased, and then he grinned at Theo. "When do you wanna?"

Felipe turned around and eyeballed them. "What are you two scheming about?"

Theo bit his lip to keep from laughing as Morris attempted to shoot Felipe an innocent look. It lasted for all of two seconds before Morris grinned. "Capes and canapés."

Felipe's eyes narrowed. "How come I get the feeling you're not just talking wedding planning?"

"We're eloping," Theo confided in a conspiratorial voice. "Before all the planning makes us certifiably crazy."

"Yeah, I want to enjoy the moment. Not be dying of nerves because something isn't planned perfectly," Morris added. "We're taking your idea. You and I can wear capes. Theo will make nibbles, and we'll get hitched on the down low at the bistro."

Trask turned around, a smile tugging at his lips. "Congrats, you two."

"Does this mean I get to be a best man twice? I can wear a cape and a kilt?" Felipe's eyes gleamed with mischief. "I'm in."

"You have to send me a picture of both. Are you going for superhero capes or something that would fit in more with the Faire?" Trask asked.

Theo hoped superhero. Hell, if they were going with the zany theme, they might as well carry it the whole way. They would look back on the day of the big wedding and laugh while everybody else ran around in circles.

"Oh, superhero all the damn way," Morris said, and Felipe nodded eagerly. "I'm thinking Superman. I love Batman, but he's moody. I don't want moody. I love Superman's blues and reds. Laila can wear a Wonder Woman getup. She'll freaking love it."

"Good plan. I'll make something for us and Lincoln too. He'll want in on it. The capes can be souvenirs." Felipe gave Theo a crooked grin. "Which I guess leaves you and Scottie out of the fun."

"Oh, don't you worry. Coming up with the cocktails and finger foods for the theme will be superheroic for us. We won't feel left out," Theo assured him. Then he considered Morris's earlier question. As tempted as he was to suggest eloping as soon as possible, he didn't think they'd get away with it now. "We should probably do it at least within the same year as the big wedding, huh?"

"Probably, though this means we can celebrate two anniversaries. That will be fun." Morris said with a laugh. "I say we rule out the winter months. I'll still be nervous, and I don't want to worry about slipping on a patch of ice and sailing off the deck into Back Creek. I can't really fly like Superman."

Only Morris would consider that a worry. "Let's aim for March. The ladies will be in full-tilt mode and easily distracted. We'll be in the middle of moving, so it'll be a nice break, and if we come across acting weird, they'll figure it's because of the move and the wedding planning. They'd never suspect an elopement."

"You are devious." Morris tapped his finger against Theo's lips. "I think I love that about you."

"And now you just took a turn down sapsville." Felipe snickered.

"Oh, we haven't even started getting sappy," Theo warned and flicked his hand toward Felipe. "Go back to torturing Trask's ears with your yapping."

"It's not torture," Trask protested. "I like hearing Felipe talk."

"See." Felipe stuck his tongue out at them, hooked his arm through Trask's, and turned back around to catch the end of the song.

Theo glanced around at the thinning crowd, then leaned over to Morris. "I say we slip away, leave Felipe and Trask to get into whatever trouble they want, and you and I go and celebrate in the back of your little car."

Morris laughed nervously. "You wouldn't really…." He gave Theo a long look. Theo smirked back and slid his hand under Morris's kilt, moving up along his thigh. Morris stood up, capturing Theo's hand before he could go any further. "Night, Felipe, night, Trask. Gotta go."

Chapter Eight

TRASK SLIPPED into the room and took a seat in one of the hard plastic chairs in the back. Long-familiar faces milled about, talking in low voices as they exchanged greetings and news. A few newcomers hovered uncertainly near the door with expressions ranging from hopeful to sullen as they were encouraged to take a seat. He didn't see Ryan, even though he wasn't closing the Den tonight, and then Trask remembered that Ryan had been splitting his time between this group and the one in Henrico as he settled into his new life.

This was Trask's home group. He'd been going to this same meeting on Monday nights for over a decade now. Coming here kept him grounded even when his mind wasn't on the program. His thoughts were definitely wandering tonight. He kept thinking about how much fun he'd had hanging out with Felipe and getting to know his friends better. His thoughts also lingered on kissing Felipe among all the cars in the dark field after they left the Faire. That felt good.

Trask did not get involved with young men still in college. He definitely did not get tangled with people in one of his immediate circles. If this game group worked out, then Felipe would be in his immediate circle. He had rules. Rules that had changed his life. Some argued he had too many rules, but he was still alive because of them. At the same time, he recognized rules were meant more as a guideline for life and it was possible to get too bound up in them, which could be just as unhealthy. The question he had was which applied to his life at this time?

Every time Trask told himself he was going to take a step back and reevaluate the growing situation between them, he found himself exchanging texts and phone calls with Felipe. He found himself not calling off that breakfast date they had with puppies before the game next week. With puppies. Trask shook his head in bemusement. He had lost his mind, and yet he felt vitally alive.

Over the last few months, Felipe had somehow managed to sink himself into Trask's mind. He hadn't realized how much until after that first date. Then bam! A thousand little memories of Felipe's wicked smile and laughing eyes rose to the surface. The challenging strut to his gait when he wanted to flaunt it, and the quickness of his tongue.

Trask glanced up as the meeting began and put his rambling thoughts away. He paid attention here in a way he'd never paid attention at the church services his grandmother had dragged him to as a child. He often wished that she'd lived long enough to see him turn his life around. Ryan would tell him that she did know, and the thought did help, but it wasn't the same as having her here.

He smiled faintly at old Joe as he opened up. The man was in his late seventies, as lean and tough as a steel nail. There were others who had the sober and clean years in that Joe did and gradually stopped coming, thinking they didn't need the meetings anymore, but not Joe. Trask hoped that one day he would be doing the same and maybe showing that the program still had a purpose, still worked, even with that many years behind them.

Trask looked down at his hands as Joe opened the chip container and contemplated the step for this night's discussion. This step hadn't given him as much trouble as others had in the past. Now he found himself looking at it in a new light with his fascination for Felipe. What was it inside him that had him seeking the young man out, agreeing to see him again?

"Anyone with twenty-four hours?"

A soft susurration of regret drew Trask's attention back up, and his heart panged as he saw Jason with his hand raised. He'd had at least three years of being clean. There had been a time when Trask doubted Jason would make it that far. Trask intimately knew the pain and humiliation of collecting that twenty-four-hour chip after managing to hold on for that long. He also knew the relief and healing it could bring to admit it to these rooms. His heart ached for Jason, caught up in the midst of his personal demons, but he was here and that was a good thing.

When Jason turned to sit back down after collecting his chip, Trask noted the bruised bags under his eyes, the trembling in his hands. He could've gone on another bender instead of coming here. Hell, he still might. Trask had done that before too. But he kept telling himself that if he just continued to come, something said within the NA rooms would have to sink through his thick-assed, stubborn skull. It had and it stuck.

As the meeting continued, Trask listened to the others' stories, gleaning from them some lessons he could apply to his own life, marveling at others, how the hell they were still alive, and contemplating what it meant to him. Old Joe caught his eye, and Trask knew if he didn't speak, he just might be called on to do so. It could still be hard for him to open up at times, though here, he'd come to be more relaxed about it. But Joe had been his sponsor for many years, and he was always on the lookout for Trask and making sure he didn't become complacent.

"Thank you for sharing, Carrie," Trask murmured with the rest and half raised his hand. Joe nodded in acknowledgment. "Hi, I'm Trask and I'm an addict."

"Hello, Trask," familiar voices replied like an old Greek chorus.

Trask rubbed his palms together. "There are some steps I really struggled over. Making amends for one. I had so much anger inside me, and I really felt that there were those who owed me amends first before I gave them theirs. But the steps all kind of work together, and I had to keep going back to tonight's step to get a handle on making amends." He'd gone several rounds with Joe over that very issue.

He paused, lacing his fingers together. "A searching and fearless moral inventory…." He pressed lips together in thought. "That's an ongoing process. It's not a one and done step like I once thought it was. I believed I'd go through the program, graduate so to speak, and I would be done. Thinking like that kept me coming back, but it tricked me too. Because I kept thinking of an end result and not an ongoing life-changing process. And I ended up right back here with a fresh twenty-four-hour chip, a bad case of whiplash, and the terrifying knowledge that I should be dead."

Trask glanced up and caught Jason's eyes. The raw desperation in his gaze was the same damned look from Trask's past. But Jason wasn't alone. None of them were.

The room was quiet with the empathy of similar experiences. "To me, this step has to encompass the good as well as the bad. As hard as it is to face all our shortcomings and flaws, to admit all the places where we screwed up without equivocation, the reverse can be just as difficult. I think the hardest thing for me to face then, and it's still difficult to grasp now, is that I am worthy of being loved. To be honest, it terrifies me and I push people away and I question my motives for wanting them near. Am I too dependent, or is this going to be another crutch? What can I possibly give someone who has no way of understanding the world I come from? I use that as a shield to keep myself safe, but sometimes I think I'm actually harming myself in the process."

He had no family left to speak of. He could count on one hand the number of friends he'd let get close to him, and most of them he'd met through the program. His last long-term relationship ended a couple of years ago. Hell, as Felipe reminded him, he didn't even have a pet anymore.

"I have lost people I really cared for because of it, and it's a destructive pattern I don't want to repeat." Only Trask sure as hell didn't know how to stop it. "So there, I've acknowledged it, wow." He shook his head. He supposed he ought to admit that he had no damned control and go with the flow, but that was a rough one for him. He surrounded himself with his rules, his false idea of control, and knowing it was an illusion didn't make it any damned easier to let go. He could spit out NA adages all night; applying them was another matter.

"I think what it comes down to right now is that I'm afraid of putting my toe back in those waters, because what if I succeed? That would mean commitment and working through all the ups and downs of a relationship, and dammit, that's real work. And deep down, there is still that nagging voice that asks me if I'm worth it. Some days the answer is a hell yes, other days not so much."

Trask met the gazes around the room with a self-deprecating smile. "I have chased relationships away when I was using. I have chased them away when I wasn't, but by my behavior, I might as well have been getting high. And I've kept them away by building this wall around myself and only letting a few people close. And I think that's where I am right now. On the other side of the wall and wondering if I should go through that damned open door."

He paused again and nodded, clasping his hands together. He hoped he hadn't let that run away from him. He really wasn't good at this sharing business, but he continued to try. "Thanks for letting me share."

Joe favored him with a two-fingered salute and turned his attention to the next speaker. Trask listened in quiet contemplation as more shared their stories. He was often surprised by what poured out of him when he spoke. Sometimes truths he had buried so deep that he didn't realize they were lingering in his subconscious until he opened his mouth. He had much to think about tonight.

Jason spoke at the end, his head down, his voice barely audible. Trask couldn't remember who his sponsor was, and whoever they were they didn't seem to be in the room tonight. It nagged at him as they gathered in a circle for the closing prayer. At a time like this, Jason needed a strong sponsor. The meeting ended, and a few made a beeline for the bad coffee at the back of the room. Some others surrounded Jason, while more groups broke off in quiet conversation.

Trask shrugged into his jacket and made his way over to Joe, who was packing up the meeting materials into a battered case. Joe glanced up, and a warm smile crossed his weathered and seamed face. "I was hoping you'd stick around afterward." Joe stood up and clasped his hand.

"I hadn't seen you since I brought you home from the hospital." Trask squeezed his sponsor's hand and tried to quiet the worry inside of him. Joe was showing his years tonight in the slump of his shoulders and the pallor of his complexion. "How are you feeling?"

"Better. The medicine seems to be doing its thing." Joe rapped his knuckles against his bony chest. "It's going to take more than a heart scare to slow me down."

Trask smiled. "You'll outlive us all just out of pure stubbornness."

"You going to speak at my anniversary meeting in a few weeks?" Joe stood up slowly and pushed the case toward Bethany, who picked it up to stow away. She shot Trask a friendly smile, and it seemed to him that those smiles had been getting a little friendlier each time they ran into each other.

Trask had never made much of an issue about his sexual orientation during these meetings, though over the last ten years or so people in the Richmond area had become much more open-minded about things as the city began to change. Joe and Ryan knew, but precious few others. Because he was so closemouthed, that meant he occasionally had to dodge an interested lady, and in all his years, he'd never found a way to do that that didn't lead to embarrassment for them both.

"I wouldn't miss it for anything," Trask assured him.

"So you've met someone?" Joe asked, crossing his bony arms. The faded blue denim of his shirt matched his eyes.

"I've known them casually for a couple years now." Trask never suspected Felipe's interest would turn toward him or how it would feel to be in his crosshairs. It was an interesting sensation, a little flattering, though it left Trask bemused if he were honest. "They've been after for me for a date for a couple months now."

Disappointment crossed Bethany's face, but then she put on an easy smile. "Seems to me you should give it a whirl." She patted his arm. "No harm in trying."

"You of a mind to get caught?" Joe asked with amusement glinting in his eyes after Bethany excused herself.

"I have, twice so far." They might as well call the Ren Faire day a date instead of describing it as a group hangout. If it ended in kisses, it should be considered a date. Maybe he was old-fashioned that way. "And have plans for a third."

"About time." Joe clapped Trask on the shoulder. "You mind coming over a little later this week? I need some help pulling things from the garage. We can talk more about your new someone and what you said tonight."

There weren't many people that Joe reached out to for help, and Trask felt honored to be one of them. "Don't mind at all, just let me know when."

Trask was actually grateful Ryan wasn't here tonight, because his share would lead to questions he wasn't prepared to field yet. Not with Ryan's dislike of Felipe and what he stood for. At least he'd been distracted lately at work, because Ryan hadn't even questioned why Trask had taken a Saturday off.

He was tied up with a visit from his soon-to-be in-laws and wedding planning, and it gave Trask a short reprieve, though he was sure he'd be dodging more concerns from Ryan soon. This would give him a chance to talk it out with Joe before Ryan stuck his opinion in there. Trask loved the man. He'd been friends with Ryan for years, but he wasn't blind to how Ryan held on to perceived slights.

"Will do." Joe shrugged into his heavier jacket and fished out his keys. "You heading out?"

Trask glanced over at Jason. The people around him had thinned. Jason was wringing his hands as he lingered. Afraid to step out the door. Trask had been there too. There probably wasn't a damn thing he hadn't tried to use as an escape when the pain, fear, and guilt got to be too much, and sometimes knowing that it would be worse when he woke up had only made him run toward it harder. Addiction was a vicious, ruthless beast.

"I'm going to go see if Jason wants a cup of coffee." Trask smiled, remembering one freezing spring night when Joe had approached him with an offer for coffee and conversation. The best way he could give back that gift would be to offer it to someone else.

"I think that's a fine idea." Joe nodded his approval with one last clap to Trask's arm, Joe's way of expressing his pride. "You go on and do just that."

Chapter Nine

"OKAY, THIS is the real test," Felipe said as he opened the back door to his car and slid in before Waldo could make his escape. He liked to hide, hence the name Felipe had given him. With the puppy's antics, he had no doubt Jaydon and the little fella would become best buds. He picked up the training harnesses and slipped them on Waldo first, then Sophie. They crawled over him, tails whipping, tongues lolling with happiness. "If you like Trask and he likes you, then I'm taking it as a good sign." Felipe was a firm believer in a dog's ability to recognize a closet asshole.

He opened the door again. Waldo made a bolt for it and then looked back at Felipe with an almost comical expression as the leash and harness brought him up short. "Don't worry. The Karlins have a fenced-in backyard. You can run amok all you want. But you might want to learn to come when Jaydon calls. Because that may give you more freedom, you renegade."

Felipe stood up and looked back at Sophie, who eyed the ground from the height of the seat. "It's okay, you can do it," Felipe encouraged. To his delight, she cocked her head and hopped down onto the floor, then onto the ground from there. "That's my girl. That's how you think through a problem."

He texted Trask to let him know they'd arrived and then let the puppies sniff around and play after being confined in the car for the last ninety minutes. Trask lived in a little complex off Broad Street, not far from his shop. It seemed like a nice enough place, but for the lack of greenery. Sometimes it sucked living in a rural county, but not when it came to the scenery. Felipe wasn't sure he could trade his views of the forest for the wash of blues and grays from the buildings, even if he had the extra company and a more exciting nightlife.

Trask ambled out of the apartment building in his shirtsleeves despite the chill and paused when he saw the puppies. "You weren't kidding. They are adorable." He crouched down, holding out his fingers to be sniffed as the puppies tumbled over to greet him. Now that was a sight guaranteed to tug at every one of Felipe's heartstrings. He was a total sucker when it came to a man who loved animals as much as Felipe did. "Hey there," Trask crooned in a soft voice. "I'm Trask."

That alone should have been Felipe's clue during his doomed relationship with Dakota. The man had no time or patience for a pet. He bet Dakota would love one if he paused long enough to see what he was missing. But he would never give it a chance.

Felipe walked over as Trask rubbed ears and wagging rumps with tattooed fingers. "Yeah. If it isn't love at first sight for Waldo and Jaydon, then I've lost my innate ability to match a puppy with the love of its life." And from the way Sophie was licking Trask's hand and wiggling so hard that her entire body was in motion, her attraction to Trask was as strong as Felipe's. Good. Trask needed some unconditional love, and Sophie needed someone who would challenge her intelligence and energy.

Trask tilted his head back, his dark eyes warm enough to light up the overcast day. "I've got a spot for them ready upstairs. Hungry?"

For a lot more than food. Felipe wouldn't mind another round of kisses like the one he'd received when he last saw Trask. "Definitely."

"I hope eggs and toast are fine," Trask said as he stood up. "I don't really make anything fancy when it's just me, and I wasn't sure what to buy."

"You could've handed me a box of cereal and some milk." Felipe's pulse jumped as Trask brushed a kiss over his mouth. "Do that again and I'll scandalize your neighbors."

"Well, we can't have that." Trask winked at Felipe and took Sophie's harness from him. "Come on. I've got some toys with your name on them. We'll pick out a few for you and your friend and send him off to Jaydon proper."

Felipe followed Trask into the ancient elevator that rattled its way to the top floor. "So what have you got planned for the game today?" Felipe asked, his curiosity nagging him. He was looking forward to role-playing almost as much as he was looking forward to spending the day with Trask. It had been over a year since he had a chance to roll the dice.

"You'll see," Trask replied with an enigmatic look. "And don't think you can cozy up to the GM either. It won't work."

Since Felipe had been considering just that, he assumed an innocent expression. "I would never stoop to such underhanded tactics."

"That remains to be seen." Trask chuckled as he unlocked the door to his place.

Felipe had an impression of a studio-style apartment before the door closed and he wrapped his arms around Trask's neck. "I've been thinking of this since our last kiss."

He locked his lips on Trask's, gratified by the man's immediate response, and didn't let go until they were both breathless. When he pulled back, he noted the bemusement in Trask's expression with satisfaction. Felipe wasn't going to be the only one thinking of doing that again late at night as he tried to sleep.

"I think that was better than a cup of coffee." Trask's gaze dipped to Felipe's mouth again. He leaned in, pinning Felipe to the door, his hands caging Felipe to either side of his hips. Felipe's pulse jumped as their lips met again in a kiss that devastated his senses. Trask kissed like he was indulging in every moment.

"Just coffee?" Felipe teased when he could think again. "Come on. A whole-milk mocha latte at least."

"If you knew how much I liked coffee, you'd take that as a compliment." Trask crouched and unclipped the leashes to Sophie and Waldo's harnesses. He pointed to a dog bed in the corner and a small pile of toys. "The bed's new, the toys belonged to Spaz. I couldn't seem to make myself toss them. There's fresh water in the dish, and I bought a little puppy kibble for them so you wouldn't have to worry about using yours."

Stunned, Felipe watched Trask walk away toward the kitchen. "And sexy on top of all that. I'm such a goner," he said under his breath as he leaned back against the door.

Sophie followed on Trask's heels without a backward glance, as if she agreed with Felipe's assessment, while Waldo moved around the main room exploring. Felipe was nosy, he'd fully admit it, and the way a man set up his living space said a lot about him. The bed was simple, big enough for two but barely, with a bedspread haphazardly pulled up. A comfortable chair sat in the corner with a bookcase on both sides and a fold-up tray stand nearby. The dog bed wasn't far from the chair, and an old rug lay underneath it for extra padding.

Waldo pounced on a squeaky toy shaped like a snake and shook his head ferociously. Felipe crouched by the bowls and half filled one with kibble. A gigantic flat-screen TV dominated one wall, with a sleek entertainment center beneath. The only decorations were a signed picture of Martian Manhunter, a gorgeous print of cherry blossoms, and several photos. Felipe crossed to the pictures. One was of Trask and a Jack Russell terrier with intelligent eyes. Another captured Trask, Ryan, and some chick Felipe had never seen before. Trask and an old man dominated the third. The final one was of an old lady with steely determination in the set of her jaw. She had to be family of some kind. She and Trask had similar bone structure. But that was the limit of the photos. There wasn't even one on his nightstand.

"Been here long?" Felipe asked as he came to the kitchen and leaned against the entrance.

"Ever since the elevator was almost new." Trask laughed lightly. He scrambled up a mess of eggs at the stove, moving around Sophie, who explored the area at his feet. "It's so close to the shop that I can walk to it unless it's a real shit day. And the rent isn't bad. The yuppies haven't gotten a hold of this part of Richmond yet. I have enough stashed away to buy a house, but I can't see needing all that space, so I've just kind of stayed."

Felipe crossed to the toaster as it popped, and he laid two slices on each plate in front of it. "Is there anything I can do to help?"

"Sure." Trask nodded to the fridge. "There's butter in there if you want it and some raspberry preserves, which is my favorite. Coffee's on the counter. Pour yourself a cup."

It smelled heavenly. Felipe did appreciate a good cup of coffee. He pulled out the preserves from the fridge. Just about everything he'd seen in the apartment was secondhand and worn with long use except for the TV and coffee maker. Trask's setup was barista level. "Wow, that is some machine."

"I take my coffee seriously." Trask slid the eggs on the plates and flipped off the stove. "Let's carry it out to my excuse for a balcony. It's where I keep my table unless it's really bad out."

The air had a bite to it, but Trask seemed impervious as he walked out in his bare feet. Felipe was not that warm-blooded, so he grabbed his jacket before following with their coffees and condiments. Trask pulled out a chair for him at the wrought iron table, then sat down across from him, propping his feet up on the railing. The pups followed, taking the opportunity to explore every nook of the balcony. There wasn't much to see but the somewhat run-down face of the city, but Felipe bet it was pretty at night.

"I'd forgotten you said you don't drink or I wouldn't have invited you out to the bar that first night." Felipe stretched out his legs and sat back with his plate in his lap.

"Don't worry about it." Trask put a good-sized dollop of preserves on his toast and tackled that first. "You go to bars often?"

"Not really. For one, there aren't that many close to home that I'd feel comfortable at. Casey Jones isn't bad, but then there's the hassle of finding someone who'd take turns being a designated driver with me. Not many people want to drive out to my place after dark. And quite frankly, the idea of getting lit up on a Friday night doesn't really have much appeal anymore."

A sympathetic smile crossed Trask's face. "Was it a bad hangover or someone you picked up that made its appeal fade?"

Felipe grimaced at the memory. "Hangover and the aftermath definitely played a part. This summer I'd gotten pissed about the relationship I was in, so I ended it and then drowned my sorrows and irritations in tequila." Bless Morris. He'd sat with him the entire night listening to Felipe bitch and whine. Felipe pressed a hand to his stomach as it reacted.

"I still can't say tequila without being sick to my stomach. I woke up with a hangover to end all hangovers and not entirely sure if I was sober yet. Morris's boyfriend was being annoying, and they were sucking on each other's faces to add to my misery. To put a cap on it, I was stuck being social with my family for the rest of the day while my mom and lola made paella. It's normally my favorite, and they kept trying to serve me more. When I finally escaped, I swore I'd never let a guy get me that worked up again."

"You are a quicker learner than I was." Trask didn't follow that tantalizing comment with more information to satisfy Felipe's curiosity.

"Not quite. A few weeks after that I got lit up after a con. It was in a brewery, of all places. And I was stuck in a car with Morris for hours the next day." Felipe shook his head at the memory. "Actually, if I'm honest, Morris was stuck with me. Two miserable hangovers in a row were enough to make me realize that I'm more of a social drinker than a binger."

Trask made a noncommittal sound, though his attention remained focused on Felipe. He was a hard read. Felipe found that a challenge.

"Besides, most of the people I hang with don't get wasted. They may have a beer or two, Morris can kill a pitcher of margaritas on a long weekend, but that's the extent of it." Felipe glanced down at Waldo, who was looking at his toast with such hope in his eyes. "Don't be a beggar. I'm not the sucker you're looking for." Felipe wagged his finger at the unrepentant pup before turning back to Trask.

"Being tipsy is fun. But I have a hard time staying still unless I'm at my sewing machine and super focused." Felipe lifted his plate onto the table so Waldo wouldn't be teased over his toast. "I've drawn a couple cool concepts for a costume while tipsy, but I once sewed a zipper on backward too. No more getting drunk for me. I don't want to be that guy, you know the one everybody snickers over because he's being a monumental asswipe while lit the fuck up."

"Yep, I have met that guy many times." Trask gently nudged Sophie away from knocking over his potted plants. "Hell, to be honest, I've been that guy."

Now Felipe was intrigued. He could not picture Trask being that asshole. "You've got to give me more than that. What was it? Inappropriate comments, thinking you're so clever when the alcohol hits you? That has gotten me into trouble a few times."

"No, I was a belligerent drunk." Trask fisted his hands and lifted them up with an inscrutable expression. "I tended to let these do the talking for me when someone else got mouthy."

"Good thing neither one of us is in danger of getting wasted around the other. Because I'm mouthy sober. Apparently I'm worse drunk." Felipe traced his finger over Trask's knuckles. Trask was one big still water. Felipe had gone swimming enough to know deep and sometimes dangerous currents ran underneath still waters. "That's pretty much my extent of drunk stories. It's a sad lot."

"No, not at all." Trask set his empty plate aside and drew up his legs. "I'm utterly incapable of just getting tipsy, so I stay away from any hint of it."

He seemed lost in thought as he looked out over Richmond and idly scratched Sophie's head as she laid her paws on the chair and stretched up to meet his strokes. "You really are a sweetie, aren't you?"

Felipe tamped down a little spark of hope. He wanted a special home for Sophie. The way Trask had talked about his Spaz, and how long it had been since his boon companion had passed, made Felipe think maybe he was open to loving another. Felipe crossed his fingers that Trask would take to the puppy as much as she seemed to be taken by him. Trask lifted her onto his lap and smiled down at her as she nuzzled him. There was none of his usual guardedness in that look. "I shouldn't do this. It'll make you think it's okay, and one day you're going to be far too big to be on anyone's lap."

"But not today," Felipe murmured.

A quick smile flicked across Trask's lips as he met Felipe's gaze. "No, not today. So, the other night you asked me why I asked you out after I said I wouldn't. I have to ask you, why me?" He gestured back to his apartment. "This is pretty much me, not much that's interesting."

Interesting was not the word, fascinating more like it. "Well, at first it was just because you're sexy and not easy. I like a challenge."

Trask frowned, his heavy brows drawing together. "A challenge? Like an itch to be scratched?"

"I'm not as flighty as all that. I prefer someone who's not all let's get it on. I enjoy a good lay, but I like to have a rapport with someone before the boom-chicka-wow-wow. It adds to the boom."

Trask's lips twitched. "I see, I think. Then?"

"You told me about Spaz." Felipe gestured to Sophie, who was trying to lick Trask's face and hands at once. "Any man who loves a dog that much is a man I want to get to know more."

"Well, come on, then. Let's go run these two around the park so they collapse into a fluffy pile of fur when we get to the Den." Trask set Sophie on the ground and stood up. "The game is all ready to go, so we have nothing to distract us until then but these two hooligans. Maybe we can work on that getting-to-know-you a little more, because I find myself wanting to see you again every time we say goodbye."

Felipe grinned up at him. Trask had a way about him that just melted Felipe like a marshmallow toasting slowly over an open fire. And what really tickled him was that he didn't think Trask did it on purpose. He wasn't saying it to score points or to get his hands all over him. It was simply the truth the way Trask saw it. Yeah, that boom-chicka-wow-wow was going to be an explosion when it happened.

Chapter Ten

"AND THAT is where I'm going to end it tonight," Trask announced, folding his game screen down across his stack of notes and books. He glanced around the table at the gathered group with a sense of satisfaction as the howls erupted.

"Are you serious?" Morris demanded, his jaw dropping.

"Aw fuck no, man, you're killing me." Dakota rocked back on the legs of his chair, then shot a guilty look at Daphne. "Sorry."

"Sadly, Jaydon's heard worse from me." Daphne glanced over at her son, who had fallen asleep in Trask's comfortable chair almost the moment he'd sat in it. Nestled up against him were two equally exhausted puppies. She shot a glare at Felipe. "You'd better find a good home for Sophie, because Jaydon's going to be asking about her constantly."

"I'm working on it." Felipe flapped his hand dismissively. "Unless you want two. Jaydon seems like he has the energy for it."

"But I don't. No encouraging my wife," Brett cut in. Then he turned to Trask. "You are evil, man."

Trask smiled slowly. He loved having a role-playing group that got into the game so much. He often spent hours crafting a session, and players like this, who created intriguing characters and then ran with them full tilt, were a joy to GM for. "I know it. So you enjoyed yourselves?"

"Are you frickin' kidding me?" Felipe waved his hands. "That was fantastic. When are we going to do it again?"

"I'm available next weekend," Jackie said as she picked up her scattered dice. "If I have to wait a whole month to find out if I make it out of that Imperial oubliette, I'm going to kill someone."

"I have to work." Lincoln grimaced. "Please don't kill me, but this is the second Saturday in a row Theo let me take off. I'm not going to push it and ask for a third. Someone can play my character if you really want to get together."

"That's a nice offer, Linc, but I can't make it either. I'm going to be up in Philly for a three-day show." Morris turned to Trask. "It's an anime-heavy convention. I know you do a lot of online sales in that area. Do you want me to bring some of your postcards?"

"Yeah, that would be cool." Trask had heard of that con, and he'd considered sending Ryan a few times, but he wasn't sure if the end result would be worth spending the money on gas, hotel, and food. If he got enough nibbles from the postcards, he might have to reconsider. "Thanks."

"No problem." Morris tucked his character away in a folder. "That was a seriously awesome game, man. I hope you'll do it again."

Trask took in all the expectant expressions. He had missed this. And the drama he'd been concerned about between Felipe and Dakota had not surfaced. A few swipes had been taken at each other, but then they'd done the same with everyone else and it had all been in character without the edge that true animosity caused.

"Yeah, I'd like that. How often did y'all say you got together?" Trask asked.

"About every third weekend if we can swing in. That'll put us the weekend before Thanksgiving." Felipe lightly punched Lincoln on his arm. "You think your nursemaid will let you out by then?"

"He's not my nursemaid." Lincoln grimaced and shrugged. "I should be able to swing it."

"Don't ask me," Brett said. He walked over to his son and gently shook Jaydon's shoulder. "Daphne's our event planner. I make no decisions around the holidays without consulting her."

Jaydon yawned and sat up, half his curls mashed to the side of his head as he looked around the room with confusion. His brows came together in a fierce, sleepy scowl as Waldo came awake with a start and a yip. Jaydon's whole expression changed to joy as he hugged the puppy to him. "Look, Dad. See, he didn't pee on me like you said he would."

"Yeah, but he's still not going to sleep in the bed with you. We bought him a nice new dog bed." Brett scooped up Sophie and sat her on the floor. As Trask watched Jaydon with Waldo, he didn't think the battle was one Brett would win.

Trask looked at Daphne, who was checking her phone with a frown. "Is that weekend doable for you?"

"Yeah, I think so, but it's going to have to be the last one until after the holidays." She met everyone's disappointed looks. "I feel you, but it's too crazy. Unless you feel like schlepping to my place and dealing with me wrapping presents and making cookies."

"The real question is will we get to eat the cookies?" Morris asked. "I'm a certified taste tester."

"Don't I know it." Daphne finished gathering their belongings and took one look at her yawning son. "See you next time, guys."

Sophie watched them go with Jaydon and Waldo, her tail wagging uncertainly until she sat down with a little whimper. Trask's heartstrings tugged, but before he could pick her up to offer comfort Felipe was on the floor with her, playing and rubbing her belly. He was half puppy himself, and half ornery cat as well. He certainly had the pride and arrogance of a cat, but this was another side of him Trask liked just as much.

Morris, Lincoln, and Jackie left not long after the Karlins. Dakota stayed behind to help Trask and Felipe straighten up. The store had closed a couple of hours ago, and the front room was dark. Trask felt a little bad that the game had gone on so long because now everyone had a trek ahead of them. Next time he'd propose they start at noon and end a little earlier. Dakota finally left after several lingering glances toward Felipe that the other man didn't seem to notice.

"What was up with that?" Trask asked after the door shut and the chime faded.

Felipe rolled his eyes. "My guess is he was looking to get a room for the night instead of heading back to Baltimore and wanted a warm body to fill it. I ignored him," Felipe said with a sniff of dismissal. "Dakota is all about the casual bang with no ties."

Trask thought about Dakota's visit to his shop and wondered if there was more to it than it seemed. He did not want to get involved in the middle of a triangle. As soon as he thought of stepping back, he rejected the idea. Dakota had his chance and he'd lost it. This was Trask and Felipe's opportunity to see what might happen, and Trask didn't want to let it slide away without a protest.

It had been a wonderful day all around. Trask and Felipe had spent the entire morning and early afternoon talking. Felipe had a way of drawing him out with unconscious ease. He sure as hell didn't know what Felipe got out of their time together other than his teasing wish for eye candy, but for Trask, Felipe was rapidly becoming a friend he could trust. Maybe it was reciprocal.

"So what are your plans for the holidays?" Felipe asked, pulling a much-battered tennis ball out of his backpack and sending it rolling across the floor as Sophie bounded after it with delighted yips.

Trask debated on how to answer that. In his experience, those with deep family connections always seemed to feel bad for those who had no one to share the holidays with. He'd spent a couple meals with Ryan, though he expected this year Ryan would want to do the whole double family thing with his fiancée. A few times he and some of the others from his home group would have a little thing on their own. He hadn't heard of any plans for this Thanksgiving, though.

"Not sure yet. I may just keep it low-key this year." Marie's Diner down the street did a real killer turkey special that came with all the trimmings plus a slice of his chosen pie on the side. It didn't take long to reheat, and the meal was always one he looked forward to. He just replaced the turkey with extra macaroni and cheese.

"If you're interested, you're welcome to join our dinner at my family's place. It's usually a pretty big mix. We have people from my dad's side who always get into an argument with people from my mom's side, often in two different languages, so it gets to be a little hilarious if you're a bystander." Felipe shot him an amused look. "Though I'll warn you we only have two settings, loud and louder."

That made Trask smile. He had a crazy mental image of a room full of Felipes all going off on their own tangents. "I'll think on it and let you know. I wouldn't want to intrude on family, though."

"Intrude away," Felipe said with an airy wave. "We do all the time. But if it'll make you feel better, there will be friends coming and going most of the day. We do an open house type thing, and there will probably be a few extra guests during dinner as well. My lola's not satisfied unless she feeds a battalion of people."

Their upbringing couldn't have been more worlds apart. Trask's old lady never cooked unless it came out of a box, and her idea of a feast was three kinds of alcohol to chase her pills down. Their holidays used to consist of going over to his uncle's house, right up until the year his dad had tried to run him over with the truck over some dumbass argument. That incident just about broke his grandmother's heart.

That wasn't to say all of his memories were bad. There had been holidays at friends' houses where Trask had seen how healthy families behaved. There had been quiet one-on-one times with his grandmother.

And since he'd been on his own, after he'd pulled himself out of the same pit his parents had been in, there hadn't been one holiday that passed where he hadn't been grateful for what he did have.

Trask felt a tugging at his feet and glanced down at Sophie, who had grabbed a hold of his pants cuff and was pulling for all she was worth. That place in his heart that had been empty since Spaz died called to him. "You are going to be such trouble," Trask murmured as he crouched down and lifted her wiggling body. One ear tried to stand at attention, its tip bent over. She was going to be at least three times the size of Spaz and just as intelligent. "A man would have to be constantly on his toes to keep you occupied and happy or you'll be into everything."

A soft, knowing smile crossed Felipe's face. "The right kind of man would consider that a happy challenge."

Trask cradled her closer, feeling that spot fill up as Sophie licked his cheek and whipped his arms with her tail. "That was your intention, wasn't it, when you brought her over?"

Felipe attempted an innocent expression that he could not hope to pull off on his best day, and Trask merely raised a brow in return. He was going to be a dog owner again, and he couldn't even be mad at Felipe for such underhanded tactics.

"I saw how much you loved Spaz. You didn't even have to say it." Felipe shot Sophie a wistful look. "I love that girl. She's the best of any of Lady's pups, and she's had some good ones. She's going to be as sweet as her ma, and I wanted her to go to someone who would appreciate her and who would give me the chance to visit. Besides, she has followed you around almost nonstop since you met. I think she claimed you first."

"Sophie, huh?" Trask sat her down with a shake of his head. "Who would ever think I'd have a lady and not another hellraiser?" He scratched her ears. "Though I expect you can be both."

He stood up, catching Felipe's triumphant grin, and pointed his finger at him. "And you are one sneaky imp."

Felipe smirked. "I guess it's good you caught on to that early." There was not one trace of guilt in his eyes, only supreme satisfaction, and suddenly Trask wanted that look there for other reasons.

"I guess I should thank you, then." Trask closed the distance between them. He had a momentary impression of Felipe's dark eyes widening in surprise, and then he had Felipe pinned between him and the round table.

"Trask…" was all that Felipe had time to say before Trask captured that generous mouth of his in a heated kiss. Felipe made a muffled sound against his lips and then kissed him back, his strong arms winding around Trask's neck.

He challenged Trask in every way, and he suspected that if he laid out every ugly incident from his past, Felipe wouldn't bat an eye. He'd demand to know why Trask was living in the past instead of in the moment with him.

The heat that flamed up between them had Trask's entire body alive and awake. He felt Felipe hop up and perch on the end of the table, and then his legs were hooking around Trask, pulling him closer. Thank heavens for sturdy furniture and locked front doors.

Every time Trask started to pull back, Felipe would clutch at him or make a demanding sound in his throat that had Trask diving back in, eager for more. He leaned over Felipe, one hand braced on the table as he eased him back. He slid his other hand under Felipe's shirt. His skin was smooth, so smooth that Trask wondered if he waxed or was this way naturally.

He pulled back, breathing hard as he tried to rein it in. One more moment and he'd be stripping that shirt off Felipe and maybe something else as well. "Damn, your kisses pack one hell of a punch."

"You've got a lot of banked fire in you too," Felipe said, his gaze still heated as he slid his fingers through Trask's belt loops and pulled him closer. "Kiss me again."

It would take a stronger man than Trask Briscoe to resist a demand like that. He leaned over Felipe, groaning softly as their cocks pressed together through their jeans. He took his time this round, tasting the softness of Felipe's lips, learning the shape of his mouth. Felipe followed his lead with a purr in the back of his throat as he rubbed against Trask.

He deepened the kiss, rocking against Felipe as their tongues tangoed and teased. Hot shivers raced over Trask's skin as he felt Felipe's hands under his shirt, skimming over his back. He broke away to explore Felipe's throat and touch his lips to the fluttering pulse there.

"Please tell me that one day you'll fuck me on this table so every time I go into a fight in a game I can scream a battle cry that will make your toes curl in memory," Felipe whispered with a wicked laugh.

Trask's brain short-circuited. He could picture that all too well. He'd never be able to sit at this table again without getting a boner. Then the realization hit him. They were going to fuck, just not today. Not in the back room of his store on one of his gaming tables. He just had to figure out a way to back off without tweaking Felipe's pride. "Not for our first time," he managed to say as Felipe's mouth latched on to his neck. Damn, that felt good and seriously impeded his ability to think.

"Good point. We'll save it for our second time." Felipe raked Trask's shirt up higher and tweaked one of his nipples. "Oh fuck, you have nipple piercings?"

"Yeah," Trask managed. "Some dive in Virginia Beach." He'd been there for some dumbass reason years ago. He couldn't remember why, but the nipple rings had been a result. That had been one decision he hadn't regretted.

Felipe pushed him back, and Trask stared at him in confusion. Felipe made an impatient gesture toward him. "Off with your shirt. I've got to see this."

Trask smiled in relief and snagged the back of his T-shirt. "I thought for a second you were going to kick me out of your future bed over a couple pieces of gauged wire."

"Oh hell no. I just want to see, and it would be cruel to send me home with my curiosity unsatisfied." Trask felt a little silly about being half-naked at his work with a raging hard-on, but the pure appreciation in Felipe's eyes as he looked him over quickly quelled that. "Oh, very nice."

Felipe made a little twirling motion with his finger, and Trask obediently turned around in a full circle. He took a couple of deep breaths, willing himself to calm down, though seeing Felipe half-sprawled on the gaming table was not helping. "That's a gorgeous phoenix on your back."

"Thanks. Took six rounds at the shop to get her finished." The result had been worth every minute of pain and every dollar spent.

Felipe sat up as Trask faced him again and ran his hands over the tattoo on Trask's chest, sending a hot tingle down his spine. "And what's this? Are you some kind of super environmentalist?" he asked as his fingers traced the outline of the Tree of Life.

"Nope." Trask caught his hands and kissed his knuckles before Felipe could get him all worked up again. "A survivalist."

As much as he wanted to continue kissing every inch of Felipe, he had a long drive ahead of him. Trask could be a gentleman and at least offer him a place to crash. But asking Felipe to stay the night was not a step he was prepared to take yet. He shot Felipe an apologetic smile. "I think we're confusing Sophie."

"Sure, blame the puppy." Felipe rolled his eyes at the lame attempt to back off. He gave the dog a doting smile and ran a hand through his mussed hair. "Do you have everything you need for her? We can run by the store."

Trask slipped his shirt back on, trying to will his body to calm down, but it was impossible with Felipe's voice, his scent, his presence. He rescued a fallen game miniature from Sophie's attention, trying to distract himself. "No," he said firmly as he pocketed it and rerolled the ball for her. "Go get that instead."

He met Felipe's gaze as he hopped down from the table and straightened his shirt. He'd half expected Felipe to pursue the idea of making out back here until they were both too horny to think. He hadn't fought it at all. Not even a seductive glance. Either Felipe was not as turned on as Trask, or he was thinking up some mischief. And damned if he didn't have Trask thinking he ought to lay his hands all over the imp until he was in the same state as he was, which just might be his plan. "I think I'm good for the night. We can hit the pet store in the morning. Get stuff for home and here."

Trask crouched by the puppy and gave her belly a good rub as she rolled onto her back, her paws waving in ecstasy. He was going to be a dog owner again. The idea still bemused him, but the sweet little mutt had caught him from the moment Felipe had shown him a picture, if he was going to be honest. In another month he wouldn't be able to pick her up. She wasn't going to stay small long.

"I'll leave her harness." Felipe gave the two of them a wistful look. "I have extra newspapers in my car just in case."

"We'll be okay." Trask fetched her harness. It was long past time she went out and did her thing. "Send me the stuff from her vet. Call me when you get home so I know you're there safe."

"I can't believe you're sending me home with blue balls," Felipe grumbled as he stuffed his game paraphernalia into a bag. "There ought to be a law against that."

"Consider yourself properly thanked. And think of it this way: it'll keep you awake on the drive home." Trask hid a smile as Felipe shot him the bird. The man turned him upside down in a good way, amused the fuck out of him, and had him thinking thoughts he hadn't had in a long time. Trask grabbed his keys and jacket to walk Felipe out the door.

"At least I know you're as turned on as me." Felipe boldly patted Trask's cock through his jeans as they walked outside. "It's going to take a while for that bad boy to die down. Any other piercings you want to show off before I go?"

"No, and you are a troublemaker." Trask caught Felipe's hand before he became even more wound up than he already was. It was going to take him a long time to get to sleep. He gave Sophie an encouraging smile. "Come on, I know it's been a while since you've been out." She looked up at him, squatted, and promptly peed all over his sneakers.

Felipe lost it. He had to lean against the building, he was laughing so hard. Trask looked down at Sophie, who wandered off to explore, her tail wagging, and at Felipe, who had his arms wrapped around his stomach as he snickered until he couldn't catch his breath.

"I can see that this is going to be the start of a beautiful relationship." Trask wasn't sure if he meant Felipe or the puppy.

"You're not mad, are you?" Felipe asked, wiping the back of his hand across his eyes. "She's just a baby."

"No, I should've taken her out when she first woke up. I'm sure this won't be her last accident." He dropped a kiss on Felipe's lips and thought longingly of asking Felipe to come back to his place. "Go home. Text me. I'll send you pictures of your baby in the morning."

"I will." Felipe opened his car door and shot Trask a look that sent an excited tingle through him. "Sophie saved your ass this time. She won't be able to next time. Fair warning. I'm getting you naked and keeping you that way all night."

Trask watched Felipe drive away, his body aching even more. He was in trouble. He had no doubt that after a whole night naked together, Felipe would make even more of an impression than he already had. And

Trask was having a hard enough time keeping Felipe from occupying so much of his thoughts. A few dates and this had gone from zero to hot and heavy. But Felipe had engaged much more than Trask's hormones, and that's what really had his attention.

Chapter Eleven

"Suero, I need your help."

Those words coming from Brenden Wade's lips almost made Felipe drop his plate of nachos. He set them down on the corner of a half-empty table and met the promoter's irritated gaze. "Did I hear you right?"

Brenden's eyes tightened. "Don't be a smartass. You heard me. I need your help. Are you happy?"

"Delighted." Felipe smirked. This was a first he wanted to milk. "I always love it when you ask instead of demand. What can I do for you?"

The set of Brenden's shoulders relaxed, which was about all the thanks Felipe was likely to get, but he enjoyed the idea of the promoter owing him. "We have a no-show for one of the panels." The look in Brenden's eyes was of quiet, contained anger. "This is the second time this person has done this to me."

There wasn't likely to be a third. Brenden wasn't a complete tight-ass, though Felipe would never tell him that. He'd give someone a second chance, especially if they'd given warning about having to miss an obligation, but that was his limit unless there was a very compelling reason.

"I don't normally accept assassination requests in public, but I might consider it if you make it worth my while." Felipe sat down and tucked in a napkin so he wouldn't get cheese all over his Slytherin robes. He'd invested too much time in sewing them and gathering his accessories to screw it up before the contest.

"I'll keep that in mind," Brenden said drily. "Look, I have a panel at two—"

"The one on cosplaying on a budget?" Felipe interrupted. "I was planning on going."

"Yeah, well, I need you to help comoderate, and I need you to behave yourself. No drama for the sake of a good show. Not today." Brenden gave him a stern look. "If it all works out, both of you come see me later. I might have a proposition for you for my big con."

"Have you been drinking?" Felipe asked, suddenly wary. "Why are you so mellow toward me?"

"Do you want me to go back to biting your head off?" An edge crept into Brenden's voice. "Because I can. If you don't want to be involved, just say so. I have other guppies to fry."

"Don't get your panties in a twist." Felipe held up his hand. "I'd love to do it, for real, thank you, man." If Brenden could back down enough to ask for his help, then Felipe could show his appreciation. It was seriously weird that once Felipe stopped banging Dakota, Brenden decided to act human instead of like an ice-cold marionette. Though, if Felipe were being honest, he'd have to admit that he'd instigated half their encounters. Brenden just made himself into a giant target. "I'm going to have to moderate this one with Abby Albion, aren't I?"

"How do you know she wasn't the no-show?" Brenden asked.

"Because as annoying as she is, she'd never pull a stunt like that." Felipe grimaced. "She'd have to be dying in a hospital before she'd not send at least an email." He was going to need more than nachos to deal with her for an hour. This called for a double chocolate brownie.

"Thanks again." Brenden rose from the table. "I've got to go check on lunch, make sure it's going to be in the green room on time. Don't forget to look for me after the panel."

Felipe watched Brenden walk away and shook his head. He guessed the guy had finally realized Felipe was not interested in hooking back up with Dakota, though why he should care, Felipe never understood. It wasn't like Felipe had made Dakota's life miserable. They certainly never argued as much as Brenden and Dakota did. He'd never get the two of them.

Felipe continued to eat the nachos as he pulled out his phone. Trask had been sending him pictures or videos of himself and Sophie every morning. As much as it had ached to give her up, he couldn't deny the obvious joy the two of them took in each other. The video from this morning was especially cute. Sophie's head was cocked, her heart-shaped dog tag hanging from a pink skull-printed collar. Trask was a sap. Felipe never would've guessed. Her face was all in the picture, half blocking Trask as she attempted to lick the phone during their selfie while Trask laughed. The sound gave Felipe all the warm fuzzies.

She'd grown in the last couple of weeks, even more than Waldo had. When he'd stopped by the Karlins' booth, they'd been full of stories of Jaydon and his new dog. Jaydon had even given up the joy of being at the con to stay at home with a babysitter and his new best buddy. Felipe loved hearing stories like that about his puppies and their new homes.

He pulled up another picture of Trask. He really had it bad. He'd had crushes, infatuations, relationships up and down, but he'd never pined before, and he was pining to see Trask again. Dahlgren wasn't that far from Richmond. He'd expected Trask to be here, but he'd been disappointed when he went by the tables for the Magick Den and only saw Ryan. He'd expressed that disappointment too, in a series of sad-faced picture texts. All Trask would say was that he had a prior commitment. It sucked. And Trask wouldn't say what the commitment was, either.

Felipe shoved his phone back in the leather pouch at his waist. He'd better go look for Abby and find out what she had planned for this panel. He did not want to go in cold. He waved to Morris as he passed by his friend's table and searched the crowd for the leggy blonde in a Scarlet Witch costume. She was hard to miss when she was six feet in heels.

There she was, posing for the cameras at the photography studio some enterprising soul had set up. Felipe had considered doing it because they promised to put whatever background you wanted on it. He could have a real Draco Malfoy photograph, looking like he was roaming the halls of Hogwarts, for his website. Yeah, he totally had to do that before the day was over.

Felipe made his way over to the booth and stood off to the side with his arms crossed as she finished her shoot. She spotted him, and her dimples deepened for a moment before she assumed that expression of lofty disdain. "What do you want, Short Round? Slytherin, huh, I might have guessed. No wonder we never get along."

She stopped beside him and leaned down to look at his leather Death Eater mask with an envious expression. Felipe was rather proud of how it turned out. Just like how he'd finally managed to make elf ears so that you had to know where to look to see where the fake ear began. "How do you do it?" she muttered under her breath as she turned the mask slowly over in her hands.

"Talent, Duchess. Some of us got it." Felipe tipped his head back to look up at her. Abby made him feel short. Morris, for all his size, never did that, maybe because he was an overgrown Pooh bear. Abby was an evil Amazon woman. Now that he thought about it, she should totally do a Wonder Woman. She would kick ass. She had the bearing. "I hear I need to bail you out again."

"Whatever, I told Captain Tightpants I can do it all on my own, but Brenden wants things run his own way." She lifted her eyes heavenward with a sigh. "I'm not sure what insights you can offer."

"I've got more money-saving tips up my sleeve than a realtor's royal whelp. You've got your family's cash to fall back on whenever you want it," Felipe retorted as a dangerous smile crossed Abby's lips. Dammit. He knew better than to jump on her heir-apparent status. There were few things that pushed Abby's buttons more than that, but she totally started it. And as always, his mouth continued it.

"Screw you," Abby said pleasantly, that smile still on her face as her eyes flashed. "Why don't you go hang around the Magick Den's booth some more, sulking because your eye candy isn't there? You worried that he's dodging you already?"

Ouch, that hurt and played into some lingering Dakota-fueled insecurities. "Ugh." Felipe threw up his hands. He had to rein this in or this would be the shortest panel ever. However, that dig called for at least one more swipe. "You're so fucking annoying."

"You're infuriating," Abby retorted, her dimples disappearing.

"You think you're right all the time. There's no talking to you with your nose so high up in the air," Felipe continued. "As for me, I'm fucking lovable."

"You're all mouth and nothing to back it up," Abby sneered. "I have dimples, and they're adorable."

A family passing by did a double take at that exchange. Felipe paused with another comeback on his lips as his sense of the ridiculousness broke through his irritation. He laughed. "In the rank of all arguments we've had since kindergarten, this has got to be one of the stupidest."

Abby tried to hold on to her annoyance, but after a moment, a smile tugged at her lips. "I guess it's a good thing we got it out early and not in front of everyone at the panel."

Felipe was sure there would be more incidents. This was him and Abby; neither one of them could hold back with a good crack if the opportunity presented itself. If Felipe was straight, he probably would've married her so they could send themselves off to early graves. It would've been entertaining. Bickering was the cornerstone of their relationship, bolstered by their mutual keen interest in being creative with their crafts.

"I'm sorry for the dig about your family." Felipe's sense of justice nagged at him.

For a moment, true unhappiness glittered in Abby's eyes, and then she shrugged it off, leaving Felipe to wonder if he'd imagined it. "I barely felt the sting." Abby looked away with a nonchalant flip of her hand. "I shouldn't have ragged on you about Trask. Trust you to latch on to the sexiest guy at the cons."

He glanced at his watch. "We have about an hour until the panel. Want to see if we can find a quiet spot in this crush to talk it over and plot our mutual demises?"

"Yeah, I suppose we should." As Abby turned around to search for an empty corner, Felipe admired the job she'd done on the Scarlet Witch jacket. It was expertly tailored and showed off every bit of Abby's skill and creativity. Damn her, why couldn't she just suck?

"Why the hell aren't we working together?" Felipe blurted out. He wanted to smack himself in the head as soon as the words left his lips. He wasn't supposed to be the one to bend first. Abby was. That was the unwritten code he'd gone by for over fifteen years.

Abby turned and regarded him in surprise. "Because there would be blood in the water, both of ours, within a month."

"And no one would believe any of our alibis if one of our bodies showed up in the morgue," Felipe agreed. She was right, it was a disaster waiting to happen, but damn, they would totally kick ass together right up until the double homicide.

"Still...." Abby's brows drew together in thought. "As much as I don't want to give you the credit, your rep is as good as mine."

Better really, but Felipe kept his mouth shut. She needed to stick to her deadlines. And if he were honest with himself, he'd do better if he was less of a diva. They could balance each other out, maybe. "We both get good hits on our websites, and my YouTube videos are really starting to get a following."

"I prefer Twitch. Too many trolls on YouTube." Abby eyed Felipe with growing interest. "Though having the word out on multiple platforms isn't a bad thing."

Even though Felipe had proposed the idea, he didn't want either of them jumping in over their heads. "Let's see how the panel goes and then meet with Brenden to hear his proposal first."

"And if we're both alive and scratch-free afterward.... Maybe we can discuss it," Abby agreed. "I think you should talk about your do-it-yourself tips during the panel. Those seem to be your most popular hits on your channel, and it's pertinent to the topic."

Pertinent. Well, no one said that a geek/nerd couldn't be gorgeous too. Some people had all the luck. If Felipe had her dimples, he could conquer the world. "And you should talk about what shops to hit and when. People always overlook the thrift stores and Army Surplus." Abby had clued him in on that little tidbit. It got to be expensive to make or buy everything from scratch. He'd found that modifying finds could be just as satisfying.

"Okay, all this congeniality is getting weird." Abby flapped her hand at him in a shooing motion. "Go bug someone else. I brought some tools and supplies to show off. You can help me lay them out thirty minutes before our panel. I'd just better have them all back at the end of it."

"Hey." Felipe pointed a finger at her as she started to saunter away. "I'm not the thief in this relationship. Crayon swiper."

She looked over her shoulder at him as those dimples flashed to life again. "Hey, learn how to become a better sharer if this is going to work."

Felipe had to be out of his mind to suggest it, but already the thoughts and plans he'd poked at in the back of his mind started to spill over. They could have a booth at some shows with a book of costumes and props they'd made. Unless there was a big project, they wouldn't have to work side by side unless they were at an event. And they interacted at those times anyway. They could call themselves Creatures & Cosplay.

He needed to talk to someone about this. Someone with common sense who wouldn't be afraid to tell him he was crazy. He walked by the Magick Den's table and suppressed a sigh of disappointment when Trask had not made a miraculous appearance. Ryan, however, caught his eye with a glare. He had not stopped at the table since the morning when he'd asked if Trask was coming and gotten a snarl in response. Felipe didn't know what had crawled up his ass to gnaw on his spleen, but he didn't feel like tracking it down either. Too bad if the man had to see him. It was a smaller con, and the same faces got recycled. Two feuds had been sort of mended today, first Brenden, then Abby. Ryan could bite him. Felipe had filled his be-nice quota.

Dakota was deep in conversation with Brenden, looking as if he couldn't decide if he wanted to strangle his brother or brain him with his clipboard. Personally, Felipe would pay to see both. Mended feud or not, Brenden had a takedown waiting for him.

"Those two just need to bone and get it over with," Morris said as he came up beside him.

Felipe did a double take, looking between Morris, who watched the brothers with an expression of aggravation, and Dakota, who was drilling his finger into Brenden's chest, his face red as he ranted. "Have you lost your mind? They're brothers."

"Not really. Foster brothers don't count, not even when they keep up with their foster family. And they didn't even meet until they were halfway through high school. They may say the words, but I don't think either one of them ever considered the other a brother." Morris clapped his shoulder. "I heard Brenden yoked you with Abby. How's that going to work out?"

Felipe tried to look away from the drama unfolding in front of them. He couldn't hear what was being argued, but both Dakota and Brenden were on fire. And the way Brenden looked at Dakota... no, no way. Morris was out of his mind... maybe.

"I need you to tell me if I'm crazy." Felipe finally turned away. His brain could not be expected to process both him and Abby, and Dakota and Brenden in one day.

"Yes."

Felipe scowled up at his friend. "What do you mean, yes? I haven't even given you the question to that scenario."

Morris grinned and lightly punched Felipe on the shoulder. "Because the answer to that question from you will always be yes." Felipe shot Morris the double bird, and Morris just laughed. "Okay, give me the scenario."

"I'm thinking about going into business with Abby Albion." Felipe gnawed on the corner of his lip as Morris let out a low whistle.

"Yep, certifiably nuts... though—" Morris broke off, his voice thoughtful. "You're both driven and ridiculously talented, and you don't actually hate each other. If you both can let go of childhood grudges, I can see it working."

Felipe breathed a sigh of relief. He could depend on Morris's opinion. The man was as steady as they came. He cocked his head as Brenden stalked away. Holy fuck, was Dakota checking out his ass? Felipe turned his back on them as Morris shook his head with a snort. "Christ, this is bizarro world today. I can't handle it."

Chapter Twelve

TRASK KEPT a firm grip on Sophie's leash as he glanced around the convention hall. Vendors and artists bustled around like a stirred-up anthill. It always amazed him how quickly a con got set up and taken down, moving with the precision of a dance. He spotted Ryan, loading full boxes onto a handcart, and walked over feeling a little self-conscious. He hadn't planned on coming today. He'd led Joe's anniversary meeting, then took care of some business at the Den, and when Gillian came in to relieve him, found himself driving out to Dahlgren instead of heading home to put his feet up.

He'd told himself it was to help Ryan out, but halfway to the con, he'd admitted it was really to see Felipe. He'd learned that lying to himself only led to bad things. And he was not about to start that nonsense with Felipe.

Ryan glanced up in surprise as Trask neared. "What are you doing here?"

"I came to surprise a certain someone." Trask eyed the products that remained to be packed and the rest of the boxes to be loaded. "And I figured I could give you a hand so it won't take so long for you to head home. I'm sure Reva is working her usual magic in the kitchen."

Ryan shook his head as he crouched down to hold out his hand to Sophie, who sniffed it curiously. "I'm glad you finally got around to getting another companion. It's about time."

"Sit," Trask commanded, pointing to the ground, and Sophie plopped her wiggling butt down. Trask fished a treat out of his pocket and she popped right back up. "Good girl. She's a smart one, listens, but her attention span doesn't hold for long. Not that I can blame her. She's been doing pretty good at the Den, don't you think?" He got her to sit again and gave her the half piece of biscuit.

"I do. She's a beaut," Ryan approved, making Sophie ecstatic with a full-body rub. "You never said where you got her."

Trask chuckled, knowing how this would throw his friend. "Felipe gave her to me. She was his favorite puppy of his dog's litter, and he saw my pictures of Spaz. So he introduced us, knowing what the results would be. Devious imp." It still made Trask marvel at how easily he'd fallen for his ploy.

Ryan shot him a startled look and then eyed Sophie thoughtfully. "Maybe he's not so bad. He seems to be prodding you out of your rut."

"What is that doing here?" Brenden appeared out of nowhere and pointed an accusing finger at Sophie. "I know you don't need a service animal, Briscoe, so unless you've got a good reason, get it out of here."

"It's too cold for her to wait in the car," Trask objected. "Have a heart. I'll keep her out of the way while I help Ryan load up."

"You're not even on the roster." Brenden frowned, looking at his clipboard as Sophie sniffed around his feet with a little whine for attention. "What are you doing here?" Brenden unbent enough to crouch and hold out his hand to the puppy, and his eyes softened as she pressed in close for a little loving attention. She was not people shy at all, which was good because sometimes there were all kinds of folks coming to the Den.

"You're here!" Felipe's joyful voice cut through Brenden's incipient lecture. He bounded through the milling vendors and con staff, his black robes swirling around him. Not many could pull off a full Draco Malfoy costume and look as sexy as Felipe did. Though Trask wished he'd ditch the platinum-blond wig. He loved Felipe's dark curls. Heedless of his costume, he fell to his knees before a madly wiggling Sophie. "I've missed you, baby. Look how big you've gotten. Tin Man's been taking care of you, hasn't he?"

Tin Man…. That wasn't the first time Felipe had referred to him that way. Where had that come from, Trask asked himself as he watched the reunion.

"I see where you rate in the relationship," Ryan said in an aside as he hefted another box.

"Never get between a man and the love of a dog." Trask met Felipe's gaze. Felipe's smile turned wicked, and he leaped to his feet again. Trask's heart thumped hard.

"Suero, how many times do I have to tell you that you're supposed to exit the con with the other attendees?" Brenden asked in a voice thick with exasperation as he threw up his arms. "Does anybody follow the rules around here?"

"I don't know how you can keep track of all your own rules." Felipe rolled his eyes. "You must have them tattooed on your spleen."

"Well, it's not like they've changed much." Trask came to Brenden's defense. He got it; it was a safety issue. Brenden wasn't a complete martinet. Dogs and nonattendees should be out of the way as the breakdown happened.

"You and Brenden and your rules." A teasing glint came into Felipe's eyes. "It's a good thing you two never hooked up. You'd never be able to find each other's dicks."

Trask stifled a chuckle as Brenden turned his stern eye on Felipe. Trask knew why he had his rules, though he had no idea what drove Brenden.

"You and you. Go." Brenden pointed to the puppy and Felipe, and then he turned that finger on Trask. "And you too if you're not loading."

Felipe held out his hand for Sophie's leash. "I'll keep an eye on her while you help Ryan and Cranky finds someone else to harass."

Trask's lips twitched until Brenden turned that steely eye back on him. "Thank you. I appreciate it."

"No problem." Felipe stole a quick kiss in front of everyone, winked, and then snapped his fingers at Sophie. "Come on, girl. Let's go cause a ruckus outside."

"No ruckuses, shenanigans, or running amok," Brenden called after him. "Do you hear me, Suero?"

Trask shook his head and started packing as another renegade vendor caught Brenden's eye. "What does he think he's doing trying to take that scaffold down by himself?" Brenden hurried off to deal with him, his voice carrying across the empty hall as he berated the vendor and called for Dakota to help.

"That man is going to give himself a heart attack before forty if he doesn't chill out," Trask said, neatly organizing the games as he went with the ease of long practice. He really needed to try out that new Pandemic expansion. Maybe he'd break it out this week and test it with whoever was hanging out in the back of the Den at the time. The designer had made several games that always left him wanting to play another round as soon as he finished the first one.

"That's Brenden's problem." Ryan lifted another box onto the trolley and then stood back to eye the remainder. "We did pretty good today."

"Always glad to hear that." Trask wouldn't call himself rich, but investments he'd made had paid off, and the collections he had in storage were worth quite a bit. He made a killing online. The biggest plus, though, was he made a living off hobbies he loved.

"How was the meeting? Old Joe made it another year, huh? How many is that?" Ryan asked as he locked up the money box and buried it in a crate.

"Meeting was good. Joe's got thirty-one now." Trask remembered when a year seemed like an impossible lifetime. When Joe had latched on to him, Trask had been out of hope, out of time. He'd go a month or two of being clean, even once managed to make it almost a year, and then dove right back into hell. That man had saved his life. He might be a cantankerous old bastard, but there wasn't a damn thing that Trask wouldn't do for him except start using again.

"So you and the kid... that's actually a thing?"

Trask wished Ryan wouldn't put it like that. It made him feel like an old lecher. "We're feeling it out. He seems to have no reservations, which is probably good because I have them all."

"Just as long as none of the reservations have anything to do with whether or not you'd be good for him." Ryan shot him a pointed look. "Your past is just that, your past. Long gone. You're not that guy anymore, so don't judge yourself by that."

Trask was oddly touched by Ryan's words and not sure how to respond, so he merely nodded and kept on packing. "Besides," Ryan continued, "I think he needs to consider whether or not he's good enough for you."

"Give him a chance." Trask sat another box on the trolley and strapped it down. "Look past his age and the fact that he's a cosplayer and get to know him. There's more to him than people think."

Ryan looked as if he were about to argue and then paused. "I still have reservations, but you're right. If you're serious about this, I'll give him the benefit of the doubt. You're usually a good judge of character."

"I think you're reading way too much into us." Trask stepped back and looked around to make sure they hadn't forgotten anything.

"We've had a couple dates. We're not jumping into anything serious, just enjoying each other's company."

A faint smile crossed Ryan's face. "Okay, my friend. Let's get this loaded so you can go find your boyfriend. I do have to remember Morris considers him a close friend. Morris wouldn't put up with a genuine jerk."

After they loaded up, Trask shut the back doors to the Magick Den's van and thumped his fist against the panel. "You're good to go." He gave a thumbs-up to Ryan. "I'll see you tomorrow."

Ryan stuck his hand out the window and waved as he pulled away. Trask had saved him a little time by helping him pack up. Now he could head home early, lock the van in the garage, and spend time with his fiancée. Trask and Ryan would worry about unloading the product in the morning.

Trask turned and searched the shadows under the streetlamps for Felipe. He was walking around the perimeter of the building with Sophie sniffing every bit of greenery she could find at the extreme end of her leash. He'd donned a cape with a hood, and if he wasn't at a con, he'd look sinister; now he just blended in.

Trask shoved his hands in his pockets and made his way toward him. He wasn't entirely sure what prompted this last-minute plan to come up here to see Felipe, other than he just wanted to see him. It had been a couple of weeks, and the nightly conversations and morning texts were just not enough anymore. Besides, if Trask was going to go meet Felipe's family for the holidays, and it looked more and more like he was going to cave, he'd like more than three dates behind them. Time was counting down. They had the game next weekend, and then it was Thanksgiving.

"Hey," he called softly to Felipe as he got closer. "Nice cape, though I love the whole look."

Felipe turned around, sweeping the hood off. "Yeah, I figured since it was getting colder it would be nice to have and not ruin the look." He cocked his head. "I wasn't expecting you. I thought you had a thing to go to."

"I did." Trask dropped a kiss on Felipe's lips, and before he could pull back, Felipe locked his arms around Trask's neck and kissed him until Trask's thoughts spun. He stared down at the self-satisfied expression in

Felipe's eyes and tried to collect his scattered wits. "I uh… wow, I forgot what I was going to say."

Felipe's smirked widened and he patted Trask's cheek. "You were talking about after your thing."

"Yeah… I thought maybe we could catch dinner together." Someplace where they could take the food out to the car and linger for a couple of hours without pissing off the waitstaff. He didn't want to leave Sophie alone.

Felipe glanced down at Sophie. "You've been taking good care of her. I can see how happy she is with you."

Distracted, Trask looked down at the puppy. "Yeah, she keeps me on my toes. She's pretty amazing. Into everything and chewing apart all her toys." Not to mention his headset, a pillow, and an old sneaker he didn't even remember he had.

"That's what the smart ones do." Felipe was watching Trask in an inscrutable way. It was a bit unsettling. Usually he was very easy to read. Despite the toe-curling kiss he'd just given Trask, he was starting to wonder if Felipe wanted to take a step back from this… whatever they had going on. "You had me pining for you today. I don't do pining. And I sure as hell don't admit it if I get into such a high school state."

Trask smiled slowly and reached for Felipe's hand. He didn't try to pull away. "Is pining when you can't stop thinking about the other person?"

"Yep, and long to be with them." Felipe squeezed Trask's hand.

"And you wish they were there so you can share something small and silly that happened during your day, that probably means nothing to anyone, but you just like sharing it with them and they listen anyway?" Trask asked as he drew Felipe closer.

"That would be it." Felipe slid his arms around Trask's waist. "I kept walking by your table to the point where Ryan started shooting me looks like he meant to brain me."

Trask chuckled because he could just picture it. "Well if that was pining, you weren't doing it alone."

"I was really hoping you'd say that." Felipe kissed the fluttering pulse at Trask's throat. "And since you did, how about we pick up some takeout from the Indian restaurant everyone is hanging out at, and then you can drive me back to my place."

The innuendo in Felipe's voice called to him. Yes. Every part of Trask's body focused on that one answer, but Trask pulled back to look at him to be sure this was what Felipe wanted. Pure male satisfaction and certainty stared right back at him. This was a temptation Trask was happy to succumb to. "I didn't bring any protection with me."

"That's okay," Felipe said with a wicked grin that stoked the banked fire that had been smoldering ever since Trask decided to head up to Dahlgren. "I have plenty."

Trask captured that smirking mouth in a quick kiss and headed toward his car before Felipe could give everyone another show. "Is it far to your place?"

"It's just over the bridge in Maryland." Felipe gestured vaguely in the general direction of the river. "Let me text Morris and let him know I caught a ride home. Did you want to pick up the takeout or raid the fridge later?"

Trask had been to the Indian restaurant Felipe was talking about, and he was tempted. They had the best food in the area and plenty of vegetarian options. But if they went there, Trask would have to be sociable for a good thirty minutes while they waited. Felipe was an outgoing soul. The complete opposite of Trask. He'd be drawn into conversations with no effort, and Trask didn't feel like being any more sociable than he already had today. He'd bared all at the anniversary meeting, and now he wanted Felipe all to himself and some quiet time. Pure selfishness.

"As much as I'll miss the dinner, I want you more." Trask opened the door for Felipe. Okay, that made it sound like all he cared about was screwing him. "I mean, I want to spend time with just you, on top of wanting you."

Felipe laughed and slid into the car. "I'll take that both ways. Don't worry. I'm sure there is plenty to raid in the kitchen."

Trask caught a squirming Sophie and attached her to the seat belt harness. When she got bigger she'd be able to see out of the window when she stood, but for now, Trask distracted her with several toys she could gnaw on so she wouldn't torment him with her occasional whine. He always felt so bad when she did.

"You put the dog in a harness?" Felipe asked with a note of incredulity. "That takes all the fun out of riding in the truck."

Either Felipe managed to train the puppies to stay off him as he drove or he didn't notice the distractions. Trask rubbed the top of Sophie's head and slid into the seat beside Felipe. "You ever wrap your car around a tree?"

Felipe gave him a thoughtful look. "I can't say so. But I'm guessing from that fierce expression on your face that you have."

"An experience I never want to repeat. Especially when I'm carrying precious cargo." Not that Trask valued anything at that time in his life. But that was long behind him. He kissed Felipe the way he'd wanted to moments ago, and Felipe responded as if he had been thinking the same. He was all sunshine and wicked eagerness, and Trask didn't make himself pull back until he heard Felipe's soft moan.

He released Felipe, his body aching for more as Felipe gave him a bemused smile. "Is there anything scandalous or dangerous you haven't done?" Felipe asked, breaking the spell that had Trask almost reaching for him again.

Trask considered that a moment, tapping his fingers on the steering wheel. "I can safely say that I've never gotten a girl pregnant."

Felipe burst out laughing. "That's good to know. Bringing home step-puppy babies is one thing. I don't know if my mama can handle step-grandbabies."

"And I've never deliberately hurt anyone. Haven't pulled a weapon on anybody." Trask studied Felipe's face as his mood turned somber. He had a lot of dark in his past, and he wasn't sure what a man like Felipe would think of it. Felipe seemed to be all laughter and living in the moment.

Felipe brushed his fingers over Trask's cheek. "The tidbits you drop about your past, I can picture it when you talk about it. I can see the echoes, even down to the brawling, but I cannot see you being scary violent. And maybe one day you'll give me the whole story."

Trask thought he could trust Felipe with the whole story. It had put some past boyfriends off. Others had tried to get him to prove that he no longer had a problem by trying to insist he take a drink with them. Though not all, some could handle it, and Trask had learned to judge them. He suspected Felipe could handle it. "I think I will."

Felipe's smile blossomed. He leaned in and kissed Trask's cheek. "You get to me, Tin Man. Boy, do you get to me."

Trask was beginning to realize that it went both ways. Felipe had tucked himself quite neatly into Trask's life with his infectious smiles and sassy mouth. Trask had some deep feelings brewing, and he wouldn't want it any other way.

Chapter Thirteen

FELIPE TAMPED down the spate of nerves that attacked as Trask turned off the main road onto the tiny lane hidden among the trees. This was ridiculous. He'd brought guys home before for wall-banging sex. And he'd had feelings for them to one varying degree or another. He'd never been nervous, not since his first time. Sex was glorious, messy fun, sometimes comical even, but never nerve-wracking.

This was different. Trask was different. Some would say it was the aura of Trask's dangerous past that drew him, but they'd be wrong. He was sexy enough without those hints. Just look at him. Trask could tattoo "totally bangable" across his forehead and everyone who saw it would nod to themselves at the truth. Felipe wanted to lick him like a melting ice cream cone in big, greedy slurps.

Maybe it was the way that Trask didn't seem to angst over the past or worry about the future. He treated Felipe the same way he treated everyone else. He wasn't the hot piece on the side that past boyfriends wanted to flaunt or hide or the fun fling that distracted someone from what they really wanted, and now that Morris had opened his eyes, Felipe planned a good brood over Dakota and Brenden later. He felt like a fucking moron. Morris had tried to warn him, and he didn't listen. He'd have to ask Morris what he thought of Trask, no old man comments allowed. He wanted his real opinion. Morris would give it to him when he realized that teasing time was over.

With Trask, he could just be himself and not concern himself with how it would be taken later.

"Watch out for the deer," Felipe commented as he spied movement among the trees.

"That's really a problem?" Trask slowed the truck to a crawl as the road narrowed even more and twisted around a bend.

"Oh yeah, those suckers come out of nowhere and all you see is a flash of brown hide and panicked eyes, and then just as you relax, realizing you didn't hit the stupid bastard, three of his friends go, 'Hey, that SOB made it. Let's give it a try.' Bam, dead deer on your bumper."

Trask chuckled. "Good to know. You weren't kidding when you said you lived in the middle of nowhere." Between them, Sophie started barking in excitement, and her tail whipped Felipe's arm.

"It seems farther away in the dark." Felipe pointed toward the light that gleamed through the leafless trees. "That's the lamp at the edge of the yard. It always makes me think of Narnia when I'm coming home at night. You can pull around to the far end of the driveway. I live upstairs in the back."

"Wow, big place," Trask murmured as the trees opened up to reveal the sprawling farmhouse. "This is seriously cool."

Felipe grinned and reached between them to pat Sophie. It was nice to have someone appreciate his home. He loved it here. "Just wait till you see the view from my deck. You can spy all kinds of wildlife: deer, beaver, eagles, and the ugliest bastards I've ever seen, turkey buzzards. They're huge. And the sunsets are awesome, but we'll have to wait for another night to watch."

"I'd like that," Trask said after a quiet, breathless moment. That was the appeal. Trask didn't have any qualms about admitting he was thinking of Felipe too. He didn't make a big deal when Felipe uttered anything sappy either or accuse him of being clingy. Which was bullshit. What was the point of being in a relationship with someone if you didn't want to spend time with them? Felipe never got that mentality.

Trask parked the car in the back, and Felipe was surprised to see the lack of cars in the driveway. He hoped he wasn't missing a family function that he was supposed to attend tonight. Trask rubbed his hands on his jeans. "Is it weird that I'm a little nervous?"

That touched Felipe in ways he wasn't certain how to express. This kind of honesty was new to him, especially after his last experience, and it prompted Felipe to be honest in return as he captured Trask's hand. "Me too."

"Is that so?" Trask turned to him, and Felipe couldn't see his expression, but he heard the skepticism in his voice. "It's been a while for me. What's your excuse?"

Felipe unbuckled his seat belt and reached for Trask, his heart beating faster. "It's my first time with you." And his initial attraction to

Trask was rapidly turning into something so much more. More than what Felipe was ready to process.

Felipe slid over to Trask's side of the truck, leaning over Sophie. Despite their nerves, he knew exactly what he wanted and that was his lips on Trask's, those sexy tattooed hands on his body, and he wanted to undress Trask slowly in the light of his bedroom lamp. As he slid his arms around Trask's neck, Trask's lips found his own.

Whatever nerves Trask might have, it sure as hell didn't show in his kiss. Felipe groaned, diving into the taste of him, the faint scent of his spicy aftershave, the scratch of his beard against Felipe's skin.

"I don't think you've lost your touch," Felipe murmured against his mouth.

Trask's lips curved. "I don't think you have anything to worry about either."

A sharp bark from between them had both of them pulling away. "You recognize home and you want out, huh?" Trask said, looking down. "Hold on, Daddy's got it."

Damn, Felipe could really fall for him and fall for him hard. He'd never been head over heels for anyone before. He'd had heavy feelings for a few, but not like this. He'd seen others around him in that state and he'd envied them, but he'd never gotten it. Now he understood why Morris wanted to hang out at the bistro most evenings. Why he got that little smile when he'd receive a text or a call from Theo. And why he'd get so aggravated when Theo took on too much work.

It was the little day-to-day moments that made up a relationship. The silly times or the mundane bits, a smile and a touch of the hand. Not so much the dates and going out to party. It was watching a man dote on a puppy. It was hearing him share parts of his past that Felipe knew he was ashamed of but trusting Felipe enough to say it anyway. Trask didn't seem to be much of the open up and sharing kind. Felipe could yap for hours about nothing, but when Trask spoke he was kind of like Yoda, cryptic and deep.

Felipe slid out of the truck, his breath steaming in the night air. The temperature had dropped in the last hour. He whistled softly. Lady appeared out of the shadows and leaned against his leg. Felipe rubbed her head and throat as she lifted into the caress, and Sophie ran around them both, barking in excitement. Felipe could almost hear the endless "hi, hi, hi" in her tone as she greeted everything she hadn't seen in a couple of weeks.

"Is the place fenced in?" Trask asked, letting the puppy's leash out as far as it would go but keeping her on it.

"No, and there are possums and other critters. I'd keep her on that until she learns to come to you all the time. Just like my girl here." Felipe leaned down and kissed the top of Lady's head. "Lady, this is Trask. He's a friend." Felipe emphasized the last word.

"Nice to meet you, Lady." Trask held out his hand to be sniffed and patted her head. "You know, I'd forgotten how dark and quiet it was in the country at night. I don't know how you can stand it."

"Try standing here on a July evening when the cicadas are out. There's nothing quiet about the country. It's just a different kind of noise." Felipe grabbed Trask's hand and tugged him toward the back of the house. "And I'm in the mood to make some."

As they hit the outside stairs that led to his deck, Trask caught him around the waist. He brushed his lips along Felipe's nape. Heat swept through him as he felt Trask's body behind his. They were of similar height and build, and he just knew they'd fit so well together. "How much noise?" Trask whispered in his ear.

Felipe smiled slowly and slid his arm around Trask's neck, then twisted to kiss him, lightly nipping Trask's lip. "Since it doesn't seem like there is anyone else at the house, an absolute spectacle."

Trask's cock pushed insistently against Felipe's robes. "I was kind of hoping you'd say that." Trask slid his hands under Felipe's cloak, searching for an opening in his clothing. His cold touch shocked Felipe's skin through the thin material.

"Bitch." Felipe pulled away with a gasp and a laugh. "That's not the kind of squealing I was thinking of."

He ran up the stairs and pushed open the door to his apartment. Despite the chill, he was burning to get more of Trask's hands. Trask looked around curiously at the small living room, cluttered with a worn-out couch, an extra mannequin draped in a half-finished costume, and Felipe's rickety craft table covered with elements for his latest project.

Felipe stripped off his cloak and tossed it over the couch as he walked backward. Trask's black-eyed gaze zeroed in on him. Felipe smiled slowly and sat to pull off his boots, then undid the hidden zipper to his robes. Trask crouched down and unclipped Sophie's harness, and the puppy took off with a happy bark of joy, Lady trotting after her.

"Are you going to strip down right here in front of me?" Trask asked, shrugging out of his own jacket.

"Yep." Felipe pulled off every one of his accessories and laid them carefully on the table. The school tie and shirt followed, neatly folded by the cloak. As much as Felipe wanted to strip down like a pole dancer, tossing his clothes every which way, he'd put too many hours into this costume to be careless with it. He smiled at Trask as he unbuttoned his pants. "And I fully expect to watch you do the same before I let you through my bedroom door."

He loved the way Trask looked at him like he just wanted to pounce and devour him in one greedy bite. A sexy silver wolf on the hunt. Felipe pulled off his pants and stood unashamedly naked in the doorway to his bedroom. "Well, are you going to join me or not?" Felipe trailed his fingers down his body to his aching cock. "Or do I have to take care of myself?"

"You are one hell of a tease." Trask stripped off his shirt as he moved toward Felipe. "From your sassy mouth to every little move you make."

Felipe grinned as he watched Trask undress. Damn, he was sexy, and there wasn't a part of him that didn't bear some kind of ink. Felipe wanted to explore every inch of him. "Do they all mean something to you?" he asked, gesturing to Trask's naked body. He could only imagine how much all of that cost.

Trask glanced down at his body. "I can't say that. Some I don't remember getting, some I got just because I liked the look of them, and I like getting tattoos, but a good number of them do have meaning for me."

Felipe dragged his finger down Trask's side. "It looks like you have a bare spot right here. Maybe I should mark it. A little imp carrying a steaming coffee mug."

"That might be an idea sometime in the future." Trask grasped Felipe's hips and guided him back into his bedroom. "I see you don't have any. You ever think of getting one?"

"I like making my own decorations and changing them with my mood." Felipe made a humming sound as Trask kissed his neck. "A tattoo is way too permanent." Not that he was against commitments, just not of the ink variety.

He flipped on his bedroom light and steered Trask toward the bed. They tumbled onto it, and Trask kissed him again, his beard scratching delightfully against Felipe's skin. He'd never given thought to how that would feel, and he realized he'd been seriously missing out on the joys of facial hair. Felipe stroked his hands over Trask's body, lightly tweaked the bars piercing those sexy nipples. Trask groaned into his mouth, his cock throbbing against Felipe's thigh.

Felipe rolled over, pushing Trask onto his back. His lips feathered over the leaf-covered branches on Trask's chest. He kissed down the intertwined pocket watch chain and the scattering of ravens down one long arm to the timepiece with the missing hands on the back of his hand, then moved to the other arm with its winding sea dragon and helpless ship. He could spend hours discovering Trask's body.

There were scars too, old and healed over, on his chest and around his knee. Trask's body told a story, and bit by bit, Felipe was going to get it all out of him. Trask's blunt fingertips danced along Felipe's spine in a caress that had him arching against the older man. "Damn, everything about you is sexy," Felipe murmured.

"I think that's supposed to be my line." Trask's hands slid into Felipe's hair as he pulled him closer for another kiss. Felipe's body went all hot and heavy. He loved the way Trask did that, how he took charge without being annoyingly domineering.

He had been thinking of this ever since he set his sights on the sexy gamer. In the months that followed, as he slowly worked his way under Trask's quiet reserve, his fascination had grown. He hadn't expected to find so much in common with him. He hadn't realized how easy it would be to talk with him once he had the man one-on-one. And he sure as fuck hadn't anticipated how Trask's kisses would set him on fire and have him wanting to surrender.

"More," Felipe said on a breathy moan, his lips tingling, his body alive. He straddled Trask's thighs, rocking against his hard cock.

Trask gripped his ass, kneading and teasing, before breaking off with a light slap. "Where's your lube and condoms, imp?"

Felipe shivered as Trask nuzzled his throat and tried to think past the demanding hormones that were cussing him out at the moment. He didn't want to move. He wanted to stay draped over Trask like a security blanket as they drove each other crazy. But if he didn't move, he wouldn't get fucked, and dammit, Felipe really wanted to get fucked.

"Screw responsibility," Felipe grumbled as he left the warmth of Trask's body to lean over and yank open his drawer. He managed to get his hand on the box of condoms and fished one out as Trask discovered his nipple. His fingers and toes curled as he let out a desperate whimper. Trask's lips and tongue sucked and demanded. His teeth nipped, and Felipe whimpered again, writhing over him. "Oh fuck, you're killing me," he panted as he pulled away to try to get his equilibrium back.

"Felipe." Trask's husky voice washed over him in a warm wave. "Get the damn lube."

Felipe shot him a glare as he reached again for the bottle out of the dangerously listing drawer. The moment his hand reached it, Trask found his other nipple. Felipe closed his eyes with a soft cry. It was his biggest weakness. He'd roll over in a heartbeat for a guy who played with his nipples just right.

"Trask…. Trask, please…." His hands fisted in the sheets as Trask moved from one point of sensation to the other.

He felt slickened fingers penetrate him as he groped for the condom. He tore the package open, his heart pounding as Trask watched him through lazy, half-lidded eyes. "You have the sexiest whimper I ever heard," Trask said, stretching his fingers as the need spiked higher.

"You tell anybody I whimpered, and I swear you will pay." Felipe tried for a threatening look, but he felt too damn good, too needy to make it effective. "I make guys whimper. Not the other way around," he said as he rolled the condom down on Trask's cock.

"Promises, imp." Trask grinned as he slid his fingers free and grasped Felipe's hips. "You think you can make me whimper? Bring it."

Oh, if Trask thought he could challenge Felipe Suero like that and be able to crawl away afterward, he had a surprise in store. Felipe narrowed his eyes with a soft growl as he leaned down and nipped Trask's collarbone.

Trask flinched back with a soft laugh. "My imp has fangs."

His body on edge, Felipe grasped Trask's condom-covered cock, feeling the slickness of the lube that Trask must've slathered over it, and eased back on it. He groaned as the hard length penetrated him. Trask's fingers flexed on his hips and his lips parted on a silent moan, but he let Felipe set the pace.

Felipe watched the pleasure on Trask's face, drinking in the moment and promising himself that he would get Trask naked again any time he could. He moaned softly as he settled all the way back, feeling the stretch and burn. Fuck, that felt good.

Then he remembered Trask's words and a slow smile crossed his lips. He was going to blow Trask's mind and stake a claim on him that Trask would remember for the rest of his life. "Mmmm." Felipe clenched around Trask's cock with a breathy moan. He crouched over him as Trask's eyes widened.

"I think I'm in trouble." Trask slid his arms around Felipe and tried to roll them both over, but Felipe clamped his thighs around Trask's hips.

"So true, Tin Man." Felipe ground back against him, taking control and feeling a little thrill as Trask let him. He rode him with hard thrusts that had Trask groaning. His hands skimmed over Felipe's body in an exploring caress.

"Fuck, you're beautiful." Trask lifted up on his arm and fisted his hand in Felipe's hair, not too rough, but just fucking right. And then his hot mouth was on Felipe's neck and Felipe moaned. He leaned into him, looking for that right angle, and cried out when he found it. Yes, right there. He clenched around Trask, moving faster to Trask's soft gasps. He was going to get that damn man to whimper if it killed him, and it just might.

Felipe bit his lip as Trask's hot mouth moved lower. If he touched Felipe's nipples again, he would come out of his skin. His lips were everywhere, branding Felipe's skin, pushing the excitement higher. Trask lowered himself back on the bed with a strangled groan. He ran his fingers over Felipe's cock and gave it a squeeze. "Touch yourself for me."

Felipe met his dark-eyed gaze and saw the raw need, the burning heat. He sat back, his eyes locked with Trask as he rode him, feeling almost as if he had a fever beneath his skin. Under that gaze, he started at his neck and slowly stroked his hands over his body.

Trask's lips parted on a moan. Close to the sound that Felipe wanted him to make, but not quite there. Biting his lip again, Felipe tugged on his nipples. Fuck, it felt good, not as good as Trask's wicked mouth but good enough to make him clench around the man with a desperate groan. Fuck, fuck, fuck, he wasn't going to make it.

Then Trask captured his hand and brought it down to Felipe's straining cock. "Right there, touch yourself. Let me watch."

Trask was a little bit of a voyeur. Felipe tucked that little tidbit of information away. He would definitely revisit that later. Felipe fisted his cock, his head falling back with a desperate groan. "Aw fuck." He ground back on Trask's cock, his body tensing. Trask grabbed his hips, bracing himself as he thrust and climaxed, a strangled note dying in his throat.

Close enough, Felipe thought, crying out sharply as his orgasm rolled through him in a long continuous wave. He rode the hot spikes of pleasure as Trask made that delicious sound again, and Felipe felt the hard throb of his cock as he came.

Felipe draped himself over Trask with a long sigh, boneless and sated. Score one for both of them.

Chapter Fourteen

TRASK STARED up at the ceiling, still wrapped around the wild man in his arms as he tried to catch his breath. He wasn't entirely sure if he could keep up with Felipe, but damn, he wanted to try. Felipe might love dogs, but he was a hunting cat in bed. A sleekly muscled jaguar ready to pounce, and his prey stood no chance once he was in his sights. As if he heard Trask's thoughts, Felipe rubbed against him with a purr and nipped his chest. "I'm hungry. Are you hungry?"

Not waiting for an answer, Felipe clambered out of bed and strolled naked out of the bedroom. Trask paused long enough to pull on his underwear before following. He found Felipe in the dim light of the kitchen, perusing the contents of the fridge with pursed lips.

"You are completely comfortable in your own skin, aren't you?" Trask asked with a soft laugh as he washed his hands. He wasn't used to that. He often seemed to end up with someone who was fragile beneath the surface, their identity and worth caught up in how someone else viewed them. Felipe was a refreshing change. "You're not just feigning confidence."

Felipe looked over his shoulder and twerked his taut, naked ass. "What's there not to be confident about? I'll admit I do bitch about the state of my thighs, but that's because I either went on a comfort food binge or because I feel like preening when my current boyfriend assures me how awesome they are."

Trask eyeballed Felipe's smoothly muscled thighs. "They are pretty spectacular, even when they're gripping the life out of me."

Felipe gave him a Cheshire smile and leaned over to rummage around. "I have some lumpia we could heat up, some beans and rice, but I think that's the limit on my vegetarian food up here. I misjudged the contents of my fridge. I was too busy thinking of getting you naked." Felipe took a bite of something and shook his head. "Nope, this lumpia has meat. Damn, you're missing out. My lola can cook."

He hip-checked the door shut. "It's not late. There are plenty of restaurants in town, or I can raid the fridge downstairs. They've got to have something."

Trask did not want to get Felipe in trouble with his neighbors. "Let's head into town. And you can tell me what happened at the con that got you so excited earlier." Trask liked the idea of lounging around with Felipe half-naked as they talked the night away. "We can bring it back and pick up where we left off."

Felipe's eyes gleamed. "I like the way you think." He bounded into the bedroom and shrugged into a hoodie and a pair of jeans as Trask got dressed. "Brenden seems to have chilled now I'm not boning Dakota anymore." He rolled his eyes with a grimace. "Morris has this crazy theory that he was so bent out of shape over us because Brenden wants to lick that particular lollipop."

Trask laughed softly. He would never get used to the way Felipe phrased things, and he hoped he never did. "I have wondered about them a time or two myself." Trask sat on the edge of the bed and tugged on his boots. "Nothing ever niggled you the wrong way when you and Dakota were a thing?"

"To be honest I never got how they were even friends. Brenden and Dakota are always arguing. If one says it's night, the other insists it's day." Felipe ran a hand through his tousled dark hair. "Though it used to piss me off that Brenden could call and ask for something and whatever plans Dakota and I had were forgotten."

Something in Felipe's tone made Trask wonder if he still had feelings for Dakota. "You ever think you two might hook up again?" Trask asked casually as Felipe searched the floor for a pair of socks.

"Fuck no." Felipe's tone was adamant. "I have zero interest in poking that stick again. If Brenden didn't kill me and stuff me in a vendor storage crate, I'd stab Dakota to death with my sewing shears the first time he tried to fob me off with some bullshit about plans changing. Besides, we get along better as friends. I don't miss him as a boyfriend. I just don't like feeling used."

Trask made a mental note not to ever break a date with Felipe unless he had a very compelling reason. "I'm glad you're not yearning for someone else. I'm too old to engage in a duel for you."

"You're not old." Felipe popped back up with his socks in hand and smirked. "You're well aged, like a good cheese or wine."

"Ouch." Trask clutched his chest. "I'm not sure if that's praise or not."

Felipe's eyes twinkled with a teasing light.

"How about you? Any exes lingering around that I can give narrow-eyed death glares to?" Felipe finished getting dressed and grabbed his keys and wallet out of the open bedside drawer.

"Nope, last boyfriend moved to Atlanta." He'd asked Trask to go with him, but Trask couldn't see uprooting himself. Which was a sad commentary on their tepid romance. It had been nice and easy with no depth to it at all. Saying goodbye had not been a hardship on either side. Relationships shouldn't be like that. They should have depth and meaning. That one had just been a slow decay.

"Good to know." Felipe caught Trask's hand and pulled him up. "Back to what I was saying, Brenden in his newfound Zen asked me to cover for a missing panelist. Then to put cream cheese icing on the red velvet cake, he asked me and Abby to head up some cosplay ideas and panels for the big con he plans on doing in Annapolis next year."

Trask had heard scuttlebutt about that. He'd been wavering on going. Tables would be expensive, and it was far enough away that he'd have to get a hotel and budget for meals. He did have enough stock in his offsite storage that he could cut prices and make a killing if people were in a buying mood. With big cons, it could be hit or miss. It depended on the number of vendors and the variety. He'd hit up Brenden and feel him out before committing. He should do that soon or else the exhibitor tables would sell out.

"That's awesome, Felipe. What ideas do you have?" he asked as he followed Felipe back out into the living room. He sought out Sophie to see what she'd gotten into while he was occupied. Lady and the puppy had curled up, snoring, in an old, worn dog bed.

"Well, I really opened a whole ball of possible awesome trouble." Felipe grimaced as he opened the door. "Brenden shoved Abby and me together. She's a kickass cosplayer who I've warred with since elementary school. I got it into my crazy-assed head that we should work together on more than just the panels. And because it's me, I blurted it out before thinking it through."

Trask trailed Felipe and paused to let himself get adjusted to the darkness outside. Felipe ignored the fact there was no way he could possibly see the stairs and clattered down them at an alarming rate. "What kind of work?" he asked as he followed more slowly.

"We both make costumes for others on the side, and we both have a pretty good following online." Felipe waited for him on the back patio. Trask had an impression of a long set of glass doors leading to the main part of the house and wondered how many apartments it had been cut up into. "I think if we work together, in a few years it might be something we can make a living off of. I've been taking business classes because I'd really like to do it full-time. What do you think? You started your own business."

"You do really good work," Trask said after a moment of thought. "And your attention to detail shows. When you go to a con, you are your own walking advertisement."

Felipe walked backward, his attention on Trask's face. How the hell he kept from tripping and falling on his ass, Trask didn't know. "I sense a but in there."

"Not exactly, except I would consider your prices. If you charge what your time is worth coupled with how long it takes you to make one of the more intricate costumes, you won't find too many who can afford you. So that's not a way to make a steady living wage. And you have to consider that this sudden upsurge in outside interest for geek culture might not last. So you need to be adaptable. Have you considered avenues of revenue other than cosplay?"

Felipe was quiet as they walked to his car. "The Ren Faire has been a staple in Crownsville for like forty years now. There are people who would pay sweet money for an elaborate costume."

"I wasn't paying too much attention to the vendors when we went." Trask opened the car door for him. "As I recall, don't they have several costume stores?"

"They do, and other vendors offer a good number of accessories, but every time I go, I manage to give away cards and get commissions. Like you said, I'm a walking advertisement, and I do my research. I have a shit-ton of books on historical fashions." Felipe rested his arm across the top of the car as he continued to lay out his thoughts. "It's something to build on. Some seasons I've even been a part of one of the acting troupes. I could always take con season off August through October next year and use it to promote at the Faire if Abby and I haven't dismembered each other yet. Then there's the costume design for the

Port Tobacco Players. It's our local theater group, but that's really more on a volunteer basis. Still, you never know what it could bring."

Felipe slid behind the wheel, and Trask considered his words as he moved around the car to the passenger's side. He'd clearly given this some thought. If Trask had had a quarter of his drive or foresight when he'd been Felipe's age… well… no sense in looking back with what-ifs because he liked where he was right now just fine.

"You ever think of making small, quick objects that you can sell to supplement your income?" Trask asked as they were making their way back down the long, winding driveway. "Accessories, masks, things that people will want, that you can charge top price for while you're working on bigger projects?"

"That's a thought," Felipe mused. "We could take pictures and post them online. We'll have to think about it. That's really projecting into the future. I figure if we've managed to find a way to work together in semiharmony by the time Brenden's big con comes around, then we'll have a real chance at doing this. If not, well, we tried and I'll have to make sure she doesn't steal all my business. How the fuck do you compete with dimples?"

Trask was at a loss for a response. "It's a factor I've never had to deal with. For the most part, game and comic book store owners aren't going to win any beauty pageants, and they definitely aren't going to charm anyone. We rely on the fact that those who come in know what they want and have ready cash to burn. If I can discuss the games and storylines with them, I don't need dimples."

Now that Felipe mentioned it, Trask thought he remembered a long, lanky woman with deep-set dimples and Icelandic eyes dressed up at many of the cons. He'd always pictured her as some kind of Valkyrie warrior. "So how long has this rivalry gone on?" he asked as they hit the darkened highway. There sure wasn't much out here in this part of Maryland. A few motels and a biker bar were all that Trask spied as they drove in. Felipe turned in the opposite direction of the bridge, and all Trask saw on either side of the highway were more trees.

"Since the first day we met. We both have serious competition issues and a mutual love of crafts. Our desire to share our projects with each other is offset by our need to outdo one another." Felipe shook his head. "I'm trying to channel that into the thought if we team up together, we can demolish everyone else. That's still competition."

"So, what would be the next steps?" he asked, fascinated by Felipe's vision. He loved the idea of taking a creative dream and running with it.

"We're going to have a meeting online sometime next week. Safer there than in person." Felipe's teeth flashed in a wicked grin. "Discuss what projects we have lined up and see if we could help each other with any issues. Compare our online platforms and make some tentative plans for upcoming cosplay panels and convention opportunities."

The lights of a decent-sized town appeared, and Felipe turned off into a strip mall tucked back away from the road. Through the wraparound window, Trask could see a packed pizzeria. "Do you think it could wind up getting ugly between you two?" Trask asked. "Sometimes working with your rival can lead to real tension, especially when you get hit with tight deadlines."

"Nah," Felipe said after careful thought. "If it didn't get ugly in high school, I doubt it will now. The worst outcome I can see is one or both of us getting tired of the bickering and deciding to bail. Other than that disastrous first encounter in kindergarten, neither of us tried to sabotage each other. That one time was enough to teach us both how bad it could go if we went down that route. So we've contented ourselves with snark mostly and trying to win all the contests that we both enter."

Frenemies since kindergarten, now that was a fucking hoot. Trask laughed. "One day you're going to have to tell me that story."

"I will," Felipe promised as he parked. "Though I'm not sure what light it puts me in."

"Oh, I'd imagine, a bit of a troublemaker with a sense of the wicked, more of a sense of fairness than you'd want to admit to, and quick on the defense." Trask caught the flash of Felipe's grin in the dim light. "How'd I do?"

"I think you've got me pegged, Tin Man. I'm not sure if I can say the same, but I'm working on it." Felipe got out of his car and stretched, and once again he reminded Trask of a hunting cat. "They've got kickass pizza here, fried ravioli that makes Morris weep, and pretty okay pasta. The perfect meal in between sex."

After the last round, Trask definitely needed some fuel. "I'm curious, why Tin Man? Is it the silver?"

"Well that adds to the effect, but not why you make me think of the Tin Man," Felipe said as they strolled toward the restaurant. "See the Tin Man thought he wasn't capable of love, thought he didn't have a heart, and never realized how much he was already giving the whole time. That's the part I think you overlook, how much you give to others." Felipe cocked his head and looked at Trask as if he worried he'd overstepped a boundary. "Not so much that you think you don't have a heart. I think you're afraid to admit how deeply you feel."

Trask nodded slowly. "I think you might have me pretty well pegged too." Trask couldn't think of the last time he'd been with a man who both understood him and wasn't put off by that. It made Trask less leery about offering more details about his past. It was taking another step deeper into this relationship, but the slow smile that crossed Felipe's generous mouth erased all of Trask's reservations.

"I like watching people interact," Felipe admitted as Trask opened the door. "And not to sound stalkerish, but I've been watching you for a while. You're just interesting."

Trask chuckled as they stepped into the warmth and light of the restaurant. Felipe had to be the first man in a long time who thought he was interesting. And he suspected it wasn't for the usual reasons. "I think I know the answer, but I have to ask. Interesting because of my mysterious and shady past?"

Felipe met his eyes and shook his head. "No, just for you."

A little flustered, Trask examined the menu above the counter. This was a first in a long time, a guy having him in knots. It sure beat the alternative.

Chapter Fifteen

FELIPE'S STOMACH tightened with nerves as he got out of the car. His parents were home, and so were his grandparents. He should take advantage of that and introduce Trask. But with Trask's premature silver it made him seem older than he was. Early forties was not ancient. Still, they'd had a few quibbles over Dakota being in a different decade. The tattoos might be an issue for his mom. Trask's sketchy past that he'd hinted at from time to time would be a stumbling block for his dad. And his lolo…. Felipe shook his head at the thought of his grandfather, who still couldn't seem to wrap his head around the concept of Felipe being gay.

At least he could count on Mariana and his lola's support. He was pretty sure they'd see what he saw in Trask. But he'd really rather save the introductions for Thanksgiving when there would be many guests and his family wouldn't focus their entire attention on Trask as one unit. That could be scary.

"Wow, looks like all of your housemates came home at once," Trask said as he emerged from the car carrying the pizza box.

Felipe winced. Fuck, he should've known Trask would assume he rented with a bunch of other nonrelated people. He had exes who took exception with where he lived, intimating that he was some kind of freeloader leech. Bullshit, but best to get it all out there now.

"Actually, those two cars there belong to my parents. That out-of-date monstrosity in the garage is my grandparents' relic. Either they were all out somewhere together, or they all returned at the same time." Felipe sighed as they headed toward the back and the safety of his apartment. "I really hope it's the second and I'm not forgetting the first or else I'll be hearing about it as soon as they realize I'm home."

"You live with your parents?" The odd note in Trask's voice stopped Felipe cold. Ugh, he was not going to be one of those judgmental twerps. Felipe refused to believe it.

"No. I rent the upstairs apartment from my parents. I pay my rent on time. I pay my share of the utilities, and I even buy my own damn groceries." Through the back glass doors, Felipe caught a glimpse of the whole clan gathered in the living room, catching up on episodes of *Modern Family* or *Black-ish* if he were to guess. Trask peered over, too, and it irked Felipe even more. So what if Trask had been on his own for, like, forever. That way wasn't for everybody. He liked living nearby. Felipe turned to face him on the stairs. "And just so you know—"

Trask held up his hand, forestalling Felipe's escalating tirade. "Chill out, Felipe. I don't care if you're still using your old bedroom and your mom is making you casseroles every night or lumpia or whatever you call it. Are you happy here?"

Felipe blinked in surprise and then narrowed his eyes thoughtfully. He could safely say that Trask might have been the first boyfriend he'd had since moving upstairs to ask him that. Still, there was something in his voice that set off little warnings. "Yes…." He began walking slowly back up the steps, his gaze still locked on Trask's face. "It's close to school and work, and I can keep an eye out in case my grandparents need anything when my parents are out."

A pained expression crossed Trask's face. "You owe no one an explanation, least of all me. It's a good thing, you being here. I was close to my grandmother once, and I wish I'd been on hand for her, too, instead of halfway across the country."

"Once?" Felipe opened the back door and heard the skitter of paws behind him, both big and small. "What happened?"

Trask's expression shuttered. "She's gone. She was sick. She didn't tell any of us how sick. I can't really blame her for that, but I wish I'd known."

Felipe felt as if he'd stepped over a line. Sometimes he didn't think before he opened his damn mouth. He knew that when his lola passed, he would be shattered. His earliest memories were of her singing to him as she rocked him in her chair or stood at the kitchen counter making him palitaw while arguing and laughing with his dad's mom. He didn't remember his abuela as much as he wanted to, but he did remember how both of his grandmothers were always together. They took care of him while his parents worked, and it didn't matter whose house he went to in the morning, the other grandmother would show up before long. He remembered the mix of languages flying by, Tagalog, Spanish, and

English, as they shared their own stories of growing up and immigrating. It was pretty much the best childhood ever.

"I'm sorry." Felipe made room for the pizza box on his coffee table. "Is she that older lady in the picture on your wall?"

"Yeah, that was her. It's okay. It was a long time ago." The distance in Trask's voice couldn't quite mask the lingering regret.

When Felipe looked back at him Trask was greeting Sophie, who acted as if she hadn't seen him in a year. It really was sweet the way they had taken to each other. He'd had no doubt that the puppy had been happy with him, but it was clear she adored Trask and Trask adored her in return. They'd needed each other.

Felipe looked down as a weight settled against his leg. He smiled at Lady, who looked at him hopefully, and reached down to scratch between her ears. Lady's tail thumped in acknowledgment as she leaned in a little more with a breathy whuff. She always seemed to know when he needed her. The easy camaraderie between him and Trask had vanished. He didn't know how to get it back again, and if he'd caused the strain with his defensiveness or if it was just another example of Trask's overabundance of reticence.

"You hungry?" Felipe asked, deciding to act as if nothing were odd. If he made a bigger deal out of it, he'd only work himself up. "Let me grab a couple of plates. You want some coffee?" Maybe he could talk Trask into staying the whole night if he played this out right.

"Sure, but just decaf," Trask called after him, his voice lighter. "Dark roast if you have it."

Felipe looked through his sad collection of coffee. He'd have to be better prepared the next time Trask came over. He'd seen the setup Trask had at his loft. The man took his java seriously. He pursed his lips and grabbed the only decaf he had. It wasn't dark, but maybe if he poured extra grounds in the filter it would compensate.

To be honest, he never made coffee himself unless he was cramming all night for a class or putting the finishing details on a costume. He usually hit up the Green Mermaid in town for a triple shot latte before heading to work instead of relying on his own kitchen skills. By the time he hit his little tollbooth from hell, he was all fired up and ready to go. Maybe a little too fired up if he were honest. Espressos and cages did not mix, especially not with a guy like himself.

While the coffee brewed, he grabbed a couple of chipped plates and talked himself out of fretting. That's what always got him into trouble. He'd take something small and make it gigantic in his mind, and when he finally spouted off about it, it ended up being a lot more of a spectacle than it needed to be. Granted, Felipe didn't see a problem with a little drama from time to time. But it could be taken to extremes. Trask already expressed a dislike of needless fuss.

Felipe poured the coffee and took a cautious sniff. It smelled okay. He grabbed a water for himself and wandered back into the living room. Trask was sitting cross-legged on the couch with Sophie settled in a comfortable sprawl between his knees. "You're not naked," Felipe pointed out, handing Trask the coffee. "I thought we decided it would be a naked pizza party."

"Neither are you." Trask set his coffee down and pulled his shirt off. "Why not start with this and we can see where the night takes us?"

"You just don't want a wiggling puppy on your naked bits." Felipe plopped down and stripped out of his own shirt as Lady lay down by the couch. He opened the pizza box and breathed in the scent. Half the pizza was mushroom, spinach, and goat cheese, the other half the same with meat added. Felipe did not have a problem with vegetables on his pizza, but there was no way he was passing up the pepperoni tonight.

"There is that to consider." Trask handed Felipe a plate. "Put some of that toasted ravioli on there too. I hope it's as good as you said it was."

"Better." Felipe put half of the appetizer on the plate next to a couple squares of pizza, then added one of the cups of marinara. It was sad, but that was almost his favorite part. He could practically drink the stuff. He filled his own plate and then sat back, stretching his legs out beside Trask.

He eyeballed the enigmatic man across from him. Felipe had been doing most of the talking so far. Maybe he could tease some bits out of Trask. He was dying to know more about the man who was seriously starting to hook him. "So, are you going to give me the Trask life story?"

"Is there anything you want to know in particular or just a general bio?" Trask took a sip of coffee and his eyes popped.

Felipe gave the mug a disappointed look as Trask set it back down. "It sucks, doesn't it?"

"No, no… it might even put color back into my hair. In fact, I'm kind of expecting it to go for a walk right out of my cup about now." Trask bit into his pizza and shook his head at Sophie when she gave him a soulful look.

The teasing note in Trask's voice set Felipe at ease. "I guess if we're going to continue to see each other, I ought to learn a little more about the art of coffee brewing."

Trask looked thoughtful a moment. "I'd be happy to teach you."

That had to be a good sign. Felipe smiled as he picked up another slice. "So, Trask Briscoe 101, are you from Richmond? You've got a twang sometimes that just doesn't seem to fit the area."

Trask shook his head as he took another sip of that awful coffee. "South of San Antonio, but I've lived in the Richmond area about twenty years now. How about you? Born and raised in Southern Maryland?"

"Yep, though when I was younger, I spent many of my summers in either Manila or Bogota visiting family. Mom and Dad were very insistent that I get to know my scattered cousins. Then the rest of my mom's sisters came here, so we haven't been back to the Philippines since." Felipe looked off thoughtfully, remembering all the sights and smells. "I'd like to go back one day. See if it's like what I remember."

"What about Colombia?" Trask asked. "You ever get there anymore?"

Trask knew his geography. Felipe couldn't remember if Trask said he'd gotten his GED, but from the number of books Felipe had seen at Trask's apartment, he had many varied interests. "Last time I went was right after graduation."

"So you're a first-generation American?" Trask tried the marinara and added a little more to his plate.

"On my mom's side, on my dad's, second. He was born down the road in the next county. Then he met Mom, bought property out here and built this house, then added on to it bit by bit." Felipe realized that Trask was getting him to do all the talking again. Granted for Felipe it didn't take much, but Trask had a way about him that just encouraged yapping. "What about you? Do you know where your folks come from?"

"I haven't a damn clue." The note in Trask's voice was final, and Felipe blew out a breath. He wouldn't poke that prickly pear today, and he was okay getting Trask's story in bits as he grew more comfortable talking about it. He'd just have to glean the knowledge or get Trask in his bed again and learn through osmosis.

Sophie seemed to realize she was not going to be able to sucker Trask out of free food. She stood up, smacked her tail against Trask's chin, and hopped down to curl up with Lady. Felipe snickered and ran his toes over Trask's side. "She told you."

The corner of Trask's mouth lifted in a brief smile, and he stretched out his legs, too, tangling them with Felipe's. "So what appointment did you have today?" Felipe asked, changing the subject before Trask got even more closemouthed.

"You talk a lot, don't you?" Trask cocked his head with a faint smile.

"I do, I really do." It had been a chief complaint of a few boyfriends and friends, though Morris usually didn't mind unless a car trip got too long. "Is that going to be a problem? I might as well know now. Because I can go nonstop. It gets me into trouble all the time."

"Only if you feel the need for me to talk as much." Trask leaned forward to grab another slice of pizza. "I'm a much better listener than I am a talker if you haven't noticed."

"I may have picked up on that." With Trask it didn't feel awkward. Maybe it was because he really did listen and Felipe's chattering wasn't just background noise to him. He listened, commented, and asked questions in return that only got Felipe talking more.

"But to answer your last question, I went to a friend's NA anniversary meeting. He wanted me to speak." Trask's expression was thoughtful. "I don't like to lead meetings, but for Joe I make an exception and don't bitch."

"NA?" Felipe thought he should recognize the term. He knew he'd heard it before.

"Narcotics Anonymous," Trask said, his dark gaze steady. "I've been going to meetings off and on since I was eighteen, though, in the beginning, it was more off than on. Joe became my sponsor about seventeen years ago. Because of him and NA, I finally was able to stay clean for more than a year. If you were looking at my pictures, he's the old man with me."

That explained a lot, actually. Felipe's dad hired some of the guys from the long-term rehab place down the road. Felipe got to know a few of them when he'd worked with them. Most of them were pretty good people, though their eyes contained some demons. One OD'd when he was only one week away from completing the program. That had been a blow to the whole crew. Felipe had never forgotten him. He had been only twenty.

"How many years do you have?" Felipe asked quietly.

"It'll be sixteen this spring." Trask's solemn expression gave no hint to how he felt about reaching that milestone, but Felipe had an inkling of how difficult it must have been at the time.

"That's pretty freaking amazing." Felipe set his plate aside and took Trask's empty one to add to the stack. "It was nice of you, about your friend I mean. I'm sure it meant a lot to him."

"I think it did. He saved my life, my sanity. I wish my grandmother had lived to see me get clean. She died when I thought I hit the bottom, and I didn't realize how much further I could fall." Trask shook his head and then fixed Felipe with a look that sent a little thrill of excitement through him.

Then Trask crawled over to him and Felipe's heart beat a little faster. "You look like a man with some serious intentions."

"I have a few thoughts in mind about what we could do with the rest of our evening." Trask's lips nibbled along Felipe's jaw. "I kinda bared it all earlier during the meeting. I'm not sure if I'm up for another tell-all tonight. But it's a start at least. Is that going to be okay?"

"I thought you were going to sidestep all my questions, but you didn't. I think I can handle it." Felipe's thoughts scattered as Trask rubbed his jaw against Felipe's. It was kind of difficult to think with Trask's beard rasping against his skin.

"I'll answer your questions." Trask pulled back, his eyes warm as he looked down at Felipe. "You have a right to know about the man you're sleeping with. But you'll probably get them in dribbles as I work up to it."

Trask told him more than he knew. Felipe was a firm believer in actions, and every time he was with Trask the attraction grew. "Despite popular opinion, there are times when I can be patient." Felipe slid his arms around Trask's neck and drew him back down. "But not when you're half-naked. We can talk later. Kiss me now."

Trask caught Felipe's mouth in a heated, devouring kiss, his callused palms sliding over Felipe's bare skin. Then he couldn't think anymore, only feel as Trask branded and claimed, giving Felipe back everything he'd dished out earlier and pushed him even further. Felipe's heart squeezed. Oh man, he was in it deep.

Chapter Sixteen

TRASK AWOKE to the insistent chirp of a phone alarm and the sensation of a warm naked body pressed against his own. Sophie yipped in excitement and scrambled onto the bed for good-morning nuzzles and licks that involved cold noses and wet tongues. Trask rubbed her head as he tried to figure out when the hell they made it back to the bed. Trask thought back on the hormone-crazed blur of last night and grinned as he remembered the stumbling, groping, heated trip in the search of more condoms.

"Fuck," Felipe groaned. "Motherfucker, I will end you if you don't shut up."

Trask opened one eye as Felipe shifted next to him, slapping the floor as he searched for his phone. "Not a morning person, huh?"

"Fuck mornings, fuck alarms." Sophie licked Felipe's face when he lay back, and Felipe cussed again. "Sophie! Cut it out. I don't want love. I want fucking sleep."

Trask snickered and began to laugh as Felipe focused a baleful eye on him, his dark hair a wavy, tumbled mess. "You find this amusing?"

"This is a whole side of you I didn't expect." Trask expected the morning to be awkward, but it wasn't at all. Not with Felipe. "You were all smiles and sunshine for breakfast at my place. You had to wake up even earlier for that. Now you're snarls and surly glares."

"That was different." Felipe poked his side. "Anticipation of a date with the most interesting guy I'd met in a long time dragged me out of bed with a cheerful attitude. The only thing I have to look forward to right now is being late for work and then stuck in a box for eight hours with nothing to entertain me but stupid drivers. I'd much rather stay here curled up with you."

That prospect did suck. Trask would go mental with a job like that. He didn't know how Felipe handled it. "Well, when you put it that way."

Felipe poked him again. Trask caught his finger and brought it to his lips. Felipe's eyes got to him on a visceral level. The deep warm brown expressed every emotion before Felipe had a chance to open his mouth. They could be warm with affection, bright with mischief, or glinting in irritation as they were now. With Felipe, he'd never have to guess where he stood. He was capable of creating drama, but Trask got the sense he was not one to play games.

Trask grinned, and Felipe's eyes narrowed dangerously as his alarm chimed again. "If you give me any kind of hippie bullshit right now, I will end you along with the phone."

"Early bird gets the worm?" Trask asked, lifting one eyebrow as Felipe glared. He was a joy to tease. "It's a new day so shine on?"

Felipe grabbed a pillow and thwapped Trask with it. "A new day means a new opportunity for mayhem and murder. I have lots of trees in the backyard. I'm pretty sure I could find a spot for your body."

Trask laughed and caught the pillow before Felipe could smack him again. He leaned up and kissed Felipe's lips. "Come on, imp. A shower will wake you right up, and you can text me all of your amusing observations from your steel cage later."

The alarm abruptly silenced as Felipe found the phone. He propped himself up on his hands, the sheets tangling around his naked waist. It was a sexy sight and one that gave Trask thoughts of lingering a little while longer in Felipe's bed. But he didn't want to be the cause of him being late, and he sat up with more than a little regret.

It wasn't that bright outside, so Trask figured it was shy of seven. If he hit the road immediately, he'd be at the shop in plenty of time to unload from the show.

"Why are you so cheerful in the morning?" Felipe threw back the covers, got out of bed, and stretched luxuriously, rising up on his toes.

Trask knelt up, slid his arm around Felipe's waist, and kissed his shoulder. "After how we spent last night, can you blame me?"

Felipe turned and kissed Trask with that cat's smile playing on his lips. "Good point. Last night was rather spectacular." He caught Trask's hand. "Come on, if we hit the shower together, the hot water may last."

It was a damn shame there was not enough time or water for shower sex. The shower was tiny, giving them little room to maneuver but an excellent reason to be all over each other. The water smelled faintly sulfurous, but Felipe's soap drove off the scent of the well. By the time they got each other washed off, the water was cooling rapidly, and they rushed through rinsing off with breathless laughs.

Felipe took one look at the clock as they were toweling each other dry and began cursing again. "Fuck, Tin Man. I've got to run. I'm going to be late. Fuck, don't even have time to go to town for my coffee."

Trask followed the cussing tornado as Felipe scrambled, searching for clothes and shoes. "I'll feed Lady for you," he called, stopping by the kitchen and locating the kibble.

"Thank you," came a muffled, heartfelt cry from the bedroom. "Can you top off her water too?"

By the time Trask had attended to the little chores and put the dishes they used last night in the sink, Felipe had emerged from the bedroom with a slightly harried expression. "Sorry to run out on you like this, but I cannot be late again this month. My supervisor will burst a vein. I'll text you later."

Felipe dropped a kiss on Trask's mouth and left, the door slapping shut behind him and letting in a cold draft of air. He took the outer stairs with a speed that made Trask wince. He hoped Felipe didn't try that in the middle of winter when ice formed overnight. He'd break his damn neck.

Felipe hadn't even grabbed a snack or a slice of leftover pizza. "Does he do this every morning?" he asked Lady, who settled herself by the doorway with a sigh. Lady thumped her tail but ignored him. Poor girl was missing Felipe already. So was he if he was honest about it.

Trask got dressed and finished straightening up, leaving the clean dishes to dry on the rack and the bed neatly made. He'd pick up Felipe's favorite coffee and something for him to eat or Felipe would be one cranky bastard by the time lunch rolled around. He thought he saw a coffee shop in town last night as they went to dinner. He managed to get a wiggling Sophie into her harness as Lady slipped out the dog door.

As they were walking down the stairs, the back door to the main house opened. Trask eyed the emerging older man and young woman with trepidation. There was no mistaking they were related to Felipe. He had Felipe's proud profile, and she had his laughing, expressive eyes.

"Sophie!" The young woman dropped her bookbag and held out her arms. "I missed you, baby. Look at how big you've gotten."

Sophie let out a soft cry of delight and scrambled down the stairs impatiently. Despite Trask's reluctance to meet Felipe's family without him present, he hurried his steps before Sophie wiggled herself off the stairs.

Damn, this was awkward. If he'd left five minutes earlier or waited for another ten, he would not be having to go through this. "Good morning." Trask touched the brim of his ball cap. He really hoped he and Felipe had not made too much noise last night. "You must be Mr. Suero." He held out his hand. "I'm Trask Briscoe."

Mr. Suero's cool gaze flicked over Trask, and for a moment Trask thought he wouldn't shake his hand in return. "Mariana, get in the car. You're going to be late for your appointment," he said with a quick sideways glance at his daughter before clasping Trask's hand firmly.

Mariana rose, a protest in her gaze. It struck Trask again how much those eyes reminded him of Felipe. "Good luck with your appointment," Trask murmured as Sophie watched Mariana retrieve her bag with a little whine for attention. Trask comforted her with a hand on her head. "It's okay, Sophie. I'm sure you'll see her again soon."

Mr. Suero waited until she was out of earshot. "Are you a friend or a date?"

"I'd like to think I'm both." In a short amount of time, Felipe had managed to get himself solidly placed among the handful that Trask called true friends and not one of the mere acquaintances he enjoyed seeing on occasion.

Mr. Suero's frown deepened. "I have to say, you're the oddest one yet. And Felipe's brought home some doozies." Trask knew that tone, knew it intimately, the disapproval and instant judgment. He met Mr. Suero's hard gaze with an even look in return and refused to comment. "How old are you?"

Well, Trask couldn't blame the man for asking that. He'd probably do the same if circumstances were reversed. "Forty-two, sir."

A cynical light appeared in Mr. Suero's eyes. "Look more like fifty." There really wasn't much Trask could say to that except offer him his driver's license, but he wasn't about to prove that he was telling the truth. He knew he shouldn't let Mr. Suero's attitude irritate him, but he couldn't help but compare Felipe's dad with his own old man. "You look like an ex-con, rock star, or gang member, so which is it?"

"You've got one of them right." It was a fight to keep his tone even. The man was only being protective of his son and Trask couldn't really blame him, but it opened up painful memories and longings. "I've never been tempted to join a gang." Even in the midst of his drug-induced nightmares, he'd known doing that would have him heading for a body bag. Sophie picked up on his rising tension and pawed at his leg with a little whine. Trask half crouched to pet her in wordless reassurance.

"I'm guessing not a rock star either or I would've heard music late into the night," Mr. Suero said with a weighing glance. "Felipe would've had you rocking out."

Trask assessed the other man's wary demeanor. Might as well be upfront now and save them all a headache later. "As much as I'd like to play an instrument, I just don't have the ear for it. I did some time back when I was about Felipe's age for something stupid, and it never happened again."

Mr. Suero nodded, and his gaze flicked down to Trask's hands. "And all the decoration? You get that while in jail?"

Trask held out his hands in fists, studying the words emblazoned across his knuckles. "Clean," "Life," "Death," "Love." They were vows, promises, and warnings. "No, some I picked up before, many after. Nothing to symbolize that time. It's a period I'd rather not revisit."

"I think you might want to reconsider sniffing around here." Mr. Suero definitely did not have his children's expressive eyes, but the words and tone were plain enough, and his stance screamed how unwelcome Trask was.

Trask considered his response carefully. If what Felipe told him was true, Mr. Suero was a man who gave others a chance to pull themselves out of the pit. Trask appreciated that. He'd done the same himself for a couple people at the Magick Den a few times. Maybe his experiences had jaded Mr. Suero, and maybe it was just protectiveness that would ease when he got to know Trask. So it would be best just to stand his ground, but not in a way to make it ugly. If it got to be too unpleasant later on down the road, well then Trask would reevaluate. He wouldn't want to get between Felipe and family. Just because he didn't have one of his own didn't mean he didn't understand the value of them.

"With all due respect, that's not your decision to make." Trask had no doubt Felipe would go off at the top of his lungs if he knew about this conversation. "I know Felipe's only twenty-two, and I'm very aware of our age difference. I also know he's a grown man who essentially works two jobs, goes to school on top of it, and pays his bills. So I think he's capable of making his own decisions." Trask forced his defensive reaction to chill as Mr. Suero's brows climbed to his hairline.

"Is that so?" There was no way to tell from Mr. Suero's tone or expression how he took that announcement.

"That's about how I see it. I'm not looking to hurt him or change him. I enjoy his company, and for some reason he enjoys mine." Trask straightened and shoved his hands in his pockets. "I also know what a rare man he is and one who ran out of here without his breakfast, so I'm going to go take care of that if you don't mind."

He touched his cap and called to Sophie as he turned toward his truck. "Have a good day, sir."

Trask felt Mr. Suero's gaze on him the whole way to the truck as he replayed the conversation or lack thereof in his mind. He could've handled that better. Hell, he'd probably fucked it up every way he could. He had his faults, many of them, but he was not some kind of old lecher preying on boys, and the insinuation pissed him off.

The way the man had looked at him awoke a slow fire of anger. Trask tried to avoid that anger. Once lit he had a hard time putting it out, and he didn't want to ruin the fine mood that Felipe left him in with a brood.

He got Sophie nestled in her harness, though it took some doing because she kept licking his face with soft whines. "It's okay, baby. I'm okay."

But he wasn't. After he got her settled, he slid in behind the wheel and spied Mr. Suero in his own car, watching him with Mariana in the seat beside him. Jesus, what did the man think he was going to do? It was clear he wasn't going to leave until Trask did.

Trask tightened his jaw and pulled out. The scenery around him was one of stark beauty, acres of trees, bare limbs reaching toward the sky with only a few clinging leaves to break up the long outlines, but Trask barely saw it. He reached the main road and headed into town. He needed some time to think before he saw Felipe again. Maybe it was time to pull things back and take them a little slower. He just didn't know.

He didn't want to be the cause of any discord between Felipe and his family. As much as he regretted it, he'd have to take a pass on the Thanksgiving offer. He'd find a way to break it to Felipe. Trask had been through enough uncomfortable family holidays of his own. He had zero desire to go through that again with someone else's. If they were still a thing by the New Year, maybe Felipe's dad would relax some. At least by then, the holidays would be over.

By the time Trask found the coffee shop and ordered them both food and coffees, he felt better. That would be the right way to handle it. He'd check with Jason, see if he needed a place to go for Thanksgiving dinner. The young man had elected to stay with his old sponsor. Still, Trask had offered to lend his ear as well. It wouldn't hurt to ask. He could look in on Joe too, though he'd likely be with his grandkids.

Trask headed toward the sleepy little toll bridge and took a gamble, aiming for one of the middle lanes in the hopes of spotting Felipe. He had to go over the bridge one more time before he found Felipe's booth.

Felipe stuck his head out the window with a grin. "I thought that was your truck, and I was disappointed I wouldn't get to see you again."

"Here you go." Trask handed out the largest latte he could get and the bag with Felipe's breakfast. "Now I'm going to go before I'm accused of bribing a government worker and am hauled in."

Felipe's eyes widened, and he inhaled a sniff of the brew. Trask smiled as he pulled off, and he had to laugh as he saw Felipe half hanging out of his booth, blowing kisses. "Trask Briscoe!" he called out after him. "I'm going to marry you."

Chapter Seventeen

FELIPE UNFURLED his whip and assumed a dangerous and sultry pose as Abby took up her spot beside him. He might have just found a signature costume. Catwoman suited him perfectly, and he knew he was turning heads in the form-fitting getup. Though it was a sore point that even in his black leather stiletto boots, he still didn't match Abby in height. His instincts had been right about her. She was made to be Wonder Woman. Together the two of them looked ready to kick comic book ass.

The one damper to his day was that Trask couldn't see how awesome he looked. Felipe sent pictures, but it wasn't the same. When he pranced by the Magick Den's table, he got Mr. Surly Ryan, not his sexy Tin Man.

That was the problem when there were several cons running on the same weekend. Felipe missed dropping in on people he wanted to see. Jackie was at the con in Gaithersburg, and Felipe had needed to talk to her about designing the new Creatures & Cosplay webpage banner he wanted to surprise Abby with since she'd gone ahead and gotten them a domain name. That had been cool of her, and he had to reciprocate.

Then there was a collectible con in Tyson's Corner, and Trask was at that. Trask was the owner of the Den. He had all the cash. So it made sense that he went to see what he could score for their store. But that con had no real use for cosplayers, and Felipe had gotten into this one for free. The prize for best costume was dank as fuck. So here he was. All those factors, though, meant no Trask-ogling for him.

Soon there would be a moratorium on convention life until after the holidays. Probably for the best because finals would be coming up soon. And his budget was taking a beating. He should've recycled his Link costume instead of staying up all night to finish the Catwoman one and blowing too much money on the boots. But the idea was so cool, and he was killing it. He'd handed out a good number of his business cards and taken a commission for his mask.

"Okay," Abby said, cutting into his thoughts as the cameras finally lowered. "Let's split up until it's time to register for the contest. I want to watch the quick-draw panel. It's always fun, despite what you think."

"If I wanted to watch someone draw, I'd go hang out with Morris." Felipe eyed the concession stand and shifted his stance. The boots were killer-looking and killer on his feet. "I think I'm going to go invest in something decadent."

"You might want to ease up on the sweets." Abby flashed him her dimples. "You don't want to pop a seam before the judges."

Felipe waved his hand in unconcern. "I'll share the wealth with Morris. After all, everybody knows that calories shared meant they are practically zero."

Abby sighed and shook her head. "Don't I wish that were true. Some of us have to live in reality, Short Round."

Please, the woman was literally an Amazon, and it showed. If Felipe had her height, he'd never have to worry about his waistline. Besides, he absolutely refused to be concerned about such things until he was at least in his thirties. Then he could angst for a decade or two before saying screw it, you only live once, and enjoy the fuck out of his old age.

Okay, a situation like this called for double chocolate brownies. Felipe crossed his arms as he stared up at the menu that sadly lacked anything remotely resembling brownies of any kind, though the oversized snickerdoodles were a nice consolation prize. As he stepped up to the counter to make his order, the guy behind the counter let out a low whistle. "Nice Catwoman."

Felipe smirked and pirouetted on the killer stilettos. "Thanks." Damn, cons were so good for his ego. He took his cookies and snuck off to the corner of the hall where he could have a few moments of quiet and watch the other attendees. He found the mix of people fascinating. He eased down onto a bench, pulled out a cookie and his phone. He wanted a little Trask time before diving back into the fray.

Hey, for Thanksgiving, want to come down the night before?

They could have breakfast in bed and watch the Macy's Thanksgiving Day Parade. They could go for a hike, and he'd show Trask the extent of their property. There were some beautiful spots out along the trails, and it was cold enough that Felipe didn't have to worry about ticks. The four-legged critters didn't bother him, but he hated the creepy-crawly ones.

I'm so sorry, Felipe. I can't commit to Thanksgiving at your place this year. Please don't get mad. I wanted to tell you in person this weekend.

Felipe stared at the message with acute disappointment as his day soured. He'd been so sure he had Trask convinced. *What happened? I thought I'd changed your mind.*

Something came up. We'll talk this weekend. I promise.

Felipe broke off a piece of another cookie and bit into it savagely. It only made him feel marginally better. Too bad all life problems couldn't be solved with carbs. Fine…. Trask wanted to be that way. Felipe could wait until the game next weekend, and he'd corner Trask then. He gave a moment's consideration to calling him, but it would be an exercise in frustration to pull words out of him. Trask was not a phone fan. Felipe could usually get him to talk in person. On a phone, he heard grunts and mmhmms.

A shadow fell across him, and he glared up at Dakota as he took the seat beside him and had the fucking balls to steal one of his snickerdoodles.

"I will stab you with my stiletto if you take another one of my cookies," Felipe warned.

"I've missed you too, Felipe," Dakota countered, taking an unrepentant bite. "You looked sulky, so I thought I'd be a friend and check in on you."

Sulky. He wasn't sulky. He was fucking disappointed. After Trask's letdown, the last damn person Felipe wanted to see was his ex-lover, who had disappointed him numerous times.

He started to deliver a scathing retort about the faithlessness of men and then thought of the game next weekend. If he said something, Dakota would get all hyperprotective the way he sometimes did. Which would only make the game uncomfortable, and Trask pretty much spelled out at the beginning that he wouldn't GM a group like that. Dammit, Felipe wasn't about to lose out on a game too.

Felipe narrowed his eyes at Dakota and stabbed a finger at him. "When I need your intervention, I'll ask for it."

Dakota regarded him thoughtfully a moment, his gaze unusually serious. "Before you think I'm just doing this in order to get you naked again, let's clear this between us. I know you've moved on, and despite what others may think, I'm happy for you. You and I were never going to work long-term. We're both too temperamental, and let's face it, both you and I know I have serious commitment issues."

This was a rarely shown side of Dakota, and it cooled Felipe's temper. Their history aside, they were friends first and always had been. "Nothing's wrong but a big case of disappointment and frustration."

"Trask is at the collectible con, isn't he?"

"That sums it up," Felipe said, letting Dakota think it was just that. "I can't get anyone to stop harping on why we wouldn't work. I've got Morris crying over his age. I've got to get him to meet my family sooner or later, and that's going to take some smoothing over until they relax. And I can't prove it, but I think Ryan's whispering in Trask's ear about the evils of cosplayers."

Dakota's mouth lifted in his quicksilver, mischievous grin. "Some people need to chill out on that debate. On both sides. Personally, I think you and Trask mesh in a way that seems as if it shouldn't work, but it does. So don't sweat the others. Really it's about the two of you, not the other people in your life. I mean, you don't drag your family into your bedroom, so why do it for the relationship?"

"Ugh." Felipe swatted at Dakota and stood up. "I will not thank you for that image in my head, but I see your point. I'm going to go check in on Morris and tell him you swiped the cookie I'd bought for him. You'd better watch your back. You know how that man views his food."

"I'm perfectly safe. With Morris's height, I can see him coming from across the con." Dakota crumpled up the cookie bag and lobbed it over into the trash can. "Yes, nailed it!"

Felipe left Dakota with a shake of his head. He'd almost asked him about Brenden, especially after that crack about family. But he decided that was between the brothers and he was leaving it alone. If Morris was seeing things, Felipe did not want to be the one to plant that notion in Dakota's head because there was no telling what he'd do.

Oddly enough, his discussion with Dakota helped him to feel better. As he neared Morris's table he noticed Morris muttering to himself, his table devoid of customers and his hands gesturing along with his internal monologue.

"What's wrong?" Felipe took up a spot at the corner of Morris's table, close enough to chat but out of the way.

"Deadpool is being an ass," Morris grumbled. "Or Iron Man... can't fucking tell which."

Now that was intriguing, because Morris definitely knew the difference between the two characters, which could really only mean one thing.

"It's Deadpool, dude, he's the definition of ass." Felipe glanced around, searching for the source of Morris's angst. "Iron Man's not too far behind him, though still lower on the scale."

"Yeah, but the comic book character can get away with it. Ryan Reynolds can too because he's adorkable. But not some jackass cosplayer with a half-assed pieced-together costume who seems to think it gives him a license to ignore every bit of con etiquette because he's in character." Morris emphasized the last words with air quotes.

Felipe's friend had a look of aggravation on his broad face, and it took quite a bit for Morris to get aggravated. "I hear that complaint about con etiquette more and more, not just about cosplayers either. It's getting to be a little more cutthroat." He scanned the crowd, looking for the man in question. They were only three hours into the show, but from the expressions on the row of vendors and artists, none of them were happy. "What did he do?"

Morris pressed his lips together in an angry line and pulled out one of his original art books. Felipe's heart sank. Morris had hundreds of dollars of work in that book. Morris opened it up to what had been a sweet watercolor of Superman that Felipe always admired. An ugly ring blurred his face and splash marks stained the page.

"Oh fuck. I loved this piece. Can you fix it?" Felipe held up his hand. "Never mind, that's not the fucking point. He set his drink down here?"

"Yeah, so he could pose for some pictures. I'd pulled it out of its sleeve to show someone who was interested in buying it. He didn't even look. Just reached back and plopped it down hard enough to spill. Like it wasn't already sweating. Then he caused a huge stink when I called him out on it and tossed the drink." Morris jerked his thumb toward the trash can behind him. "He had the balls to demand I buy him a new one. I told him I would be happy to when he paid for the picture. I was about to close on an eighty-dollar sale. And it just went to shit from there."

It was jerks like him who made it difficult for all cosplayers. Felipe clenched his jaw and scanned the crowd, looking for the bastard. Sometimes you just had to police your own. "Did you complain to Tiffany?"

"Tiffany doesn't give a fuck. She already got my table fee. She doesn't want to deal with the drama." Morris tucked his book away. "Hell, I don't want to deal with the drama. Last time an artist got into it with this dude, he got all his friends riled up online and they harassed him for weeks. It tainted the whole con."

Felipe caught sight of Abby and gestured her over. "Don't worry, Morris my man, I've got this."

"Felipe." Morris said his name with a note of warning. "What are you going to do?"

"Hey, it's me. Trust me." Felipe marched to intercept Abby. "Duchess, have you seen Deadpool around?"

"Which one? The straight-up Deadpool or the mashup with Iron Man?" Abby glanced at her watch, then toward the panel rooms. "The quick-draw panel's getting ready to start, sure you don't want to go?"

Wow, a mix of Deadpool and Iron Man. Felipe wasn't sure one costume could hold that much ego. "Nope, I have business. The mashup sounds like the dick I'm looking for."

"Last I saw him, he was in the far aisle, catcalling anybody in a costume. One of the guys from the Magick Den was trying to chase him off. So now he's grandstanding in front of the booth." Abby rolled her eyes. "When I ran into him he offered to use my lasso for a little bondage and tried to grab my butt. Not that I have much. You have more curves than me. But they are mine."

Felipe ground his teeth and clenched his fists. Okay, this dude had fucked with two of his friends now. And he was pissing off Ryan. Felipe was already on the man's bad side, and this would just clinch his opinion of all cosplayers. "I hope you told him off."

"You know I did. Wait, what are you doing?" Abby asked as he stalked off.

Several options ran through Felipe's mind. He wished this was the Escape Velocity con. The Klingon Security would've already taken him in line. Or one of Brenden's cons. Oh man, between Brenden and Dakota, the guy wouldn't have started a damn thing.

"I'm going to challenge him to a snark-off." Felipe shot Abby a sharp smile as he caught sight of his prey. The jerk had his phone in his hand, music playing on its loudest setting, as he did the Macarena in front of the Magick Den's stall. Felipe winced at the expression on Ryan's face. He looked ready to stuff the dude into a bag of holding for eternity.

"Oh, heaven save us," Abby muttered under her breath as she grabbed his arm. "Felipe, I'm not sure that's the best approach. Talk to me. Tell me what's going on."

"It's better than me cold-cocking him." Felipe put his hands on his hips as he faced her. "He disrespects you and he ruins a watercolor of Morris's. And it's people like him who give us a bad rep. I don't want to hear weeks of bitching online as the vendors and cosplayers go at it again."

Abby grabbed his arm again as Felipe started off. "Wait. Your snark will lead to him cold-cocking you. He can't compete with your mouth."

"Then he's wearing the wrong damn costume." Felipe flicked his claws disdainfully at the guy when he started in on the Cha Cha Slide as the music changed. "He shouldn't suit up if he doesn't have the lip for it."

Abby had a point, though. A snark-off would take time, and they'd be blocking the Den's table even more. He had to lure the dude away. Then he'd have a few words with him in private. "Hold that thought. Actually, this calls for Catwoman. I'll meet you by the green room."

Felipe sashayed off, lightly tapping the coiled whip against his thigh as he moved with a lazy grace toward his target. The dude didn't even notice him. He was too busy panning for the cameras and quoting movie lines. The idea for his costume was clever. Felipe would give him that, but he'd cut corners, and it showed, from peeks of his day clothes underneath to one of the armor panels starting to slip off due to his exertions.

Ryan saw him coming and threw up his hands with a roll of his eyes. Felipe would deal with him later. "What do we have here? A dick in a box, but without Timberlake's sexy suaveness to pull it off," Felipe purred as he strutted by.

Deadpool stopped midstep and put his hands on his hips. "Awww, did I piss in your kitty litter? Scamper off, unless you mean to use that whip."

Felipe idly flicked the end like a cat's tail and laid the back of his hand against his forehead, miming a swoon. "Darling, you couldn't handle me and my whip, but say pretty, pretty please and maybe I'll be a good little kitten and not the vixen of your nightmares."

"Ramble on…. You're blocking my photo op." Deadpool held up his phone. "The Electric Slide is up next."

"I warned you," Felipe murmured. He snatched the dude's phone out of his hand and skipped down the aisle, waving it in the air like a prize. "Catch me if you can, Deadbeat Man," he trilled. "Or did the cat steal your tongue too?"

"Hey!"

Felipe snickered and quickened his steps. He'd had practice in making an escape on stilettos and slipped through the crowd with ease. Abby waited by the green room with her arms crossed and her expression stern. It only added to the whole Wonder Woman effect. He'd have to compliment her when he wasn't being chased. He tossed the phone to her. "Hold on to that for me."

Abby caught it one-handed and groaned. "Felipe, what did you do?"

"Give me my phone back!"

Felipe turned to face Deadpool as he came around the corner and blew him a kiss. "I'd love to play with you more, Deadbeat Man, but I have other fish to fry." He grinned at Abby. "Catch you on the flip side."

He scampered off again, heading for the exit as Deadpool closed in. They'd gathered a small crowd who apparently thought this was some kind of staged show. Which gave him an idea for him and Abby to do some quick skits at the next con they attended. Once outside, Felipe made his way around the corner of the building and then took up a position leaning against the wall.

Moments later Deadpool followed and stopped short when he saw Felipe. "What the fuck is wrong with you? That's not funny."

"Neither is ruining someone's artwork, or touching a woman without permission, or deliberately trying to sabotage a vendor's sales by showboating," Felipe snapped as he straightened.

"Don't be—"

"I'm not done, fucker." Felipe advanced on him, and the guy took a stumbling step back. "Now, you've got two choices. You can leave right now, and I'll even give you your phone back, but I swear I'll have you blackballed from any con I have influence with." Which pretty much just meant Brenden's cons, but he knew Dakota would back him.

"But—" he started, and Felipe didn't want to hear his excuses.

"I'm not done!" Felipe snarled, holding up his finger and pointing the claw at him. "Second choice, you go to Morris Proctor's table and pay for the painting you ruined. Then you go and apologize to the vendors and any lady you offended, and not only will you get your phone back, and a new soda, but I'll keep my lips shut about what a menace you are."

"I'm the menace? You—"

Felipe held up his finger again. "Nope, don't wanna hear it. I'm in a mood. Make it snappy because it's almost time to register for the contest and I'm not being held back from that."

"Fine. I'll pay for the stupid picture," Deadpool said in tones of deep aggravation. "But if you think I'm going to forget this, you'd better watch your fucking back."

Felipe closed the distance between them until his nose was only a half an inch away from the dick's. "Bring it. Oh, and if you touch my friend's ass again, I'll cheer her on while she mops the fucking floor with you. Ta-ta, bitch."

Chapter Eighteen

IT WAS a fine fall day for working outside. The chill held a bit of damp in it, but Trask's exertions kept him warm and limber enough. People hustled in many of the yards in Joe's active adult living community, hauling out decorations or taking care of yard work. Leaden skies and leafless trees didn't bother Trask. He liked watching the seasons march along. The scent of woodsmoke and the promise of the holidays to come warmed him almost as much as the work did. It seemed like autumn was one holiday after another from Halloween to New Year's. And a few early souls were already dolling up their yards and houses for Christmas.

Trask moved the ladder over to the next window and picked up another framed insulation panel. Only two more to go and Joe's house would be set for the winter. Next Sunday, they'd do Ryan's place. If Felipe stayed over after the game, maybe he could cajole the imp into helping and hanging around for that. He'd be able to introduce Felipe to Joe and Reva, and then he'd know all of Trask's closest friends. It seemed like the right thing to do even if he planned on taking this relationship slow.

"Heya, Trask," Joe called from the doorway, over the sound of the low music coming from Trask's earbuds. "I have some fresh decaf coffee brewed if you're of a mind to have a cup."

Trask considered the remaining work. The sound of the leaf blower had stopped some time ago. And he'd spied Ryan's truck with a load of firewood pull up midmorning. He ought to have that unloaded and stacked by now. "I'm almost done here. I'll be along in a few."

He switched the music on his phone to The Mighty Mighty Bosstones and clambered back up the ladder, taking the insulation pane with him. After he finished tapping the panes into place, he stowed the ladder away and headed toward the house, more than ready for that cup of coffee and maybe a scrounge of Joe's fridge for a little something to eat before he headed off to the Den.

The scent of coffee and cinnamon greeted him as he opened the front door. Rubbing his hands together to get warmth back into them, Trask made his way toward the murmur of voices in the kitchen. "Yard looks good. It didn't take you that long to take care of the leaves," he said as he pulled down a coffee cup.

"Long enough," Joe replied from his spot at the table, where he was tucking into a slice of coffee cake. "Thanks for your help."

Trask gave him a salute, poured himself a cup of coffee, and inhaled its fragrance, rich and dark. Now that right there was heaven. He pointed to the coffee cake ring and looked at Ryan. "Reva's baking again?"

"She's either baking or redesigning something or looking for a house to flip. I don't know where she finds the time to work on wedding plans, but she manages. Want a slice?" At Trask's nod, Ryan pulled out the knife and cut a good-sized chunk. "I was getting ready to tell Joe about the con yesterday and the antics your Felipe pulled."

His Felipe. Trask took that as a sign that Ryan was starting to warm up to him. "He's an imp, that's for sure." Trask glanced at Joe and nudged his chin toward Ryan. "And this one's an incurable gossip, so only pay half a mind to what he says." Curiosity got the better of him. Felipe had mentioned an incident in his texts but hadn't gone into any details. "What did he do?"

Ryan grinned, a look of pure delight that Trask had never seen on his face when he talked about cosplayers. "So that jerk showed up to the con, you know the one that's been running around the area, acting more entitled than most and causing one disruption after another both at the con and online?"

Trask nodded and began eating his coffee cake as he listened to Ryan's story. He remembered that young man well. He'd pissed Trask off a time or two. He usually showed up at a con with a pack of his cronies in tow to act as a self-made audience and admirers rolled into one. He'd heard they could be pretty rabid online, but he'd never engaged them. Personally, he didn't have much patience for social media and the headaches that went with it. He let Gillian handle that aspect for the Den and mostly stayed offline himself.

"Well, he must've decided to up his game or had some kind of chip on his shoulder this Saturday because he was especially obnoxious. I made the mistake of telling him off." Ryan reached into the fridge and pulled out a container of pumpkin spice creamer.

Trask winced as Ryan poured a hefty stream into his mug. He couldn't see ruining a perfectly good cup of coffee with that. He swore pumpkin spice was a cult thing. Whoever was behind it had plans to take over the world. "Let me guess. He parked himself outside of the booth."

"Yep, and he seemed perfectly content to remain there until registration for the costume contest, blaring his music and line dancing." Ryan grimaced with heartfelt exasperation that Trask echoed.

"Sorry you had to deal with that." Trask gave him a sympathetic smile. At least at the Den, they could kick out anyone being too disruptive.

Joe's bushy eyebrows climbed up to his hairline. "Kids," he grumbled. "Always have to be the center of attention."

Trask was sure every generation said something similar. He thought it was more of an individual thing. Take Felipe for instance, that was one who would not hesitate for a moment to be right in the center of things, but he wasn't one to try to steal someone else's spotlight in favor of his own. Now his best friend, Morris, he was more than happy to take a back seat and just observe what was going on around him.

Ryan glanced at Trask to see if he was still listening. "Get on with it," Trask encouraged. "How did the imp get involved?"

"Word is the cosplayer did something to mess with one of Felipe's friends. I never did get the full story. Everybody was so busy talking about the fallout they didn't want to give details about the cause. Well, anyways, I'm stuck watching this fool gyrate in front of our booth, knowing that anything I say was only going to make the situation worse. And he was all up and down the booth, so nobody could get around it to look at the games. Then your man sashays up in a Catwoman costume." A reluctant smile crossed Ryan's face. "I've got to give it to him. No one struts like Felipe."

Trask grinned because he could just picture it. Damn, he wished he'd been there that day. He hoped someone took a video of the encounter. "He does have a way about him."

"The two exchange some sassy words, and I'll admit I wasn't happy to see Felipe at all. I thought they had staged the whole act between them. Then before the guy could start shit again, Felipe swipes his phone and goes skipping off, skipping mind you in heeled boots, like he really was Catwoman. I swear every vendor in the row clapped when the other dude chased him and Felipe led him right outside the building."

Felipe really was something else, and the more time Trask spent with him, the more he wanted to. Felipe just warmed him up, filled places that Trask hadn't been aware needed filling. "I take it that means you're softening up on the imp."

Ryan shrugged. "Maybe a little. Honestly, it was more that he took the repercussions without complaint. At least not out loud. The other dude is still bitching online even though he got his phone back and wasn't booted from the con."

"They kicked him out?" Trask's heart tugged for Felipe. He knew he'd been looking forward to the contest, and his costume looked amazing. Felipe poured his heart and soul into his cosplay.

"Yep, for being the cause of such a big stink. However, a number of the vendors got together with the promoter and laid out the truth, so he's not permanently banned. Morris Proctor led the charge on that one. Many of the cosplayers backed Felipe up. It was kind of odd having the two groups come together for the troublemaker." Ryan shrugged and held out his hands. "Gotta give it to him. He sized up the situation and handled it. Maybe not how I would've handled it, but it got the job done and none of us were harassed anymore."

"Okay, now I'm intrigued." Joe rose and nudged Trask's arm. "After all these small hints from you about him, I want to know what this guy looks like."

Trask dug out his phone as Ryan smirked. He felt a little self-conscious. He wasn't one to go around showing off pictures or talking about the guys he was seeing. He pulled up one of them together that they'd taken in Richmond with the dogs piled around them. It was a favorite if Trask was honest. That was the day Sophie had claimed him, and Felipe looked so damned happy. Trask liked that look on him.

"Christ, Trask." Joe glanced at him and then went back to studying the photo. "He's a little young, don't you think?"

"Age is just a number, Joe. You ought to know that." There were times when that observation made Trask wince, though most of the time he was of a fuck-it mind-set. Of all the differences between him and Felipe, age was probably the most minor. "It's not like we're making permanent commitments. We're enjoying each other's company. That's all that needs to be said."

Joe handed the phone back with another shake of his head. "Seems to me you have plenty to say on the subject, more than you normally do. Sounds like the imp, as you call him, is going to turn your hair more silver than it already is. It's my job to voice concerns."

"I can't believe I'm saying this, and this goes no further than us." Ryan shot Trask a pointed look. "He's an imp in a good way. He's pulling Trask out of a rut. Hell, he gave him that sweet mutt that's just as much of an imp as her former owner. You don't have anything to worry about, Joe."

"Felipe would have heart palpitations if he heard you defend him." Trask gave Ryan an amused glance. It was good to see him letting go of preconceived notions about Felipe.

"I said this goes no further," Ryan scolded with exasperation. "He'd use it as an excuse to chat my ear off the next time he comes to a con and you're not there."

Joe made a noncommittal sound. "You spending the holidays with him?"

Trask felt a little bad about backing out of it, and he knew Felipe had to be irritated. It was for the best. Felipe would see that when they had a chance to talk over the weekend.

"No, he asked, and I considered it. We're still new enough that I don't want us to be under a microscope from his family. Besides, I asked Jason to have dinner at my place with me. His sister flat-out told him he wasn't welcome for Thanksgiving." Trask grimaced and shoved his hands into his pockets. That was something he'd never had to face. He chose not to visit his so-called family. He hadn't been kicked out. He didn't blame Jason's sister, but it did make this season hard for those struggling, and he didn't want Jason to be alone.

"I thought he was keeping his old sponsor." Joe cut himself a second slice of the coffee cake. "Nobody can bake like Reva. You tell her I said so, Ryan."

"Truth." Ryan grinned and nudged Trask with his elbow. "You should've said something. We can shove over a couple more seats at our table for you and Jason. I'd assumed you were going to be with Felipe."

"You and Reva have been more than generous in opening up your home to me." Trask lifted his coffee mug in a salute to Joe. "You and your family as well. I would've had many an empty holiday without you. Thanks for the invite. I'll pass it along to see if he's interested. He may just want to do something low-key. As for your question, Joe, his sponsor will be out of town, visiting a new niece I believe."

Trask glanced at his watch. "I'm going to go relieve Gillian before she starts texting me emojis."

"Good idea. Once she gets started, it roller-coasters from there." Ryan poured himself another cup of coffee as he eyed the remainder of the cake. "See you tomorrow."

Joe waved his hand and went back to his second slice. Trask drained his cup and set it in the sink. It was late afternoon, and he'd left Gillian alone long enough with the new hire and a back room that would be half filled by now.

Trask went to the back door that looked out on Joe's fenced-in backyard. It seemed as if Sophie hadn't stopped moving the whole morning, exploring the space from end to end, running through piles of leaves before they'd picked them up. She would sleep hard when they got to the Den. Trask really needed to think about getting a new place for her. His girl deserved a yard where she could run rampant, not his pint-sized loft.

Sophie was streaking toward him before he even had the door all the way open. "Ready to go to the Den?" Trask leaned down to give her a pat as her ears pricked forward at the sound of his voice. "Yeah, you know where we're going when I say that word."

"Thanks again for the help," Joe said as he walked Trask to the door.

"Anytime." Trask lightly clapped him on the shoulder. "See you at the meeting. Come on, Sophie."

Once he had Sophie settled in her harness and his phone set up in its holder, he directed it to call Felipe. He wanted to hear the imp's voice, and not just on a recording.

"What's up, Tin Man? Can't talk long. Big Brother is watching me in my iron cage." Sophie barked at the sound of Felipe's voice and wagged her tail wildly. "Hey there, Sophie." Felipe's tone warmed.

Trask patted Sophie until she settled down. "I heard what happened at your con. I just wanted to make sure you were okay. I know that was a disappointment."

"Whatever," Felipe said in a tone thick with disgust. "I should've known that *pendejo* would've gone crying to Tiffany. And she didn't want to deal, so she sided with him to shut him the fuck up. What a fucking whiner. At least Morris got his money back, but still, the little bitch ruined his art, and that pisses me off a lot more than getting kicked out of a stupid con. I'd do it again."

Trask wished Felipe wasn't so far away so he could swing by with a cup of coffee, a little something to put a smile on Felipe's face. "I have no doubt you would. You're a good friend, Felipe."

"Yeah, I guess so. His friends have been harassing me online. Nothing I can't handle. Bunch of amateurs if they think they can one-up me with words. Besides, I'm not going to have to see his ugly face for a long time. Tiffany can have him. I'm not doing another con of hers again, and Dakota is making sure he won't cause trouble at one of Brenden's cons. The dude is on the Chessie Con shit list. It's a short but notorious list, and once you're on it, Brenden isn't known for softening his attitude. Look, I've gotta go. Any chance you can come over tonight?"

That was tempting but not practical. "I wish I could. But I have to close tonight and open tomorrow. It's one of those times when it would be nice if we lived closer together." Even if there wasn't much traffic between Southern Maryland and Richmond, it was still a haul. "Maybe you can come down the night before our game?"

"I'm working the late bridge shift. Damn, this sucks. Gotta go." Felipe made a smacking kiss sound. "We'll figure something out."

Trask sighed as the call ended. That imp sure had put some kind of spell on him. He'd been well and truly snared. He glanced down at Sophie. "What do you think?" Her tail thumped against the seat. "Yeah, me too, girl, me too."

Chapter Nineteen

As soon as Felipe got his hands on Trask, he was going to get some answers out of that man. Something was going on, but damned if he could figure it out. He thought it was frustrating when he was dating Dakota. It was three times more frustrating with Trask in Richmond. He didn't roam around like Dakota did, going from one venue to another interview and then off on tasks for Brenden. Trask stayed put for the most part, but Richmond was too far away for Felipe to just pop on over there every time he wanted to scratch an itch. Or nail Trask down so he could figure out what was up with him.

Maybe he was just being paranoid. Maybe he was just disappointed over Thanksgiving. He'd been looking forward to it, and he didn't like the idea of Trask dining alone. Or maybe he was picking up the weird vibe in the air.

Felipe muttered darkly to himself as he stomped up the stairs with Lady running on up ahead. "I really can pick them, can't I?" he asked his dog as she waited patiently for him to open the door instead of dodging through the doggie door as she would've done when she was younger. "They all make better friends than fucking boyfriends."

He was supposed to meet Abby online tonight to go over some tentative plans for their joint website. He couldn't bail on her, no matter how tempted he was. He hated it when people bailed on him. And despite his feelings, this situation with Trask was not an emergency. He'd pin him down when they met over the weekend. He'd already arranged to work late on Sunday, so he could take his time getting his answers.

Felipe threw his coat over the back of his couch and groaned when he saw the pile of schoolbooks on the coffee table. What had possessed him to add this venture with Abby now? After the holidays he'd have his associate's degree and plenty of time to launch into a brainless new project. But the momentum was there now. He and Abby were on the same wavelength for once, and he didn't want to mess that up by backing out.

He closed his eyes and deflated, then felt a heavy head on his knee. He rubbed his hand over Lady's ears. She always knew when he was moody. "You wouldn't desert me, would you girl?"

She licked his hand, her eyes bright. "Yeah, I love you too." Felipe patted the couch beside him. "Come on, you can cuddle with me as I suffer over accounting."

His main door opened and Felipe almost snarled in exasperation. Only one person walked in unannounced. "Mariana, I told you to knock. Fucking knock. My place, you know. Even if I was still living downstairs and you were coming to my bedroom, knock!" One of these days, his baby sister was going to catch him in a very compromising position, and dammit, she'd have no one to blame but herself. Felipe didn't see the need to lock his door when no one ever came back here without pinging him first but her.

"If Mama hears you cussing at me, she's going to lose it." Mariana plopped into the worn wide armchair across from him, her expression plaintive. She knew what a sucker he was when she gave him that look. He couldn't stand seeing his little sister unhappy. "Can I study here with you? Dad's been in a mood, and I don't want to listen to another one of his lectures."

Felipe winced in sympathy. When Dad got started, it didn't end until he was dead certain you had soaked in every bit of the wisdom he was dishing out. And he could trust Mariana would not only actually study, but she'd get on him if he slacked off. "What are you working on?"

"Essay on *Antigone*. Those Greeks were a mess. Nobody could be happy." Mariana pulled out her little laptop and curled up on the chair. She was small and lithe, with the body of a dancer, a razor-sharp mind, and an ability to focus that Felipe envied. He could only concentrate if he was invested. "If I was a Greek back then and I ran into an oracle, I'd just off myself then and there and save myself the agony to come."

"If you were in a Greek tragedy, the knife would break so you couldn't off yourself, and to add to the insult, the attempt would put you in a situation that only made things worse." Felipe shook his finger at her. "Never try to thwart the gods. They get pissier than a drag queen who lost out on the last pair of Jimmy Choos in her size."

Mariana shook her head with a smile and bent over her work as Felipe pulled up his accounting project. If he got this done before his online meeting, the night would be a win despite his irritation. As much as he bitched at his sister for completely tromping all over his rules, her presence soothed him. Nothing got Mariana worked up. She was like a mini lola. Between her and Lady, his night was looking up.

"I met your new boyfriend."

Felipe looked up sharply. She was frowning at her computer, idly twirling her pencil in her hair. "When the hell did you do that?" Then his eyes widened. "Oh fuck, the morning after he stayed the night. Fuck."

Mariana looked up this time, her brow furrowing in a frown, and Felipe tried to remember to put a damper on his foul mouth. He'd wanted to introduce Trask at Thanksgiving. He'd mentioned him to his parents a couple times. Showed pictures to his lola and opened up about Trask to her. He knew Trask would be a hard sell at first, but once they got to know him, he knew they'd like him. They just had to give him a chance. And somehow it had already happened without him and Trask hadn't said a damn thing!

"What did you think?" Felipe asked cautiously. Mariana was usually open with her opinions.

"I didn't get much of a chance to form an impression. He was real polite, though." Mariana looked up at Felipe and wrinkled her nose. "He's kinda old, don't you think?"

"He's not as old as he looks. The silver sexiness has to be a genetic thing." But even if Trask were fifty, Felipe would want him. He pondered Mariana's words with foreboding. "Why didn't you get a chance to talk to him? Trask run off? He can be a little closemouthed around people."

Mariana shook her head and went back to her essay. "Dad shooed me away so he could talk to him."

The sense of foreboding struck full force. Trask and Dad had been alone together. That might explain why Trask backed out of Thanksgiving and was acting so fucking weird. And why his dad had been giving him the stinky side-eye all damned week. "Excuse me."

"Wait, where are you going?" Mariana asked, her dark eyes widening in alarm.

"Going to talk to Dad." He'd get some answers, too, and then he was taking this up with Trask. If he and his dad got into it, he had a right to know, dammit.

"Wait!" He heard Mariana scrambling to her feet. "Calm down. Take a deep breath."

Felipe waved her back. "If my computer rings, answer it and tell Abby I'll be right up."

He marched down the back steps with Lady in his wake, already whining. She hated it when he and his dad fought. He gave her an absent pat as he saw his parents through the glass doors, sitting on the couch, watching TV. His grandparents weren't in sight.

Then he glanced at his watch. Yeah, they were in bed, which was for the better. They'd take sides and it would become a whole family thing. Felipe slid open the door and stomped through the kitchen. His dad hit Mute with the remote. "Something wrong?" he asked.

"What did you say to Trask?" Felipe demanded, his hands on his hips as he stared his dad down.

"So he went crying to you, huh?" His dad crossed his muscled arms over his stomach, his face weathered from spending more time outdoors than he did inside. Donato Suero looked like a man who spent his life building, his shape blocky and enduring. "I wondered if that was going to happen."

"No, he didn't," Felipe snapped, waving a hand in emphasis. "But he did back out of the invite to Thanksgiving dinner. I was wondering what the hell happened, and then Mariana mentioned that you two met and had hush-hush words."

"He's not coming?" His dad nodded in thought at Felipe's glare. "Probably for the best. Your lolo would not have stood for him being there."

"Lolo would deal," Felipe said from between clenched teeth. He and his grandfather did not get along most of the time. They saw the world through completely different viewpoints, and nothing would ever change that. Lolo could not wrap his head around Felipe, and he wasn't about to tone himself down for the man's comfort. "Sorry, Mom, but it's true."

"I'm staying out of this one." Ratree held up her hands, curled her legs up on the couch, and reached for a book. "Just don't start cursing at each other. I won't put up with that."

Felipe was keeping a hold of his mouth through a pure effort of will.

"I'm not your grandfather. I don't care if you bring a boyfriend to a family dinner. But this Trask is something different. He looks like he's a step away from retirement. I don't understand why you can't meet men your own age," his dad continued.

"I do meet plenty of men my own age and they're all immature assholes." Felipe shot his mom a guilty look as she gave him a reproving frown. She was even smaller than Mariana and twice as intimidating as his dad when her temper got worked up. "Well, they are. I like Trask. We share many of the same interests. We have amazing conversations. He's thoughtful and responsible and a good guy if you'd give him half a chance."

His dad tapped his fingers together, giving a Felipe a measuring look. "Did you know he is an ex-convict?"

"Oh, Felipe." His mom looked up from her book, her expression worried. "You can't expose Mariana to someone like that."

Felipe clenched his jaw again, his temper rising as a headache began to form. He'd suspected that might be the case, but he'd wanted Trask to tell him his story in his own time. There were obviously lots of painful bits in his past, and he was getting it slowly as Trask grew more comfortable with him. He treasured those times that Trask shared because it showed his trust, and to have his dad digging around pissed him the fuck off. "He's not dangerous, Mom. He's not."

Someone who was dangerous did not treat puppies the way Trask did. The man was capable of a great deal of love and loyalty. You just had to look beneath his quiet surface. Felipe considered himself a good judge of other people, and what he'd seen of Trask, what he'd heard between the man's words just drew him in.

"He got awfully defensive with me," his dad said with that stubborn tilt to his chin that Felipe had seen too many times. There was no talking to him right now. He had to let him stew it out before he would be able to get his dad to look at it from a different angle.

"Wouldn't you have? Christ, Dad." Felipe threw up his hands.

"Felipe Suero!" His mom leveled a finger at him, her mouth tight. "Do not bring that language to my house."

Felipe took Mariana's advice and took a deep breath before trying again. "You judge him on his age, his past, without really knowing his past. Knowing you, you probably told him to break up with me or something equally asinine, and I bet he refused and that just pissed you off even more, and he probably picked up on that."

His voice was rising and he knew it was rising, and he could tell from his mom's flinty expression that she was about to tell him off hard core for his language. "But you never bothered to ask me how he treats me, did you? You never thought to ask me how I felt about him. This is me, dammit." Felipe tapped a finger against his chest, his eyes stinging. "Can you honestly see me staying with anyone who's not going to treat me how I deserve? Screw that. And on that note, I'm out of here."

He bit his lip hard before he could tell his dad to fuck off, but dammit, it was there ready to fall from his lips, and he knew if he stayed around, the fight would only escalate. Felipe didn't want to say anything he would sincerely regret later, and he'd only learned through painful lessons that leaving until he calmed down was the best action to take.

He turned around and stormed out of there before his mom could call him back. She always tried to play the peacemaker after his dad and he argued. It just pissed him the fuck off. How could his dad sit there so calm when he was screwing with Felipe's life? His dad wasn't the one sleeping with Trask. He had to live his own goddamned life and stay the hell out of trying to make Felipe's decisions for him.

He took the stairs two at a time and forced himself to pause and take a breath before he flung open the door and demanded Mariana leave. It would only make everything worse, and he'd be riddled with guilt later on. Taking his anger out on Mariana was like picking on a sweet puppy, a totally sweet puppy that just wanted to love you and be loved in return. Poke her enough and she nipped back, and those nips hurt. Felipe didn't want to deal with that any more than he did the hurt feelings.

Felipe looked down at Lady, who was waiting patiently by the door. He just wanted to take off as he had so many times as a teenager. Go for a drive along the county roads. Or go to Morris's place and whine. But he had adulting things to do. Fuck adulting. With a sigh, Felipe opened the door and composed his expression.

Mariana gave him a sympathetic look. "I don't know how you manage to project your voice all the way up here, but you did."

"It's the vents." Felipe threw himself down on his couch and waited for Mariana to call him out on his bullshit.

"I think you should invite him to Thanksgiving anyway." She rested her chin on her hand as she eyed her brother. "He was really polite to me, and Sophie seems so happy. She wouldn't be happy if he was a secret jerk."

Felipe stared at his screen, waiting for Abby to log on. "At this point, I think it's going to take an excavation truck to extract him from Richmond." He had some new messages on his site from that dumbass cosplayer. The man's buddies were getting bored with the harassment, but not dickwad yet.

"He didn't seem like a coward to me," Mariana said with a sniff. "He could've ignored us. Instead, he walked on up, introduced himself, and shook Dad's hand."

That ought to have scored some points with his dad. He was normally a sucker for shit like that. "I'll talk with him when I see him this weekend. You finished your homework?"

"I have my outline done, so I can take a short break." Mariana set aside her laptop and gave him a pleading look. "Does this mean you're going to boot me out?"

"No, I'm not going to make you leave, but I have a business meeting. So it might get boring." Felipe went through and took a perverse delight out of deleting each message. The idiot was just repeating himself, and Felipe already had his fun out-sassing him. Besides, the deleting seemed to be pissing him off more than the sassing did. There were times when Felipe could be a petty man, and he didn't give a fuck who thought it.

Excitement lit up Mariana's dark eyes. "Are you making a new costume for someone? I heard a bunch of messages coming in. Everyone loved the homecoming dress you made for me. Would you make my prom dress?"

"Slow your roll there, sis." Felipe held up his hand. "Senior prom's a big deal. Mom would pretty much buy you whatever you want. Something special."

"It's special if you make it," Mariana argued. "Then I have a one-of-a-kind Felipe Suero dress, and I know you'll make it better than anything I can get at the store."

Pleasure softened the anger that still lingered. Damn, his sister knew just how to make him feel better. "Okay, but it can't be black. You look too good in bold colors. You have to make a splash for your senior prom. And you can't promise any of your friends that I'll design dresses for them too. This is for you and you alone. Got it?"

Mariana beamed and blew him a kiss. "Got it. How about a ruby red or something like a garnet? I can borrow that necklace Dad got for Mom for their anniversary."

Felipe eyeballed his sister as he mentally went through colors and styles. "I think I can work with that."

Chapter Twenty

TRASK'S HEART wasn't entirely in the game, and it all had to do with a pair of subdued dark eyes. Subdued and Felipe did not go together. At least no one else in the group seemed affected, and the game rolled out with drama limited to characters. The only other one who noticed was Morris, who kept giving Felipe occasional glances and nudges. Best friends. You couldn't hide a damn thing from them. Ryan, who eventually chalked his broodiness up to holiday blues, had hounded Trask a few times himself.

Trask painted the new scene for the motley crew of troublemakers, on a deserted outstation on one of the fringe planets, with a dead contact and an Imperial ship on the way. "Well, folks, what do you do?"

"I examine the body to be sure they're dead. Carbon-based beings are so fragile. I don't know how they work with those bodies," Lincoln said with a doleful air.

"Of course she's dead, you metallic moron. Spines don't twist that way, and look at all that purple blood," Dakota replied, shaking his head.

"Are you sure you intercepted that transmission right?" Morris asked with a frown, staring at the layout on the table map.

"Pretty sure," Brett replied. "They'll be here within an hour, and it's a sure bet they'll have a lot more manpower than we do. If we don't find the information she hid, they will."

"I'm searching the body for credsticks." Felipe scooped up his dice. "Do I find anything?"

"Hey, man, have some respect." Jackie pushed her miniature over to confront Felipe's.

"Look, I'm a smuggler. I'm not some high-minded Senator like him." Felipe pointed to Morris and then turned his finger on Brett. "I don't have any loyalties to the Rebels like him. And I sure as hell don't think your Force mumbo jumbo gives a damn whether or not the credstick rots with this woman's corpse or helps me out. I have bills, you know. We have bills since you'd partnered with me to buy this damned ship."

"Welp, I found the gal you wanted me to find." Dakota smirked at Morris. "You can pay me now and I'll be on my way."

"The contact is no good to me dead," Morris protested.

"Her status was not specified in the contract. Isn't that right, Y-X8?" Dakota looked at Lincoln.

"Correct, sir. The contract was to locate this poor woman and to bring Senator Venau and his friends to her," Lincoln intoned. "However, I do believe that we—"

"Save me the lecture." Dakota flapped his hand at Lincoln and turned toward Morris. "But just because I'm a bounty hunter doesn't mean I'm completely amoral like that smuggler. Let's say another 15 percent and I'll locate that information for you before the Imperials get here."

"I'm not risking my ship by sticking around," Felipe insisted.

"Don't you think we should find out who did this to her?" Jackie argued. "Search the body for clues, not profit? We'll find another way to pay our bill."

It was so much fun to sit back and listen to good characters argue a situation out. Trask started a timer on his phone. If it went on long enough it might be a moot point, and he'd love to see what they'd do if that Imperial ship showed up before they came to an agreement.

He caught Felipe's eye and gave him a faint smile. He'd missed him in the last couple of weeks. It had been hectic, more hectic than he'd been expecting as sales picked up both online and in the store for the upcoming holidays. It seemed he'd never had time to chat as much as Trask wanted or work out his moodiness. He had no damn reason to be moody, and it was time to get over it. One man's opinion should not bug him. Even if that one was the father of the man Trask was falling for.

Felipe raised a brow and did not smile back. The imp was upset about something. Trask should've known when he decided not to come early, as he had last time. Trask hoped he still wasn't mad over the canceled Thanksgiving plans. The decision to go had been up in the air, so it wasn't like he had confirmed and then backed out on him. Trask could understand how Felipe would get his feelings hurt over that, given his history.

The argument between the players went on for more than twenty minutes, growing more heated until Morris threw up his hands. "Fine!

Another 15 percent. Freaking mercenaries. And don't worry about your ship. I paid for the repairs last time, didn't I?"

"Only after we threatened to shove you out an airlock." Felipe shot Morris a glare. "Don't make me threaten that again. I know you have more creds than you claim."

Trask glanced at his timer. That ate away almost half their time before Imperial arrival, and it was getting late in reality. Seemed like a good place to end it and leave everyone on tenterhooks until the next time. One thing he'd learned was to always leave the party wanting more.

"Glad you came to an agreement." Trask folded up his game screen. "And on that note, I think that's where we'll leave it for tonight."

"Nooo! Are you kidding me!" Brett jumped up and ran around the table as his wife looked on in amusement at his antics.

Sophie rose from her dog bed, watched Brett with a cocked head and lifted ears. She glanced at Trask, and he patted his leg. "It's okay, girl."

"Chill out." Daphne shook her head. "It's almost eleven. And if you think you don't want to stop now, think how you'd feel if it had been midbattle. We do have a babysitter waiting for us."

"There are going to be no battles, got it?" Jackie said with a stern stare around the table. "Felipe and I just got the ship running again."

"Good luck believing that." Dakota stood up, grabbed his miniature, and stowed it in its case. "There's going to be a battle."

"Maybe I can talk our way out of it." Morris tucked his character sheet away.

"Yeah, that went soooo well last time." Felipe rolled his eyes. He was the only one not preparing to leave, and Trask took that as a good sign. He wanted a chance to talk to Felipe alone, and he hadn't had the opportunity all day. He didn't think it would take much to get Felipe to tell him what was bothering him. Then they could move on to catching up. Trask had missed him.

One by one, their friends left, taking what was left of the foodstuffs they brought. Trask had been prepared this time and cleaned off the sideboard so they could have room for the Crock-Pot and trays. Boy, had they delivered too. Trask hadn't eaten that well in a while. He'd have to get the recipe for Jackie's mac-n-cheese.

And he was letting his thoughts wander because Felipe was sitting there silent, boring holes into him as Trask felt increasingly awkward while he tidied. He hated dealing with this kind of relationship issues because he never knew which foot to stand on. But he figured confronting Felipe head-on was better than letting him stew.

"You're mad," Trask finally said as the quiet grew taut.

"No shit, Sherlock." Felipe's eyes flashed with unreleased anger.

Trask scratched his head, trying to think of what he could've done. The last time he'd seen Felipe, he was yelling about marriage. A word Trask did not want to even think about. Their conversations on the phone hadn't seemed off, but it was hard to judge because Trask wasn't a fan of the phone much and tended to keep calls short and sweet. "Is it because of Thanksgiving? I thought that was up in the air, not the invite, but whether I could... would go or not."

"I guess it depends on why you're not coming." Felipe crossed his arms on the table and stared Trask down. "If it's because of my dad, yeah, I'm really going to be pissed. And I'm a little more than irritated that you had a confrontation with him and never once mentioned it to me. Didn't you think I should know?"

"Is that what he called it? A confrontation?" Trask laid his hands on his hips as anger sparked. Well, dammit, he hadn't figured on Mr. Suero as a man to tell tales. He'd suspected that a situation like that would upset Felipe, which was why he hadn't said anything. Fights with his own old man were most likely to end in ugliness, and he hadn't wanted to be the cause of one between Felipe and his dad.

"I didn't think of it as that at all," Trask continued. "We had a conversation. He expressed his concerns, rightly so I guess about my age, and he questioned my past. He wouldn't be the first man to do that. There was definitely some measuring up. But it didn't come down to raised voices or name-calling. He made his point and I made mine. That's not a confrontation."

Felipe stood up. "Did the conversation piss you off?"

Well, Trask could hardly deny that. "A bit," he admitted. "I don't like being judged, but that has more to do with people in my past than your dad. I don't have much experience with dads who are protective, so I'm thinking it could've gone a whole lot worse. I think we both got each other's message." That he was still irritated was his own damn issue and went back to his inability to let things go.

Trask gave Felipe a wary look. "Why, what did he say to you?"

"That you got defensive." Felipe walked toward him like a damn cat stalking through the grass, and it made Trask nervous. Felipe was unpredictable at best, and Trask just could not figure out what he was going to do next.

"I'm ashamed to admit that's true. I let him get my back up, but that's more on me than him." Trask tensed as Felipe stopped in front of him. Oh man, there was pure fire in Felipe's eyes. It had never occurred to him that Mr. Suero would've said anything to Felipe, but now all those questions Felipe had been flinging at him over the last week made sense. "Did he mention that I did jail time once?"

"He did," Felipe replied evenly.

Trask kept waiting for the explosion to happen, and the fact that it hadn't worried him. He fully expected that bomb. All of Felipe's pent-up energy had to go somewhere. He searched Felipe's face, but there was no judgment there. Not like there had been on his father's. "It was for a DUI, and since it hadn't been my first offense, I got a year. Ended up serving the whole time on account of not behaving myself."

"You didn't have to tell me that. I was waiting for you to be ready," Felipe murmured, the anger draining away from his stance as he rubbed his hands over Trask's arms.

Trask relaxed and reached for him. "It's not like it's a secret. I just don't talk about it much. It happened, one more incident in a long string before I finally got the damn hint that if I didn't get clean, I'd be dead. I know it seems like I dole my life out in small doses. But really you have the crux of it. I abused drugs and alcohol. Got into trouble for it countless times. If we sat here and did a biographical account it, would probably take days, and some of my memories are sketchy at best."

"Yeah, I have the gist, but there are gaps. Stuff you really haven't done more than hint at. Like your family." Felipe held up his hands as Trask stiffened. "Which is fine for now. I know there were some real bad parts. I can also see what you've made of yourself despite your past. I'm not screwing the twenty-two-year-old Trask. I'm pretty damn sure I would've told the twenty-two-year-old you to go sniffing elsewhere until you got your shit together. But one damn day, if this keeps going, and I'd like it to keep going, I'd like to know. It's a part of what shaped you."

"I suspect if the twenty-two-year-old Trask came sniffing around, your dad would've chased me off with a shotgun, not exchanged concerns." Trask pulled Felipe closer, relaxing now that the worst seemed to be over. That wasn't so bad at all. "Though the thought of you with a younger me is one I don't like. He was a selfish asshole, and you deserve better."

He leaned in to kiss Felipe and was shoved back by a hand on his chest. "Oh hell no. We're not done." Felipe glared at Trask. "First you had words with my dad, and you still haven't said what those were. Not really. Neither has he, but I'm guessing part of it has to do with staying the hell away from me. Which brings me back to why you bowed out of Thanksgiving dinner."

"Look, I'll give you the rundown how I remember it." Trask leaned back against the wall and recited the conversation as Felipe listened with a frown. "I'm sorry if you felt that I was keeping things from you. In my mind it was over with."

Felipe cocked his head. "You really told him it was my decision to make?"

"I really did." Trask shoved his hands into his pockets as he eyed Felipe. Maybe this would be the end of the grilling and they could put this behind them.

Felipe was silent a long moment, and Trask could practically see the thoughts tumbling around in his head, he was thinking so hard. "And about Thanksgiving?"

"What about it?" Trask wasn't sure he should admit one of the reasons he'd backed off was because of Mr. Suero's attitude. Felipe would probably insist on him coming, then, and that really wasn't the only factor.

"You're dodging the damn question," Felipe said through gritted teeth. "What are you doing for Thanksgiving?"

"There's a young man who's going through a real rough spot right now, and he was going to be alone on the holidays." Trask had gotten used to not having family around for these times, but for Jason, an empty table was a raw wound. "I've invited him over to spend the evening."

Felipe's eyes went flat with fury. "Is he cute?"

Trask frowned. He could not keep up with Felipe's emotional leaps. "I never really considered it. Even if he was, even if he swung in my direction, and I don't know that he does, the last thing he needs right now is the drama of a relationship." And Trask didn't date within the meeting rooms. If a relationship didn't work out, he didn't want to feel like he needed to find another group. It would leave him homeless in a way.

"So now I'm being overly dramatic." Felipe's voice lowered to a dangerous level.

Trask pursed his lips and studied Felipe's flashing eyes. That fury was still simmering there. Felipe never acted how Trask expected. He was waiting for curses and arm-waving at the least, not these still waters. There was a whirlpool stirring underneath, and Trask suspected he was about to get caught in the undertow. "Judging from the death glare I'm getting right now, yes, I'd say you are."

Felipe grabbed him by the front of his shirt and pulled Trask closer. For one breathless moment, Trask wasn't sure if Felipe was going to kiss the sense out of him or deck him, and he couldn't have said what the hell he'd done to earn either.

"Fuck you." Felipe smiled sweetly, let go of him, and sauntered out of the store.

Trask heard the front door chime and scratched his head. He looked at Sophie, who looked back at him with the same confusion. "What the hell just happened?" She turned her attention to her toys, and Trask sighed. "You're no help."

He went to the door, fully intent on calling Felipe back so they could finish this discussion, but when he got there Felipe's taillights were already pulling out of the parking lot. "Well, hell." Trask stared until the red glow disappeared, an uneasiness in his heart and utterly clueless on how to fix it.

Chapter Twenty-One

"YOU NEED to tell your client he's a fucking idiot." Felipe tossed his phone on the table with an irritated huff. "We cannot do everything he wants within the time he wants it and at that ridiculous discount. I'm not working for pennies, and you'd better not either."

Abby's dimples flashed as she set down her own phone. "I agree with your sentiment, but not the phrasing. If we go around telling potential troublesome buyers what we really think of them, we won't be in business long." She tapped her nail on the screen. "He may be an idiot, but he's a potentially useful idiot. I say we use him."

"That sounds cold-blooded and devious," Felipe scoffed. And dammit, intriguing. He looked at Abby with new respect. This was why Abby sometimes managed to best him. Felipe was too impatient to use the devious route.

Those dimples deepened. "So you're in, then?"

It was on the tip of Felipe's tongue to say hell yeah, but he paused. He really needed to be better about not jumping in headfirst without at least one moment of reflection. "What do you have in mind, Duchess?"

"Hold that while I get another round of coffee. I want to think this through." Abby uncoiled her long legs from the seat and stood up. "Another latte?"

"Sure, why not," Felipe said without much enthusiasm. The scent of roasting beans in the air was driving him nuts because it kept making him think of his first date with Trask. He missed the jerk. More than he'd missed Dakota when he tried pulling the same bullshit, always making other plans and setting aside their time together. Then he'd just been mad. Now he was all-around discontented.

To make matters worse, Trask didn't seem to be all that upset about their argument. If he missed Felipe, it sure as fuck didn't show. He still texted Felipe, sent pictures of Sophie, asked how he was doing. He'd even called a few times, but he didn't seem to be moping like Felipe was moping, and he sure as fuck wasn't groveling. Felipe desperately wanted to see him, but if he heard one more excuse about why some other guy was more important than him again and plans had to be canceled because of it, he might lose what self-restraint he'd managed to hold on to.

Abby returned and set a cup in front of Felipe as well as a small plate of raspberry thumbprint cookies, cut into heart shapes. "That heart looks like it's bleeding," Felipe said moodily as he picked up one and broke it in half.

"Okay, what's the problem?" Abby eyed him as she took her seat. "You've been in the weirdest mood all day. I can't tell if you're mad or sad or just hormonal. But it's definitely not this potential commission that's got you all worked up, so spill it."

Felipe wasn't sure if he could open up to her. He usually shared all of his relationship angst with Morris, but it was impossible to whine to someone who was deliriously happy in their own relationship. It wasn't that Morris and Theo didn't argue. They did. Theo had a temper, and when Morris decided to get prickly, the spines lingered until he chilled. But they weren't serious arguments. It was more spats that led to incredible makeup sex. At least that's what Morris boasted about. Felipe wanted incredible makeup sex for himself.

Felipe eyed Abby. "So there's this guy I've spent the last couple months chasing, and he finally let me catch him."

Abby's eyes widened as she picked up a cookie. "So you and Trask actually did hook up. You know, until the rumors came out about you and Dakota, I never realized you were gay. How crazy is that?"

"For real?" It was Felipe's turn to stare at Abby in disbelief. "How many fucking years have we known each other? How many times have you seen me in a skirt?"

"It never came up in conversation. It wasn't like we had heart-to-hearts. I didn't want to assume." Abby nibbled on a corner. "I mean, when you put it that way, yeah, I guess it's obvious. But sometimes obvious is overlooked when you've known someone as long as we have. You were always hanging out with the girls in high school. Sue me. And Tasha Mack swore up and down that you two were screwing senior year."

A reluctant smile crossed Felipe's face. Tasha Mack. Wow. He'd had a serious soft spot for Tasha back in school. "Actually, Tasha is now Terrence. He's a dancer in DC and dating an accountant of all things."

Abby shook her head as she stirred some creamer into her tea. "The revelations keep coming today. Just between me and you, did you get it on with Tasha, or did you wait for Terrence?"

Felipe smirked. "A gentleman doesn't tell."

"Ugh, you're impossible." Abby grimaced. "Whatever, you're gay and I should've known. I just figured you were a hell of a lot more comfortable with yourself than most guys our age were. So spill it. You've been chasing Trask, and I'm guessing caught means sex. So what? He dump you right after? Start acting like a royal jerk? Do I need to stomp his foot with my heel?"

Felipe was a little touched that she was jumping to his defense. "I don't know," he admitted with a sigh. "I can't remember ever being so worked up over a guy before. I guess it's because I don't know where I stand with him. He's not demonstrative. He's definitely not into PDAs. But get him in private and he lets loose, oh wow." Felipe paused to appreciate that memory until Abby tapped his knuckles with her spoon and gave him a get on with it look.

"I wanted him to come over for Thanksgiving because he doesn't have family nearby." Felipe paused as he looked back at his reasoning. "And I wanted him to meet my family, 'cause damn, I really like him, Abby. Maybe that's too big of a step and I freaked him out."

He hadn't thought of it that way. He'd just gotten Trask to start dating. Just got him naked in bed and suddenly he wanted to spring his family on him. And it wasn't like Felipe had a small extended family. His family sprawled. And they were all up in everyone's business. He never thought of it because he was used to them, and guests were in and out of his house all the time and they didn't seem to be bothered. He just couldn't see Trask being intimidated by a loud family, no matter how reticent he was.

Abby frowned. "Your thoughts are rambling again. What happened? You asked him to Thanksgiving and what? He broke it off?"

"Well, he seemed to be giving it some fairly serious consideration. At least that's how it looked to me. Then apparently him and my dad got into it, though he denies it was a 'confrontation.' And suddenly he's made other plans."

Abby shot him a glare of exasperation. "Why didn't you lead with that? That tidbit changes everything. So Trask and your dad had words, and I'm guessing you weren't around if you don't know exactly what went down. Did either of them mention it to you?"

"Neither of them told me a damn thing," Felipe said bitterly and took a sip of his latte. "I had to find out from my little sister. So I snarked at Dad first. He thinks he's protecting me. Bitch, please, I can protect myself. I'm just asking he give the man a chance, get to know him before he passes judgment. And yeah, I know Lolo is going to throw a fit. But I could be dating the President of the United States and the old man would still throw a fit because he cannot grasp the concept of his grandson being gay. So I'm not giving him any consideration."

"I have to admit, neither side telling me would piss me off too." Abby stared down at her tea. "Okay first, I have to get this out of the way. I hate you, Felipe. I mean that in the nicest way possible. Trask is the sexiest guy at all of the cons, hands-down. I had no clue he was gay either, so apparently I have zero radar, and you managed to snag him. As far as I know, he's never been snagged by any con-goer."

Felipe had to smile at the little boost to his ego. And she wasn't making any comments about Trask's age. Felipe was done with that too. If people didn't like age gaps, then they didn't have to get involved in that kind of a relationship. He did. He always had once he discovered he clicked better with men older than him.

"Okay, before we get off track." Abby met Felipe's gaze. "So Trask and your dad had words. Your dad thinks he's protecting you. What did Trask have to say about it?"

"He said that my dad made his point and that Trask made his in return about me being capable of my own decisions." Which was cool, though the fact that it was a secret still irked him. "He admitted to getting a little mad and defensive, but he seemed to think it wasn't much of a big deal. And he seemed genuinely confused as to why I was upset about him not saying anything. Who wouldn't want to know?"

"Like I said, I would've been irked too if I'd been the subject of an argument and neither my dad nor my boyfriend mentioned it. I'm speaking from experience." Abby took the other half of the broken cookie. "So what happened next?"

"He called me a drama queen, so I left." In pissy, huffy glory, which had felt good at the time, not so much now. There was too much unsaid, and now it was festering. With any other boyfriend, Felipe could have his fit and then return once he'd calmed. But the distance would always be a stumbling block to that response. He'd really have to rein that in if they wanted to go further.

The corners of Abby's mouth twitched, but she couldn't stop the dimples from making an appearance as Felipe gave her a sour look. "Felipe, you are a drama queen."

Damn her for having a point. It was something that Felipe usually embraced, but not right now. "I wasn't being one then."

Abby's brow lifted, and she took a sip of her tea as she waited him out. Felipe replayed the argument in his head. Only he supposed it wasn't much of an argument, because Trask had gone about it in his usual mild way when Felipe had been feeling anything but mild, and maybe that had irked him too.

"Okay, maybe I was a smidge of a drama queen, but I had reasons. One, there was something off about Trask from the moment he found out I was subletting the upstairs apartment from my parents. He denied it, but I know it was there. I'd seen it before. Two, there was the whole confrontation with my dad that he neglected to tell me. Three, he's having Thanksgiving with some other dude who he'd never mentioned before, and he had the audacity to call me dramatic when I called him out on it."

But now that he'd replayed the conversation in his head he realized that he hadn't heard what Trask was trying to tell him. He'd only focused on parts of it. He banked on the hopes of having a good argument and wild makeup sex on the gaming table, and Trask hadn't bitten.

It was impossible to argue with someone so fucking reasonable. And Trask hadn't exactly broken their plans like Dakota used to break their plans. Felipe had invited him to Thanksgiving dinner. All Trask had said was that he'd think about it and get back to him. Just because his answer wasn't one that Felipe wanted to hear didn't mean he was guilty of pulling the same shit.

And Felipe owed him an apology. Fuck. He sucked at apologies.

He glanced at Abby, who was watching him in amusement. She irritated the hell out of him too. She knew exactly what was going on in his head. "Okay, I get your damn point. You don't have to say it. I'll talk to him."

"Well then, my job is done. And when you talk to him, find out about this other dude so I'll know if I have to stomp him or not."

Felipe shook his head. "No… you don't have to stomp him. If I'm going to be fair, I might as well be all the way fair. Trask did mention that this other guy had nowhere to go." And he'd acted like a spoiled-rotten teenager, immediately latching on to only the fact that Trask was celebrating the holiday with another man. Now that he wasn't being such a bitch, he bet it was someone from his NA group and not a potential rival.

Abby, bless her, did not comment on that bit of asshattery. Instead, she gave him a smile and a shrug. "At least you're seeing Trask and not that other dude from the Magick Den. The dude that hates cosplayers. I'd have to call you a sellout."

"Oh, fuck no, that pain in the ass who'd love to see me out of there? Ryan?" Felipe shook his head. "No, Trask Briscoe, Mr. Tin Man Silver Fucking Fox." Felipe sighed and then grabbed her hands. "I think you're my new BFF, for real. When I told Morris I was planning on seducing Trask, he called him an old geezer."

"Morris's taste is suspect." Abby sniffed in dismissal. "I heard he was engaged to a short line cook."

Felipe snickered. He couldn't wait to repeat that rumor to them. Theo would laugh and Morris would bristle for him. "He's not really that short. He's my height, but anyone next to Morris is a shrimp. And as much as I love the gossip about him being a line cook, if I don't correct that, Morris might kill me. Theo owns his own restaurant and is the chef. You probably heard of it, the Chesapeake Bistro down in Solomon's Island."

Abby's eyes brightened. "Oh yeah, we ate there all the time as a kid. Family place, right? I used to hang out with one of the daughters, Robin, whenever Dad had business dinners there that went on forever." Then she held up her hands and shook her head. "Okay, we're off topic again. Let's get back to the client."

Now that was an annoying entitled twerp, but he was a client. "If we must."

Abby sat back and opened up the client's message on her phone. "Want to hear my idea?"

"Yes, Oh Devious One." Felipe pressed his palms together and gave her a little bow.

"We give the costume to him at the price he wants and negotiate on the timing. Hold up, hear me out." Abby lifted her palm as Felipe drew himself up, ready to deliver an indignant retort. "However, in return, we get free advertising on his website for the next convention and a free table in a decent location."

Felipe calculated the cost of the table and the contacts they were likely to make at that show. The guy would still be getting a bargain in his opinion, but in the long run, it should work out in their favor. "Sometimes I like the way your mind works. But he can't be a dick about how long it's going to take us to make this for him, and he can't go spreading how cheaply he got it. I'm not trading our talent and hard work all the time."

"Just on special occasions?" Abby asked with a laugh.

"Exactly so." Felipe picked up his latte, stood up, and kissed the top of her head. "On that note, I'm driving to Richmond. I have makeup sex lined up. You'd better get to work putting the finishing touches on your costume for the final show for the year or I'll whip your skinny little ass during the contest." He was recycling his Link costume. He missed that one, and he'd never run with it at this con, so he might have a chance at the prize.

"At least I took out that bastard at Tiffany's show." Abby smirked, her eyes glinting. "Winning a contest never felt so good. He's not still harassing you, is he?"

"Nah, he's moved on to the next person who's irritated him. I suspect if he shows up at the same con I'm at, he will attempt to renew hostilities. But I'm not playing anymore." Felipe shook his head and shrugged into his coat. "Life's too awesome to be worried about it. A guy like that is going to be perpetually upset at someone, and he'll never understand the part he's played in his own drama."

Felipe paused as he grabbed his bag. "Hey, if I ever get like that, shoot me."

Abby laughed long and loud, her eyes sparkling with sudden mischief. "It would be my pleasure."

"Duchess, sometimes you're scary." Felipe pointed to his eyes and then at her to indicate he was watching her.

"You'd better believe it."

Chapter Twenty-Two

TRASK LEFT the Chinese takeout on the top of his truck and released Sophie from her harness. She let out a bark of delight, her whole body wiggling. "I think you like this place even more than the loft."

They certainly spent enough time at the Den, where Sophie had her own bed, her other box of toys, her admirers, and the little fenced-in yard she could hang out in when she wanted to be outdoors. She didn't even have to wait for Trask to get up like she did at the loft. When Trask built the space years ago for Spaz, he'd added a doggie door, and Sophie adopted the practice with joyful abandon.

"Sit," Trask ordered, pulling out her leash and a small treat.

The puppy immediately sat down, head cocked as she waited with semipatience for the treat in Trask's hand. He had to give it to her. She caught on quick. She wasn't the biggest fan of the leash, but this was Richmond, not Felipe's backyard, and Trask wasn't going to take a chance on her getting hit. "That's my good girl," Trask cooed, giving her the treat as he leaned down and received a wet swipe of her tongue across his cheek.

"We'll go to the store tomorrow and get you a new collar and harness since you're growing so fast, and a new leash since you've half chewed this one to pieces, again. Then we'll go to the park and chase the ball until one of us collapses first. I suspect it'll be me."

She barked her agreement, her tail waving madly as she leaped to the ground.

"Come on, Sophie. Let's go relieve Ryan so he can get home. Then it's going to be just us tonight." Trask retrieved his dinner and headed for the Den. It should be a fairly quiet night. The kids playing Pokémon and Magic would be leaving soon. A couple of the war games crews had booked one of the tables until nine, but they'd be engrossed in their own world and unlikely to lift their heads until it was time to go.

He tried to figure out the odds of getting Felipe to engage in a conversation with him and decided they weren't good. Man, when Felipe got mad, he took it seriously. And Trask had zero ideas of how to fix the situation, but he was beginning to think that forty-eight hours of disquiet was enough. It was either time to say it had been fun and walk away or make the drive up to Maryland to see if he could get Felipe to smile again. And there was no question about what his choice was. He missed the imp. If Felipe still wanted to sulk, well then he'd reevaluate their options.

Ryan lifted his head from the magazine as Trask and Sophie entered. There was a sour look on his face that Trask recognized. He only got that expression when one person came around. Trask's heart skipped a beat. Wow, he didn't really think that was a thing. He'd always thought that was some nonsense that romance writers made up. But that was a definite skipping.

Trask shook his head and pushed his thoughts into a more practical bent. No, he was reading too much into it. Felipe would not come all the way to Richmond without texting first to see if Trask was available. It was too long of a drive on a maybe. People didn't do that, even if Felipe did not fit into any usual category.

"What's put that look on your face?" Trask asked. He set the food on the counter and bent down to release a dancing Sophie, who was so excited he had a difficult time unhooking her. As soon as she was free, she raced to the back with joyful barks. Trask winced and told himself she'd settle down soon and then he wouldn't have to worry about her taking off like that. "Kids screwing around in the back?"

"Sophie!" A very familiar voice from the back room tugged at Trask's heart. He shot Ryan a sharp look.

"When did Felipe get here?" Trask hadn't expected he'd return without cajoling after Felipe stormed out. But now that the moment was here, Trask had mixed feelings about it. Felipe had put him in a state of agitation, and Trask didn't much like that situation. The man had him turned around, that was for sure. Oh, screw it. He'd been this close to driving up to see him. He wasn't going to take that back because his feelings might have been a tad bruised.

"About fifteen minutes after you left." Ryan folded his magazine and tucked it into his messenger bag.

"And you didn't text me?" Trask asked in exasperation. That had been two hours ago.

"I didn't realize you wanted an alert every time a customer walked in here," Ryan responded in a cool tone as he grabbed his coat and slipped it on. "He's been keeping himself occupied and out of trouble, so I thought it best not to bother you."

Ryan had been hoping Felipe would get annoyed and leave again. He didn't understand Felipe's patience when he had his mind set on a goal. Which begged the question, was he here to talk or to end things? He'd thought Ryan's animosity toward Felipe had faded after the con, but it seemed like it had come roaring back. "Anything else I should know about?"

"Nope." Ryan shouldered his bag. "Just tell me one thing. You planning on letting that kid catch you again? I know who's put that brood in your eye, so don't deny it."

Trask smiled faintly at Ryan's phrasing. "Probably." Ryan made an exasperated sound and headed for the door. "Who says I want to escape?"

Ryan shook his head and left without another word, which made Trask feel a lot more comfortable. He didn't think he should be airing his laundry at the Den where everybody could overhear it. Ryan's attitude toward Felipe would probably swing a few more times, but overall he seemed to be softening. As he turned toward the register, he caught a glimpse of Felipe out of the corner of his eye.

Trask faced him with a wary look. He did not want a scene at his store, and he was never quite sure which way Felipe was going to jump. Felipe's expression was subdued, which was a look Trask didn't like on him because it just didn't suit. His heart panged as he held out his hand to him. "Come here, imp."

A relieved smile crossed Felipe's face and he bounded over, engulfing Trask in a hug. Trask held him close and shook his head as Felipe drew back. "No kissing, I'm at—" Felipe's lips were on his before Trask could finish the thought, and his hands fisted in Trask's hair.

"Some rules are made to be broken," Felipe said with a chuckle as he released Trask.

"You are a shameless rule breaker." Trask tapped the end of Felipe's nose, feeling much lighter than he had a moment ago.

"I behaved. I didn't kiss you the way I wanted to kiss you." Felipe shot him a flirtatious glance before his expression turned more serious. "Can I stay tonight? I wanted to talk to you, and I need to say I'm sorry."

Trask had half expected Felipe to want to hash it out right away and was grateful he had been wrong. He definitely hadn't expected an immediate apology. "Tonight works for me." He tapped the bag on the counter. "Hungry? I have some bean curd in a brown sauce. Pretty good. Some steamed rice to go with it."

Felipe peered into the bag with a shake of his head. "You really are serious about this vegetarian stuff, aren't you? Do you ever cheat?"

"I don't fall apart if I accidentally eat something that someone made that has meat in it. And there have been times when I've been given tea and coffee with caffeine in it. That's a little more irksome, but I've dealt." Trask did not want to go back to caffeine headaches and insomnia. "The rest I'm very serious about. I go to NA meetings every week, and I won't use or drink. Those are the only inflexible rules."

"It's good to know you have priorities and it's not all one way or no way." Felipe set the bag aside. "I'll take a pass this time. I've already eaten. And since you're at work and a stickler for these things, I'll return to entertaining the masses in the back while you be productive."

Trask caught his hand before Felipe could disappear on him. "Thank you for coming." He brushed his lips over Felipe's cheek, and Felipe squeezed his hand in response. "To be honest, I was going to head up your way after we closed. This whole situation was making me antsy."

"I'm glad I wasn't the only one moping." As Felipe strolled toward the back he shot Trask a look that swept heat right through him in more ways than one. He looked forward to satisfying that gleam in Felipe's eyes even as his heart tugged again. Trask had been hooked and hooked hard by a pair of warm brown eyes and a mischievous smile that promised years of trouble.

He sat down behind the register and rubbed his chest. He'd been in lust before. He'd been in relationships both quiet and compatible, and others that were combustive and dangerous, but not one of them had sunk into him like Felipe had. It was a little scary.

Trask made himself a plate and realized he couldn't walk away from what was growing between him and Felipe. He was a selfish bastard, but Felipe made him feel good in a guilt-free way. Trask enjoyed his time with him. Felipe's observations about life and others entertained the hell out of him, and behind that sharp tongue was a sensitive man who he wanted to get to know more. Not that he expected it to last longer than a season, but it would be fun while it did.

It was funny how the threat of having it disappear made Trask realize that he didn't want to keep Felipe at arm's length anymore. Once Felipe knew the whole story, well, at least he'd be prepared for Trask's past and how it influenced everything he strived for now.

The back room cleared out thirty minutes before the Den closed, and Trask locked the register and went back to see how much of a mess they left it in. Felipe was gathering the few abandoned cans and the empty wrappers of deck expansions that some of the kids had bought after the final round of play. "You didn't have to do that, but thank you," Trask said, and Sophie lifted her head at the sound of his voice.

"I know how you like everything here to be neat." Felipe tossed the trash into the basket and tied the ends of the bag together. "I know you're not closed yet, but I can't sit on this any longer. So here we go." He straightened as if he was getting ready to face a firing squad.

"You don't have anything to apologize for." Trask tucked a stray chair back in its place and searched for something to keep his hands busy. He was better at conversations when he was doing something.

"No, I do." There was a rueful tone in Felipe's voice. "And for the record, I hate apologizing, but I'm not above doing it when I make an ass out of myself. I didn't listen to you. I didn't even try. I had it in my head what the situation was and stewed on it for too long. So when we finally got to talking, anything that didn't fit my version of events didn't get heard. I wanted a good fight and you weren't giving it to me. It just pissed me off even more."

Mystified, Trask stared at Felipe. "You wanted to fight? Why would you want to fight?"

"Because!" Felipe threw his hands up. "Yelling lets off steam and gives me an excuse to claw you during makeup sex. It's just… I like a good argument followed by spectacular makeup sex." His arms dropped to his sides, and he looked defeated. "Which I suppose is just the kind of drama you don't want in your life. Getting upset means you care, and you didn't get upset."

Trask set down the miniatures he was organizing and caught the front of Felipe's shirt. "Come here," he said gruffly, sliding his arms around Felipe. "If you'd dragged the group into it and got them all worked up, if you'd ruined the game, that's the kind of drama I don't want. A little arm-waving and raised voices aren't going to scare me off."

"No?" Felipe asked in a hopeful voice, his mouth muffled against Trask's chest.

"No." Trask kissed the top of his head. "I'm not going to get mad and yell. I'm just not. But it doesn't mean I don't give a damn. And it doesn't mean I'd turn down a little clawing makeup sex either."

Felipe snickered, nipped Trask's collarbone, and held him closer. "Good to know."

"I need to apologize too. I should've told you that I met your dad and he wasn't too pleased with the thought of me and you together. The situation concerned you too." He felt Felipe stiffen against him, and when Felipe lifted his head, that spark of anger was back.

"You never told me what else you said to him. And I know I didn't let you, but I'd like to hear it now."

"There really wasn't much to it." Trask shrugged and let go of him. "Not much more than what I already said. I admitted to doing time, though I didn't say what for." He glanced at Felipe to gauge whether that would set off another storm of emotion. "And I told him you needed your breakfast and I was going to see to doing that."

"Is that it?" Felipe asked with a disbelieving glance.

"Mostly." Trask tugged on his ear, replaying the conversation. "I might've told him to have a nice day, but not in a douchey kind of way. At least I hope not."

Felipe leaned back against the table and shook his head. "So I pretty much jumped to every wrong conclusion. I was sure there was something about me living upstairs that got under your skin. You had this look in your eye that I misjudged, but it pretty much set my back up, so I was misinterpreting every damn text you sent me. Then when you pulled out of Thanksgiving, I took it as a sign I was right, and you even tried to tell me about your friend and I still didn't listen because sometimes when I get my head fixated on one thing, it stays fixated until someone smacks some sense into me. And to be honest, I think I have an automatic hate for people canceling plans, even plans that aren't really set, and I'm sorry. That's my past drama coming up to affect you and that's not fair."

Well dammit, if Felipe could be that honest about his shortcomings, then Trask could admit his own hang-ups. "There was something about you living upstairs that got to me and talking with your dad, just not what you think. But I don't care that you rent from your parents. I really don't."

"I knew it!" Felipe straightened and crossed his arms. "I wasn't imagining things. So what the hell is it, then?"

Trask winced and looked away. He felt like an asshole for even letting it take ahold of him. "This is hard for me to admit, but I was jealous, that kind of scratch-your-eyes-out envious angst that I didn't think I was capable of anymore."

Felipe stared at Trask in bafflement. "Why? Of what?"

"You have a family. I don't. And even when I did, they didn't give a damn about me and I sure as fuck didn't give a damn about them. The thought of my family living under one roof, even if I could come and go like you without having to encounter them… that would've been ugly more often than not." Trask had been so damned tired of the ugly. Getting out of there had been his only priority, and nothing could've induced him to stay.

"I see you, I see people like you with families that support you, dads willing to come out and say hey, I'm not sure if you're right for my son, and it's this crazy combination of damn… what's that like? I want that. And terror that I wouldn't even know how to live that kind of life if I had it." Trask shook his head with a sigh, unable to look and see the pity in Felipe's eyes.

"I am very stingy about who I let in close." He looked down at his tattooed knuckles. "I can count them right here." He lifted one hand. "I don't know if I can do more. But I'm willing to try."

"Whoa, okay." Felipe sat down in a chair. "That's a lot to churn through your mind."

Trask looked up at that. There wasn't any pity in Felipe's gaze, just a whole shitload of confusion. Not that Trask could blame him. How could he comprehend what it was like to have no one, though Trask would far rather be alone than be stuck with the family he was born in. How could he understand the ugly?

"I think that's what my problem was. It went from, I don't know… we were testing the waters with each other. It was more than a casual thing, but not quite a relationship." Trask crossed his arms and leaned back against the wall. "And I realized that, damn, I did want something more with you. A whole hell of lot more, but you came with extras that I hadn't prepared for."

"So you had the confrontation with my dad, and instead of feeling like it was time to walk away, you decided you weren't going to play hard to get anymore?" Felipe muttered to himself something Trask couldn't quite hear in another language, and it didn't sound complimentary. "So why opt out of Thanksgiving if that's the case?"

"I wanted your family to get a chance to get to know me, to get used to the idea of me and you before we celebrate a family holiday together. To be honest, the idea of trying to stomach a meal with a lot of animosity…." Trask shook his head. "I had enough of that bullshit growing up. I'm not going to start that with your folks just to prove a point."

Felipe pressed his lips together, processing all that. Trask watched the emotions cross his face as if Felipe were trying to decide to be forgiving or aggravated. "So just tell me this. Do you really have someone to spend Thanksgiving with, or was that a lie to make me feel better?"

"Damn it all, Felipe." Now Trask was insulted. "I wouldn't lie to you."

Felipe just softened. There was no other way to describe it. The tension fled from his body, his eyes sparkled, and that heavy bottom lip curved in a sexy smile. Trask's heart thrummed as Felipe slid his arms around Trask's neck. "Well then, how about that makeup sex? Right here on this table?"

Trask stepped out of the reach of temptation. "You are more than an imp. You're a whole camp of them. We're still open and this is still my workplace."

Felipe wrinkled his nose at him. "You know you've been thinking of fucking me on this table ever since we made out right here." He patted the smooth finish and shot Trask a wicked smile. "Now you're going to be thinking about it a little more. I can be patient. It'll make it all the sweeter when you finally cave."

Trask shook his head as Felipe grabbed the bag of trash and sauntered out. He had no doubt Felipe was right and they would end up naked back here at some point. He was in over his head. But he had to admit, since he said yes to Felipe, he'd had more fun than he'd had in a long time.

When they got back to his place, he had every intention of giving Felipe all the back-clawing makeup sex he wanted, and he'd consider the scratches as badges well earned. He shook his head again with a disbelieving chuckle. His imp had him right where he wanted him.

Chapter Twenty-Three

DAKOTA EYEBALLED Brenden as he ran through his spiel, laying out his ideas for the new and improved Chessie Con to a potential vendor. Once Brenden made the commitment, all the parts started to fall into place. Dakota would be very surprised if they hadn't. Brenden never committed without thorough research and methodical planning. Whereas Dakota just jumped in balls to the wall and got shit done. Together they made a hell of a team. Whether they were trying to kill each other or not.

Felipe had it all wrong about them. Yeah, they argued all the time. They definitely got in each other's faces and annoyed each other to distraction. But it was fun. It was one of the many ways they showed their affection for each other. Dakota relished his spats with Brenden, and he knew Brenden did too. Getting along all the time would be dead boring.

"I think we hooked him," Brenden said with a self-satisfied note as the man walked away with a flyer and application.

"The spots are filling up fast." And they would need to make a hefty payment on the convention hall at the start of the year and squirrel money away for the ad campaign that Dakota designed. Which brought Dakota right back to his current scheme and how the hell he was going to get Brenden to agree with it.

The best way to get Brenden to go along with Dakota's plans was to surprise him. And the best way to surprise him was to wait until he was neck-deep in his thoughts and lists. Then Dakota could lay out his idea and hammer Brenden with all his arguments.

It always came down to strategy and surprise with Brenden, because if he gave the man the time and wits to argue back, he won. He was just smarter than Dakota, even if Brenden hated hearing that. He didn't like it when he thought Dakota was talking down about himself. But some things were just the truth. Brenden was smarter, but Dakota had all the charm. He'd take that.

With that in mind, Dakota rode out the con, holding his peace next to Brenden, until the show started shutting down. At least it wasn't one of theirs. All they had to do was pack up the materials on their promo table and roll out. Brenden would be distracted, but not too distracted.

"So, I've been thinking. Being responsible and all that, making a budget." Just as he figured, Brenden's gaze zeroed in on him at the words responsible and budget. "I'm going to move back in with you." Best not to ask and just lay it out there. If he asked, he'd probably get a hell no. Dakota gave Brenden a sunny smile at that comment and then leaned under their table to grab their packing gear.

"What do you mean you're moving back in?"

Dakota stifled a snicker at the panic in Brenden's tone. Brenden tried to hide it with his usual cool stare, but Dakota had known him since he was fifteen years old. There was a telling sharp note to his voice, and his eyes had widened before he caught himself. For Brenden that was almost the equivalent of a girlish scream at the sight of a rat.

"Come on, I'm not that much of a slob. You won't even know I'm there." A complete bald-faced lie, and they both knew it. Dakota's grasp of putting things away was practically nonexistent, but in a way that worked since Brenden had a compulsive need to tidy. In fact, Dakota was doing him a favor by giving him an outlet for his ways.

"Bullshit." Brenden put one hand on his hip and shook his clipboard at Dakota with the other. There was something about the prissy line of his mouth that always made Dakota want to kiss him.

Brenden had shut down that idea years ago, spouting off nonsense about upsetting the family, yadda, yadda, yadda. Whatever, it wasn't like they really shared genes. And it wasn't like their family even needed to know. It was just a little kiss and snuggle between friends. One of these days he was going to lay one on him just to watch Brenden sputter and flail. It would be epic. Dakota loved to make Brenden sputter and flail.

Brenden's eyes narrowed dangerously and his nostrils flared. "Did you hear a damn word I just said?"

"You know, you're awfully sexy when you glare like that," Dakota said, neatly sidestepping the fact that he had tuned Brenden out the moment he started lecturing him about his habit of leaving clean laundry on the couch. It was clean. What was the big deal?

"I'm fucking serious, Dakota." Brenden's cheeks flushed as Dakota mimicked his words back at him. Damn, he could be so much fun to tease. Dakota adored the anal-retentive jackass. "Dakota!" Brenden planted his hands on his hips. "Please tell me what's wrong with your place? I thought you loved living in Baltimore."

Dakota did love Baltimore. The town was always hopping. He had season tickets for the Os and could jaunt on over whenever he wanted. Little Italy was amazeballs. And Geppi's was his home away from home. The comics museum was situated right at Camden Yards, so Dakota could indulge both of his loves in one go. It had been his dream to get Brenden up there in Baltimore with him, but Brenden did not seem inclined to dislodge his delectable ass from his little house in Bowie, so apparently Dakota had to return to him.

Bowie. God save him. Nothing fucking happened in Bowie, Maryland. If he didn't love Brenden so much and share his dream for this big con, he'd never settle down there. And, truth be told, he missed Brenden. He missed living with him, putting up with him, and just having him around, even when it was damned inconvenient when Dakota's imagination ran off with all the things he'd like to do with Brenden if given the chance.

"Loving B'more is not the point. One day you will understand its charms. Look, it's like this. We need the capital for that big Annapolis Chessie Con. The bills are piling in the closer we get to it. If we live together, we cut our expenses in half." Besides, living by himself was starting to get a little boring and lonely. It had been nice at first, no one to complain about him walking around naked, bitching about his dishes and desire to switch off tacos and pasta every other night.

"I've already told you, I'm not taking your money," Brenden said flatly.

Dakota drew himself up and drilled his finger into Brenden's chest. "The fuck you are." Prideful bastard. "You've stretched yourself as far as you can go. And you're going to take Uncle Trev and Aunt Evelyn's money when they offer it. Because we're fucking family, Brenden. Our foster parents believe in us. They believe in this dream of ours, and they know you well enough to trust that you'll pay back every damned dime whether it succeeds or not. So stuff your attitude before I stuff it for you. We're partners, right?"

Brenden threw up his hands with a huff. "Fine, do what you will. You always do. Go ahead and move in if you really think it's necessary."

"Thank you." It was a good thing Brenden knew when to back down.

"But this is between me and you, got it?" Brenden gestured toward the Chessie Con paraphernalia. "This is our dream. Trev and Evelyn have done enough for us. We're not taking anything from them. Okay? Especially with all of Aden's school bills."

Dakota crossed his arms and met Brenden glare for glare. "You know what, I'm going to leave that one alone. If you want to fight them on it, then you can. I'm going to stay out of it. And good luck, 'cause you're going to get your ass handed back to you with a big ole bite taken out of it."

"I'll take my chances." Brenden set aside his clipboard and began taking down their banner. "I still think moving in together is a bad idea, disastrous if I'm being honest. Don't you think we're both happier in our own corners?"

Dakota had expected a little pushback, but not this. Brenden was practical to a fault. This was a logical step. Why the fuck was he resisting? He should be happy. Yeah, they clashed, but that was normal, and it was never an ugly clash. Dakota had missed Brenden, and he was a little irked that Brenden didn't seem to be missing him at all. Especially when Dakota was thinking of the long, lonely drive ahead and wondering if he could get Brenden out for dinner one-on-one instead of their usual group.

"Seriously, Bren, what the fuck is your problem?" Dakota gave his shoulder a shove. "Do I really make you that miserable?"

Brenden glanced over at Dakota's hurt tone, and his expression softened. "No, you don't. I'm sorry. It's just, you know how I get. How I like everything a certain way, and I hate changes. I'd just gotten used to being alone it seems like. It's not you. It's all me and my issues."

Well, Brenden was particular, that wasn't a lie. But he wouldn't quite meet Dakota's eyes, as if the task at hand required his vital attention. It was a little unsettling. Dakota should know where he stood with Brenden after everything they shared. Sometimes it seemed like Brenden was holding back from him, keeping a distance, and Dakota just didn't get it.

"I'm glad that's settled because I already put in my notice to my landlord." Dakota grinned at Brenden's long-suffering sigh, but his foster brother didn't comment on Dakota's tendency to act a little too soon sometimes.

"You can have your old room back." Brenden glanced at his watch and then shook his finger one more time at Dakota. "And I don't want naked lovers in the living room unless they are my naked lovers."

Dakota started to tease him about bringing over someone, but then the idea of Brenden having a lover hit him. He'd always been very circumspect about who he was seeing, to the point where Aunt Evelyn worried that all her boys would be bachelors forever. Brenden was just choosy. Which was a good thing because Dakota didn't want just anybody dating Brenden. It had to be somebody worthy of him who would appreciate his wit and loyalty, who would tease him when he got too serious, and who'd appreciate his intelligence and drive. Brenden scared off a good many who couldn't see beyond his sardonic tongue to the gentle man beneath. Idiots didn't know what they were missing out on.

Dakota always suspected that when Brenden finally fell for someone, it would be for life. He'd have to make sure they understood how damn lucky they were. And if they broke Brenden's heart... well, they'd never see Dakota's fist coming.

"You're not seeing someone, are you?" Dakota asked. Not that he really cared. It would be good for Brenden to get laid. Dakota had just been looking forward to the thought of them hanging out like they used to. He was selfish. He didn't want to share his time with Brenden. They may get on each other's nerves, but Brenden was his best friend in the end. The one man Dakota trusted to rein him in when he needed it.

"Off and on." Brenden folded their banner into its case and checked off an item on his clipboard with the air of a man contemplating the fate of the universe. "You?"

"Nobody steady, not since prima donna broke up with us." Dakota looked over his shoulder, searching for Felipe. He'd had a fondness for Felipe that he couldn't deny. Felipe had a charm all his own, and watching him bicker with Brenden had always been amusing because they could be so much alike at times. It was cool to see Felipe so happy with Trask. He deserved it. "Did you hear about the fiasco at Tiffany's con?"

"Oh yeah." Brenden's mouth thinned. "It never should've escalated to that point."

"Don't blame Felipe on that one." Dakota neatly stacked their business cards and postcards, then put them in their own boxes. "He shouldn't have had to take matters in hand. He wouldn't have had to if we'd been in charge."

Brenden's frown deepened, and Dakota could practically hear the argument in his head. Siding with Felipe just went against his nature. "True," Brenden admitted reluctantly. "As much as the idea of the prank he pulled annoys me, the fact that there were so many pissed-off vendors for one man's antics annoys me more."

Dakota would never get a better opening than that. "Speaking of that. I think we should make sure that guy doesn't make trouble at one of our cons. I'm thinking that he should be banned from the cosplay contests, if not the shows themselves." That would be ideal.

It had been Felipe's idea to blackball him, and Dakota agreed with him all the way. But he had to present it as his idea. Brenden had a huge blind spot where Felipe was concerned, even if he'd been easing up on that attitude.

Brenden paused and set down his clipboard. "Give me an argument for it. On the one hand, I agree with you. This isn't the first time he's disrupted a con, and quite frankly, I don't want to deal with Felipe's reprisal if he does try it. But so far he hasn't pulled this shit at any of our shows. We'd be starting the bad blood this time if we made the first move."

That was Brenden's sense of fair getting in the way of things again. Screw fair. The jerkwad didn't deserve it.

Dakota pondered an argument that would sway Brenden that would not involve invoking his ex's name. "You know it's just a matter of time. A guy like that only gets worse. He doesn't learn his lessons. So we've been lucky so far that we haven't had to put a boot up his ass, but it will happen. And I don't want it pulled at the Annapolis Con when we might be too damned busy to deal with it directly."

Brenden didn't look entirely convinced, though he was considering Dakota's words. "I definitely would agree to not giving him a free pass if he requests one."

Dakota glared at him. That was not nearly enough to deter the jackass. "Are you going soft on me, Bren? That's all based on an if. Not only that, if we're going to give out free passes, they should go to Felipe and Abby first. Wait—" Dakota retorted and pointed a finger at Brenden when he started to object. "They obey the rules… mostly. We've never had a complaint about them from vendors except for that guy from the

Den, and he complains about every cosplayer. And they do panels for us. Well-attended panels that people enjoy."

"You do have a point." Brenden folded the tablecloth into a neat little square. Dakota didn't know how he managed that trick. Every time he tried it, it ended up in a messy pile. "My concern is, if we make the first move and ban him, he'll consider it an act of war and he'll immediately hop online with all his jerk buddies, and that's not the kind of publicity I want at this stage. I have no problem cutting him out when he does act out, and I'll make sure security knows who he is. That way, he's always the bad guy and we're not giving him any excuse for sympathy."

Brenden did have a way of troubleshooting all scenarios, and it made sense, even if it irritated Dakota. He was of the "fuck 'em" mind-set, and if the guy tried to start anything, he could do it to Dakota's face. "You know what, let the bastard come to our shows, but I say give Abby and Felipe free passes for life. That'll get back to him and make him squeal like a crab going into the pot. Serves the little prick right."

A faint smile crossed Brenden's lips before he quickly suppressed it. "You're going to make me interact with Suero for life. That's just wrong."

"Admit it, you surly bastard, you like Felipe." Dakota shook his head as Brenden tried to level him with a warning look. Dakota was immune to Brenden's 101 death stares.

"I will not," Brenden insisted, and then he softened with a shrug. "But dammit, I agree with you on one point. Felipe deserves the chance. He's really come through for us. And he and Abby make a crazy team. However, I do not want them dominating every contest."

"Trask will keep Felipe in line. They seem permanently attached now." Felipe was way too young to shack up for life. Hell, for Dakota ninety would be too young. "Felipe deserves to be happy. And I like Trask. Oddly enough, they really balance each other."

"Just like you and I, the odd couple." Brenden searched his pants pockets and pulled out his keys. "When do you think you'll start hauling your stuff over to the house?"

"I'll probably start next weekend, do it in bits, then get the bulk over by March when my lease goes out." Damn, he was really going to miss his apartment, but being front and center to harassing Brenden twenty-four seven would totally make up for it. "This is going to be awesome, you and me against the world again."

Brenden looked away, the set of his shoulders stiff as if he was about to face an execution. Dakota shook his head with a shrug. His anal-retentive friend would chill out once they were together. Dakota just needed to give him time to get used to the idea and not take it personally that Brenden wasn't as excited about the move as he was.

"Hey, it'll be okay, I promise." Dakota gave him a nudge with his elbow and crouched to lash down their boxes.

Brenden gave him a faint smile, his eyes warming with a light that few got to see. "It'll be a disaster, but there's no one I'd rather be a disaster with."

Chapter Twenty-Four

"WHAT PROJECT are you working on now, Felipe?" Lola asked, patting the couch beside her. "I haven't seen you in weeks you've been so busy."

With a twinge of guilt, Felipe flopped down, determined to stop moping. He had been busy, between a new project for school, his new enterprise with Abby, and a delicious distraction in Richmond. His lingering irritation with his dad had him staying away too. None of which was fair to his lola.

"You remember Abby Albion?" Felipe asked, taking her hand. He loved his lola's hands. He'd spent a lot of time looking at her hands as she taught him how to sew, how to cook, and a hundred other lessons she imparted to him. His mother had the same hands, hands that had soothed every childhood illness he'd had and a complete inability with crafting. He'd always found that funny. The talent had definitely skipped a generation.

"Oh yes, Abby. The girl who stole your crayon." Lola's husky voice enveloped Felipe in a thousand comforting memories.

Felipe cracked a smile at her oh-so-serious tone that meant she was gently teasing him. All around them their family buzzed, talking over each other in cheerful chaos, the way they did at every family holiday. The little ones ran all over the living room, tumbling over each other and squabbling. The teenagers sat in their little spheres of isolation, their faces over their phones, except Mariana, who flitted from one group to another, like she hadn't seen anyone in decades when they'd all gotten together just on Labor Day and they'd see each other again at Christmas and New Year's. Felipe's family was never far away.

"That would be the one," Felipe admitted.

"The same Abby who dated the gentleman you were pining for in tenth grade." Lola's memory was as sharp as ever. Felipe was embarrassed to remember that jerk. He was glad Abby had the sense to drop him as soon as he started making her life miserable. Lola was the only person in his life who knew about that guy. She'd been the first person he'd come out to, and she'd held on to his secret for years.

"True, but I nabbed the guy she wanted for prom." Not that Abby ever figured it out, considering her surprise at his orientation. He still didn't get how she didn't clue in on that one.

"You didn't go to prom." She narrowed her eyes at him as Felipe smirked.

"True, and she didn't go with him either." Prom night Felipe had been getting it on in the barn out back. They'd had a candlelight dinner, music, and a really sweet bed made up in the loft. That memory had carried him through the rest of high school. There were some things, though, he couldn't tell his lola. "But that's a different story. So you know she's been competing with me at shows, doing her own cosplay thing, and pretty much trying to drive me as crazy as I probably drive her."

"You had told me that. Sounds like she's doing good for herself, even if it ties you up in knots. We need people who will challenge us." She glanced fondly across the room at her husband. Frankly, Felipe never understood what she saw in the old man. He was cranky, set in his ways, and convinced he was always right. He never hesitated on giving his opinion, whether Felipe or anyone else wanted to hear it. He annoyed the hell out of Felipe.

"Well, we're kind of working together. We've picked up a demanding project that's going to take both of us to finish. And doing some shows and panels." It still made Felipe boggle. They were being civil to each other, and it was working. The sniping had been outrageous fun, but this was its own kind of fun.

Lola considered that a long moment, absently patting his hand. "I'd like to see what you come up with. Bring her by. I haven't seen Abby since your last day of elementary school."

Felipe groaned. Damn, Lola really did have an amazing memory. "Do you remember every single one of Mariana's misdeeds, or is it just me that gets the special treatment?" He and Abby had gotten into an epic food fight that last day, and since both of his parents had been working, it had been up to his lola to pick him up from the principal's office. Abby had been right by his side waiting for her dad, and they'd bonded over how much trouble they were going to be in.

Her dark eyes sparkled as she tweaked his earlobe. "Certainly, I do, but perhaps there is not as much to remember for her as there is for you. Mariana is quiet like me, like your mother. You, you are fiery like your lolo."

Felipe looked out at his family again and caught his dad's eye. Trask had made him look at the situation in a different light. Felipe had blown it out of proportion, and he really shouldn't have come downstairs cussing at Dad like he had. His dad would like Trask if he just gave himself a chance to get to know him. His dad was quiet and steady too. Felipe was the oddball of the family. His gaze slid to his lolo, who was teasing Felipe's mom with a sly smile. But he was not like that man in any way.

"I can agree with fiery," Felipe said grudgingly. "But I draw the line there."

He wished Trask had come. Mariana had asked about Trask's whereabouts more than once, much to his parents' discomfort. Felipe pulled out his phone and curled in closer to his grandmother. "Smile, Lola. I need to send a picture to a friend of mine." He snapped a photo and admired the image before sending it to Trask. *Thinking of you. Happy Thanksgiving.*

"The young man you were telling me about?"

"He's not that young, Lola." Felipe felt that he had to point that out. Not that Trask was as ancient as everyone else complained about either.

She laughed her warm, rich laugh. "At my age everyone is young."

His phone dinged, and Felipe pulled up the picture of Trask with Sophie, curled up on the floor of his apartment. *Miss you too, imp.* Felipe's heart panged. He really wished he was with the aloof twerp. He had so many emotions where Trask was concerned, deep emotions that he'd once longed for but now wasn't sure what do with. He wanted to talk about it with his grandmother, but he couldn't with the bedlam surrounding them.

Lola took the phone from Felipe and examined Trask's picture through her bifocals. "He considers you an imp?" She gave Felipe a fond glance. "I think that name just might serve."

Felipe loved the way Trask said imp. There was a warmth and affection in his tone when he did, as if he didn't wish Felipe to be any other way. "Yeah, I'm his imp, and he's my Tin Man."

"He has kind eyes." She handed the phone back to Felipe. "The eyes don't lie, Felipe."

"Yes, he does." And he had a kind, quiet way about him, a steadiness. Felipe liked that. Morris was similar, though Trask made Morris seem downright extroverted. "Dad doesn't like him."

"That's not precisely what I heard. You have an old soul, Felipe, but a young mouth that speaks too fast sometimes." She patted his hand again and looked at her husband. "Like others. You both butt heads because of your similarities, not your differences."

Before Felipe could respond to that bit of nonsense, she got up. "Come on. I've stolen enough of your time. Let's see what game Mariana has pulled out for us."

After-dinner family games at Thanksgiving and Christmas were a ritual that he didn't dare back out of, even if he'd rather trade pictures and chat with Trask over his phone. The spot next to his dad was open at the table and Felipe slid in next to him, feeling like he had in high school when he'd really opened his mouth too far and regretted it. Felipe stole a look at his dad, and guilt squirmed like a living thing. He'd been the one to etch those lines around his dad's mouth. It was a holiday. He shouldn't have let these bad words between him and his dad linger for so long.

Felipe nudged his dad's arm. "Can I get you a fresh cup of coffee?"

His dad turned his dark eyes on Felipe. Felipe looked more like him than his mom, but he had none of his dad's personality. His dad was grave and serious, worked hard and spoke little. His dad, hell, his mom and sister too, were blindingly smart. Not that Felipe was stupid, but he didn't have the same intellectual drive they did. On rare occasions it made him feel inadequate, like he wasn't living up to some nameless potential. Though, if he were fair to himself, both he and his dad preferred to work with their hands and being their own boss. Which was why his dad formed his own company and found his own success. Felipe wanted to do that, too, just with sewing and crafts, not construction.

"I think I'd like that," his dad said cautiously. "Do you want some help getting the coffee maker started?"

It was an opening, and now that Felipe had made the overture he had to follow through or he'd regret it later. He looked down at his hands and nodded, his throat tightening. Whether or not he'd deserved to be angry, Felipe hated it when he was at odds with anyone in his family. They were too tight-knit for that to be a comfortable situation.

The kitchen was quiet now that the remains of the meal had been packed away, and no one was ready to tackle dessert yet. Felipe filled the coffeepot with water as his dad spooned beans into the grinder. "I'm sorry, Dad," Felipe said in a low voice, casting a quick glance at his dad's stern visage. "I shouldn't have cussed you out like that. I should've waited until I'd calmed down and then talked to you."

A faint smile touched the corner of his dad's lips. "Let's be honest, Felipe; calm or not you would've cursed. There are other ways to get your point across without F-bombs." His dad turned to face Felipe and leaned back against the counter. "But mouth aside, I owe you an apology too. Sometimes I forget that you're an adult with adult responsibilities and making adult decisions. Your friend reminded me of that in no uncertain terms."

"I think you'd like him, Dad, if you gave him a chance." Felipe regarded his dad seriously. "He's a good guy. I know he has a past and he's been through some real shit, but if I've met anyone who's learned from their mistakes and grown from them, it's him. And he didn't stalk me like some old lecher either. Hell, it was probably the other way around."

Okay, it was definitely the other way around. Felipe did tend to zero in on a guy when he was interested. Trask had been no exception.

His dad sighed, a frown of concern still visible between his brows. "I believe you did the chasing, but he didn't have to let himself get caught." He held up a quelling hand as Felipe straightened. "I'm not as progressive in some areas as you'd like to believe. Relationships require compatibility, and a big age gap can hamper that."

Felipe did not see any problems in that area at all, but he did know better than to equate chemistry with compatibility, which was why they were taking things slow. And Trask was definitely not one to dive into anything without testing the waters three times or more. It would've been frustrating if Felipe hadn't been enjoying the slow build. Besides, it wasn't like Trask was ducking him. He was just one to make sure no one got hurt, and Felipe definitely wasn't interested in being hurt again.

"I'm just asking you to give him a chance. Talk to him in a nonjudgmental way. Let's face it, Lolo will be doing all the judging for everyone." Felipe cast a look at his grandfather. He would have to let him know before Trask came over for a family dinner and let the disapproval storm its way out. At least once it was over, Lolo usually moved on.

"I thought you had invited him over for Thanksgiving?" His dad filled his mug with fresh coffee as Felipe grabbed a cup for himself. "Did you back out of it because of our argument?"

"I don't back down." Felipe pulled out the creamer and shook the carton at his dad. "You know that. Trask had a friend who had no family to be with, so he's having a little celebration at his place."

His dad nodded thoughtfully as he took a sip of his coffee. "How long has he been clean?"

"Since I was still throwing a fit over not having two recesses in grade school." Felipe doctored up his brew, piling on the cream and sugar. "He's been on his own a long time. Owns a successful business that I suspect is more prosperous than he lets on. He mentors others. In all the years I've seen him at shows, he's never lost his temper, even when he had the provocation."

"Enough, Felipe, *entiendo*. You don't need to list all of his good qualities. I suspect you could entertain me for an hour and I would learn more than I wish to." His dad smiled as Felipe shot him a wicked grin. "Maybe sometime soon we can have dinner together, you two and me and your mom."

Felipe swallowed around the sudden lump in his throat. "Thanks, Dad. I really like this guy. He's really got me right here." He pressed a fist against his chest. "You should see him with Sophie. Those two, it was love at first sight." Felipe suspected he was playing second fiddle to a dog, but he completely understood unconditional pet love. "He's got so much in his heart that he doesn't let many see, but it's there if you look."

"What does Morris think of him?" his dad asked. He had a real soft spot for Morris, probably because he felt that Morris looked out for him, but it was a pretty mutual friendship. Felipe always had Morris's back too.

Felipe let out a huff. "He teases me and calls Trask an old geezer. But in all fairness, I give him a rough time about his choice in a fiancé. Morris has adopted his soon-to-be brother-in-law and is protective of him, and he has no qualms about bringing Lincoln to Trask's place for our games. If he didn't think Trask was a good match for me, he'd say something, not just tease." Like how Morris had tried to warn him about Dakota. Felipe might not listen, but Morris would try.

"That does ease my mind." His dad laid his hand on Felipe's shoulder. "It's not that I don't trust your judgment, but you're someone who throws their whole heart into an endeavor from the beginning, whether it's a new guy or the business you've been working to develop.

I would just like to see a little more caution from you. Because I hate seeing you get hurt."

Well, Felipe could hardly blame him for that attitude. He'd definitely given everyone who'd listen a bitching earful when he'd parted ways with Dakota. The man was still his friend, by some miracle, but Felipe was very grateful the relationship had ended. They'd been all wrong for each other despite their chemistry in bed. Sex wasn't everything. And he couldn't believe he'd actually had that thought.

"Come on." Felipe nudged his dad. "Mariana has pulled out Boggle. You know that means it's going to get cutthroat." He sucked at Boggle, but it was always entertaining to watch his family argue over whether a word was real or not, and to make it more challenging, house rules said not all of the words had to be in English. Mariana and he had to learn to be on their toes because everyone would try to sneak past a word in Spanish or Tagalog.

"Just as long as no one starts bleeding on the linen. Your mom will make us pay if she has to pause in her domination to give someone first aid."

Chapter Twenty-Five

TRASK STARED at the picture of Felipe and his grandmother. It was clear that they were close. He could see that in their body language. It made him miss his own grandmother. She'd looked like an angel and had a spine of steel that had never broken. She'd been loving when Trask needed it, and he'd drank in every bit of her attention. She'd also been stern when he needed it, and he had to admit he'd deserved equal doses of that with the love. He liked to think she looked down at him and was happy about where he finally ended up. She was the one person in his family who understood him, who gave him a sense of home and family. Trask blessed her memory often.

Felipe would've shocked her to her sensible Southern core. Trask smiled at that. Yeah, but once she recovered, she would've adored the imp as much as he did. He wished she could meet him.

Sophie came up to his chair, set her paws on his leg, and lifted up to nuzzle his arm. "I'm being maudlin, aren't I?" Trask crooned in a low voice. "And you can sense it, can't you, sweetie?"

Just like Spaz had. Trask looked over the remains of his single meal. Jason had never shown up. He didn't want to think that the man was in the middle of a bender or had come off one and was ashamed and didn't want Trask to see the signs. It was crazy how people could delude themselves so much while they were using. Trask remembered thinking he was so damn clever and no one would notice the mood changes, all the little clues. Then looking back later, he realized how much of an obvious idiot he had been. But there wasn't a damn thing he could do about Jason, and sitting here by himself on Thanksgiving night wasn't good for his state of mind right now either.

The idea of spending a holiday alone hadn't bothered him in years. He had plenty of books. A day off from the store and instead of relaxing, he was restless. It was time to get out of Richmond for a bit. There was a show in Pittsburgh at the beginning of December. One that he often attended as a ticket holder instead of a vendor and picked up some odd stock that no one else had, and at crazy bargains. There was nothing in the rules that said he had to go alone.

He picked up the phone. *Doing anything the first weekend in December?*

Trask began putting away the food and cleaning up. He could bring the Cornish game hens to Joe tomorrow. The old man would appreciate it. He'd pack up some of the sides, too, or he'd be eating them for days. The apple pie, though, he'd save. He did have a weakness for hot apple pie and cold ice cream. As he moved around the kitchen Sophie approached him with a squeaky toy in her mouth and dropped it at his feet. The look she gave him was so full of hope that Trask laughed.

"Are you looking to prove how smart you are?" Trask asked, picking it up with an amused smile. "We're going to have to show Felipe this game." He grabbed a small handful of treats. "Sit. Stay."

Sophie plopped down, her bright eyes fixated on the toy. Trask was curious to try this game in a bigger place. Somewhere where she'd really have to look. A loft-style apartment didn't give many options for hiding spots. He went around the bed where she couldn't see what he was doing and slipped the squeaky toy under his chair pillow. When he went back to the kitchen, Sophie remained where she was, her body tense with anticipation. "Go get it."

She shot off in a blur of red-gold fur and bounded around the bed. Trask followed, enjoying watching the process. She sniffed around the bed, nosing behind the bed skirt, where Trask had hidden it in the past, before nudging over the wastepaper basket, another favorite hiding place. Then she rose up on her hind legs, and Trask laughed as she shoved her nose under the chair cushion. "Almost, Sophie. You've got this."

With a sharp bark, Sophie grabbed a hold of the pillow and yanked it off the chair before she retrieved the squeaky, her tail waving madly. "Good girl." Trask crouched down, holding out half a treat, and then gave her a full-body rub. She seemed to enjoy the rubdown and the approval in Trask's voice far more than the treats. She picked up the squeaky again and nudged it against Trask's hand.

She could play this for hours, even more than fetch. He'd have to find other games to work on her smarts, maybe find an obstacle course at a nearby dog park. He bet she would love that. "Okay, sit. Stay."

Trask put the toy on the bottom shelf of his pantry and left the door ajar, then putzed around another thirty seconds. He had no doubt she was listening hard to every move he made. "Go get it, girl." There was a scramble of claws on the floor as Sophie raced toward him with a happy bark. Trask's phone chimed, and he moved to the table to pick it up, watching Sophie's waving tail.

Nothing I can't change around if I get to see you. I can study at your place as well as here. Man, don't ever play Boggle with my family. I'm getting my ass kicked in three languages.

"Good girl, Sophie," Trask said as the puppy dropped her squeaky toy at his feet. He enjoyed a good game of Boggle, and he might be able to come up with a few words in Spanish, but he wouldn't be able to compete with a trilingual family.

Good luck. I'm going to be in Pittsburgh, buying up some stock. Was wondering if you wanted to hit the road with me.

A few months ago, Trask would've gone alone and not even thought about inviting anyone. Now it seemed a little lonely. He'd have to find a hotel that accepted dogs, because there was no way he was leaving his girl behind. She was just a puppy, and bonding was important. He reached down and snagged the toy. "One more round and then we'll go for a walk. We shouldn't be holed up all night."

He left Sophie waiting with impatience as his phone dinged.

You realize that is the ultimate test of our relationship?

Trask couldn't quite figure out that line of reasoning, but Felipe was often two steps ahead or sideways from him. *How so?*

Trask knelt on the side of the bed and hid the squeaky toy between his knees. That ought to give her a moment's pause. "Come on, Sophie. Find it."

A red-and-gold blur came toward him with a happy bark, and at eye level, he realized how much she'd grown. She dove right into her search and soon was pawing at him. Trask shifted with a laugh, the toy squeezed, letting out a plaintive squeak, and Sophie went nuts, barking at his knees and knocking him over. The toy forgotten, she licked him as Trask laughingly fended her off. They needed a new place. One where she could bark and not piss off his neighbors. Where she could run around outside, and if Trask had visitors he'd have room for them to hang out. He'd start looking once the holidays were over.

"Wanna go for a walk?" Trask asked, picking up his phone to see Felipe's response as Sophie carried her prize off to her doggie bed.

You will be stuck with me in a car for hours. Lesser men have been known to be struck with terror at such a thought.

Trask had to smile at that. Felipe's chatter was a part of his charm. Trask liked to hear people talk. He ran a comic book and game shop. People came in and nattered at him for hours. He considered it vastly different from socializing. That required putting out as much as taking in. As long as Felipe wasn't bothered by Trask's quiet, Trask would enjoy the pleasant flow of his observations.

Good thing I'm not a lesser man.

Trask shoved on his boots and shrugged into his jacket. Sophie came running the moment she saw him put his hand on the harness, moving in dizzying circles around him. Yeah, it was past time for a walk.

Ain't that the truth. Felipe added a gif with wagging brows at the last text. Damn, Trask was missing out on seeing him.

He should've considered meeting up with Felipe after dinner with his family. Even if Jason had shown up, he wouldn't have been there all night. There would've been time for a drive up to Maryland and post-dinner private celebration. Hell, he still might do it. Give Felipe a surprise and put a smile on his face. Trask did love it when the imp smiled.

A knock came at the door, just as he was prepared to open it. Trask paused to collect himself with mingled irritation and relief. So Jason did decide to show. Three hours late. Trask hoped to God he was sober.

But it wasn't Jason on the other side of the door. Trask stared at the cop with a sudden sinking in his gut. "Can I help you, officer?" Sophie sniffed at the cop's shoes, and Trask caught her attention with a snap of his fingers. "Sit, Sophie."

"Are you Trask Briscoe?" The cop had a stern face, which fit just about every cop Trask had run into. Thankfully it was a rare occurrence since he'd gotten clean. It rattled Trask to have one on his doorstep now.

"Yes, sir." Trask leaned down to pet Sophie. "Friend, Sophie."

"I'm Officer Duras." The cop spared a brief smile for Sophie, who watched him with a cocked head. "Nice dog. I'm trying to locate the next of kin for Jason Guy. You were one of the contacts listed for an emergency on his phone."

A slow, sad weight settled in Trask's stomach. "Why don't you come in? I can get you a cup of coffee if you'd like."

Surprise flickered in the cop's eyes. "Thanks for the offer, but I have a cup waiting for me in the squad car."

Trask stepped back and let the cop in. Sophie whined and danced impatiently as he shut the door again. "I'll take you for a walk soon," Trask promised as he crouched down to unclip her leash and take comfort from her presence.

"As far as I know, him and his family aren't on speaking terms. They're in Ohio somewhere, outside of Cincinnati." Trask sighed and scrubbed a hand through his hair. "What happened?"

"He OD'd." The cop looked around the small apartment, and Trask was glad he had a chance to clean up before he came knocking. "He's lucky. Someone found him passed out on a park bench and called an ambulance. He's at Henrico. It's touch and go right now."

That eased some of the sick churning in Trask's stomach. Okay, there was still a chance, and maybe this would be the reality smack that dragged Jason back from the abyss. Until Trask heard something to change that, he would operate on the belief that Jason would pull through. "Let me see if I can find the name of his sister, in case the docs need to contact her, but I wouldn't expect a welcome."

"You wouldn't know where he scored the drugs he had on him, would you?" the cop asked as Trask searched through his texts with Jason.

"Nope. I haven't been in that scene in a long time." Trask shot the cop a level look. "I'm not his dealer. He knows not to bring that shit around me."

"Do you know where he was planning on being tonight?" The skeptical look remained in the cop's eyes. But Trask felt he didn't have to convince him of anything. The chance of finding out where Jason got his stash was low. There were plenty of dark pockets in Richmond.

"He was supposed to be here, having Thanksgiving dinner, but he never showed." Trask shoved his hand in his pocket as he continued to scroll through his texts, but he was pretty sure he had nothing. Jason kept his mouth shut about his family almost as much as Trask did about his own. "Since you've seen his phone, I'm sure you've seen the pokes I sent him."

"Actually, I haven't gone through his texts." The cop shot him an easy smile that didn't quite reach his eyes. "Waiting for the warrant to come through, which should be soon. We just hit you up because of the emergency contact."

Trask scrubbed a hand over his face and sat down, suddenly weary. "You can look into me all you want to tie up loose ends. You'll see that my record has been clean for a long time. I suspect I'm there as his contact because I'm trying to offer him a hand. He's dug himself into a pit, and his old sponsor doesn't seem to be around. He's nibbled, but not bitten."

Officer Duras studied him a moment, reassessing. "You can't save them all."

True. Very true, and Trask tried not to let those drag him down. He couldn't make anyone's decisions for them, just as no one had been able to do it for him. Still… "Doesn't mean you stop offering that hand."

He shook his head as he reached the end of the texts. "I'm sorry. It doesn't look like he told me anything more than what I've given you already."

"Thanks for your time." The cop nodded and settled his cap back on his head. "I hope your friend pulls through."

"Me too." Trask walked him to the door, Sophie dancing at his feet, her leash in her mouth. If he didn't take her now, she'd start shredding the bit of leather. "Happy Thanksgiving. Try not to let all those midnight shoppers drive you crazy."

Trask clipped Sophie's leash on and led her out. The walk would help clear his head, give him time to think, as well as make Sophie happy. He thought of Felipe with regret. It looked like he'd have to wait until their trip before he saw the imp again. He'd be spending his evening checking on Jason at the hospital and seeing what local rehabs had beds available. He couldn't make Jason go, but he could let him know what his options were.

He passed by a row of homes with the lights on, glowing cozily out into the street as Sophie tugged him along, sniffing at everything. He needed to work with her on heeling next before she got any bigger. She was smart enough to pick up on it quickly.

He dragged out the walk with reluctant steps. He did not want to spend the evening at the hospital. But he also knew the feeling of waking up alone in one and knowing no one cared enough to stop in. And if Jason didn't pull through, well, no one should die alone either. The man might never know Trask was there, but Trask would.

His thoughts flitted back to Felipe sitting with his family, playing Boggle. Trask wondered if Felipe tried to watch his language when he was with them or if was still unapologetically himself. And wished the thought didn't make him feel so damned alone.

Chapter Twenty-Six

TRASK HAD to be tired of listening to Felipe talk. He hadn't stopped from the moment Trask picked him up that morning until after they hit the Pennsylvania border. There was lots of catching up to do, at least on Felipe's side. The only words Felipe heard from the man's lips were "Good morning" and his coffee order as they hit up the Green Mermaid before heading up the road. That might be an exaggeration, but not by much.

He even brooded every time they stopped to let Sophie out for a little stroll at various rest stops. Felipe would be sure he was being tuned out if it wasn't for the occasional glances Trask would send his way as Felipe recounted their Thanksgiving and where he stood on his projects, both for school and for the cosplaying, or the even rarer grunts of acknowledgment. Trask made silence a fucking art form.

Felipe clamped his lips together, studying Trask's profile as they merged onto the Pennsylvania Turnpike. Trask drove casually, gripping the steering wheel with one hand, his elbow propped up by the window. Sunlight gleamed on the silver in his hair, revealed the furrow etched in his brow. Occasionally he'd switch hands to reach between them and scratch Sophie's head or take Felipe's hand for a couple miles.

After a few minutes of continual quiet, Trask glanced at him with a curious look. "Think you'll finish that school project before the due date?"

He was still listening, not just letting the words flow by. Felipe should be used to it. Lady listened to him all the time and never talked back, but Felipe knew she listened. Trask was similar.

"I refuse to accept anything less." Grinning now, Felipe stretched out his legs, impatient for the trip to be over. "I've invested too much time to fall short now. I'll turn it in next week, and it will make all the other projects beg for attention. Then I can look toward graduation."

Felipe planned on skipping the whole ceremony. There were other celebrations in December that he preferred. Just give him the paper he'd earned and he was out of there.

Trask made a noncommittal sound and turned his attention back to the road, but when Felipe didn't resume his one-sided conversation, Trask gave him a baffled look. "Don't tell me you've run out of things to say."

Felipe laughed at the incredulity in his voice. "Hell no, but this is usually the point where Morris begs for me to pull out my headphones to give his ears a break. I know I've hit his endpoint when he sighs and goes 'For the love of God, Felipe.'" Felipe lowered his voice to emulate Morris's deep tones, and Trask chuckled.

"I think my ears have another hour or so in them," Trask assured him.

"That's good to know, but I'm in the mood to hear your voice." And maybe he could tease out what Trask was brooding about. He recognized those signs. Even if he didn't, Sophie's behavior would've clued him in on it. Every time they stopped, she looked to love all over Trask before he reassured her and she went back to gnawing on her toys.

"So what new and amazing things has my girl been up to? Jaydon sent me a picture yesterday of the remains of Waldo's dog bed. They had a hell of a time finding him too. After he realized he might be in trouble, he managed to wedge himself under Jaydon's bed."

Felipe was rewarded with the slow smile that crossed Trask's face as he chuckled softly again. "I'm sure he wasn't in trouble with Jaydon. Kid was probably thrilled to have an excuse to sneak Waldo into his bed. Sophie stays in her bed most of the time unless the fire alarm goes off. Then I can't get her off of me when we get back up to our place."

"Does it go off often?" Felipe asked as he rubbed Sophie's ears. He didn't want her traumatized.

"Once every week or so." Trask shrugged. "Kids on the floor above me think it's a hoot. I think it'll be a while before it happens again. Their mama figured out it was them and was laying into them hard the last time."

"Oh man. My ma would've...." Felipe shuddered. "I don't even want to think about it. It would've been dire."

Trask frowned fiercely. "She lay hands on you?"

Felipe shot him a startled look. "No, not in the way you think. I've earned a swat or two from her or one of my grandmothers more than once, that's for sure. But she never beat me. She's tiny but intimidating. Let's just say it would've been a long-assed time before I ever had the energy or inclination to think up mischief like that again, and if I did,

I definitely would've thought twice about going through with it. She would never let it rest."

Felipe worried his lip. It made him wonder, though, if Trask had to live through that, his mom hitting him. Trask glanced over and took Felipe's hand. "Stop fussing. I knew when my old lady was in a mood, and I got out of her line of fire. I'd hole up at a friend's or my grandmother's place. My parents would go at it until the cops came by or they passed out and it was safe to come back."

"I don't like people who take swings at those who are more vulnerable than them, and I definitely have evil thoughts about those who take what's supposed to be a haven and make it a place to be feared. No kid deserves that." Felipe wished he could meet Trask's parents. They'd never forget him as long as they lived. Bastards.

"Seriously, don't worry about it." Trask squeezed his hand gently and drew Felipe out of his thoughts for dire revenge. "Sophie learned a new game. I make her sit while I hide her favorite squeaky toy. She finds it every time and wants to play again."

Felipe grinned at Sophie, who lifted her head at the sound of her name. "I knew you were the smartest one of the bunch."

"She's pretty proud of herself. She's managed to gnaw on a few things she shouldn't have, but for the most part, I'm able to distract her." Trask looked down at her, his whole face lighting up. "She seems to have a preference for shoes, the older and more disgusting the better."

Dogs. Felipe shook his head. Sometimes they were so weird. "How was your Thanksgiving? Did you find a tofu turkey?"

Trask hesitated, and Felipe narrowed his eyes. Score. Something about the holiday was bugging Trask. "You told me you were having a guest for Thanksgiving."

Trask shrugged again and pulled his hand back with a wary glance. "I was. Got some Cornish game hens for him, too, but he never showed."

Felipe pondered that, trying to decide if he should make a fuss, though he wasn't sure if he was more irked for Trask or himself for missing out on seeing him. "You should've called me. You could've dropped in at my place."

"I was planning on it, actually."

Felipe waited, but nothing else emerged from Trask's lips. The man was fucking exasperating. Felipe bet that whatever happened that stopped him from coming was behind Trask's brood, but it looked like he would have to pry it out of him. "You got lost? Sophie tripped you and knocked you out and you lay for two days on the floor with a concussion?"

"You amuse the hell out of me, Felipe. No, no, it was nothing like that." Trask sighed. "I wanted to surprise you, so I didn't say anything about my plans. Then a cop came by as I was taking Sophie out before we left. The guy who was supposed to come over OD'd. Lucky for him, someone found him and called for an ambulance."

Felipe frowned down at his hands. Getting anything out of Trask involved yanking and prodding and pushing. Trask wasn't the only one who could listen, dammit. He hoped the man didn't have some crazy delusions about needing to shelter Felipe. He'd have to make sure he knew better.

"Is he going to be okay? What did the cops want with you?" Felipe's imagination took off. What if they'd arrested Trask and that's why he'd been so lost in his own thoughts? That would explain him not being able to show up and his general broodiness. "Morris's dad is an awesome attorney if you need one."

"Christ no. I'm good. They were just looking for Jason's next of kin in case any medical decisions needed to be made. I was an emergency contact in his phone. That's as far as it went. I'm sure Morris's dad is amazing, but I'd prefer to never have to deal with lawyers, cops, and courts. I went to the hospital to be with him."

Trask fell silent again, and Felipe decided he could exercise some patience. Maybe. Or then again, maybe not.

"Will he be okay?"

"That's up to him at this point." After a few minutes, Trask sighed and continued. "He pulled through. I recognized that look in his eyes when he woke up. Like he knew he should be dead. We got him a bed at a long-term rehab center not far from the hospital. They'll see him through the holidays. Help him find a new job and housing."

Those were all good things, in the end, leaving Felipe thinking there was something else that Trask wasn't saying. "You did everything that was in your power to help, right?" Felipe waited for Trask's nod. "Then what's eating at you?"

"Nothing that I can control, which means I've got to let it go. Not one of my strengths. He made his own decisions. He's going to keep making his own decisions. It just sucks to witness sometimes and to wonder if I could've done something or said something to make the outcome different." Trask leaned his arm against the window again as the brood came back to his expression. "I'll be okay, just need to work it out in my head."

"You could talk to someone," Felipe pointed out with the air of it not really mattering. "Throw it all out there. Sometimes it's less about getting opinions on what you could've done and more just venting."

"I don't like talking too much about details to Ryan or Joe… feels too much like gossiping." Trask grimaced and dragged a hand through his hair. "I hated feeling like people were talking about me behind my back, even if I was giving them a reason to do so."

"I kinda like it. Makes me want to give them something to yap about." Felipe smirked, and then he turned serious. "You could talk to me."

Trask looked at him with another one of those slow smiles. "Yeah… I could talk to you. I know it seems like I don't, but some things I talk about better in person. I'm not a phone guy, really."

"I've noticed," Felipe said in a dry voice.

"If it makes you feel any better, I was coming over for comfort and snuggles before I got the news." Trask cast a look his way that seemed sincere and not teasing.

Felipe lifted his brow. "Comfort and snuggles? For some reason, those words sound odd coming from your mouth."

"I was feeling lonely," Trask admitted. "I wanted to see you. And I'll admit, I was hoping to lure you upstairs with the promise of getting me naked."

Trask was flirting with him in his own understated way, and it completely charmed Felipe. "I don't know." Felipe tried to keep a straight face as a smile kept tugging at his lips. "Are we talking about you being already naked in bed or doing a striptease for me? After all, there was pie and coffee downstairs."

"And trilingual Boggle," Trask said wryly. "I'm not sure a striptease can compete."

Felipe slid his hand up Trask's thigh. "That is tough. I think when we get to the hotel room you should show me what you've got. Then I'll judge."

Trask caught his hand before it could go any farther and kissed his fingers. "You're on, imp."

Felipe's cock surged to attention. He had not expected that answer, and now that he had it, he was impatient to see what Trask would do. "Trask."

"Yeah?"

"Drive faster."

Trask laughed, the sound filling the truck, and Sophie barked in response. It made Felipe smile to see the moodiness disappearing from his expression. "You light me up, you know that, Felipe?" His eyes softened, and he ran a hand through Felipe's hair. "You just light me up."

Felipe's heart beat faster. That almost sounded like an admission of affection, and for once, his tongue was tied up in a knot. He wanted to admit that he was falling in love with Trask, but he didn't want to scare him off when they were coasting along so smoothly. "Good, you need a little light. Sophie and I are going to make sure you get all the sunshine you can handle. Aside from that, anytime you want to vent, I swear, I do know how to shut up and listen."

"I have noticed that." Trask frowned at the road ahead. "I guess I don't get through things by venting. I handle it better by doing. Doing something positive, like going to this show and getting stock for the Den. By enjoying your company for a long weekend away. It helps me to put it all into perspective."

It warmed Felipe to know that he was able to help, even if it was just by his presence. "Good to know. I have to make sure my man is okay. I have an insatiable need to look out for the people in my life."

"Who looks out for you?" Trask asked with a searching glance. "Who makes sure you take a break from work? Or picks you up when you're down?"

Felipe pursed his lips. Nobody had ever asked him that before. "Well, there's Lady."

"Never underestimate the love of a good dog," Trask murmured, running an affectionate hand over Sophie.

"Morris has always been a good sounding board for me, though lately he's been pretty wrapped up in Theo and Lincoln, which has forced me to focus my attention on Abby. I've vented to her some, which is weird and quite possibly amoral. But she has a way of dragging reactions out of me." Felipe wrinkled his nose. "I've managed to get her to unload some too."

"I think it's quite possible you two are better friends than you want to admit."

"Don't blaspheme." Felipe shook his finger at Trask. "There's you too. I love the fact that you actually listen to me and don't half-ass it. Mostly, though, I'd say it's my lola, my grandmother. There's probably nobody who knows me like her."

"Grandmothers are a special breed." There was a wistful note in Trask's voice. "Nothing else like them on earth."

"You'll get a chance to meet her." Felipe tugged his portfolio out of his bag and started going through the different design ideas he had for Mariana's prom dress. "Dad wants us all to go out to dinner together. Well, us and my parents."

Trask made a noncommittal sound and went silent again as Felipe began to talk about all his current projects. He had enough sewing and designing to keep him engaged for the next couple of months, and other than Abby's dipshit client, most were beyond easy.

In between them, Sophie laid her head on Trask's lap with a mournful whimper.

Chapter Twenty-Seven

TRASK HAD discovered this beauty among the hodgepodge of items on sale in the antique barn. He ran his hands over the wide expanse of the triangular-shaped tabletop as he mentally reviewed Felipe's apartment space. That should fit in the corner quite nicely. But he wanted to be sure. This was Felipe's gift. It had to be just right. Only there was no easy way to pop over to his place to take measurements. He'd eyeballed the space when he'd picked up Felipe for their trip to Pittsburgh, but the imp hadn't let him out of his sight long enough pull out his tools.

He sat back on his heels and pondered the problem. There was only one real solution. It was one Trask was reluctant to take. Trask studied the table. Time to suck it up. This was for Felipe. He took out his phone and scrolled through to the group text Felipe had set up so they could discuss dinner plans together. A quick flutter of nerves hit him, and he ruthlessly quashed it. Felipe's father had extended the invite. The least Trask could do was to meet him halfway.

He found Donato's number, took a quick picture of the table, and laid out the measurements. He composed and erased several messages before settling on one. *Would you mind doing a favor for me? I'm looking at this table for Felipe, but I want to be sure it will fit in the corner of the living room where his crafting tubs are. Would you mind taking a couple measurements?* He hit Send and pushed away the uncomfortable feeling. It was done. No sense angsting over it.

A weekend alone with Felipe had hooked Trask hard. Despite Felipe's worries that he'd talk too much, there had been plenty of times when he'd been silent while he was working on his schoolwork or on the sewing project he'd brought along. Trask had taken advantage of those times to enjoy the silence and read. It had been good to share those quiet times, to share calm without it being awkward. As much as he enjoyed quiet, Trask had a surfeit of it in his life. When he wasn't still, Felipe was always entertaining. Trask was sure he aggravated Felipe more than Felipe aggravated him.

But a little exasperation was good. Kept them from getting complacent. One thing Trask had learned over the many years of failed relationships was that they took work, and if both parties weren't willing to work at it, they might as well put a halt to it quickly. Felipe wasn't one to back down from a hard conversation. He might flail and stomp off and engage in other dramatics, but he always returned to have it out, and he listened, which had been a surprise, Trask would admit. He was a never-ending revelation. Those who took him for a shallow diva were missing the chance of getting to know an amazing man.

Felipe had eased Trask's brood over the events of Thanksgiving. Of course, he'd shoved him right back into another brood over this damn dinner with his parents. Christ. Families. Trask just didn't know how to deal.

Trask crouched to examine the table closer as he waited to see if Donato would respond. The surface was nicked and scarred but nothing he couldn't fix with some sanding and varnishing. It had been made from red oak, and it would shine when Trask had finished fixing it up. Felipe would love every inch of it. Trask could almost picture his excited delight, and it put a smile on his face.

One of the legs was wobbly, and Trask ducked underneath to investigate. The side panel of wood against the leg had rotted through. He could replace that easy. There were half a dozen cubbies and drawers, perfect to organize Felipe's tools and supplies. It would be so much nicer for him to have them on hand instead of storing it all in those plastic tubs he had around his apartment. One of the drawers stuck. On the same side as the rotting plank. Wood had probably swelled too much, warped the runners. It would take many hours of manual labor, but Trask could do it. He'd sweet-talk Ryan into letting him use his workshop.

His phone dinged, and Trask pulled it out. *That thing is going to need a lot of work.*

The man had to see the beneath the surface. *Yeah, but nothing a little TLC won't fix.* And a visit to the lumberyard to see what he could find to match. Some of the wood was beyond saving, but not most.

You have an eye for potential.

Trask hid his grin as he got back up and dusted off his seat. That was an encouraging sign. If it didn't fit just right in the corner, it could still take the place of Felipe's rickety table. The corner was ideal because it would give him more room. Felipe's space wasn't as limited as Trask's, but it was still tiny. *Thanks. I'm getting it before someone else sees this potential.*

I'll double-check the measurements, but I think you have a winner.

Trask put his phone away, a little more confident that their dinner plans wouldn't be the awkward affair he dreaded. He set off, looking for a staff member to negotiate with.

If he played this right, he could get the table at a steal and it would be a beauty when he was done. Probably wouldn't get the repairs finished before Christmas. Time was just racing by. But there was no rule that said a gift couldn't be given on any day for any reason, and Trask couldn't wait to see Felipe's whole face light up when he saw the finished piece.

He had just loaded the purchased table onto his truck when his phone rang. A slow flush of pleasure filled him as he recognized Felipe's ringtone. The imp had stolen his phone and programmed his own song with Timberlake announcing that he was bringing sexy back. It absolutely fit his sass and confidence and never failed to make Trask smile when he heard it.

"Yeah, imp?" Trask slid into his truck and set it on speaker before he pulled out. "What's going on?"

"Every dangly bit I own is freezing solid. Especially the fun ones," Felipe grumbled. "My heater is acting up. Dipshits don't know how to shut off their fucking windshield wipers, and if I get struck in the face one more time with dirty, icy water, I'm going to shove a Christmas tree up their ass and make them my own personal angel tree topper. I'll even make them wings."

Trask winced at the imagery. "Damn, that's vicious."

"So's ruining my eyeliner and making this damn job more miserable than it already is." Felipe sighed. "Did you get the picture I sent you?"

"I did. I like the look on you." Eyeliner made Felipe smolder. He didn't need it, but Trask wouldn't complain. "You know I've always wondered. When you wear those skirts or women's costumes that you sometimes do at cons, do you wear women's underthings as well?"

"Always wondered, hmmm?" Felipe's voice dropped to a seductive purr. "Did you wonder this before we hooked up?"

"Maybe a time or two." Trask was only human, and Felipe was the sexiest man to ever strut into a con. It wasn't so much his looks. Those weren't bad. It was his confidence. It just oozed from him. Confidence in his look and in his skill in pulling it off.

"Why, Trask Briscoe, you naughty man," Felipe teased with glee. "I love it. Just you wait until I get my hands on you. What are you doing tonight?"

"Closing up the Den." Trask thought of an evening with Felipe with regret. He'd learned to recognize that tone from Felipe, and it stirred his blood every time. He wasn't sure when he'd get the chance to see Felipe again and have him make good on the promise in his voice.

"Why don't I come over after I get off? I can grab Lady, pick up something to eat for us on my way down, and we can relax together until it's time to go meet my folks this weekend." Felipe did not sound at all worried about a situation that filled Trask with dread. The thought of Felipe being with him tonight gave him something else to anticipate. "Do you have to be at the Den tomorrow too?"

"Yep, we're going to be packed. Full day of events." Trask's loft was too small for two good-sized dogs, but Sophie and Lady got along just fine, and they'd survive the crowding for a couple of nights. There was more room at the Den, especially when they had access to the outside. Trask doubted they'd see Lady again after she found the doggie door. "Gillian is going to close up for me, so we can leave in plenty of time for dinner. Come on down. I'd love to see you, Felipe."

"I'm mentally already there. Ugh, the cellmate the tollbooth over is giving me the side-eyes. Probably going to report me for being noncompliant. I'll see you later."

Felipe was trouble and a half in the most delightful way. He just skated through life. Obeying the rules when it suited him, flipping the rules off at other times, and somehow managing to always stay mostly on people's good side. And though there could be a bite in his words, there was no deliberate maliciousness in him. He was simply himself with no apologies to anyone.

At least Trask felt that he'd lightened the man's day a little bit. He knew Felipe was all ready to go job hunting when the New Year started and he had his degree in his hand. There had to be more job opportunities for him in Richmond than Southern Maryland. Trask wasn't sure how Felipe would take the suggestion, though. He bitched about the county he lived in, but it was clear that he loved it too.

Trask pulled up in front of Ryan's house. His friend was at the Den, taking the morning shift, but to Trask's surprise, Reva's car was in the driveway. He'd expected Ryan's fiancée to be out, getting last-minute Christmas shopping done or running errands for the wedding early next year. Well, he couldn't ignore her while co-opting Ryan's workshop. That would be rude.

Trask stuffed his work gloves in his back pocket and went to ring the doorbell. Reva opened the door with a wide, welcoming smile, the scent of baking wafting out. There was chocolate in the air and pecans. Next to coffee and macaroni and cheese, fresh baked goods were a weakness of his. "Smelling good there, Reva. It lured me all the way to the door."

Reva smiled with her whole being, not just her mouth. She had a diamond-shaped face with a long, narrow chin and broad cheeks. She beamed at him now and opened the door wider. "Trask. What brings you here? Ryan forget something? Come in. I just pulled some cookies out. You can take a box to the Den."

He was not one to turn down Reva's oatmeal pecan and chocolate chip cookies, especially hot out of the oven. "I need to shove something in Ryan's workshop. I know he's not working on anything at the moment, and I'd like to borrow it for a few weeks."

Reva had the house all decorated for the holidays, from stockings going up the staircase to a Christmas village set up on the sideboard in the dining room. Down the hallway, the tree was decorated with scarlet bows and candy canes, fully lit, and holiday music played on the radio. She'd made a home for his friend, a warm, welcoming home, and Ryan deserved every bit of that happiness.

"Wow, Reva, you've really done it up." Trask nabbed a hot cookie off the tray and inhaled its scent before taking a bite. Maybe he should pick up some Christmas decorations, nothing crazy, but something that he and Felipe could put up tonight. It might make it seem homier for him.

"If you're going to do it, do it all the way." Reva slid another tray of dough into the oven. "Let me grab my jacket and I can help you."

"Thanks." It would definitely go faster with two people, and the table wasn't that heavy with the drawers taken out, just awkward to get in and out of a truck all by himself. "I found something special at one of those places they call an antique barn when half of them are full of junk. But repurposed junk could turn out mighty nice."

"I can't wait to see what you've dug up." Reva pulled her hair out of its messy knot and jammed a battered hat over the long black locks. She'd never been one to mess with her appearance, and Trask almost never saw her in makeup, but she had an appeal to her that went beyond beauty.

"Oh, she's gorgeous," Reva said when Trask pulled off the cloth covering the table. "You don't have room in that dinky place of yours. What are you planning on doing with it?"

Trask gave her one of his slow smiles to let her know he was teasing as they eased the sucker down. "You angling for a wedding present, Reva?"

Her dark eyes turned serious. "You being there as Ryan's best man is the only present we need. Don't think I don't know what you did for him. How you helped him out of that nightmare."

"Ryan's a fighter. To me, sponsoring someone helps me out just as much. Keeps me on the right path." Trask fumbled the gate latch with one hand and nudged it open. "I'm really proud of Ryan. He's come a long way in four years." And in that time he'd become one of Trask's closest friends.

"What are you doing for Christmas?" Reva asked as they maneuvered the table into the little workshop.

"Not entirely sure yet." Trask ran a hand over the tabletop, envisioning it done. He couldn't wait to get started, but it couldn't happen tonight, not with Felipe visiting. "I suspect Felipe will have a large say in that."

"Felipe… that the boyfriend Ryan told me about?" She didn't have an edge to her voice, for which Trask was grateful. It meant that despite Ryan's dislike of cosplayers, he hadn't been telling tales to Reva. Maybe Ryan had decided to wait and see before passing any further judgment.

Boyfriend. That label didn't fit Felipe. He was more than a boyfriend. Trask wasn't quite sure what he was or how he'd gotten to feel so right in only a few months, but he couldn't deny it. "He's Felipe. He's undefinable." Trask carefully covered the table with the worn blanket again. He'd get to work on it the moment their weekend was over. "He's going to go nuts over this."

"There's a house for sale down the street," Reva said with a thoughtful look in her eyes. They left the workshop, and she pointed down the way. "Small place, though considering your loft, it'll probably seem palatial. It's got a big fenced-in backyard for your girl."

Buying a home. Trask shoved his hands in his pockets. That was a big change. Maybe one he'd been considering for a while, but not something he would want to rush into. Still…. Trask paused to take a look around him. The neighborhood was nice, older with lots of trees and a few hidden parks. Though there was nothing about it that made it seem like it was near the city, they weren't actually that far from the Den. A ten-minute drive on a bad day.

He had the money for a good-sized down payment, the credit to negotiate a decent mortgage… it was a big step, though. "Where's it at?"

Reva grinned, her eyes gleaming with delight. "It's the little Lowcountry-style house, corner lot at the end of the street. It's been on the market for a bit."

Trask knew what that meant and gave her a sideways glance. "I take that it needs work."

"Nothing that a man who likes that sort of thing would mind. The covered porch is rotting and needs to be redone. The roof needs to be replaced, but the foundation is sound. The interior is dated, but I doubt you care about that." Reva gave him a friendly nudge with her elbow. "I'll admit I looked into it. I was thinking of flipping it with Ryan's help, but then I thought about how happy he'd be to have you down the street and how happy your girl would be to have that yard. It's a win all around."

Trask couldn't deny that Sophie needed more space. It wasn't fair to keep her so penned in. The loft had been a welcome space when he'd moved in after his last stint at rehab. But that was a long time ago, and if he was honest with himself, he'd admit that he'd been feeling for a while it was time to move on.

"I suppose it wouldn't hurt to take a look at it." Trask tucked his work gloves into his back pocket. "Know any good contractors if I'm interested?"

Reva beamed. "As a matter of fact, I do."

Trask couldn't help but smile in return. "Somehow I thought that might be the case."

He talked with her a few more minutes while she packed up a box of cookies and then rode down the street until he saw the house Reva mentioned. The flowerbeds in front of the windows were overgrown with weeds. Trask would probably just plant some no-fuss bushes. No reason to get fancy. The place needed a good coat of paint, a little sprucing up, but nothing he hadn't taken care of at Joe's place.

Trask got out of his truck and peered through one of the windows. It looked as if there was more space on the inside than it seemed from the outside. Reva was right. It might only be one level, but his entire apartment could probably fit in this living room. Trask shoved his hands into his pockets, attempting to quell the little shot of excitement. No sense in jumping into something because of pure emotion, but damn, he did like the bones of the place.

He went around to the backyard and smiled. Oh wow, Sophie would just go nuts. There was room to play fetch, to race around in circles, shady trees for her to flop under when she finally wore herself out. The sun porch was a sagging mess that would have to be completely torn down. But then he could expand it another few feet out. He loved being out on his balcony in almost any weather. This would be even nicer.

Whistling to himself, Trask grabbed one of the realtor's business cards, tucked it into his pocket, and headed to pick up Sophie before going to work.

Chapter Twenty-Eight

FELIPE LOVED the Den. He loved everything about it. The scent of paper with lingering traces of powdery incense. The sounds of geek talk and the rolling of dice if a game was going on in the back. And the best of all, Trask's slow, welcoming smile and Sophie's bark of recognition. It made Felipe's heart leap and gave him a sense of coming home. Don't get him wrong, he loved his apartment. He loved being so close to his family, and he valued his own space. But lately, coming home felt a little lonely.

"Sophie, stay," Trask ordered when the young dog would've raced pell-mell through the store to greet Felipe.

Felipe smiled in sympathy as her whole body quivered when she obeyed with a little whimper. Lady was long past that stage as she walked sedately beside him, sniffing the air. "Hey, baby," Felipe crooned as he got down on his knees and hugged Sophie. "Want me to take them outside? Sophie can jump all over me there until she's satisfied."

Trask leaned down and brushed his hand over Felipe's arm in a warm welcome. Felipe knew better than to expect to be kissed breathless when there were customers in the store. Dakota wouldn't have let that stop him, but then again, Dakota had zero care for niceties like that. No wonder he and Felipe had driven Brenden nuts. Neither one of them cared if they were giving others an eyeful. This, though… the anticipation was really nice because he knew when Trask did lay his lips on him, he would be all in the moment with him.

Felipe tipped his head back to meet Trask's gaze. There was a wicked glint in his dark eyes that made him catch his breath. "I don't know," Trask said in a low rasp. "You going to let me do the same later on?"

Felipe grinned at him and stole a quick kiss anyway. "I think I can be persuaded if the offer is tempting enough."

"I'll keep that in mind," Trask promised. And oh, it was a promise that made Felipe tingle. He should definitely engage in more phone sexy talk if this was the reception he received.

The Den was hopping. Customers browsed through the shop, making a mess of the games and trade paperbacks. Ryan was checking in on the games in the back and restocking the snacks. Every table had something going on, and Felipe itched to check them out. No, first he'd see to the girls. Then he'd see if Trask wanted some help straightening up the front. Then maybe he could horn in on a game.

"Hey, Ryan," Felipe called as Sophie ran for the doggie door, diving between the legs of a guy standing at the war game table. Felipe winced. He should've held on to her collar or brought the leash. He had to remember she was still learning. He looked down at Lady. "That's your daughter, not mine. Go on, girl." He nudged her after Sophie.

"Felipe, how is it you always contrive to make an entrance?" Ryan asked in exasperation.

Felipe eyeballed him. He had a pretty good radar for when someone found him annoying. But like Brenden, Ryan's prickly attitude seemed to have abated slowly since he began dating Trask. Maybe Trask was some kind of secret asshole whisperer. "There is nothing contrived about my entrances, thank you. It's just art, baby."

Ryan snorted and shook his head. "Whatever you say."

"I say I'm going to go wear out those two for a bit." Felipe jerked his thumb toward the backyard. "Then I was thinking of picking up the shelves up front. It's a mess."

"Thanks." Ryan's grimace softened. "A whole flock of teenagers came through. They heard about the two-for-one deal and put a serious hurting on the graphic novels. I didn't want to face it. Last time that happened, some fucknut spit chewing tobacco inside a few of the books. I wanted to hunt them down and strangle them."

That was just some demonic shit right there. The holidays brought out the absolute worst in some people. "Man, I would've totally given you an alibi. Strangling's too good for them."

With a shake of his head, Felipe joined the dogs outside. It was one of those cold, misty days where the damp sank right into Felipe's bones. He warmed himself by chasing Lady around, then letting himself be chased by Sophie in return. He played with them until Sophie's run became a trot and when he tossed one of her toys, she just looked at it as if trying to decide if she had the energy to fetch it. She'd nap with her mama for a good bit now.

When he came back in, Ryan gestured toward the stockroom. "If you're going to organize, you might as well restock. My fiancée baked some cookies. Feel free to take some."

"Thanks, man." Cookies sounded good, but not as much as a hot cup of coffee. Felipe rubbed his chilled hands together and sought out Trask's pot. Trask was ringing up an impressive sale of miniatures and paints, but the pot behind him was freshly brewed. Felipe slipped in behind him and resisted the urge to squeeze Trask's butt. He should get a fucking medal for his restraint.

"Where are the girls?" Trask asked in a break between conversations.

"Lady will stay outside all day if you let her. She's sprawled out in that little shelter in the yard, and Sophie's found a warm spot snuggled in next to her and is snoring by now." Felipe took a sip and sighed in delight. Oh, that was just what he needed. "I'm going to restock your graphic novels."

Trask shot him a grateful look. "You don't have to do that, but I appreciate it. It's been crazy."

"I also didn't grope you in front of the customers," Felipe said in a low aside and preened at the amusement in Trask's eyes. "Do you appreciate that too?"

"That's more of a mixed bag," Trask murmured as another customer approached with a stack of board games. "My sense of what's appropriate is grateful. The man who's been missing you, not as much."

Felipe lightly blew across the back of Trask's neck and laughed softly at the goose bumps that formed. "I'm sure you'll thank me later."

"Oh, trust me, imp, you'll get what's coming to you."

Snickering, Felipe carried that promise with him as he got to work cleaning up the mess that browsers left behind. He finished up the game section, replenishing the shelves and making notes of what Trask was out of when the store cleared for a few blessed moments of quiet.

"So, the loft I have, you'd say it's too small, wouldn't you?" Trask asked in the lull.

"It's small, but you've somehow kept it from feeling cramped." Felipe glanced over his shoulder at Trask, who had poured himself a cup of coffee and was taking the opportunity to sit a moment.

"Yeah, I'm sure that'll change when Sophie gets full-size," Trask said in a contemplative voice. "I've been thinking I should move, someplace bigger, you know. A friend clued me in on this house for sale."

"Whoa, you're thinking of buying a house? Where?" Felipe paused in the middle of reorganizing the Vertigo trades.

"Neighborhood not far from here. Quiet place, lots of trees. I think you'd like it." Trask leaned his head back and closed his eyes as he took an appreciative sniff of his mug.

"I didn't know there were neighborhoods around here with lots of trees." Richmond had many different scenes, from rows of strip malls to crowded old neighborhoods with wandering streets and worn exit ramps off the interstate. But the only areas he saw with trees were the neighborhoods near the racetrack, and those houses looked as if they cost a shit-ton more than what Felipe wanted to contemplate.

"There are plenty of spots. Richmond's not everything you see from the highway." Trask let out a sigh, the familiar sound that escaped every time he took the first sip from a fresh cup of coffee.

Felipe's hands went back to what they were doing, though he'd ceased to see the books he was shelving. Did that mean he was thinking of taking their relationship to the next level? Felipe took a firm hold of his inner romantic and gave it a rough shake. That was ridiculous. This was for Sophie, not the two of them. It was too soon to think of moving in together. But it might happen. Dammit, Felipe wanted it to happen. He was in love with the silver twerp, and the oblivious man couldn't see that. Felipe wanted to tell him, but that just might scare his Tin Man off for good. He seemed to be leery of talking about his emotions.

"Something wrong? You've gotten awfully quiet."

"How long have you been sitting on this?" Felipe's whirling thoughts needed a vent.

"Just heard about it after we talked this morning," Trask replied, neatly bursting Felipe's rant that was dying to come out. Trask hadn't been holding out on him. "Ran by the place. It needs some work, but—"

"What kind of work?" Felipe jumped all over that as he turned around, putting his hands on his hips.

"Well, I'm not quite sure yet," Trask said slowly. "I only got a quick look around. I sent a message to the realtor, but I don't expect to hear from her until Monday. Though it's been on the market awhile. She might pounce sooner."

"Trask Briscoe, you're not thinking of biting, are you? You need to get an inspection first." Felipe paced up and down, waving his hands. He'd seen some real messes. New homeowners who'd come to his dad expecting miracles. No way he would let Trask go down that road. The man needed a damn keeper. To further his irritation, when he glanced up, Trask had the audacity to look amused. "What's the damn address?"

Trask crossed his arms. "What are you thinking of, imp?"

"I'm thinking that I'm a contractor's son. I've seen my share of money pits. I want to examine this place before some lady in a pink suit and matching shoes makes you her bitch." Felipe drilled a finger in his direction.

Trask's lips twitched, damn him, and Felipe sent him a narrow-eyed glare, silently daring him to smile. "I would feel relieved if you took a look at it," Trask said solemnly. "I wouldn't want to be anybody's bitch but yours."

Trask was teasing him, and any other day Felipe would stick around to give him the same in return, but he had a place to check out before that realtor called back ecstatic over hooking a sucker. Felipe retrieved his jacket as Trask stood up, his eyes widening in surprise. "You're going now?"

"Yep, text me the address. There's still a little daylight left, and you said it's not far." Felipe needed some time to get his spinning thoughts, hopes, and fears together. "Won't take me long. That way if the realtor calls, you can let her know if you're interested in a walk-through."

He felt Trask's gaze on him as he walked out, but he didn't try to stop Felipe. It didn't take him long to find the place. The houses were too close together, but considering this was on the edges of the city, Felipe couldn't really complain about that. And he could not see Trask living in the middle of seeming nowhere like Felipe did.

Still, he liked the feel of the place. Old trees thrust up into the sky, filling the horizon and giving the neighborhood a sense of home. This was worlds away from Trask's studio with its steel and concrete view. The little house could easily hold both of their apartments, probably had two bedrooms at least.

Felipe sat in his car for a good fifteen minutes, eyeing the house and gnawing on his lip. Just say Trask was thinking of asking him to move in. Could he be happy here? It wasn't like he could pitch a fit after the place had been bought. Slowly, Felipe emerged and walked around the place. The yard would take some serious work to keep up. It wasn't his favorite thing to do, but if he could get Trask shirtless and outside on a hot summer day, that would be worth the sweat.

He peered through the window and wrinkled his nose. The space was great, but damn, it really needed new paint and light fixtures, and that ugly-assed carpet had to go. He bet there were some sweet hardwood floors under the gray, spotted funk. Probably smelled musty. And there were three bedrooms. What the hell was Trask thinking of, going from a loft to three bedrooms, though one of them was perfect for a sewing room.

Felipe closed his eyes and shook his head. Nope, no, he was not going down this road and imagining himself there. Trask was probably just thinking Sophie needed a yard and that it was close to the Den. And it wasn't like the place was huge. He'd be just fine in a house like this with no company. Felipe had no idea what he was planning. And that was the problem.

He could just ask…. The thought crept in. Yeah right, and then he'd be labeled the clingy, pushy boyfriend again. Trask was perfectly comfortable with his own life without Felipe inserting himself into his future. Their relationship was going just fine at this pace.

Felipe scowled at the house and then tromped up to the door to grab a business card. He'd make sure the company was legit, get some recommendations for inspectors and contractors for Trask. The rest was out of his hands.

Damn, though, he wanted his mark on the house… and the man. Permanently.

Felipe got back in his car and pulled out his phone. He needed some advice, and there was only one person he could think of to ask. Felipe trusted Morris's opinion. He wasn't one to jump into things either, and look at him—he was engaged and ridiculously happy. He'd straight-up tell Felipe that he was taking his wishes for Trask too far, just like he'd tried to tell him about Dakota.

"Hey there, stranger. I haven't seen or heard from you in weeks. What's up? You've got our gamemaster locked up in your sex dungeon?" Morris teased.

Now there was a titillating thought. Felipe had never much been into that scene. Submission was not his style, and he couldn't really picture Trask giving someone else control, but damn… that might be sexy as fuck.

Felipe growled under his breath. *Focus, Suero, for the fucking love of all that is holy, focus.*

"How did you know you were in love with Theo?" Felipe demanded.

"Are you serious?" Morris asked after a startled moment.

"No," Felipe said with heavy sarcasm. "I'm giving up sex and going to seminary school. Fuck, Morris, you really think I'd ask you that for kicks?"

"Chill out, I'm sorry. I thought this was just a fling between you and Trask, nothing serious."

"I don't do flings. That's your shtick." Felipe stared at the house in the growing dusk. Trask would probably get worried soon if he didn't hear from him. "He's thinking of buying a house."

"Oh," Morris said in surprise. "Oh...."

"And I don't know if I'm reading too much into it, or if I want to read too much into it, or—" Felipe heard his voice rising and tried to rein himself in. Most of the time he enjoyed working himself into a state of drama, but sometimes it sucked.

"Okay, shut up and take a breath. In fact, take several," Morris ordered firmly.

Felipe closed his eyes and obeyed, starting to calm down, grateful for Morris's voice. He didn't know what he'd do without his friend, who kept him grounded when he needed it. "Okay, I'm better."

"Don't laugh at this confession or I'll make you pay, but I realized I was in love with Theo when I got pissed at him. We'd had this argument, and I was sulking because my freezer was filled with meals he'd given me and I just wanted a frozen pizza. It became a whole stupid metaphor for me until the pizza burned my mouth and I realized I was being an idiot. I loved Theo, and I wanted to figure out where the relationship was going." Morris paused and let out a heavy breath. "That was my profound realization."

Felipe closed his eyes and shook his head. "Only you, Morris."

"Shut up. I told you not to laugh. So, tell me. What's going on?" Morris said in a gentler voice. "Trask is buying a house and now you're questioning whether you want this to go further?"

"No, I definitely want it to go further. I...." Felipe leaned his head back against the headrest. "I love him. He's... he's so far from what I thought I'd want. He's not overly demonstrative. He's never going to do something wildly theatrical for my benefit. He can have his prudish moments. But dammit, he's quiet and kind, and he makes me feel cherished in a hundred little ways. I just don't know if he wants to go further. I'm a jump-in-the-moment and make plans kind of guy, and he's one of those long-term slow planners."

Morris remained quiet after Felipe stopped, and Felipe braced himself to hear how much of an idiot he was being.

"You know, I had my doubts. Not just about you chasing after an older guy. To be honest, I thought you'd scratch that itch and be gone, even if love 'em and leave 'em isn't your style. You were due for a rebound, but damn, Felipe, I've never heard you like this. Have you told him?"

"No." He'd never held back on his feelings before, but look at where that had landed him with Dakota. "I don't want to pressure him into something he's not ready for or even thinking about. I have no idea how he feels about me."

"That's bullshit," Morris said firmly. "And I never thought I'd hear that kind of bullshit from you. Because if you didn't think he gave a damn, you'd have either bitched about this before or kicked him to the curb a while ago. So go talk to him and then call me back when you're done, 'cause I'll die without an update."

Felipe stared out at the growing darkness and gnawed his lip. He'd never been so damned nervous about confessing his feelings before. He definitely had not second-guessed himself this much either. Which were two big fucking clues that this was the real deal. Now it was time to straighten his panties and be entirely honest with Trask about how he felt.

"Okay." Felipe dragged his hand through his hair, stomped down on his nerves, and continued with more conviction. "I'll do it."

Chapter Twenty-Nine

IT WAS probably wrong of Trask to find Felipe's moods entertaining. Mercurial was the only way to describe him. He danced from one emotion to another. He supposed some might find it exhausting or live in fear of Felipe's flashfire temper, but those darker moods of his were like summer storms. They swept in, made a ruckus, and then it was all sunshine again. Trask didn't mind getting a little wet during the process. Not when he had the pleasure of seeing Felipe's smile beam again.

Now Trask, his moods usually involved a long week of leaden skies that threatened rain that never came. One wasn't necessarily better than the other; it was just interesting to watch how people operated in their own ways.

And Felipe was endlessly fascinating.

Something had sent him into a whirlwind, and Trask had learned the last time not to let the man chew on it for too long. So he poked at him, drawing Felipe's thoughts on the house out, teasing him into a few smiles as he considered his next move. He knew Felipe expected they would go back to Trask's place after they shut the Den down, but Trask was thinking he ought to give Felipe a surprise. Felipe sure shocked him in the past, so it was time to turn the tables.

He could hear Felipe in the back, talking to Lady and Sophie as Trask shoved the bank envelopes into the safe. Felipe had been of immense help. He'd brought back dinner from a local deli along with his sulks. He finished straightening and reorganizing the front without complaint. He'd even racked up a considerable sale when he'd talked a guy into a Sisters of Battle set for his daughter, who had discovered a shared love of war gaming. He left with two squads, painting supplies, and kits for scenery, plus a little something extra for himself.

Trask imagined that family's Christmas afternoon was going to be spent putting minis together. Trask hadn't done that in a long time. He didn't have the room at home to work on miniatures, and he kept getting interrupted at work. He could have some space set aside in the new house for hobbies like that if he bought it. War gaming took up space.

He finished locking up, taking extra care to be sure the door was secure, and dimmed the lights in the front of the store. He put some holiday music on and went to join his wayward lover. Felipe was sprawled out on the floor, snickering as Sophie kept trying to grab his Santa hat. He'd fend her off, then pretend to look the other way as she snuck back up on him. Trask hooked his thumbs through his belt loops and leaned against the entryway to watch. Felipe was so full of life, living every moment to the fullest. He definitely had taught Trask a few things, like the difference between being cautious and being stagnant.

If the price was right and the inspection came through, Trask was buying that house. No more waiting for the perfect time. There was no such thing. He had the stability and the need for a new place. Time to just go with it.

Just watching him, seeing the way Felipe's face lit up when he laughed, made Trask's chest tighten. He might not be able to identify exactly what Felipe was to him, but he knew it was important. He knew he wanted this relationship to last, and he was more than willing to put in the effort to make it work.

"Hey there, imp," Trask said, and those velvet-dark, laughing eyes turned on him. Felipe pushed himself up to a sitting position and yelped as Sophie took advantage of his distraction and pulled off the Santa hat. Trask laughed as she ran toward her dog bed with her prize. "You're not going to be seeing that in one piece again."

Felipe stuck his tongue out at him. "Glad to be your personal jester."

Trask walked over and held out his hand to help Felipe up. "You okay?" he asked, cupping Felipe's jaw. "You seem a little all over the place today."

Felipe gave him a careless shrug. "The holidays usually have me up and down."

"I thought that was supposed to be my thing," Trask murmured, lightly nipping Felipe's lush lower lip before turning his attention to the tempting curve of Felipe's neck.

"You don't get a monopoly on it." Felipe slid his arms around Trask's neck and pressed closer. "Just so much going on. Finished my finals, which were a nightmare. Have this thing going on with Abby. That's still weirding me out some. And then there's us."

"Sounds like all good things." Trask rubbed his hand over Felipe's back. The heat of him, his scent and nearness had Trask's head spinning. All day long he'd been thinking of having Felipe alone, been counting down the minutes, and now that it was here, he wanted to linger over the sweetness of the moment.

"Trask… what do you think of us?" Felipe asked in a low, hesitant voice. "Together I mean."

Trask lifted his head and looked into Felipe's hazy eyes as his heart squeezed in a tender way. "Us? I think we're pretty damn special together."

Felipe's eyes softened and lit up with that inner warmth that always seemed to spread to include Trask. "For real?"

"Yeah." Trask smiled slowly and touched his forehead to Felipe's. "Thank you for fixating your attention on me and luring me out of my little bubble."

"Thank you for letting me." Felipe's gaze hinted at a vulnerability that he rarely showed. "Do you love me?" he asked in a low voice.

It seemed to Trask that Felipe was letting him look right into that sweet soul of his, and it took his breath away that Felipe trusted him with this, with him. His throat tightened as he brushed his knuckles across Felipe's jaw. "Do kittens cause havoc?" It was such a dumbass way to respond, but it seemed the only response he was capable of right now. There weren't words to describe how he felt, not words that Trask could form, and he felt like he was screwing the moment up.

"That is such a Trask answer." Felipe chuckled as his eyes lit up again. Trask's worry eased. Felipe understood him, understood what he meant. "'Cause I really, really love you," Felipe said, peppering Trask's lips with soft kisses.

Trask's pounding heart calmed as he drew Felipe in and deepened the kiss. "Those words, you, are the best gifts I've ever received." Right then he did feel like the Tin Man when he realized he had a heart the whole time.

Felipe sighed and melted closer. They held each other as Trask enjoyed one of the rare times that Felipe was still. Trask had discovered he enjoyed cuddling, but he only got to indulge in the mornings when Felipe hadn't quite woken up yet or just before they both drifted off to sleep. All too soon, Felipe stirred and began to pull back.

Trask kissed the warm spot under Felipe's ear, just to keep him near a moment longer. "Are you going to show me what you're wearing underneath those jeans of yours?"

"Maybe I'm not in the mood to indulge in one of your lurid fantasies." Felipe wiggled his way out of Trask's embrace with a light laugh.

"Maybe I'm in the mood to indulge one of yours." Trask caught him around the waist as Felipe turned away, and nuzzled the back of his neck. He felt Felipe's slight shiver and smiled. "Didn't you say I could pounce all over you until I was satisfied?"

"Only if the offer was tempting enough," Felipe replied in a breathless voice. He twisted and gave Trask his catlike smile. "What are you offering?"

Trask walked him toward the gaming table that Felipe had tried to seduce him on more than once. "To give you that battle scream you've been begging for."

Felipe let out a soft moan, his body going pliant. "For real? Now? Don't tease me, Tin Man."

"Yeah, you've had the idea planted in my head for months, and I've been obsessed with what you're wearing underneath your clothes all damn day." Trask tightened his arms around Felipe and kissed him deeply. "Bend over, imp. Let me play with you."

With another low moan, Felipe obeyed, bracing himself on his arms as he folded over. Reverently, Trask knelt behind him and ran his hands over Felipe's ass and thighs. This was better than opening a Christmas present.

Felipe looked over his shoulder, his eyes bright with held-in laughter, and wiggled his ass. "Would you be disappointed if I was naked underneath?"

"Only a fool would be disappointed." Trask flipped open the button of Felipe's jeans and skimmed down the zipper. He slid his fingers inside, felt the lace, and his cock hardened in response. Slowly he inched down Felipe's jeans, revealing the scarlet web of flowers with emerald-green-tipped leaves. "Oh God, Felipe, you don't do anything halfway, do you?"

Sheer black stockings encased his legs, with the sexiest damn tiny scarlet bow on the back of each thigh. Barely breathing, Trask slid his hands up Felipe's legs to where the lower curve of his ass peeked out from the lacy edge. With a groan, he pressed his cheek against the fabric and breathed in the scent of Felipe's arousal as his hands continued to skim up and down, fingering the edges of the garters and panties.

"You okay back there?" Felipe asked with a laugh in his voice. "Now I'm really glad I stopped off at home to change before coming here."

"I'm discovering fetishes I didn't know I had." Trask knelt back on his heels. "Who would've thought I had a kinky side."

"Untapped depths, my love." Felipe shimmied the rest of the way out of his jeans and toed off his shoes. "I hope this table of yours is sturdy."

Trask had to taste every damn inch of him. He leaned forward, grasping Felipe's thighs as he tongued around each garter, licked along the lacy edge of Felipe's panties. The skin between his thighs was so warm, scorching to the touch as Trask pressed his hand up. Felipe's breath hitched on a soft moan.

Trask palmed the firm globes of his ass, drinking in the sexy sight of the way the lace clung to his skin, making it seem even fuller, and the musky male scent of him. He slid his finger along the cleft, edged it under the lace. "I'm going to make you whimper for me this time, imp."

Felipe glanced over his shoulder and wiggled his ass again. "Good luck with that." He slid his hands down to grip his own ass. "All I have to do is touch myself while you're watching and you're putty in my hands."

Trask did have a fondness for watching Felipe. He oozed confidence and sex. He was turning Trask into an unapologetic voyeur. He wasn't about to spar with words anymore. Felipe could easily hold an argument all night long. He'd just show him with actions that he was serious. Trask kissed his clever fingers, then took advantage of the fact that Felipe was leaving himself wide open. He eased aside his panties and teased his tongue along the exposed cleft.

"Oh fuck," Felipe said in the tones of a man who knew he was screwed and didn't give one damn. Trask laid his hands over Felipe's, spreading him wider as he thrust his tongue deeper until he felt the ridge of Felipe's puckered hole. Felipe moaned with a sound of surrender that Trask hadn't heard in his voice before. Trask wanted to hear more of it and lingered, teasing Felipe, stretching him with his fingers until he was panting and pushing back with soft little whimpers.

Trask stood up with a feeling of triumph and fished the small tube of lube and a condom out of his pocket. He'd felt a little naughty for having them there waiting all day, but when it came to his imp, Trask always wanted to be prepared. "Whimpers sound good on you, Felipe."

Felipe looked over his shoulder, his eyes glinting wickedly. "Somebody has been thinking of this. Very naughty."

"So says the man who tempted me with texts and wore this getup." Trask lightly slapped his ass, and Felipe gave him an unrepentant grin. Then his gaze went hot, and he spread his legs more and jutted his ass out.

"Don't make me wait any longer."

This was a temptation that didn't worry Trask. He palmed Felipe's ass again, then picked him up and sat him on the edge of the table. "I want to watch your face. I want to be able to do this." He caught the nape of Felipe's neck and kissed him hungrily.

Felipe groaned and kissed him back, his fingers fumbling with Trask's button and fly. He cupped Trask's cock and squeezed it with a muffled wicked sound against Trask's lips. Trask caught the edge of the table as his knees threatened to buckle under the wave of lust. Felipe chuckled throatily. "You may have made me whimper, but I can bring you to your knees."

"You already did." Trask extricated himself before Felipe got any other ideas and slipped the condom and lube on. "When I was worshipping that fine ass of yours."

Felipe preened as he lay back and draped his legs over Trask's chest. "My fine ass wants to feel your cock, and if you don't—" He broke off with a groan as Trask eased his way into Felipe's warm and willing body. He felt so good, and Trask half closed his eyes as he savored the feel of him. Felipe pulled his shirt up and ran his hands over his chest, his lips parted in an expression of pleasure that made Trask hungry for more. He braced his hands on either side of Felipe and thrust into him again.

Felipe gasped, wiggling underneath him, gripping Trask's arms. "More," he groaned, clenching around him.

Trask obeyed, his heart pounding, and with every snap of his hips, every time he buried himself deeply into Felipe, his lover demanded more in a voice that Trask was helpless to resist.

Trask eased Felipe's legs down around his waist so he could lean over him. Felipe gripped him with his strong thighs like he didn't want to let Trask go. Trask kissed his throat and jaw, murmuring tenderly, words that didn't make sense when strung together, but expressed how Felipe made him feel. He knew Felipe would understand him.

Felipe caught his hands in Trask's hair. "I love you." He kissed Trask with a greedy moan.

"Me too," Trask replied when Felipe finally freed him enough so he could speak again. He never felt about anyone the way he did Felipe. He'd come close. He'd seen the edges of it, but he'd always pulled back and never let himself fall. With Felipe, he didn't even see that edge coming, and it filled him with an indescribable joy that it had been Felipe. He was worth the wait.

"More," Felipe gasped, arching against him. As they gripped each other's hands, white-knuckled, Trask pounded into him with lust and love and sweet aching need until they both tumbled over the edge and Felipe gave that wild battle cry he'd promised.

Trask would never look at the damned gaming table the same way again.

Felipe went limp, his arms and legs sliding from Trask's body. Trask stayed right where he was, his heart starting to slow as he held on to Felipe. "I think that changed my outlook on life," he murmured, and Felipe laughed out loud.

"That's some transcendental sex," he said and nipped Trask's ear.

Trask lifted his head and smiled down at Felipe, flushed and warm, his eyes half-lidded with a sated, sexy look. "No, it's just you." He slid his hand through Felipe's dark curls. "You're transcendental. You've got me hooked, Felipe, so don't go anywhere, okay?"

Felipe lifted up on his hands and brushed his mouth over Trask's. "That's one thing you don't have to worry about."

Trask wrapped his arms around Felipe and nested his chin on his head. He had him, now he just needed to figure out a way to keep him. Because he never wanted Felipe to have to choose between his family and Trask. He'd never make him. He just hoped it wouldn't come down to having to pull back and slow down a bit, because he loved this ride that Felipe had him on. It was one he could see staying on for life.

Chapter Thirty

FELIPE CHECKED himself in the mirror again, fiddling with the top button of his dress shirt. Maybe he should wear a tie. He should've brought a fucking tie. He frowned fiercely at his reflection and leaned in. "Get a fucking hold of yourself, Suero." Christ on a stick, this was dinner with his parents, not a night out at the theater. He could not lose his shit now. This was too important.

The bathroom door shoved open, crashing into him as Lady crowded in. "Girl, there is not enough room for two fat asses in here. Get out." He pointed imperiously at the door, and Lady slunk out again, only to be replaced with a scampering Sophie, who made a grab for the edge of the towel he left dangling off the counter before he shooed her off too. It was a good damn thing Trask was thinking of a bigger place or Felipe would be driven mental before long.

Felipe gave up on panicking in front the mirror and returned to the main room to find Trask half-dressed, his shirt hanging from his fingertips as he thumbed through his phone. "What's up?" Felipe asked.

"Nothing. Some chatter from friends in my NA group." Trask tossed the phone on his bed and shrugged into his shirt. "You sure your parents and grandparents want to come all the way to Richmond for dinner? We could've gone up to them or met in DC."

"I think they were looking forward to getting out of town." Felipe was nervous about Lolo's last-minute decision to join them. He'd been hoping his grandfather would've opted to keep Mariana company. Too bad his sister had not been able to finagle her way into coming along. With her and Lola, it wouldn't have felt so much like they were facing a judgment of their peers.

Felipe flopped on the bed and watched Trask finish getting dressed. He'd freshly trimmed his beard and cropped his hair on the sides and back, leaving the top in its fuller sweep. Felipe had a serious hard-on for his hair, mostly silver with just enough black left in it to be edgy, and the crisp way it felt when he ran his hands through it. The baby-blue button-up shirt and black dress pants looked good on him. Felipe bet he would rock the hell out of a tux. It just might make his hormones explode if he saw that.

"How late would it make us if I stripped that right back off you and licked you all over?" Felipe asked, running his toes up Trask's thigh.

"Let's just say we'd miss dinner altogether." Trask smiled slowly and knelt on the bed to steal a kiss. He cupped Felipe's face in that sweet way he had, his thumb brushing over Felipe's cheek. He could always tell Trask's mood when he did that. If his thumb played with Felipe's cheek, he was feeling loving. If it was Felipe's lower lip... well... that was a whole different kind of fire. "Do I make you happy, Felipe?"

"I don't think you should be dependent on other people to make you happy, and I know you feel the same." He'd heard all about Trask's philosophies for life. Felipe slid his hand to the nape of Trask's neck and drew him down for a kiss. "But when I'm with you, there's nowhere else I want to be."

"Yeah, me too." Trask gave him a tender kiss and, to Felipe's disappointment, pulled away. Probably for the best, if Trask had lingered, Felipe would've made sure they were late. Trask was already on edge enough without adding tardiness to the mix.

He rolled up and searched for the dress shoes he'd brought. His overnight bag was open, and one shoe was missing. "Sophie," Felipe said in a low growl. He glanced toward her dog bed and saw the shoe buried among her toys. He stomped over and fished it out. To his relief, it was a little gnawed, but not so bad that it was unwearable. "I'm surprised you haven't tried to eat the Christmas tree." He shook the shoe at her as she appeared, watching the waving leather with avid eyes.

"Even she pities that thing." Trask glanced at the tiny tree, strung with delicate white lights and snowflakes. Felipe had slipped two small packages under there, but to his aggravation, Trask had not commented on them.

Felipe winced at the time on the clock and shoved his shoes on with a sigh. "We'd better get moving or we're going to be late."

Trask nodded and grabbed his dinner jacket. He slipped it on and turned toward Felipe, his hands outstretched. "How respectable does this look?"

"Screw the looks. There are lobbyists on K Street who look respectable and are steaming piles of shit as human beings. You're the quiet kind of respectable that doesn't look for any reward, and that's what matters." Felipe dropped an airy kiss on Trask's lips and jammed a winter hat on. The temperature had plummeted over the last week, and he was not looking forward to going out into that chill. Not when he could stay inside instead and get naked and warm with Trask.

He knew Trask was not looking forward to this dinner. It was everything he hated. Possible family tension. The spotlight would be on him with the expectation of him opening up and sharing. And Trask had not uttered one word of complaint. It made Felipe ache with how much he loved him. He would make damn sure they took it easy on him and gave Trask a chance.

Felipe adjusted the lapel of Trask's jacket and gave him a wicked smile. "Personally, I think we should act scandalously. Then being our normal selves afterward will cause no shock waves."

"You would say that." Trask leaned over and unplugged the tree, then pointed at Sophie. "You stay out of trouble. We'll be home soon."

Home. Felipe liked the sound of that connected with Trask, and he was growing used to the idea of relocating to Richmond. It wasn't that far from his family. His business with Abby was all online. He was done with his degree except for the formality of grabbing his diploma. There was a whole variety of work opportunities. However it all it played out, he wanted a future with his Tin Man. He caught Trask's hand and squeezed it. "Let's do this. You nervous? 'Cause I'm fucking dying."

"I am," Trask admitted. "I don't want there to be drama."

That was something about Trask that Felipe had pondered long and hard. He kept saying it yet didn't seem to mind any of Felipe's moods or behavior. The more he thought about it in connection with Trask's own past, he realized that what Trask really meant was that he didn't want to be the cause of drama, not after he'd been in the front and center of it for too many years. Felipe thrived on that kind of scrutiny and proving people wrong, but he had to remember he didn't carry the same weight that Trask did.

"I promise to be on my best behavior." Felipe laid a hand over his heart as he gave Trask an innocent look.

"Somehow, imp, that doesn't fill me with a whole lot of confidence." Trask held the door open for him and swept Felipe a bow as he walked out. "Our audience awaits."

Trask was quiet the whole way to the restaurant, and for once Felipe couldn't seem to find anything to say. He'd never felt like this, not even when he'd introduced his first boyfriend. That had been a fiasco. That dude had been so high-strung he'd made Felipe seem boring. It hadn't taken more than a few acidic comments from certain parties to reduce him to tears. Trask was made of sterner stuff, though. It would take more than a bigoted old man to frighten him off. This would've been so much easier if Lolo had stayed the fuck home.

The restaurant was in a converted tobacco warehouse down on the canal by the James River. His mom had been gushing about it for a week, some big seafood joint. They did love food from the bay and would steam their own blue crabs in the summer, eating them in the backyard with beer in the cooler and citronella candles burning to keep off the mosquitoes.

"You sure there will be something for you to eat?" Felipe asked as they crossed the street to the restaurant.

"Yep, I looked online. They have a lobster mac and cheese. I'll just tell them to let the sucker live until the next carnivore comes along." Trask gave him an easy smile. "I'm the worrier, not you, so relax. I'll have a salad, too, and it'll be a feast."

The inside of the restaurant was all dark wood and burnished leather offset with snowy white linen. Felipe shoved back his nerves one last time as he scanned the place and saw his family at the large table set in the middle of the restaurant floor. Great, then everyone would have a view of the gay couple running the family gauntlet before the holidays.

"I see them," Trask murmured as he waved off the waiter and guided him toward the table with his hand at Felipe's back. It made him feel like he was being herded to his doom, and he resisted the urge to scowl. That would just set everything off on the wrong foot. *Get it together and don't make a scene.*

Felipe scanned expressions as they neared. His mom and Lolo looked grim. His dad was always hard to read, but since he was the one reaching out, Felipe would give him a chance. Mostly he focused on the welcoming twinkle in Lola's eyes. At least one person was happy to see them. Felipe clung to Trask's hand and assumed a bright smile. "Mom, Dad, Lola, and Lolo. This is Trask Briscoe." Felipe glanced back at him, and this time the smile became genuine. Screw the nerves. It might take them a while to warm up, but once they got to know Trask, they'd love him.

He stood back, making the individual introductions as Trask greeted each one of them with his own brand of gruff politeness. His dad was a stickler for manners, so the ma'ams and sirs would sit well with him. Felipe blushed slightly as Trask pulled out the chair for him and Lola chuckled. She reached across the table and gave Trask's hand an approving pat. "I saw from your picture that you had kind eyes. I'm happy to see the same in person."

"Thank you, ma'am. I hope you didn't run into any problems on your way down," Trask responded. They continued to make polite, noncommittal conversation as they perused the menus, and Felipe realized that Trask was more nervous than he'd let on. He sucked down water like it was Johnny Walker Black and paused each time before he spoke as if he was looking for the perfect words that weren't abrupt.

"Felipe tells me you own a gaming store. How long have you been running that?" his dad asked after drinks were ordered and the bread passed around. Felipe eyed his dad. He seemed a little mellower around Trask, but Felipe wasn't certain if that was his hopeful imagination or not.

"About twenty years. It's been steady, though business picked up quite a bit when I expanded to online sales. I have a few employees, and this one has been making himself handy lately." Trask smiled at Felipe. "I think he's angling to kick out my manager and make himself boss."

"Hell no, Ryan would b—" Felipe caught himself before the curse word slipped out. Of all the nights, this one he had to be on his best behavior. No sense in antagonizing his mom over his language. "Ryan would kill me with complaints. I know who your second-in-command is, and it's not me."

"Felipe's got a job." Lolo punctuated that with a tap on the tabletop. "A good government job that will keep him through retirement. Retail's no good. Too many uncertainties. With his degree, he can do better."

Felipe gagged at the idea of staying at the Department of Transportation until he retired. No way he'd make it. No fucking way.

"You have a point. The trick is changing with the ups and downs." Trask shifted in his chair as all eyes returned to him. "The store has made adjustments over the years as interests changed."

Felipe decided it was time to draw attention away from Trask and let him catch his breath. "No way I'm staying in a toll booth for life. Now that I have my degree, I'm looking for another job. Once I find the right place, then I'm out of there so fast they won't even see me going."

He planned on finding a job that would give him the flexibility to really make a push with Creatures & Cosplay.

"You could take that business degree and do the books for your father." His mom gave him a smile of encouragement. "It'll give you some practice while you wait for that project of yours to take off."

That was a thought. Felipe eyed his dad, who shook his head empathically. Felipe had to smile at that. "What's wrong, Dad? Don't trust my math skills?"

His dad smiled fondly at him. "No, I just think we'll end up butting heads even more than we were the last time we worked together, but if you want a job like that, I can ask around."

Felipe wasn't sure any longer that he wanted a job in Southern Maryland. He'd hate to jump into something if he ended up relocating to Richmond. He'd feel like he was ducking out on a commitment. "I'll let you know. I just want to get my final grades and know I aced the last semester. Hey, Dad, you know any contractors with a good rep in Richmond?"

"Why?" his mom asked, her eyes widening with alarm as Trask squeezed his knee in warning under the table. What the hell was that about?

"Trask is looking at this place with a yard. For Sophie, you know. She doesn't have anywhere to run around at his apartment." It needed a lot of work despite Trask's assurances that he could do some of it on his own. Felipe gave Trask a cautious look, but he could be hard to read too.

"I've grown out of my loft," Trask added, "but I've stayed because it's so close to work. This new place isn't much farther. Felipe's concerned because it needs a little TLC. I'm going to meet with the realtor next week and see about it. I promised him that I'd have it inspected before I committed to anything. It needs a new roof, but I think the foundation is sound."

"That's a good plan," his dad approved. "If you're still interested after the walk-through and inspection, let me know. I can get you a list of names."

"Thank you. I did get a few contacts. A friend of mine flips houses. She's the one who clued me in on the house." Trask reached for another piece of bread and slipped it onto Felipe's plate. Like he needed the extra carbs, but he'd been eyeing it anyway and Trask must've picked up on it. "She wouldn't be interested if it wasn't a good project."

Felipe frowned at the lingering worry in his mom's eyes as they ordered their meals. He didn't see the big deal or why Trask wasn't pleased about him mentioning it. He felt like he was wading through one of the swampy areas near his house, with sinkholes on one side and water snakes on the other.

"What's wrong with the lobster?" Lola asked with a look of concern after the waiter left. "Are you allergic to shellfish?"

"No, ma'am. I'm a vegetarian." He held up his hand with a smile as Ratree began to apologize for the choice of restaurant. "It's okay. As I've told Felipe, as long as there is a good mac-n-cheese, I'm happy."

"Yeah, the first place I invited him to was a BBQ joint." He gave Lolo a wary look, determined to bring him into the conversation on something he could smile over. "You would've loved it. They do all the smoking in-house, and it smells amazing."

His grandfather crossed his arms on the table, watching Trask with a penetrating gaze. "You say you've had this business about twenty years?"

"Yes, sir."

Felipe touched Trask's hand, felt the tension in him, and wished he could help him relax. All in all, he thought this was going rather well. It might go a little smoother if Trask would volunteer a little more instead of responding or waiting to be asked, but that wasn't Trask's way at all.

"You would've been pretty young, about this one's age." Lolo turned that penetrating look on Felipe, and he silently cursed his grandfather for putting their age difference right back in the forefront of everyone's mind. "Where'd you get the capital for a new business?"

Trask's fingers flexed. "Inheritance," he said shortly, tearing apart the bread on his plate into crumbs. "I'd been living here for a couple years, working at whatever I could find, trying to save for it. The money came in handy."

Felipe's mom straightened, her eyes brightening. "So you do have family. How often do you get to see them?"

Trask went still and shook his head. "No, ma'am, no family. There are those who share my blood, but they aren't family. And none of us wish to see each other." At Ratree's look of distress, he smiled faintly, though it didn't reach his eyes. "Here in Richmond, I have friends who I consider family. We've stuck by each other. Felipe knows Ryan, but I still need to introduce him to Ryan's fiancée and to Joe." This time, the smile did warm his gaze. "They will love you, imp."

Felipe would like to meet the others who made up Trask's world. He knew Joe was important to him. If Trask talked about anybody, often it was Old Joe. "Yeah, Ryan's cool, even if he was super protective of you when I first started asking you out. He seems to have chilled since then."

"And you make enough money selling comics to buy and renovate a home?" Donato asked as their meals arrived. "I'd heard that many of the brick-and-mortar stores aren't doing well. It seems like every comic book store that comes into town only lasts a few years and then it goes belly-up."

"Actually, that place by the county line has been there for over a decade," Felipe cut in. "And that shop is smaller than Trask's operation. He sells more games than he does comics and has a room in the back where people can come and play."

"Richmond is also a good-sized city," Trask added. "Geeks know where to go to get what they want, and they're willing to travel a bit to get it."

"You get a lot of kids hanging out there?" Lola asked, and her smile widened as Trask nodded. "It's good for kids to have a community place to go."

Felipe's mom did not look convinced, and she kept eyeing Trask's tattoos as if they could come to life in front of her. Felipe shot her a quelling glance. His cousin had almost as many tattoos, and it didn't make her a bad woman.

"Still, that doesn't seem like a steady business. Kids hanging out doesn't lead to sales. Felipe would hang out at his comic shop, but he didn't have money to spend."

Lolo leaned forward with a huff of impatience. "She's worried. She knows you have a past and wants to make sure nothing illegal is going on while her son is there, but she won't come out and say it."

Felipe straightened, outrage leaping into his throat and strangling him as Ratree leaned forward to level her father with a suppressing glare and angry hiss. Beside him, Trask stiffened.

"I've never dealt drugs, not even when I was using, and I've never targeted kids. My place is a safe place for those who come to hang out, and everyone knows my hard rules."

Lola patted Trask's hand again as Felipe struggled to come up with something to say that did not involve a string of curse words. "Felipe would never be with someone who did. A fact that everyone here at this table should remember."

Trask gave her a strained smile. "I can see why Felipe talks about you with such love, Miz Madel."

"Nonsense, call me Lola," she said with a pointed glance around at everyone at the table. "Stop poking at them and give them a chance to relax or they won't be able to eat a bite with all this tension."

"I hear you also extend a hand to others who need help." Felipe's dad gave Trask an approving smile. "You give back. That's a good thing."

Felipe stared at his dad. Was he coming to Trask's defense? He knew he'd promised to keep an open mind, but Felipe hadn't expected this.

"Felipe is too young and thinking with his hormones to be a good judge of character," Lolo stated. "I mean, look at his boyfriend. He has no business—"

Felipe jumped up with an angry growl as everyone nearby turned to look. He was so furious he was shaking as he shook off Trask's calming hand. "Felipe...." He heard the warning tone from multiple voices and ignored it. It was Lolo they should be warning, not him, but they were happy to keep their damn mouths shut while he ran his mouth on about Trask. Why the fuck did they even bring him?

"You don't get a say in who I'm with, Lolo. You've never had anything good to say about anyone I dated. I don't know if it's because I'm gay or you're just a cranky bastard, but I don't care." The ring of shocked faces staring at him made Felipe squirm inside and only fueled his anger and tongue more. "If I want to have wild, kinky sex with him, that's my business. If I want to run away and marry him, that's my business too. I don't need your approval, your judgments, or your mean-assed comments."

Felipe turned his glare on the rest of the table, including his grandmother and Trask. "And I don't want to hear a damn thing from any of you, because I didn't curse once." Then Felipe realized his mistake and clutched his hair.

"Excuse me." Trask folded up his napkin and set it beside his plate, and then to Felipe's astonishment he grabbed his coat and walked away.

Silence fell over the table as everyone watched Trask stalk out. Felipe stared after him, tears stinging his eyes. Fuck, it was all a crumbled mess and he didn't know how to fix it.

Chapter Thirty-One

TRASK SHOVED his hands in his pockets and leaned against the wall outside. The air hit him with a cold slap that he ignored. Walking out had been stupid. But he didn't trust himself to maintain a civil tongue, so he'd have to settle for being rude. He could not take another minute of the tension at the table. Too many memories caught him by the throat. He had to remind himself that the situation was different in a hundred different ways from his own family. Their tension came from care, when his parents had never given a damn about anything but themselves and their next fix.

He laid his head back against the brick and stared up at the stars. And he'd gone down that same road for so long. Even if he pulled himself out, could he blame Felipe's family for being worried?

And Felipe. He didn't know whether to be pleased that Felipe had defended him so passionately or seriously irritated that he'd made such a humiliating scene. But he had to give Felipe credit for reining it in as much as he had. And because Felipe had, Trask tried to let go of the anger gnawing at him. He didn't need to add fuel to this outrage.

He turned his head as Felipe came out of the restaurant, waving his arms and muttering curses in a number of languages. "You should've told them to go fuck themselves."

"I think you did that for both of us." Trask studied Felipe's expression, trying to gauge if there was hurt there or just anger, and he caught Felipe doing the same to him.

"You okay?" Felipe asked, sliding his arms around Trask in a fierce hug.

"Yeah, it was the tension that got to me, the scene, not their poking." Trask sighed as a look of discomfort crossed Felipe's face. That was an expression Trask had rarely seen with Felipe, no matter the outburst.

"I'm sorry," Felipe muttered. "He just pisses me off so much. This would've been smoother if he hadn't come."

Maybe, but eventually, it would've come out. Better that it happened sooner. Trask just wished it hadn't been in a public place or during a meal. He wished for many things, and he wasn't sure what he could do to keep them from slipping away. "I suppose we should go back in and see what we can salvage out of this." Christmas was coming. Felipe shouldn't be at odds with his family.

"Oh fuck no." Felipe stepped away from him and waved his arms again. "If it was just Lola and Dad, hell, even my mom I could handle, but if I see Lolo again I'm just going to go off, and no one wants a repeat of that."

Relief washed over Trask, and then he noticed Felipe shivering. "Where's your coat?"

Felipe flapped his hand toward the restaurant. "I left it behind. I didn't think. I wanted to check on you."

Trask rubbed his hands over Felipe's arms and shrugged out of his own coat. "Here."

"Where are you going?" Felipe demanded as he turned to go back inside.

"Grabbing your coat and our dinners," Trask replied, steeling himself in case there was any further commentary. But better him than Felipe or there would be another scene. Thankfully, he stayed outside. Their waiter was handing Ratree to-go boxes that he assumed contained their food, since everyone else's dinner was on their plates and Felipe's coat was over her arm.

He met the distressed gazes of Felipe's family as he approached. He could see the apology and embarrassment in Donato, Ratree, and Lola's eyes. Lolo stared back at Trask with his chin tilted to the same defiant angle that Felipe got. At another time, in other circumstances, Trask would've found that amusing.

"I—" Trask paused, but the right words eluded him. "Felipe's happiness, his relationship with his family is very important to me."

Ratree studied him, searching his face before nodding. She handed over the boxes and Felipe's coat. "I believe you'll do what's right."

Lola drew herself up, saying something in a language Trask didn't recognize, her eyes flashing angrily. He didn't need to understand. He recognized the tone of a reprimand when he heard one. The table erupted, words sizzling back and forth as Trask slipped away.

Felipe spun to face him as Trask emerged, and he could see that he'd worked himself up into a furious state again. Trask handed Felipe his coat and caught his hand. "Did you tell them off?"

"No. Come on, we'll get sick if we stay out here half-naked. Let's get you back to my place."

"I don't know why you didn't tell them to fuck off," Felipe fumed as they made their way to the truck.

Trask had been tempted. He hated being judged, hell, even when he deserved it. It got his hackles up every time. And times like this, when he didn't deserve it, it dug under his skin even more, making his temper simmer. "What would it have solved other than drive a deeper wedge?" Dammit, he hated uncomfortable family situations, hated them with a holy passion. He slid behind the wheel and rested his head back against the seat. "And damned if I can't see their point."

"Don't you fucking dare take their side." Felipe twisted to face him. "All I asked was for them to give you a chance, not jump all over you. I don't care about the twenty years between us. And dammit, your past has made you the man you are today. So yeah, it fucking sucked, and you put yourself in some shitty places, but you got yourself out of them too."

Trask shook his head and started the truck. Felipe had his points, but if Trask was a dad, he was pretty sure he'd have serious reservations about a forty-year-old man hooking up with his son or daughter. It had taken him a bit to warm up to Reva, and she was amazing. But he could be protective of those close to him, too, and Ryan was like a brother. So he got it.

Felipe huffed out a breath and let out a few more choice oaths. His phone rang, and he ignored it. "So you said you inherited the money for the store. Who from? I thought you and your family didn't get along."

Trask sensed that Felipe was asking more out of a need to distract himself than curiosity, but he had to stop dodging the questions or giving only partial answers. Might as well tell all tonight. There was no reason to hold back anymore.

"My grandmother, but I had to be clean to collect on it. And man, I wanted that chance. I wanted her to see that I could build on what she left me. That I wouldn't be like my parents. I wanted her to be proud of me. So I found myself a program, got clean, showed up back in Texas a year later with my paperwork, test results. Pissed my old man off to no

end. He was hoping to contest her will and take the money for himself."
Trask sighed and scrubbed a hand through his hair.

"How long did you stay clean after that?" Felipe asked softly.

"Almost another seven months." Trask shook his head, his hands
tightening on the wheel. "Once I'd bought the place, got everything
settled, inventory in stock and the initial flurry of activity was over, I
convinced myself that one drink to celebrate wouldn't hurt anybody. I
could handle one damn drink. Goddamn, I was wrong."

Trask had zero recollection of the next few nights. "All I know
is that I finally came out of it several days later, naked in some damn
flophouse, with a shit taste in my mouth, fresh track marks, and too many
bruises."

He glanced over to find Felipe watching him with wide, solemn
eyes. "And a whole shit pile of shame and guilt?"

Trask nodded. "You nailed it, and I couldn't face it, so I went right
back to using. I couldn't face her memory, knowing how upset it would
make her if she saw me."

Felipe caught Trask's hand and lifted it, studying his knuckles
before laying a kiss on them. "Maybe for a while, but you found the
strength to fight it back again and again until you were able to say you
have almost sixteen years clean. You ever think that your grandmother
looked at you and didn't see a man who kept failing but instead saw the
man who kept picking himself up to wage that war again?"

Trask's throat tightened to an unbearable ache. He'd never looked
at it quite that way, but knowing his grandmother the way he had, yeah,
he could see that. Felipe opened up such a wellspring in him sometimes,
emotions that had been shunted aside so he could deal with the day-
to-day, that the intensity of allowing himself those feelings almost
physically hurt. He tugged Felipe to him. "You're incredible, you know
that?" he asked as Felipe wound his arm around Trask's shoulder. "She
would've loved the hell out of you."

"And I would've adored her." Felipe smiled at Trask. "I'm definitely
a grandma's boy."

"I do like your lola." Trask thought that if given the chance, he'd
like Felipe's grandpa too. They both spoke their minds, that was for
certain, and damn the consequences.

"Well, that settles it. They're just going to have to deal," Felipe
declared as they pulled up to Trask's apartment building. "You come

over for Christmas dinner. It'll be fine, you'll see. They just need to see you around, get used to you. Then they'll open their minds enough to get to know you."

"Oh hell no." Trask couldn't think of a worse nightmare while sober. A tense family dinner was one thing. He could see himself agreeing to another after the New Year, but he'd seen enough from Joe and Ryan's family to know that holidays with a real family were supposed to happy affairs, not awkward, strained ones.

Felipe stared at Trask, his mouth falling open. "I'm not letting you spend another holiday alone."

"That's my decision, not yours," Trask said firmly and went on as Felipe looked like he was about to protest. "I am not going to be the chain you jerk between you and your family. I'm not, Felipe."

"You're not my fucking chain," Felipe ground out. "You're the man who's a big part of my life. I mean, you're looking at houses and…." Trask stared at him in horror. "What? You weren't thinking of asking me to move in with you if you get a bigger place?"

Sharp, panicky claws gripped Trask's insides. Felipe was twenty steps ahead of him. Trask was just getting used to the idea that he was in love with Felipe, and Felipe already had the rest of their lives mapped out. Trask had been on his own since he was seventeen, and though he'd had lovers before, he'd never shared his life that intimately with them. Damned if Felipe didn't make him want to try, but this was not a leap he was prepared to take blindly.

"I think we need to take a step back," Trask said seriously as Felipe gave him an incredulous look filled with betrayal. "What you want for your life is something I've never looked for or wanted. I don't want to give you a false impression that this is going anywhere more than where it is now. We need to slow this down a bit."

Felipe pulled away, his lips tightening into a hard, unwelcome line. "Are you saying that this is just a casual thing between us? Because I've done that bullshit, and I'm not looking to take second place again."

"There's nothing casual about you, Felipe. All I'm saying is what we have now is good. Maybe it'll lead to more, but we've only been seeing each other for four months. Your family hates the idea of us as a couple. Some time and space will give you and I a chance to figure out what we want. It'll give your family time to adjust to the idea of me." Trask stopped trying to make his argument because the set look on Felipe's face warned him he was getting nowhere.

Felipe leaned closer, his eyes glinting dangerously. "Look, I know exactly who I am and what I want, and if you can't handle that, Mr. I've Got This, then that's your own fucking boggle. Take your space and your time and shove it up your ass." He got out of the truck, slamming the door behind him.

"Felipe." Trask got out as well, watching Felipe storm toward his car waving his hands in the air. Trask could hear his diatribe from halfway across the parking lot. "Come upstairs. Let's talk. You shouldn't drive home mad." He did not like the thought of Felipe walking away hurt and angry.

"No!" Felipe spun around to face him. "I don't want to see you right now. I don't want to see anybody. Merry fucking Christmas and happy goddamn New Year."

Trask's stomach clenched as Felipe slid into his car and slammed that door as well. He shoved his hands in his pockets and started walking toward Felipe's car. He'd talk him into coming inside, soothe his hurt, and then Felipe would see the sense in slowing down. He'd taken no more than a few steps before Felipe pulled off, going faster than what Trask thought was reasonable.

Trask swore and stared after him, tempted to follow, but that just might make Felipe speed more in the mood he was in. Trask wasn't about to involve the imp in an accident. What a shitty night all around. He'd better at least text Trask when he got home to let him know he'd made it safely.

Scowling, Trask went up to his own apartment. He'd give Felipe some time to calm down. Then maybe the man might be willing to listen to reason. And they'd also have a long conversation about Felipe's habit of driving off whenever he heard something he didn't want to instead of dealing with it. That was not the way to handle things. It drove Trask nuts that he had to wait for a few days for Felipe to calm down so they could talk.

As Trask opened the door, an anxious Sophie and Lady crowded toward him, seeking reassurance. Trask sat heavily on his bed and comforted himself with comforting them. Well, Felipe wouldn't get far. Not without his Lady. Which meant he would be back as soon as he realized he didn't have her, and then they could talk.

Maybe in the back of his mind, he was seeing Felipe in that little house. That didn't mean he was ready to ask him to live together. And it didn't mean he never would. Just one step at a damned time. He hadn't even bought the place yet.

Lady's ears perked up and she headed toward the door, her tail madly waving. That could only mean one thing. Trask opened the door just as Felipe lifted his hand to knock. "I really need to give you a key, imp."

Shock flickered across Felipe's expressive face. His eyes glittered with tears, and his mouth was set in a mutinous, angry line. "What?"

Trask pulled him close and kissed the top of his head. "I may not be in the same place as you are, Felipe, but we are on the same journey. Stay with me. Please stay."

Felipe's arms came around him in a fierce hug. "You make me so mad sometimes, and then you turn around and say something like this and it's hard to stay mad. It's irritating."

Trask shut the door and held him closer. "I'm sure you'll remember."

Felipe lifted his head and gave Trask a challenging look. "I love you."

Trask brushed the back of his fingers across Felipe's cheek. "I know, I do too. I know it right here." He tapped his fist against his chest.

The smile that flitted across Felipe's face was the only answer Trask ever needed.

Chapter Thirty-Two

"IT IS Christmas Eve. What the fuck are we doing hanging out at a coffee shop?" Felipe demanded, staring out at the rain-drenched streets of DC. A warm front had come through, completely killing his hopes for a white Christmas. Not that it ever happened, but a man could dream. Now the view from the window completely suited his dour mood.

"Avoiding our families," Abby said with a sigh, stirring her tea with an equally moody expression. "Maybe if we elope, we'll have an excuse to not return for a while."

"That's a thought." Felipe folded his arms on the table and set his chin on them. This coffee shop was nothing like the one he'd been at for his first date with Trask, but the scents and sounds reminded him of the man with every whiff of roasted beans and clink of a spoon against glassware. It didn't help that thinking of his family twisted him with guilt and lingering anger. He'd never not been home for pre-Christmas festivities. They were probably all getting ready for church right now and would leave a spot in the pew empty just in case he decided to show. "Think any of them would buy it?"

"Dad would be too overcome with horror to even contemplate the likelihood of that." Abby gave him a sad smile. "The thought of his only daughter running off with a mixed-race son of immigrants, come on, you've met the man."

Yeah, Felipe had recognized him for being a condescending fuck even as a kid. He caught Abby's fingers and gave them a squeeze. "Don't rub this in my face, but I really don't miss squabbling with you."

Abby's smile brightened, and her dimples appeared for the first time that day. "You realize that if we'd figured this out in high school, we could've conquered the world?"

"I was too much of a little shit in high school to make nice, and you had your nose too far in the air." Felipe shrugged and drained the last of his latte.

"True. Does that mean you're going to stop calling me Duchess now?"

Felipe smiled and leaned across to kiss her forehead. "You'll always be Duchess to me. Tell your dad to stop trying to hook you up with his friends' sons. You deserve more than those daddy-boy snots."

Abby shook her head, resigned. "He isn't going to listen. He thinks he knows how I should live my life. Which is quitting this costume business, which is fine for a hobby, but if I continue it on the side, I should drop the cons because I'm better than that. Then I should go back to work for Albion Realty because business is booming in good old Chuck County. And Mr. Raley's son has followed him into banking and he's thinking of running for county commissioner in a few years and we could be the next power couple."

"He doesn't know you at all, does he?" Felipe asked softly. It made his own troubles seem piddly in comparison. His family might annoy him, and he might still be pissed at his lolo, but at least they understood him. They wanted to protect him. They didn't want to further their own ambitions at Felipe's expense. And they loved him, even his lolo.

"He never has." Abby's mouth turned down again.

It made Felipe appreciate his family even more. He knew that if he showed up, even after all the strain and worry these last couple of weeks, he'd be welcomed. Hell, Mariana would be just devastated if he didn't show, and the thought of the disappointment in her eyes had Felipe getting up from the table. "Come home with me. You know you're always welcome."

Abby hesitated, staring down at her mug of tea, and then she shook her head. "Thanks for the offer, but I think I'd be pretty terrible company over the holidays."

Felipe was a bastard for not realizing how desperately lonely she was all these years. "There's a pretty awesome guy in Richmond who's probably all alone tonight too. You should go be bosom buddies with him so I know you're both not alone."

Abby tipped her head back to smile at him, though tears shimmered in her eyes. "You'd better make up with him or I just might scoop him up."

Felipe made a sound of frustration. "He has made it clear that he doesn't want anything to do with my family for the holidays." Which Felipe couldn't blame him for. On the other hand, Trask probably had no idea how tight families could disagree and still manage to be together at times like this because that's what families did. They bitched at each other, then rallied around. "And he wants me to back off a bit."

And Felipe was trying to give him space, trying not to nag him into coming or press him for more of a commitment than Trask already had. He needed to remember who he was dealing with. Trask moved slow. He'd just admitted to loving Felipe, though he actually hadn't said the words. He had to hold on to that warm feeling.

"Just don't back off for too long." Abby squeezed his hand, then settled herself deeper among the cushions.

"I promise, but only if you make a promise in return." Felipe shrugged into his jacket and tried not to think about the rain outside instead of snow. "Come by later. If you don't want company, you can hang out with Lady until you do, but don't be at home alone, okay? I can't bear two of you being miserable."

"What am I going to do when you move to Richmond?" Abby asked with a shake of her head. "I would miss these weekly chats at the coffee shops. Online is cool. In person is better."

"That remains to be seen." Felipe scowled at the rain-lashed windows. Then an idea struck him. "Though if I did, you should come with me. The art scene is kickass, seriously underrated. I think we'd actually do better there than in DC. Besides, you'd be almost two hours away from your family. That would be a good buffer."

"I never really thought of that. It's not that I don't love them and they don't love me. It's just we want wildly different things, and at this point, separation might be the best thing. Maybe then we'd come to understand and appreciate each other." Abby nudged him away from the table. "Go make nice with your family. Then you'll feel a little better. When you feel a little better, you'll be up to going to stage a scene at Trask's and reminding him exactly why he loves you."

"Yeah…." Felipe didn't know what the hell to do about Trask Briscoe. It was like he was completely afraid to risk it all. He'd only engage his heart so far, and then it was all stop. And he didn't think doing a full-out assault and fighting for him would work this time. It would only drive Trask further away. So he was trying something different and entirely alien to his being and exercising a little patience. Trask wanted some space, a little time to think, so Felipe would give it to him… up to a point. There was only so much a man could take.

"Love you, Duchess. Merry Christmas." Felipe kissed the top of her head and slipped the little present he'd made for her into her bag.

"You and Morris, you're the best friends a guy could have. You always make me feel better."

"Love you too, Short Round." Abby's lips widened into a warm smile. "I'll be around tomorrow for dessert, okay? Merry Christmas."

Felipe ducked his head as he went outside and shoved his hands into his pockets, making his way rapidly toward the Metro stop on the corner. He hated to say it, but Trask might have been right. This separation had settled a few things in his mind. Living in his little apartment had been the right thing for him at the time. And he had loved it, but it was time to move on. Once school was over and he found a new job that wouldn't make him scream with boredom, he'd look for his own place.

He and his family had to come to appreciate each other as adults. And that was a little difficult when he was still living upstairs, separate, but still at their beck and call.

The Metro was crowded with last-minute shoppers, but the numbers dwindled as they crossed the Maryland border. He checked his watch as he raced to his car. Well, he'd completely miss Mass, but maybe he could get home, get the coffee going, and lay out the desserts that Lola had made for the after-church celebration.

He searched in his bag for his keys, and his fingers encountered a small, hard package. Felipe peeked in and grinned at the present wrapped in whimsical silver-gilt paper. He and Abby were too much alike. He'd wait, savor the anticipation, and open it tomorrow.

The traffic had died down, and Felipe made good time as he tore down the road. His family would linger after church a bit, greeting friends and exchanging good wishes. That would buy him a little more time. The house was dark except for their Narnia lamppost, and Felipe hid his car around the back of the house.

The thought of seeing their faces, the surprise and happiness, made him grin as he let himself in. Lolo looked up from where he sat at the kitchen table, his weathered face even more lined than Felipe remembered. He stopped cold, looking at the old man warily. "Why aren't you at church?"

Lolo's brows drew together in a familiar glower. "Why aren't you at church?"

Felipe threw up his hands and decided fuck it. This would give him the chance to say a few things to his grandfather before his family returned. He draped his jacket over the chair and went to start the coffee. "Because I wasn't done sulking. Now I am. You?"

Lolo sighed, clasping his hands together on the table. "The thought of them being upset got to you, huh? You always did have a big heart."

Felipe opened the cabinet door to pull down coffee cups and glanced at Lolo. "Maybe, a little. Dammit, it's Christmas. I can't be mad at them at Christmas."

"How about me?" Lolo watched him with rheumy eyes. "You still going to be mad at me?"

Felipe set the saucers on the counter with a little more force than was necessary. His dad had been trying to give Trask a chance to prove himself. His mom, well, she was his mom and would be overprotective, and there wasn't a damn thing he could do about it but show her that Trask made him happy. She'd come around. But the shit Lolo had pulled crossed a line. "You were rude, bordering on asshole, and I don't think you're sorry for it. So yeah I'm mad."

"I called it like I see it. You do the same, Felipe, only with more curse words." Lolo sighed and tapped the table with one long bony finger. "Sit down a moment. There are some things I need to say to you."

Felipe pressed his lips together. He didn't want to admit his grandfather had a point or consider that maybe he'd hurt the old man in return with his words. "I wanted to set up everything for when they came home."

"This won't take long, and I'll help you." Lolo regarded him steadily a moment. "Please, Felipe."

Reluctantly, Felipe pulled out the chair and sat down. He couldn't remember Lolo ever using that pleading tone with him. "I'm listening."

Lolo nodded, staring down at his hands, gnarled from long years making his living as a fisherman, first in the Philippines and then here on the waterways around the Chesapeake Bay. "I don't want you to think that I have any issues with you being gay, because I don't. We all knew you were different since you were a little boy. You were more comfortable with your lola's sewing basket than your dad's tool belt. You never walked when you could prance. You were unapologetically you, and I loved you for it, for the confidence you've always had in being yourself."

Felipe stared at his grandfather, at a complete loss for words. "I...." His throat tightened. "I never knew you felt that way."

"Well, that's on me. I should've told you. I should've told you that I'm proud of you more often. The thing is… this is a whole different generation. Your way of doing things is not our way of doing things. When I was a young man, you found a job and you stuck with it. And if there was something you wanted to do, like your costumes, you did it on the side, because providing a home and food for your family came first. I was completely against your mom going to nursing school, but we see how I lost that one. I have my opinions. They are bred into me, but you do have to live your own life. So do what you're going to do and I'll live with it. And you'll have to understand that the thought of you quitting a stable government job to flit off chasing a dream makes me twitch because I worry about you. And I'll probably make comments and they will be testy, but that doesn't come from dislike of you. It comes because I don't want to watch you go through hardship."

"Okay." Lolo had given Felipe a lot to process, and it made him look back at the years of contention between them differently. "Wow, I… I need to think this over."

Felipe got up and flipped on the Christmas tree lights before moving on to the other decorations. He couldn't think while sitting still. He had to do something. Lolo got up as well and laid out the coffee cups and desserts on the table. It seemed like all his life, Lolo had been the one he'd contended against. For Lola's attention and love, to get his own voice out. They'd butted against each other, two feisty bastards who wanted to be right every time.

"I'm sorry I cussed at you in public," Felipe said in a low voice. "I know you all are worried about me. But if you knew Trask the way I do, you'd understand. If you would just lay off the judgments for a bit. Have a few conversations with him, like real conversations. Granted, sometimes it takes him forever to warm up, but when he does, you'd see how smart and kind he is. Hell, he's probably out doing some do-gooder thing tonight instead of celebrating. If he hurts me, it won't be out of carelessness. It'll be because he's too cautious."

"The first time I saw your lola she struck me right here." Lolo tapped his fist against his chest. "I was delivering fish to the market. She was angry at one of the men at the stalls, complaining about the freshness of some of the fish he was selling. She was seventeen, Felipe, as pretty then as she is now, and never one to be taken for a fool. So I offered her some of my catch and asked her to walk with me later."

"She said yes and you went for your walk and fell in love?" Felipe asked, charmed by the romanticism of it.

Lolo chuckled and shook his head. "She was appalled I'd asked. Her father had money. I worked for every coin I had and found ways to make it stretch further. But the next time I saw her at the market, I gave her the same offer. My friends and family thought I was crazy to pursue her. Her friends encouraged her to keep me in my place, but I wore her down, and when I finally got that walk, I fell in love."

And it had lasted over fifty years. Felipe wanted that for himself. He wanted that with Trask.

"When your mama met your dad they were both young, fresh out of school, and your mama had already won the argument to go to college. He was visiting the Philippines on some building project for his church. I raised some fierce objections to her seeing him too. I knew he'd take her away from me because I'd seen that look in her eyes when she was with him. I see that same look in your eyes when you're with Trask. Our family, we fall hard and fast, and it sticks. So I'll try to keep an open mind about this. I don't want you pulling the same stunt that she did."

Felipe snickered as he rejoined his grandfather at the table. "Don't worry, Lolo. I won't move halfway across the world, just to Richmond." He pulled out his phone and quickly texted Trask. *If it makes you feel better, I made up w/ my family. Wish you were here tho.*

"I guess I can live with that alternative." Lolo smiled faintly, then cocked his head. "Do you hear that? Family's home."

Felipe looked toward the door, anticipation warming him. "You know, we're going to totally blow their minds when they see us sitting here like this."

Lolo shot him an impish grin. "It'll do them good. Complacency's the devil."

Felipe's phone pinged in return. *Wish I was with you too. Been busy. Joe's sick so I'm taking care of him. Working on a project is keeping me wrapped up. But I miss you, imp.*

Damn the man for making Felipe want more than Trask was ready to give right now, but he could be patient. He would be patient. Because Trask mattered, and Felipe was not going to give up without one hell of a knockdown fight.

Chapter Thirty-Three

TRASK CAREFULLY fitted the drawer onto the new runner he'd made and tested it out. The drawer slid smoothly into place, and Trask smiled in satisfaction. That hadn't been too bad of a job. The next step would be the cabinets. Then all he had to do was sand it down and apply the varnish and it would be done. He'd be able to give it to Felipe for the New Year.

He stood up, his knees aching from kneeling on the cold floor. Even though he'd laid a blanket down, he'd been at this for a while. Ryan's portable heater didn't do much more than take the bite out of the air.

Sophie scrambled to her feet, her tail already wagging as she barked. "I know, time to go out and let you run." Trask stuffed his work gloves into his pocket. "I need to stretch my legs too. Shh, girl, it's Christmas, we don't need to alert the whole neighborhood."

He opened the workshop door, and Sophie shot out to explore the fenced backyard from one end to the other. Trask shoved his hands in his pockets, his breath steaming the air. The rain that hit last night made the temperature drop to a raw, icy chill. He'd have to check in on Joe before he went home and make sure his walkways were resalted. He went by in the morning for a holiday hot chocolate and cleared the ice so his friend could get to the car safely. The last thing Joe needed was a broken hip. Not with winter just getting started and him getting over that bad cold.

Once the sun set, everything that had partially melted over the day would ice over again, and Trask doubted Joe would be leaving his grandkids until well after dinner. It made him wonder how Felipe was faring with those stairs of his. The thought of him racing down them the way he normally did was a little terrifying. He had faith that Donato had gone out first thing in the morning to take care of the outside.

He suspected he might have a lot in common with Felipe's father. The man had called to apologize after that fiasco of a dinner. The conversation had been short but appreciated. Then they had texted a few times as Donato followed the progress of Felipe's table and offered a few suggestions.

Trask whistled sharply as Sophie began to dig near the fence. "Sophie." He waited until he had her attention. "No. Come on, let's go for a walk before you get into trouble. No digging." Especially in someone else's backyard.

The deck door opened, and Trask stifled a groan as Ryan stepped out onto the landing. He didn't want his friend to feel obliged to invite him in. This was a special time for them. Ryan's gaze zeroed in on him, and though it had to be early afternoon, he was still dressed in pajamas and a robe. Sophie noticed him and ran over to greet her buddy. "Merry Christmas, Ryan."

"Merry Christmas. Come on in, have a cup of coffee." He crouched to greet Sophie. "Where's Felipe? You show him what you've been working on? I knew you wouldn't be able to make it until you were done."

"Felipe's at home with his family." Trask had been so relieved when he'd gotten that text last night. He'd stewed and worried over that situation and gone to another meeting to stop himself from all the agonizing over something he had no control over. He couldn't force Felipe to forgive his family. He couldn't make the family suddenly decide that the two of them were okay as a couple. The only thing he could control was his own reaction.

He hoped time would ease their fears because, despite Felipe's annoyance with him and Trask's desire to slow things down, he could really see the possibility of a future with Felipe. At least until Felipe decided that settling down with a guy twice his age with a quarter his charm was not what he wanted for himself.

The thought made Trask a little melancholy. It was bound to happen. He had to remember that or else the loss would cut even deeper. But he sure as hell would not be the guy who held Felipe back from flying.

"Why aren't you with him?" Ryan's gaze flicked to the workshop. "Meeting him later for dinner?"

Trask shook his head as he made his way toward the deck. "Nope. That's family time, and they're not too certain about me yet. His dad's coming around. His grandmother is laid-back. But his mom and grandfather are the sticking points. Felipe had some crazy idea about cramming me down their throats and making them choke on the idea, but I put my foot down about that."

Ryan studied Trask, and he hoped his friend wouldn't get all prickly and defensive on his behalf. "How'd the diva take that?"

"His outrage toward his family was probably heard all along the waterfront, and his anger toward me for suggesting a step back was almost as epic." Both incidents should've embarrassed Trask more than they had. He'd been too concerned with Felipe himself to fuss over the idea that anyone might've witnessed their words. By the time he looked back on the whole incident later on and thought of the spectators, the instinctive cringe wasn't as bad. He had too many other cares to worry about the opinions of strangers.

Ryan hesitated, indecision warring in his expression. "You know the idea of you and Felipe has grown on me. I've misjudged him. He busts his ass even when he doesn't have to. He doesn't make himself a nuisance at the cons or at the Den."

Ryan leaned against the railing and gestured with his coffee cup. "He's good for you, Trask. When he comes around…. It's like you come alive. I think you would've been perfectly content with your life if he hadn't attached himself to you, but now that he has, you're going to find a big void if you try to pull away. This guy's special to you."

"I don't think I'm the one who's going to pull away." Trask watched Sophie as she ran off to chase a squirrel that dared to show its head. She was another one he had thought he'd been content without, and then she was there and Trask's heart had filled to accept her. Just as another space in his heart had been completely filled with Felipe. Spaces and room he didn't know he'd had.

"I think you do him a disservice," Ryan said quietly, then straightened. "Now come on in, have a cup of coffee."

"Naw, I'm good. I don't want to intrude on your Christmas. I—" Trask shut up as Ryan shot him a hard glare.

"I swear on the Almighty that if you give me some bullshit excuse about holidays and family right now, I will sic Reva on you so hard you'll never recover." Ryan stabbed a finger in his direction and then turned it on his back door. "Last I checked you were family. Even looks like we'll be neighbors, so accept our Merry Christmas welcome and come in and have a damn cookie."

Trask smiled faintly and whistled for Sophie. "I don't dare refuse an invitation like that."

Hours later, Trask opened his apartment door juggling the food Joe's family had pressed on him when he went to check on his friend and the box of cookies from Reva. He'd never be able to finish it all, but at least he'd have a Christmas feast. It had been nice to be included, but it made it harder to come back to an empty apartment.

Sophie looked up at him with a little whimper, as if sensing his melancholy, and pressed her body against his leg. She was getting big, and the solid weight against him was comforting. "I'm okay, sweet girl." Trask rubbed the silky fur at her throat and leaned down to kiss the top of her head.

Felipe should be perched on the edge of his bed with a Santa hat curled rakishly over one ear. Trask would have to call him to hear his voice. He'd wait a little longer, just to be sure he wasn't interrupting Christmas dinner. He put some holiday music on and went over to the little tree he'd bought with Felipe. Poor thing's branches were weighed down by the tiny string of lights, but when Trask flipped them on, the splash of cheer made him smile.

He glanced down at Sophie and gestured to the little boxes waiting for them. "I think we should open our presents, don't you?"

Trask opened the box for Sophie first, taking his time because he couldn't remember the last time he'd had presents under a tree, even if it was a tiny thing. Sophie's tail began thumping the moment she saw the stuffed chicken. Trask pushed the open box over to her, and she didn't hesitate to seize her prize. The chicken let out a squeak of distress, and Sophie's tail whipped around in delight as she wrestled with her new toy.

Trask pulled out his phone, took a video of her rolling around, and sent it to Felipe. *She loves it. Poor thing will be in pieces before she's done.* He paused, staring at the phone after he hit Send. *I miss you.*

He picked up the other present, neatly wrapped in ridiculous reindeer paper. He could picture Felipe picking it out, searching for the perfect print that would make the recipient grin. The box underneath was plain, and taped to the top was a key ring with a steaming coffee mug charm and two notes tagged on. The first note was slipped through the key ring and read *for your new home.*

Trask ran his thumb over it. The papers had been signed. The house was his, the second most expensive gift he'd bought himself next to the Den. The crazy thing was, after all the legalities had been taken care of and he'd been left at the house with Sophie, he'd been seeing Felipe everywhere in that place. The room on the backside was made for a sewing room. It had windows on two sides overlooking the backyard and letting in plenty of light. It would hold Felipe's mannequins and new craft table without leaving him feeling crowded.

He could picture Felipe back in the living room, working on new project ideas or snuggled with Trask on the couch. The kitchen, the bedroom, even the room that Trask thought would make a good game room had Felipe's stamp. Trask heard his laughter and saw that wicked flash of his smile everywhere.

He'd been wrong. He hadn't bought that house just for himself or to give Sophie space to play in. He'd bought that place for both of them. So they'd have a home together. He'd even made sure there were plenty of trees.

The problem he always had with relationships was that he'd only let people so close and then put up a wall preventing them from getting any closer. Then the relationships just fizzled away. It was easier that way, safer. He didn't have to worry about losing anyone again, having his heart broken, and wondering if he'd have the strength to fight through it or if it would send him on another bender. It scared the hell out of him.

But Felipe had slipped under his guard. No matter how many times Trask told himself that this wasn't serious and Felipe would move on to someone far more interesting, he'd gotten engaged anyway. He sought Felipe out, created reasons for them to see each other, and didn't resist when Felipe came to him.

And now was hooked by a pair of laughing eyes. After all those years of dodging. At least he was pretty sure that's what this feeling was that seemed to be equal parts of terror and joy. The desire to see that Felipe was happy and to be a part of that happiness. He wanted Felipe with him, in that house, and it was crazy because it was such a permanent step. One he wasn't sure Felipe even wanted despite his upset when Trask had shut down his suggestion for moving in. It would mean leaving his family, and Felipe was big on his family even when he was pissed at them.

Trask rubbed his finger over the key ring and slipped it onto the chain with the rest of his keys. He'd put the house key right on it.

The other tag on the box read. *I told ya I'd get him.*

Mystified, Trask unwrapped the box to reveal an angel tree topper with a suggestive *O* of surprise on his lips and widened shocked eyes. Trask pressed his lips together, but that didn't stop the laughter that escaped. Trust Felipe to find the only angel tree topper in existence that looked like it was getting buggered. Trask laughed until his eyes watered, and Sophie crawled all over him, licking his face.

Trask picked up his phone, overcome with the need to hear Felipe's voice. He held his breath, and after several agonizing rings, Felipe picked up. "What? My Tin Man is uncreaking enough to call me? Did the ghosts of Christmas past, present, and future come pay you a visit and now you're on your way to my house to sing carols under my window and beg my forgiveness?" The teasing note in Felipe's voice cut out the bite of his words.

"You have me all emotional over a suggestive tree topper," Trask said with a rasp in his voice that he couldn't hide.

"Emotional is good. Gotta let it out sometime. Have you and Sophie been out all day?"

"Pretty much. Working on your present for a good portion of it. Got suckered into a late brunch with Ryan and Reva, then appetizers with Joe's grandkids. They'd all opted to go to his place at the last minute." Trask could hear the murmur of Felipe's family in the background. It sounded as if they had a full house. "I don't want to pull you away from your family. I just wanted to hear your voice and to say Merry Christmas."

"It's winding down. We just had our glass of spiked eggnog. The kiddos had hot chocolate. You know...." Felipe's voice took on a wheedling tone. "That angel tree topper isn't your real present. That was just for fun. When I saw it I had to get it. Your real present is here. And believe me, I agonized over the perfect gift."

In Trask's opinion, the real present was Felipe himself. "I have a present for you, too, but it's not done yet. So I'm afraid you're going to have to be patient for a little while longer." But he couldn't wait to see the expression on Felipe's face when he saw the table.

"If you want to give me a present, you could come over and keep the other side of the bed from getting so cold. It's Christmas. I don't want to be alone."

The suggestion tugged at Trask's own loneliness. He had friends he could be with, but it wasn't the same, not when he really wanted to be with Felipe. "Truce for tonight? We can talk about our future another time."

"If that's what it takes to get you here," Felipe replied, his frustration evident.

"No, Felipe, I'd come regardless. I want to be with you too." Trask closed his eyes, bringing up Felipe's image in his mind. "Just know that I'm not looking to screw with you. I'm serious about us, even if I ask for a slowdown. Hell, I'd even agree to coffee with your family if it'll make you happy." Though if Felipe took him up on that offer, he prayed it would be a quick cup.

"I think you can safely dodge that tonight. By the time you get here, I'll be done socializing and not want to share you." Felipe's voice took on a warmer, welcoming note. "Don't keep me waiting."

"I won't." Trask scooped up his keys with a lighter heart, and Sophie's ears perked up. With all the traveling he and Felipe did back and forth between their places, their dogs could probably lead them blindfolded. "See you soon."

Trask hung up the phone and carefully set the angel on the top of the tree, chuckling again. It was just terrible and perfect. And dammit, he loved the silly thing. "Come on, girl. Let's go celebrate Christmas."

Chapter Thirty-Four

FELIPE LISTENED hard for the sound of Trask's truck, ignoring the background chatter in the kitchen. He'd already managed to sneak out once to stash the good coffee upstairs, along with some vegetarian sides they could nibble on when they got hungry. His aunts were packing up leftovers to take home and gathering Felipe's cousins, and he figured it would be fairly safe to slip away soon without bringing too much attention to himself.

Mariana hugged him from behind, laying her chin on his shoulder. Felipe smiled and squeezed her hands. She'd been all over him ever since they returned from church last night, as if she couldn't believe he was there and staying. "Trying to anchor me in place?" Felipe asked, and she nodded.

"You're eyeing the door and watching for what Mom and Dad are doing, which means you're thinking of cutting out on Christmas early." Mariana's grip eased. "You've made yourself scarce for what seemed like forever. Come on, you can't leave now."

"It's almost 9:00 p.m. That's not ditching too soon." And they'd been up ridiculously early. Neither of them had broken the childhood habit of waking up at dawn on Christmas morning. They'd sat by the tree, trying to guess what was in the packages while waiting impatiently for everyone else to get up.

"No, but we could put on *Doctor Who* Christmas reruns." That had become almost a tradition with them. Mariana didn't enjoy the show on the regular, but she loved the specials. They rewatched their favorites over the week every year.

"We can do it tomorrow. Trask's coming over," Felipe said in a low, confiding voice. And maybe they'd have a chance for a long overdue conversation. Which was partially his fault, though he wouldn't take all the blame. Trask had offered to continue their argument when he'd come back to pick up Lady, but Felipe didn't much see the point when he'd doubted he would get Trask to change his mind. It had just been easier to screw and hold each other instead. And Felipe had slipped away the next morning before he said something he regretted or pushed Trask into doing the same.

The last few weeks had given them both time to think… and to sulk if Felipe was being honest. However, it also gave him the chance to look at it from Trask's point of view. Slowing down didn't mean stopping. Hell, in Trask speak that meant *hey this is important to me*, so he wanted to be sure he was doing it right. Patience wasn't Felipe's strongest skill, but he'd try for Trask. The man was certainly giving him plenty of practice with patience, and the funny thing was, he found that it was working out in other areas of his life. Like with his lolo.

"Oh." Mariana was quiet a moment, and then she gave him another squeeze. "That's good. I like him."

Felipe rolled his eyes and turned to look at her. "You met him for five minutes."

"So?" Mariana shrugged.

"That didn't give you any time to form an opinion," Felipe said with exasperation. Her blind loyalty wouldn't help him to win over their parents.

"I saw Sophie and how happy and healthy she is. And I can see you. Even when you're mad at him, you go all sappy-eyed when he texts or calls. Last guy you were mad at disappeared and we never heard about him again."

"You make it sound like I ninja assassinated him." Don't get him wrong, Felipe had considered that a couple of times, and now he wondered how he'd let Dakota and Brenden tie him up in such knots. His feelings for Dakota were nothing like his feelings for Trask. He eyeballed Mariana. Maybe she wasn't so blind after all. He tensed as he heard the faint rumble of a truck. "Gotta go."

"I'll run interference for you. Not that I think it's necessary. Everybody's occupied with goodbyes." Mariana let go of him and went straight for their mom.

Felipe caught Lola's eye and blew her a kiss as he grabbed his coat. He slipped out the door before anyone could comment and shivered in the chill that had descended when the sun set. It was going to be another balls cold one in good old Southern Maryland. Felipe made his way over to the sound of Sophie's barking, keeping an eye out for any ice slicks that might've formed. Then he forgot all about them as Trask came around the corner with Sophie trotting at his side.

Felipe took off running with a war whoop, and Trask halted in his tracks, his eyes widening. His duffel bag fell to the ground as he caught Felipe when he leaped and held him close. Felipe buried his face against Trask's neck with a happy sigh. Now it felt like Christmas. Everything he needed was right here. "Promise me you'll give me a welcome like that every night?" Trask asked with a laugh in his voice.

"Even when I'm irritated with you." Felipe pulled back and landed a smacking kiss on Trask's mouth. He grabbed Trask's hand and tugged him toward the outside steps. "Come on, we have some talking to do. I promise, nothing too crazy. There's just a few things I need to say."

"I suppose I ought to get used to you being ready to talk when you're ready and not before. At least you do eventually talk. Seems like I'm the one digging in my heels this time." Trask shook his head and reached down to scoop up his bag as he looked around for Sophie. "I think she went through the dog door to your parents' house."

Felipe glanced over his shoulder at the chaos in the kitchen. Sophie was jumping on Mariana, who greeted her enthusiastically. "She's in good hands. My sister will be overjoyed to play with her a bit. She was always kind of hoping she'd be able to convince Mom and Dad to let her stay. If she wasn't leaving for college next year, she would've probably won."

Now everyone knew Trask was there, well, at least they wouldn't question Felipe's disappearance. He probably ought to prepare him for the idea of possibly being invited to breakfast. He knew Trask didn't want to feel like he was intruding, but Felipe knew his parents. They'd extend the invite if Trask was still there in the morning. Especially after the last fiasco. They all wanted a chance to start over and try meeting Trask with an open mind.

Felipe quickly led Trask up the stairs before they decided to invite him in for coffee. He shut the door, suddenly nervous. He'd rehearsed all the things he wanted to say while he waited for Trask to arrive, and now that he was here, for once in his life he found that he couldn't talk. Somewhere, on another plane of existence, Morris was laughing his ass off. He'd encouraged Felipe to open up his heart to Trask weeks ago, and if he had then, and not stopped halfway, he might not be here now. Trask had distracted him with awesome gaming table sex that still made his toes curl in memory.

Felipe turned away from Trask, staring at the scraps of leather and the hot glue gun he'd left on his table from his latest project. He really needed to pick up this mess. He heard Trask move behind him, felt his strong hands gently grasp his shoulders. Felipe blinked back the stinging in his eyes.

He looked over his shoulder at Trask. "I don't want to argue, please. I don't want you telling me that you just want something casual. Because if that's the case, I just can't do that again." Felipe bit his lip before he went any further. He hadn't meant for all that to spill out. Not until he knew where Trask stood.

"I'm sorry, Felipe. I was wrong to push back, to distance myself the way I did. I don't know why I do that. I want to be with you, not hold you back at arm's length." Trask gently turned Felipe around, his gaze open and sincere, and Felipe felt the tension gripping his insides ease. "I never regretted pushing somebody back, never really missed them when they're gone. But you're entirely different. I miss you when you're in the next room. I was afraid. I don't want to hurt anyone else like I have in my past. I don't want to be hurt."

Felipe continued to worry his lip as he thought about what Trask said and meant with those words. Because with him, there was always so much more beneath the surface. "The guy you were back then, the guy who hurt people, hurt himself, he was careless. You're not him anymore. You're the opposite and maybe a bit too cautious, afraid to risk yourself, afraid to risk others, so you just stay in your bubble. And sometimes that can have the same result."

Trask drew him closer, wrapping his arms around Felipe. He closed his eyes, laying his head on Trask's shoulder, listening to the rumble of his voice. "I think you have a pretty good gauge on me."

"I love you," Felipe blurted out. "And I want a forever future with you."

Trask pulled back and stared at Felipe in bafflement. "Why? I'm not exactly lovable. I'm not into grand romantic gestures. And I find it difficult to say what's in my heart. I'm definitely not a brilliant conversationalist. I'm never going to be one who gets all gushy and talky feely. Can you really see yourself being with someone like that forever?"

Well, that wasn't the reaction Felipe expected or feared. At least Trask wasn't running screaming, but how he could not understand how much he had to offer, Felipe didn't know.

"You put up with me, my dramatic scenes, my moods, my mouth—"

Now Trask looked offended as he gave Felipe a gentle shake. "There's no need to put up with you. That's bullshit. You're not someone to be endured. And if anyone ever made you feel like that, they're an idiot," Trask said fiercely. "I'm a moody bastard. At least your moods are easy to recognize from across a room. And your mouth is just fine. You say exactly what you mean. Maybe the language is a bit out there, but you make me laugh, you make me comfortable. Hell, Felipe, I'm content when I'm with you. I'm happy."

Trask let go of him and took off his cap, twisting it in his hands as Felipe stared at him in stunned disbelief. For Trask that was tantamount to shouting from the rooftops how much he cared about him, and damn if that didn't make him want to grin. Felipe stuck out his chin, gathering all the hurt and confusion of the last few weeks and banishing it. Trask looked so befuddled, so anxious, and Felipe realized he'd never seen him so raw without that calm and cool façade he hid behind. Time to tell him just how he lit up Felipe's life too.

"You bring me coffee in the morning before I've had a chance to get up and complain. You send me pictures of Sophie when I'm stuck in my cell at work because you know they will make me smile. You listen to my rambles, not just tune into them all half-assed. You hold me at night like I'm a dream you're afraid you're going to wake up from. You even tried to shield me from a split with my family, misguided or not. That's why I love you, because you love me and you tell me in one hundred ways every day. Just not with words, but I hear you anyway."

"I—" Trask broke off, almost twisting that worn cap into pieces. "Well hell, Felipe." The panic in his eyes would've worried Felipe if he wasn't reaching for him at the same time.

"What's got you so tied up, Tin Man?" Felipe whispered, sliding his arms around Trask as he was held tight. "The fact that I love you or you love me?"

"Both," Trask admitted. "I've never let myself feel this way. And I couldn't imagine anybody feeling that much for me either, beyond friendship I mean. It took me a while to accept that."

He fell silent, and Felipe made himself be still, recognizing that Trask needed that as much as Felipe needed the chatter and movement. It was nice to be held with such tenderness. Giving his love through touch and actions over words.

"I'm sorry I stormed off like that."

"You came back." Trask held him tighter. "And I'm pretending it's because of me, not because Lady was there."

"It was a little of both," Felipe admitted.

"As much as we say we want to talk things through sometimes, both of us do better when we give ourselves time to cool off and think it over." Trask rubbed his hand up and down Felipe's back in that loving way of his that just made Felipe gooey. "Otherwise we just argue in circles and our emotions get in the way. We both needed time to process in our respective corners. The problem is, our respective corners are far away."

"I don't want them to be." Felipe hated how forlorn he sounded, like a damn lost puppy.

"Me neither." Trask traced his finger down Felipe's cheek. "I think by the time that little house is all fixed up and ready to be lived in, I'll have gotten used to the idea that I'm not alone anymore."

Felipe couldn't help the smile of pure glee. "Are you asking me to live with you, Trask Briscoe?"

"I guess I am in a roundabout way." Trask smiled back. "I've been wondering what you'd do with the place if you had your chance to get your hands on it. About the only thing I've been able to think of is expanding the deck when we redo it and maybe turning that back room with all the sun into a project space for you."

"I have a few ideas," Felipe admitted, completely charmed that Trask had planned out space for him already. He adored Trask to bits, but the man was a minimalist, and with a little attention to detail, that house would be a place where both of them could come that would feel like home. "Nothing too outrageous."

Trask laughed and pulled him into another hug. "I'm not sure I entirely believe that, but after the New Year, what do you say we meet with the contractor of your choosing and start going over some plans?"

If Felipe got any happier, he'd spontaneously combust. He had his Tin Man, and he was never going to let the man go. And he would make damn sure that he never regretted giving Felipe his heart.

"Sounds perfect." Felipe scraped a hand through Trask's hair and brushed his lips over Trask's. "I love you. Merry Christmas."

"Me too, imp. Me too. I love you, I mean." Trask shook his head with a look of exasperation. "Take it as I mean it and not how awkward I damn well sound. It's not a state I thought I'd ever find myself in." Trask held up his hand as Felipe's mouth opened. "Now just wait and hear me out, okay? I don't have as much practice talking as you do, and I want to get this right."

Felipe cocked his head, a soft smile on his lips. "Okay, I'm listening."

Trask hooked his thumbs into his pockets, a nervous look coming back to his gaze. As if he was afraid this was going to come out all wrong. Trask didn't realize how much he said, how much he showed. The words weren't always necessary.

Trask cleared his throat. "If having someone else's happiness be as important to you as breathing… if being with them, even when you're irked with them, makes your day better than being without them. If seeing them smile just lights you up inside and makes all the dark places warm… then yeah, I love you, Felipe."

Felipe slid his arms around Trask's neck. "You got it right."

Relief lightened Trask's expression. "Well then, let's celebrate our Christmas now that we're together."

Felipe grabbed Trask's hand and pulled him toward the bedroom. "Now, I think I promised you presents, but that's going to have to wait. Because if I don't have you naked in the next five minutes, I'm going to stage an epic scene."

Trask swatted his ass with a laugh. "At least you give a guy some warning."

Chapter Thirty-Five

TRASK PULLED up at the back of Felipe's place with a sense of growing excitement and more than a few nerves. The deed was already done, and Donato was waiting for him, so there was no damn sense in being nervous about it. Things had been pretty chill since Christmas. He and Felipe had found a new balance. A part of him still couldn't believe the imp loved him. But maybe Felipe didn't need somebody like himself who was able to discuss all that stuff that made Trask squirm inside. Felipe must be crazy for loving him… but crazy seemed to suit him, and frankly, Trask didn't want him any other way.

The back door opened and both of Felipe's parents emerged. Trask blew out his breath and unhooked Sophie's harness. "Time to do this, baby girl." If Felipe and he were serious about moving in together in the spring, then he had to get used to being around Felipe's family, and they needed to get to know him.

"Morning, Trask," Donato greeted as Trask climbed out of the truck and held the door open for Sophie to jump down.

Trask touched the front of his cap. "Thanks for agreeing to help with this. I'd never get Felipe's present up the stairs by myself. Morning, Miz Suero."

"I must admit, you have my curiosity bitten." Mrs. Suero stopped by the truck bed and peered inside. "Donato hasn't given me a clue, and Mariana got Felipe out of the house by nagging him into some clothes shopping at the mall."

Trask smiled as he clambered into the truck to unhook the belts around the table. "I'm sure it didn't take all that much arm twisting."

"Nah." Mrs. Suero tucked her hands into her back pockets. "I need to apologize for that scene at dinner. That wasn't what I intended when I asked for Lolo to come with us. And for my own part in it."

"I have to add mine as well." Donato approached the tail of the truck. "I know I said it over the phone, but I'd like to say it again in person."

"I'm sorry, too, for walking out like I did." Trask made sure the blanket was still secure around the table as he considered the rest of his reply. "But I think Felipe's the one who was owed the apology from his grandfather, and I gather from what he said that they came to an understanding."

"A long overdue one," Donato said with a faint smile as he helped lift the table out of the truck. "Once we set this up, why don't you come downstairs for a cup of coffee while we wait for the others to get home?"

Trask clamped down on the trickle of unease. He would never get comfortable with them if he hid every time they reached out a hand. Bad enough that he'd missed the post-Christmas breakfast invite. He'd been out the door at dawn so he'd be at the Den when the doors opened. The day after the holiday was usually a busy one as people came in to redeem gift certificates or Christmas money. "I like coffee."

"So Felipe tells me." Mrs. Suero watched them maneuver the table. "I'll go put a pot on while you get settled. Then I'm coming up to look."

"He also mentioned that you bought the house and asked him to move in with you," Donato said as soon as she disappeared. His tone was so even that Trask had no clue how he felt about that new development in their relationship.

Trask cast a quick, cautious glance in Donato's direction, then concentrated on moving backward up the stairs. "I did. If he isn't tired of me by the time we've completed necessary repairs. We're looking at late spring, probably."

"You don't think less than a year is rushing things?" Donato's weather-beaten face was set, but Trask wasn't sure if it was because of the conversation or the task at hand.

"To be honest, for me, anything under five years is probably rushing in," Trask said with a wry smile as they set the table down in front of Felipe's door. "Your son has an unnatural influence on me, pushing me out of my comfort zone. I often wait too long, biding my time, and then I lose out. I don't want to lose out with him."

And that was saying a hell of a lot more than Trask intended to say. He propped open the screen door with a plant container and opened the main door to see Lady sitting and waiting. Sophie wiggled her way around him and made a beeline for Lady's toys.

He pointed toward the corner where he'd envisioned Felipe's table. There were a few of his plastic tubs in the space, but they could shift them out of the way, and once his rickety craft table was gone it would actually appear more spacious. "I was thinking of putting it right there."

"Well, let's see what we're dealing with." Donato eased the cover off the table and let out a low whistle. "Felipe will lose his mind when he sees this."

Trask smiled and ran his hand over the finished top, the newly varnished wood glowing in warm tones. "It was pretty beat up when I found it, but it came together beautifully. It had too much potential to leave it behind. I have the drawers and cabinet doors individually wrapped in the truck." He wanted it completely set up before Felipe came home so he'd get the full effect.

"You do a good, patient job. The pictures didn't do this justice." There was a warmer gleam in Donato's eyes when he looked at Trask. "Did Felipe know you had something in the works for him?"

"He did." Trask began moving the tubs of supplies. "He's been hounding me to let him take a peek. But I didn't want to rush it."

Donato clapped him on the shoulder and helped him shift Felipe's supplies. When they set the table in the corner, it gave Trask a sense of satisfaction. It fit just as he pictured it would. Working together they grabbed drawers, and Trask fitted the glass paneled doors on the hinges. He hoped his imp didn't linger at the mall.

Mrs. Suero came into the apartment and let out a low sound of appreciation. "Oh, Felipe's going to want to get to work immediately." She shot Trask a smile that was pure Felipe. "I love reclaimed furniture. Seems a shame to me to throw something away that can be reused if given a little attention."

"Only you expect me to give it that little attention," Donato said with a fond glance.

"Just as you expect me to attend to all your splinters and other war wounds." Mrs. Suero studied the table a little longer with her hands on her hips, and then she gave it a satisfied nod. "Come on, let's go have that cup of coffee. I think there might even be some biko leftover, too, if Mariana hasn't gotten into it."

Trask thought he'd heard Felipe mention that dish a few times with a gleam of appreciation in his eyes. He glanced around, saw Sophie wrestling playfully with a hank of rope, and whistled to her. "Sophie, let's go."

The scent of brewing coffee greeted them as they came downstairs. The Sueros puttered around in the kitchen, going through cabinets and rifling around in the fridge. Trask looped his thumbs through his jeans and studied the pictures on the walls. Generations of family decorated the place, mostly in casual shots that Trask believed always revealed more about their subjects than the formal portraits did.

"That one was always a favorite of mine," Donato said from over his shoulder, pointing to a snapshot of two dark-haired, dark-eyed women laughing as one bounced a toddler on her knee and the other wrangled a young boy. Trask would know those laughing eyes anywhere. "The lady snagging Felipe is his lola. The other is *mi madre* holding Mariana."

"It's a sweet photo. Felipe always talks about the both of them with a great deal of love." Trask turned around and accepted the mug of coffee Donato handed him. On the table was a little plate piled with what looked like sticky rice cakes. "Thank you. Those look delicious, Miz Suero."

"Call me Ratree, and I can't claim any credit for them. My mother does most of the cooking around here." Felipe's mom fussed with the napkins, betraying the nerves that Trask also felt.

Donato waited until they were seated and each had a serving of the cake before he spoke again. "Felipe's different. He's always been different, and I've always worried that he wouldn't find someone who appreciated that about him. I haven't had much of a chance to see you two together, but what I have seen and heard, you do seem to value his creativity and feelings."

Trask laced his fingers together and contemplated Donato. The judgmental expression, the tightening around his eyes that Trask had seen before, was no longer there. Even Ratree seemed to have softened some, though she continued to worry her lip. "I don't think you have to be concerned about Felipe settling for the wrong partner. It's just not in him. He's an all or nothing kind of guy. If we hadn't worked together, he'd have left me ages ago and never looked back."

"He's a romantic dreamer." A worried frown puckered Ratree's brow. "He's had this wish for settling down for years now. He's tried to not let it show, but Felipe can't hide much."

Trask smiled in appreciation for that comment. Felipe certainly didn't keep much in. He took a bite of the biko and savored the sweetness as he considered his words. "He's a romantic dreamer to an extent. He has his dreams and isn't afraid to work toward them, but he's pragmatic enough to realize when something isn't working and cut his losses."

It was an intriguing mix. One that Trask didn't see often. People could probably say the same about him. He'd always wanted that storefront, a place for geeks to be geeks with no apology. He'd rolled with the changes as they came, though, not sticking to one way because it differed slightly from his original vision, and because of that the Den had evolved to what it was today, and it was thriving.

"Have you two addressed the age difference?" Donato asked and bit into his own biko with an appreciative gleam in his eyes.

"Not so much." Trask stroked his fingers through his beard. "I had a few qualms when he started flirting. But he's an adult, and he sure as heck makes his own decisions. I for one cannot fathom why he set his sights on me, but he did. At this point, the age difference isn't really all that profound."

Forty years down the road, that was a different story, and there were times when Trask was nagged with guilt over it, but he knew exactly what Felipe's opinion of that would be. "The truth is, I don't think either of us expected to develop any real feelings beyond friendship and companionship, but we did. I can't in good conscience pull back and hurt him because I worry about what the future might bring. I tried that when I wanted him to focus on his relationship with y'all, and that didn't go too well."

"Yeah, he's never been one to be told what to do." Donato grimaced. "It's why we butted heads so often when he worked for me."

"To be honest, if I'd suspected we'd be headed down this road when I asked him out for coffee, I'd have held my peace." Trask stared down at his coffee and thought about everything he would've missed out on. "And I'd've been wrong. So I guess it's a blessing we cannot see our own futures."

Donato nodded and studied Trask a moment. "I get the feeling you and I are going to understand each other well."

Trask smiled slowly with a sense of satisfaction and relief. "Yes, sir. I think we will."

"It's a mother's job to worry," Ratree cut in. "And I'd worry no matter who Felipe ended up with, or what job he takes, or where he lives. But as he reminded me, not giving you a chance is exacerbating the issue. So I'm late to the party, but I'm willing to give this a chance because Felipe loves you. I can see that."

The tension that Trask had been carrying around since he arrived eased. "And you all are a reminder that not every family is bad. Sometimes I forget that. I like knowing that Felipe has y'all to fall back on."

They talked for the next hour as Donato and Ratree drew Trask's life story out of him by sharing tidbits of their own pasts. Trask sensed that Felipe's father was another soul who found it difficult to share, and he appreciated the effort and relaxed even more. Then Felipe's grandfather joined them and Trask was immediately wary. But his concerns over Felipe coming home to him being grilled were unfounded. It was like the scene at the restaurant never happened, other than a gruff apology.

It was amusing to see Felipe in the old man's tart observations. Trask's phone dinged, and he glanced at the incoming message. *What do you say about an overnight? I can be in Richmond in a couple hours.*

How about your place instead?

Trask grinned at Donato. "I expect Felipe will be home right quick now."

Lolo snorted and rose to pour them all more coffee. "Driving like the Ghost Rider most likely."

"Not with Mariana and Lola in the car or one of his dogs," Donato cut in. "He has more care for others than himself."

"You like comics?" Trask asked, and Lolo turned toward him with a gleam of appreciation.

"I love Ghost Rider and the Punisher the most. Helped to improve my English. I devoured every one when I came to the States." Lolo returned to the table with a reminiscent look. "When Felipe started showing an interest in comic books, I'd let him read them when he came over. His mama threw a fit."

"Not exactly the kind of reading material we wanted him to have at that age," Ratree added drily.

You sure?

Trask wished he were with Felipe so he could see the expression on his imp's face. *Seeing as I'm already here, drinking coffee with your grandfather and parents, yeah I'm sure.*

Not long after that, Trask spied Lady getting to her feet to trot out the door, and Sophie scrambled after her, barking in excitement. "I think that means Felipe received my message."

Donato waved him on with a smile. "Go reassure my son that you've survived coffee alone with us. I suspect we'll see him soon enough."

"He'll make it a point to glance in and glare threateningly at least once," Lolo added.

Trask emerged as Mariana and Felipe came around the house arguing heatedly, with Lola bringing up the rear. Felipe's face was drawn in concern, but his expression lightened when he saw Trask. "Are you okay?" he demanded.

Mariana rolled her eyes. "You didn't need to hound me to drive faster just because he was here. Hey, Trask."

"Mariana, Miz Madel." Trask nodded to them both as he smiled at Felipe. "I'm fine, imp."

"What are you up to?" Felipe stopped in front of him, hands on his hips. "Why are you here having coffee with that cranky crew?"

"Well, technically, I'm a cranky old man too," Trask teased, just to watch Felipe's eyes flash in warning. "Do I have to be up to something?"

"Yes. You drove all the way here without telling me. You had a reason. Was it to make nice with Dad when I wasn't here? So I couldn't tell him and Lolo to knock it off if they were stepping over the line?" True to Lolo's prediction, Felipe opened the kitchen door to give the occupants of the table a hard look.

Miz Madel patted his shoulder as she passed, her eyes twinkling merrily. "Happy New Year, Trask. I'm happy to see you again."

Trask grinned at her. It was impossible to not respond to Felipe's grandmother. "Same here, Miz Madel."

Felipe turned toward him with a narrow-eyed glare as Mariana watched with interest, and Trask held up his hand before he could jump to conclusions. "Let's address your first concern. I'm fine. Your parents and grandfather are fine. We had a very cordial conversation, and I think we understand each other a little better now. I already know your sister and grandmother are on our side, so I guess we may be in the clear."

"You think you've got it bad," Mariana scoffed. "Try being the baby and a girl."

"Your second concern," Trask cut in as Felipe turned his baleful eyes on his sister. "I'm here without you because I wanted to surprise you with your present, and I contacted your dad because I needed his help with it." Trask watched Felipe's conflicted emotions with amusement. The imp didn't know which way to jump first. "Now before you rocket off with your one thousand questions, why don't we pop upstairs and take a look at what I've been working on."

Excitement won and Felipe grabbed Trask's hand. "Have you been practicing that argument?"

"I just hoped once I mentioned your present your curiosity would outweigh your need to hound me for details," Trask admitted as he followed Felipe's dash upstairs.

Felipe flipped him off but didn't stop his forward momentum to argue. It was immensely gratifying to see his excitement. He threw open the door, and his squeal could be he heard downstairs. "Where the hell did you find that?" He threw Trask a brilliant smile and bounded into his apartment. "IKEA?"

Before Trask could answer that insult Felipe was kneeling before the table, running his hands over it as he crooned. "Oh no. This baby has seen things. It's been around awhile. I love it. I'm going to call it Clarence."

Trask watched in bemusement, amazed at Felipe's endless capacity to surprise him. "You're naming your table?"

"Of course I am. Doesn't everybody?" Felipe laid his cheek on the surface before exploring every drawer and cabinet, exclaiming over each one like it was a new treasure.

Trask leaned against the doorjamb, unable to take his eyes off Felipe as warmth suffused him and his heart ached with tenderness. He'd had many moments of gratification inside the NA rooms, moments when the time and care he'd put into another had yielded long-lasting friendships that sustained each other. Felipe was the first person who gave him the same feeling outside those small circles.

"I'm glad you like it." It made every hour he'd poured into the project worth it. He suspected that was how Felipe felt when he delivered a costume commission. Though it was so much better when it was a loved one whose eyes lit up like that.

Felipe whirled around and pounced on him. "I do. I love it. I'm sorry I didn't say that right away."

"You don't need to." Trask brushed his lips over Felipe's. "Most of the time with you, there's no guessing."

"It's perfect." Felipe spun back around to run his hands all over the table again. "I can't wait to send Abby pictures. She's going to be so jealous."

Trask waited until Felipe had gone through every nook again and cleared his throat. Felipe glanced at him with questioning eyes. "I was wondering, my anniversary meeting is coming up." He shoved his hands into his pockets, trying to quell the sudden nerves. "I'd like for you to come to it."

Felipe frowned. "I thought NA meetings were for insiders only. Wouldn't I get you into trouble if I went?"

Trask shook his head. "Anniversary meetings are a bit different. It's a celebration, and if we have any family or close friends who support us, they're invited. Hell, half of Joe's grandkids showed up for his last one."

He'd never had anyone outside of the program who he'd been close enough to that he wanted to come. And the people from the program that he was closest to would be there, no questions asked. "I'd really like for you to be there."

Felipe's eyes softened. "Then I'll be there."

"I'm going to ask Ryan to speak." Trask smiled gently. "Since he gave me my most recent come-to-Jesus moment. I think he'd be pretty damn pleased to see you there too."

Felipe laughed and shook his head. "So it looks like the both of us have conquered our respective dragons. Ryan was breathing fire over you about as much as my family was breathing fire over me."

Felipe gave Trask the craziest mental images, and he wouldn't want it any other way. He caught Felipe's hand and gave it a squeeze. "I guess there's nothing standing in the way anymore. Now it's just you and me."

"And two crazy dogs." Felipe slipped his arms around Trask's neck. "Happy New Year, Tin Man. I get the feeling this year is going to be even better than the last, and the last one rocked."

Epilogue

TRASK RESISTED the urge to scratch at the healing tattoo on his side. He was only reacting out of nerves and what the new tattoo represented. Felipe was charmed by the little image, but then again he would be since it was for him, a catlike imp with a steaming cup of coffee. He'd wanted to gauge how Felipe reacted to that little bit of permanency before he moved on to the next step. He should've known Felipe would be delighted. Trask was the only one who felt like he needed to take things in slow steps.

At least that's how he'd lived for the last fifteen years. Slowing down until he was crawling along. Felipe had made him speed up some, but after this decision, well, he was really jumping into the future.

He had to remind himself that the more they worked on their house, the more this felt like the right step. Just natural. Despite his concern when he'd broached the topic to Felipe's family, they'd been delighted instead of worried. Funny what a couple of months could do.

"What the hell am I thinking?" Trask touched the lump in his pocket with a spurt of panic as he peered through the black curtain separating the con from the panel rooms. He did not profess his undying love in front of a group of people. He most certainly did not let it be known to Felipe's friends that he planned to do so. They filled the small room near to bursting. Who the hell knew Felipe had so many damned friends? "This is not the way to go about this. It should be private, quiet."

Like at their home, though it was anything but private and quiet with workmen trotting in and out all day following the well-laid plans of Reva and Donato's friends. Yeah, at least here there were plenty of people rooting for them.

Ryan gave him a nudge of commiseration. "It would not stop the panic, believe me. And when he's looking at you, you're going to stop feeling that panic. You won't even be aware of the rest of us. Besides, you can't back down. I won't let you. He took down Deadpool. If you don't ask him to marry you, I'm booting you out of the Den and making him our official mascot."

Both the thought of Felipe out-sassing Deadpool and Ryan sticking up for him had Trask smiling. "I've been telling Felipe for months that I'm not into grand gestures, and he's okay with that," Trask grumbled a little more. "Why did I decide that I needed to do a grand gesture for this?"

Ryan squeezed his shoulder. "Because you love the diva, and you know that by doing it this way, he'll know without a doubt you mean it, because you sure as hell never would if you didn't."

Ryan had a damned point. Besides, Trask had been dreaming of this surprise and the look on Felipe's face ever since he'd bought the ring. It wasn't easy to get one over on his imp, and he knew Felipe was clueless about what was about to happen because if he'd picked up on it, he would've hounded Trask until he spilled.

Trask eyed Felipe's animated face as he answered some cosplaying question that Trask hadn't even heard. He shoved his hands into his pockets to hide the trembling. He'd bared his soul in NA rooms with memories that still had him squirming in shame sometimes. He could bare his soul here with a lot more joy if he'd just stop overthinking it.

"Any other questions?" Abby asked with a pointed look toward the curtain at the back.

Trask wouldn't let it be said that he punked out on one of the more important moments in his life. Not this time. Not when it came to Felipe. "Actually, I have a question for Felipe, if that's okay." He slipped through the curtain and walked halfway up the aisle. As he did, the people thronging the room, the strangers and friends, ceased to matter as Felipe turned his gaze on him.

His eyes brightened, and a grin curved that generous mouth of his. "Trask, are you looking to do the Tin Man thing for real?" His expression took on a wicked note that Trask knew all too well. "I give private lessons."

Abby elbowed him in the side with a hiss as Brenden let out an exasperated sound. "Family show, Suero."

Felipe rolled his eyes and then narrowed them as Trask continued toward him until he had come around the front of the table and paused by Felipe's chair. He glanced around the room, then looked back at Trask. "Okay, what gives?"

"I had a couple things I wanted to say now that we have our little house, even if we're living in the middle of a mess as we fix it up. There's no one else I want to live in the middle of a mess with than you." Trask thought he might never be entirely comfortable with talking about his feelings, but Felipe made it easier than most. "Back when you set your sights on me, you gave me a glimpse of a future that I didn't know I wanted, and then it became something I needed."

"Trask Briscoe, you are messing with my head." Felipe fisted his hands over his heart, and the look in his eyes just filled Trask up with the light that Felipe gave him. "Don't joke with me."

Trask smiled at him and reached into his pocket, closing his fingers around the little box. "That future showed me waking up next to you. It showed me the imp in your smile and your attention to detail whether you're making a costume or a home. It showed me you chattering at me nonstop."

"Wow, that's serious love," Morris said, making the room chuckle.

Felipe flipped him off without ever taking his eyes off Trask as he went down on one knee and held out the little box. "I want you to be my partner, my best friend, my other half."

"Shut the fuck up," Felipe whispered, tears welling in his eyes. "Stop screwing around."

Trask grabbed his hands and folded them to his heart. He'd never seen Felipe so off-balance. If this was what grand public gestures did to his imp, Trask would have to make the effort to do it every once in a while. "Felipe, you know me. You know I don't mess around when I'm serious." He smiled faintly. "I have a rule, you know."

Felipe nodded, his throat working before he finally managed, "Yeah, I know your rules."

"Will you marry me, Felipe Suero?" To Trask's everlasting panic, the tears spilled from Felipe's eyes. "Don't cry. For the love of God, don't cry. I'll take it back if it'll make you feel better."

"You can't take it back. I'll brain you." Felipe grinned through his tears and flung his arms around Trask's neck. "I can't believe you made a public spectacle of yourself for me. I love you more than puppies."

Trask laughed and got up, pulling Felipe into his arms. "Is that a yes?"

Felipe opened the little box and slipped the ring on his finger. "That's a fuck yes, Tin Man."

MARGUERITE LABBE has often been called both Trouble and Sunshine by those who know her. She's not sure how she manages to make both those nicknames work together, but apparently she does. She's a New Hampshire gal who married an Alabama guy, an Air Force brat who has somehow managed to settle herself firmly in Southern Maryland, with one overgrown son and two crazy cats.

Marguerite loves to spin tales that cross genre lines, where stubborn men build lifelong ties of loyalty, friendship, and family no matter the odds thrown against them, and where love is found in unexpected places. She has won the Rainbow Award for Historical Romance with Fae Sutherland, as well as the Rainbow Award for Paranormal and the Rainbow Romance Award for Excellence, also in Paranormal.

When she's not working hard on writing new stories, she spends her time reading novels of all genres, enjoying role-playing and tabletop games with her friends, and helping out her husband with Apocrypha Comics Studio.

Website: www.margueritelabbe.com
Twitter: @MargueriteLabbe
Facebook: www.facebook.com/marguerite.labbe.3
Email: margueritelabbe@gmail.com

MARGUERITE LABBE

BOOK
—— // ——
I

A LITTLE SIDE OF
GEEK

THE
GEEK LIFE

Geek Life: Book One

When opposite worlds collide, it's anyone's game.

Proud geek and comic book artist Morris Proctor wants nothing more than to live in semiseclusion with his devil cat and gamer friends. Despite what his well-meaning family thinks, he's perfectly content with his status quo. The last thing he needs is to date another nongeek hell-bent on changing him.

Then he meets his adorkable new neighbor, Theo Boarman, who doesn't know *Star Trek* from *Star Wars*, but who tempts him like no other.

Theo has spent the last year recovering from the loss of his parents and trying to play both roles for his teenage brother, while working to keep the family restaurant afloat. Dating is the last thing on the menu, especially with a man who thinks the height of dining is shoving a packaged meal into the microwave.

But if Morris gives him one more shy smile or flaunts that kilt he wears so well, Theo will be forced to convince him that a hot summer fling is just the recipe to let off a little steam.

When that fling gets serious fast, Morris has to decide if he's willing to give his heart to Theo on the chance that they're a perfect mix.

www.dreamspinnerpress.com

MAKE ME
WHOLE

MARGUERITE LABBE

After a grueling battle in ancient Greece, lovers Dexios and Lykon committed their lives to each other in the name of Goddess Cythera. After the war, fearing the strength of his love for Dexios, Lykon abandoned his vow and returned home. Heartbroken, Dexios called on Cythera, who changed him into four unfinished statues. In that form he would wait for his fickle lover to return, break the curse, and make him whole.

Thousands of years have passed when Galen Kanellis finds the disassembled pieces in the storeroom of a Seattle museum and makes them the focus of his new exhibit. Needing information, he contacts his ex-lover Nick Charisteas. Nick has a lifelong dream of finding the Dexios Collection, and the last thing he expected was for it to wind up in the hands of the man who broke his heart. As both men search for answers about the statues, worries of abandonment and fear of loss test their renewed relationship, threatening to separate them again—this time permanently.

www.dreamspinnerpress.com

OTHER SIDE OF THE LINE

MARGUERITE LABBE

Caleb Hudson and Hal Zimmer became best friends the day they stood up against the schoolyard bully together. Life's complicated enough with their friendship crossing racial lines in 1960s Charleston, South Carolina, but as time passes, they realize it's more than their friendship that sets them apart from other kids. At first, Caleb denies his feelings for Hal could be more than companionship. He supports his friend when Hal admits he's gay, but Caleb isn't ready to face his own truth.

Hal becomes a staunch antiwar protester, and the divide between them widens after Caleb is drafted. But when Caleb returns from Vietnam, the time for denial is over. His homecoming sets off a series of events that force Caleb and Hal to confront their desires and what lines they're willing to cross to get what they truly want out of life.

www.dreamspinnerpress.com